Feet in the Valley

Aswini Kumar Mishra is a familiar name in the world of poetry, both in his native state Odisha and outside. He is the current Secretary of the Odisha Sahitya Akademi.

A retired officer of Odisha's state civil service, he served the state in different capacities for more than three decades. This is his maiden English novel.

Feet in the Valley

ASWINI KUMAR MISHRA

RUPA

Published by
Rupa Publications India Pvt. Ltd 2016
7/16, Ansari Road, Daryaganj
New Delhi 110002

Sales Centres:

Allahabad Bengaluru Chennai
Hyderabad Jaipur Kathmandu
Kolkata Mumbai

Copyright © Aswini Kumar Mishra 2016

All rights reserved.
No part of this publication may be reproduced, transmitted,
or stored in a retrieval system, in any form or by any means,
electronic, mechanical, photocopying, recording or otherwise,
without the prior permission of the publisher.

This is a work of fiction. Names, characters, places and incidents are
either the product of the author's imagination or are used fictitiously and
any resemblance to any actual person, living or dead,
events or locales is entirely coincidental.

ISBN: 978-81-291-4008-1

First impression 2016

10 9 8 7 6 5 4 3 2 1

The moral right of the author has been asserted.

Printed by HT Media Ltd, Noida

This book is sold subject to the condition that it shall not,
by way of trade or otherwise, be lent, resold, hired out, or otherwise circulated,
without the publisher's prior consent, in any form of binding or cover other than that
in which it is published.

To Alokita (Sona), the apple of my eye, who would confidently leaf through this work of her grandad some day...

Acknowledgements

I would like to thank my wife Nirupama, son Nayanansu and daughter-in-law Nishipadma, for their love and support.

I am indebted to my friends Prafulla Kumar Tripathy and Jatindra Kumar Nayak, both renowned scholars in English.

I am thankful to Rupa Publications India, for taking good care of my work.

1

THE RAIN WAS streaming down. Somen came out of his living room, stood in the verandah and gazed at the sky, without seeing the good Lord anywhere. Although he had passed twenty-eight, he was unemployed and had been tossed aside like a heap of unwanted debris by society and pushed to the brink of decay. He therefore considered the great Almighty as his main rival although he still questioned God's very existence. Was it all madness that this wounded spirit sprang out from the mind of an educated youth? From now onwards a bright lad like him would be clearly branded as an unemployed one. Somen consoled himself, 'Are you late?' 'No', his conscience replied. 'Some day I still hope I will have a dignified job,' Somen murmured. 'They simply can't go on disqualifying me time and again. Listen,' he said to himself, 'you have to consolidate your own strength. Don't allow your ego to be shattered by an interview. You can easily reshape it. A single event in life shouldn't incapacitate you.' As if there was nothing attractive on earth, Somen looked at the sky allowing his eyes to submerge with the dark clouds floating about. From where could he trace that silver lining? The dark clouds hovered just above the roof of his residence and the rain fell like poisonous fluid from a venomous creature. The viscous vapours rose against the horizon and the rain kept falling incessantly.

The midsummer whirlwind earlier had blown dry leaves to the front of the house. The jackfruit tree stood alone in the corner and a few of its dangling fruits fell to the ground like wounded birds. At times, flashes of lightning knifed across the horizon. The monsoon air was refreshing, but its coolness failed to remove the heat from Somen's mind. He was getting disappointed that his confidence would soon disappear.

Somen felt embittered by this new *fatwa* on him. It was nightmarish because his talent had never been put to such hard scrutiny in the past. His personality, which had long been a metaphor for intelligence, had come to an abrupt halt. His merit so long taken for granted in schools and colleges, in essays and debates, would come under the public radar of instant surveillance. The citizens of Beethalgarh would regard him just like any other commonplace lad, moving on his bike to either the post office or marketplace. What a shame!

Such a spectre of public mandate dismissing his ruling intelligence troubled him a lot. It was as if Somen wanted more than ever to prove the inward strength of his own intelligence, almost as much as he wanted to have another chance to demonstrate his competitive ability either before the Government or any corporate house. Just then Minati came with a cup of tea. The rain had almost eased off. Mrs Roy, his mother, switched on the verandah light, removing the darkness.

After finishing his tea, Somen went out of his house with an umbrella and started walking along the newly laid railway lines. He faintly remembered the then railway minister, who was no more, inaugurating the lines. Somen was a young kid then and had gone to the event with his baba. He had seen an old man in a khadi cap and dhoti speaking in a patriotic tone. Thunderous clapping followed his speech and the lamp was lit to the accompaniment of the blowing of hundreds of conch shells in order to prove that God favoured this holy project. People distinctly remembered the minister's promise that connecting Samastipur with Beethalgarh would be accomplished within a span of five years. Those five years ultimately dragged to more than fifteen years. Even today, a stretch of more than a hundred kilometres was without rail lines. Irrespective of which party was in power at the centre, the contestants took up the cause and it became an election plank that the political parties used every five years to come to power. Somen brooded over the infinite patience of the people of this region. They, of course, hadn't allowed their zeal to die down and waited every year for staking their claims in the railway budget. Hopes were rekindled time and again but construction went on at a snail's pace at the rate of three–five kilometres a year. Every time there was a call attention motion in Parliament, the Railway Minister came out with a stock reply of 'resource constraints' and that was enough for the people to wait for the next year. This had nothing to do with the personal lives of the railway employees stationed nearby. Beethalgarh was the railway junction, situated about two hundred kilometres from Samastipur town, and was supposed to be the commercial nerve centre of this zone. Anyone transferred here had to bow before the authorities for this prize posting. The ticket collectors were fortunate enough to avail of this type of opportunity. However, Somen's dad, Roy Babu, a small-time railway employee, was an exception. As a booking clerk, he did not hesitate to impose freight charges on his son's luggage when he left Beethalgarh to pursue his postgraduate education in Samastipur. His honesty meant little to his colleagues. Somen's elder sister Minati was still unmarried. She was above thirty and had only recently found a job. The railway authorities had opened a crèche and Minati had temporarily been appointed as a craft teacher. But what about train ticket inspectors and other railway employees of the colony? Consumed by greed and keeping to the rules they had let loose a reign of terror on villagers travelling without tickets. This upset many passengers but being defenceless, they escaped by parting with their hard-earned cash. Under such exigencies, the business community sometimes had to part with their merchandise such as toothpaste, shaving razors and purses etc., in exchange for clemency. Somen's father was the only employee to raise his voice against such misdeeds but he lacked the power to be effective.

Somen pondered over this deep-rooted practice. So how would things change even if there was a railway connection between Samastipur and Beethalgarh? These predators would lose no time to collect their booty from users of the new lines.

The humidity was making Somen uncomfortable and he felt compelled to return home where the airing of the ceiling fan would cool him down. In the gathering dusk, he discovered a tree without blooms and leaves and a crow perched on its pale-brown bough. It was busy flapping its wet wings, looking here and there at the ground.

'Wasn't it justifiable to despair about not qualifying for a job, then?' Somen muttered.

'Somen, where have you been? Your food is ready!' shouted Mrs Roy, his mum, from the courtyard. He rushed inside his house. Mrs Roy went to the kitchen and fetched a plate of pakoras, his all-time favourite.

She handed the plate to Somen saying, 'My dear! What are you thinking about? Don't take this small fact to heart. Remember "In a war small battles are lost." Be ready for the next one. Only a little hard labour will do. Carry on. I am with you.' Somen made up his mind to make another attempt to prove that his lost chance had not dampened his spirit, leave alone those of his ageing parents.

2

SOMEN HAD BECOME tougher and bolder as if the no-win had given him a new lease of strength from within. Every day was a challenge for him to approach his studies strictly on a competitive basis. He stayed awake all night so that his luck would not break in the next interview. His parents and Minati even took to sleeping outside so as to not disturb him in their solitary bedroom. Every month, his baba placed orders for the books and periodicals his son needed. The family spent less and less on their needs. Roy Babu even gave up having tea or paan outside. He managed with just two pairs of clothes.

The booking counter got crowded when the arrival of the Mumbai-Howrah Express was announced. The idle atmosphere was plunged into sudden alertness. Arati struck up the office computer for allotment of berths and other activities. She suddenly slammed the ticket window shut unconcerned that a group was still shouting at her for something. Arati mistook them for non-travellers. To her, they lacked the minimum dignity that was expected of express passengers. The situation became tense. There were blows on the wooden shutters, 'Didi, Didi.' Arati was going to get into unnecessary trouble. Roy Babu came to her rescue at once. The window was opened once again. On seeing Roy Babu in her seat, Arati dragged her chair near Dolly's and concentrated on a women's magazine. But it didn't last long. 'Arati, what is that you are going through?' asked Dolly. 'Just an article on marriage.' 'Wa...Wa... Let me have a look.' 'Amazing! Even educated guys prefer stay-at-home partners,' said Arati. 'Perhaps to keep them as plastic toys in glasscases,' added Dolly. Like two cats fighting over a cake, they snatched the magazine from each other. Dolly went through some lines while commenting, 'See, Arati! In a foreign country like China a man is at liberty to become a member of a woman's family. A child can pick either of its parents' titles.' 'Oh! So nice. I don't want to change my title even after my marriage. I am so much in love with it.' The Senior Station Master entered their booking office and their discourse came to a natural halt. 'Why are you sitting so close to her?' The SSM expected Dolly to reply. Some other colleagues tried to suppress a laugh. Dolly was at a loss for a quick reply. How could she convince the SSM of her innocence? After all it was Arati who pulled her chair beside hers. Would Dolly be instantly made to look a little more ridiculous? Seeing all of them mum, the SSM didn't prolong his query. Instead, he introduced one khadi-clad 'neta' accompanying him as the representative of the local Member of Parliament. He had come with a letter from the MP seeking to reserve berths for six persons who were travelling to Mumbai the next day to attend a meeting of their political party. Roy Babu brought out another such letter from his drawer. It was from the MP of their neighbouring constituency with a similar request. Roy was blunt in his reply, 'Excuse me, Sir, we have only five berths to allot. We have to divide them equally as per the principles laid down in our code.' 'What code?' thundered the stranger accompanying the SSM. 'Our railway code,' Roy Babu replied coolly. 'Hell with it, we need berths at any cost. We are the government. Do you know who the Railway Minister is?' Sensing that something was about to happen, everyone including the SSM preferred to remain quiet. 'These people are experts in interpreting the law according to their whims. He can oust all persons standing for tickets and insist that all berths be reserved in his favour. He can dictate terms according to his own choice of things, as he happens to be the representative of an MP,' murmured Roy Babu. Instantly three berths were reserved in his favour. The SSM promised to arrange the rest from the quota available at the nearby station. 'The fire of democracy is so flamboyant!' Dolly remarked to her colleagues sitting closer. As fresh recruits, they had never experienced such a scene before. Many of them had digested it in shocked silence. The SSM and the leader eventually left the place. Gradually everyone including Roy couldn't stop laughing. 'Are there going to be further onslaughts from the duo?' Dolly seemed like she was presiding over a seminar to discuss this with her other colleagues. Everyone present took pity on her. The focus was more on the lackadaisical attitude of the SSM. An innocent lady like Dolly, who seemed comparatively sober had unnecessarily drawn someone's ire. However, the moment slipped past as the candid laughs lightened everyone's spirits.

The old colleague, sitting beside Arati and Dolly, advised them on how to combat such wrangles from outsiders in case they happened again.

'Be cautious, the public chair is always sensitive. You have to act diligently,' said Roy Babu to Arati and Dolly.

Arati and Dolly took up their mindful chattering with the old veteran, knowing that this seasoned mind could redeem them from any such unpleasant encounters or crises that may occur in the future.

3

BEFORE THE YOUNG and old of Beethalgarh could discuss Somen's unqualified talent and before he could be portrayed like a model of failure for young competitors, Somen threw himself wholeheartedly into the flow of preparation with full vigour. All types of magazines relating to competitive examinations lay scattered on his table. By now, he had had enough time to speculate on what could be his next course of action in life. He cast a fleeting glance at the cover of one such magazine, which bore the smiling photograph of an IAS topper. Somen detested it so much that he flung the magazine on the ground. 'What a farce!' he muttered. 'I don't know how success comes to just a handful on earth.' His baba couldn't afford to send him to a standard coaching institute. Even though Somen had laboured hard and studied for fourteen to sixteen hours a day, all his determination to enter the All India Services had led to nothing. Years of concentrated efforts had yielded no results. Somen, although intelligent, now found it difficult to take stock of his unfortunate situation. Without a job, how could he pilot himself or his future family through the rest of his life? His parents' expectations made him restless. Perhaps Somen was not gifted with an exceptionally brilliant brain. Such questions hit him again and again. Had he prepared himself for the examination the right way? A friend of his father had commented, 'Somen, you laboured too hard but for better memory you should have relaxed at times to allow your brain to recharge itself.' Madam Sarita, the principal of Joseph School and a friend of his mum's, said candidly. 'Did you really revise all the compulsory papers? I don't think so. You must not have done your revision systematically.' One of the neighbours, a friend of his baba's, argued how rural youths lacked the smartness to appear before bigwigs in an interview to present their points convincingly. Unlike students from big cities they weren't as fluent in English as well. Somen had overheard so many such dialogues that were uttered just to frighten him off. He felt terribly disappointed by the arrogance of these commentators. What they really wanted was to keep other people's children at the same level as their own. He didn't like to burden his mind by listening to such silly dialogues aimed at him. For him there was nothing uglier than an employed young man flashing a boastful smile. He felt a void in him.

4

THE TRACT OF land was filled with shrubs and boulders giving it the look of a dressed-up playground for flying creatures and reptiles, vertebrates and invertebrates. In the centre, dotted with fallen nests and feathers, stood the office known as Panchayat Samiti alias Block involved in the process of achieving Rural Development. It was adjacent to the Railway Colony. The theoretical aspects of plans engineered in places like Delhi and other capital cities of this country were translated into action at this grassroots point. Pasayat, the Block Development Officer, was the chief executive looking into all these affairs of effective planning. The BDO and his team of officials were implementing the policies on rural upliftment. Repair and maintenance of rural roads, excavation, maintenance of fishery tanks, childcare, distribution of essential commodities, and amelioration of poverty through agricultural planning were the priority sectors. Somen, unlike others, had failed to perceive the sacred figure of 'Bapu' behind the functioning of this three-tier Panchayat Raj. There had been a great transformation in the lifestyles of agents who were supposed to work as middlemen between the block-level functionaries and the rural populace. Somen had observed the groups of contractors and officers through his window. When he had peeped through the casement, he had seen the Inspector of Civil Supplies riding pillion on the motorbike of a retailer. Couldn't one officer walk a short distance of just a few metres from his residence to the office instead of depending upon a person against whom several complaints had already been filed? The young inspector had already received a sizeable fortune from his recent marriage. He preferred not to use the two-wheeler he had received in the dowry fearing that it would be scarred and soiled by the dirty roads. 'Stupid!' Somen shouted at him like a ventriloquist.

There had been competitions in the colony to spread the gospel of consumerism. The entire region was reeling under a dry spell, yet the dwellers in the colony, particularly the employees, had come forward to bathe in material refreshment. Following the severe drought, the government had sanctioned special grants to provide labour-intensive work for the poor. This in turn had helped the associates of the executing agencies to grab substantial portions of the expenditure in terms of percentage, a very popular practice amongst corrupt elements in bureaucracy. Apart from their salary and other perks, the employees in the Block office had found means of extracting more from the system. The official setting was designed in such a manner that people had to part with some money to get their work done through these people.

Rout, the Stipendiary Engineer of the Block in league with rural touts, would prepare false bills under the head 'million wells programme'. The scheme, as envisaged by the Central Government, was to dig wells for agricultural purposes. The Government would then reimburse the entire amount provided that the beneficiary was a small or marginal farmer belonging to a backward ethnic group. The officers monitoring this scheme, in connivance with vested interest groups, would claim that an ordinary pit was a proper well, or if it didn't exist, prepare false bills and obtain signatures from ignorant beneficiaries and embezzle the entire amount. Essential commodities like sugar and rice were scarce and thus controlled by black marketeers, who in turn would sell them in the open market at exorbitant prices. Hota, the Inspector of Supplies, through improper gratification would turn a blind eye towards such illicit trade. Both Nanda and Patel, Junior Engineers in charge of rural engineering, were the most cunning employees who chose to overlook the preparation and payment of bills in exchange for their cut. They prepared false bills exaggerating earthwork in villages on the eve of the rainy season and kept the Measurement Book open without making any entries. After the incessant rain had eroded the pits, they would make backdated entries in connivance with BDO Pasayat, who certified that they had been checked. They would wade through water without getting wet. In the gathering of *moroom*, JEs invariably exaggerated the collection and prevailed upon Sub-Contractors to spread it on dry rural roads before conscious citizens or investigation authorities came to know about it. In case this was closely scrutinized, they manipulated the records by showing the lifting as 'head load' instead of 'cart load' or by adding extra items like watering the road to settle the dust or the clearing of shrubs from the site. This secret romance between the Sub-Contractors and JEs to line their pockets was carried out in full view of the innocent labourers for whose benefit the popular Government at the centre took up such emergency measures.

When it got dark, Panda, the Gram Panchayat Extension Officer, would sit in his chair flanked by two or three persons. His office peon would welcome the clients who arrived with a smile. Panda would then start tampering with the Measurement Book and Case Records that the Gram Panchayat secretaries had submitted to him. Although the Government had imposed a ceiling on the maintenance of rural roads, his supervisory authorities like the BDO and District Panchayat Officer never came down heavily on him for blithely exceeding the amount. The reason was obvious. Seth, the peon attached to Panda, could be seen transporting bags full of vegetables and fish to the residences of his bosses under the cover of darkness. The quantum of fish, netted from rural ponds, was never recorded accurately. The entries in the cash book remained much below the actual amount. The inspecting authorities cleverly avoided such omissions and everyone knew the reasons. Although the state capital was equipped with functionaries to do the checking, it hardly bothered about the effective implementation of all procedural formalities at the grassroots. Corruption, like an octopus, had spread its tentacles to devour the whole of the Block office and Beethalgarh. People had failed to discover if these people had any integrity in their professional outlook. The Panchayat Raj Department deliberately sent a BDO like Pasayat to destroy the integrity of the staff working under him. No one, including him, ever bothered sending the higher authorities their biannual property statement. A man of questionable integrity had been selected as BDO and he never hesitated asking the cashier of the office to deduct a substantial amount from the interim or final bill of the Awas Yojana, which was exclusively meant for the poorest of the poor. The local newspaper, *Daily Mail*, published from Samastipur, never carried a single line about such activities more because of the fact that a close relative of the newspaper's owner was hand in glove with the Block office. Tiwari, the local journalist of the *Daily Mail*, sought help from the BDO and Extension Officer, Co-operative, to solicit official advertisements from different societies. The BDO, along with the Assistant Registrar, Cooperative, even went out of his way to provide funds for the advertisements. This was done without prior budgetary allocations. As a result, news on corruption hardly appeared in the *Daily Mail*. Beethalgarh in its own way had become a sanctuary for white-collar employees. Pasayat, the BDO, remained the kingpin of all such affairs and spent his days like Amarnath's ancient Shiva lingam, sometimes waxing before his subordinates and at other time waning before his superiors, and again enlarging himself before his subordinates while consuming both the nectar and the poison from the churning of an ocean similar to that of an Indian myth.

All day long and well into the evening, Pasayat sat in his office, flexing the muscles of both hands to pick up the telephone and say 'hello' to someone, run his fingers across the keyboard of the computer, push his pen through file notes or press the button of the bell to call in some of the rural poor loitering in the verandah outside.

As evening approached, the office employees began to melt away and several familiar faces from the town who had styled themselves as Sub-Contractors or public representatives made their way into the Block premises with the intention of deepening their friendship with Pasayat and his staff. Gossiping and chattering meaninglessly, each one took his turn to come closer to him, while at the same time indirectly eyeing the profitable assignment that would appear intermittently on the noticeboard. Many said that they were exactly the person who should be transferred here to head this office. 'How nice the administration is now! There has never been one with such a sound functioning,' they said point blank. 'Yes, even my superiors will agree with you,' Pasayat told them unhesitatingly. The waiter, a dhoti-clad, middle-aged man, pushed the spring door and welcomed the visitors inside, that is, if there were any empty chairs. One usually came with paan or a packet of cigars, the BDO's preferred brand. He handed them over to the waiter and tiptoed silently into the chamber. Many of them had devised a plan to make him happy by echoing his negative views of the poor and their upliftment. Before them, Pasayat conducted himself like a visionary, telling them how averse he was to the belief of showing sympathy for hungry folks, precisely because of his penchant for hard labour and inborn merit instead of banking on Government charity or subsidy.

The State Government, on the other hand, followed an idealistic path of ameliorating the conditions of the hungry so that they did not crumble into dust. It had envisaged guidelines for the public servants, except of course for those of the lowest grade, to prepare confidential character reports on the basis of one's attitude towards the weaker sections.

How come a man with his anti-poor stance was posted to an office that was primarily aimed at improving their lot? 'Oh, I am not in the clutches of the administration. I can never be. If the authorities so desire it, let them transfer me. I am only true to my own conscience. Yes, hard labour and inborn merit...nothing else,' he repeated.

5

NUMBING ONESELF INTO inaction was the best course of action for the official functionaries operating from Beethalgarh's tallest building, known as the Notified Area Council office. Whenever a taxpayer asked for a street bulb or for a handful of bleaching powder or for some *moroom* stacking to cover up the obstructions on his path, the first answer he would receive was a 'no'. Paucity of funds was the slogan mouthed by the newly posted Executive Officer, R.S. Das. People didn't like to bring their problems to him, as he was new to this small town and was yet to become acquainted with their minds and spirits. A senior employee of the secretariat clerical cadre, he preferred to rule the roost as an executive in a small town rather than fade into insignificance in the state capital. He had resorted to ample manoeuvring to win the hearts of the Minister and the Director, Urban Development, for this prized posting. He seemed unruffled by the strong resentment he faced from the general public caused by non-availability of funds for developmental works. He readily offered every simplistic explanation to convince people at large. In spite of this so-called impediment, he went on gratifying himself endlessly. Money, collected by way of octroi, was diverted towards the remodelling and distempering of his official residence. The lifestyle of his better half, his two daughters and his own scaled new heights. Shanti, his wife, wanted to shine with the glory of material possessions. She would never ever return to the emptiness of the clerical hive. She entered into feverish competition with the other women in the colony. In the process, she tried her best to get everything she never had when she lived in the state capital. The opulent Goddess Laxmi herself came down to open the floodgates of prosperity for her. Shanti went on chanting: *Namastestu Mahamaye Sripitha Surapujite, Sankha, Chakra, Gada Haste, Maha Laxmi Namastute*. The results were spectacular. She, like Sriya, the worshipper of Laxmi, was gifted with untold wealth. Shanti, craving for more silk saris, took a stroll with her husband to the nearby Samalpuri Handloom House and introduced herself voluntarily to the shop owner, Agrawala. He conducted them into the inner chamber of the showroom, offered them seats and ordered coffee. Shanti responded enthusiastically. What would her husband's position have been amongst the long queue of white-collar professionals in Bhubaneswar?

She selected two silk saris. One was the colour of copper sulphate with a magenta border. It had magnificent tie and dye in the border and warp-ends. The other was an exquisite *bomkai* model with a violet body and grass-coloured warp ending. The cloth merchant assured them that the colour would not fade even after repeated washes. Shanti wanted to take them on credit. Das whispered something to the owner and the latter seemed obliging. At home, she wanted to test the genuineness of the silk yarn. She asked the orderly to fetch a little hydrochloric acid from the chemistry laboratory of the college. She took out sample fibres from both the saris and boiled them for half a minute in the acid solution. To her good luck, it immediately dissolved the silk yarn. Shanti heaved a sigh of relief. Das was impressed by his wife's intelligence. While embracing her closely, a muscular grin appeared on his face and he said, 'Did you notice the trader's fear of me? He is so afraid of the octroi tax.' Shanti didn't understand what 'octroi' meant. She was only aware of the power her husband had enjoyed at that time. Her face lit up with a smile. She murmured, 'Please wait to see me in my new saris.'

6

BEETHALGARH HAD SLOWLY become the breeding ground for malarial mosquitoes and the menace started plaguing the whole township. After two patients succumbed to their illnesses in ward No. 21, people staged protests at the NAC and subdivisional hospital in groups. There was a special meeting of the executive body of the NAC to discuss the matter in great detail and an agenda was drawn up accordingly. Councillors, including the Chairman and Vice Chairman, cutting across party lines, started repeatedly pointing out the severity of malaria. They all wanted to know in specific terms what steps the EO and his staff had taken to arrest its spread in the town. They also insisted on issuing a red alert to inform the higher-ups and were seeking substantial aid from the Government to combat the crisis. The agitated members wanted to know in detail the amount of funds the EO had spent during the last quarter in administering DDT, phenyl and bleaching powder. Das, in return, immediately asked both the health inspector and the storekeeper to table before the body all these required items. After scrutiny, the amount seemed inadequate keeping in view the growing population of the area. Some of them guessed its true utilization and started maligning the NAC administration for not coming up to the expectation of the people at the time of their distress. Mohan, a young Councillor, came to the rescue of the EO and the other officials before the matter could take an ugly turn. The angry Councillor of ward No. 21 had even raised his fist to threaten not anyone in particular but to assert his strength in general before the gathering. Das was unprepared for such pandemonium and confined himself to his chair. He couldn't handle the hustle and bustle of the council members. The comparatively younger members had even whistled. Beethalgarh could be so primitive! The Councillors' meeting proved to be a sordid affair. It appeared like a dungeon of drunkards and cut-throats. The EO had never come across such awful scenes before. The secretariat services were far removed from all this. Nonetheless, he didn't lose his temper but stood helplessly for a while. The fury subsided slowly. Someone from the office hinted to Das that the anger of the Councillor of ward No. 21 was not because of the malaria death but because his man had been deprived of the opportunity of carrying out the improvement of the road adjoining his ward. The Sub-Contractor himself was there, peeping through the window, enjoying the whole episode. Das retorted promptly, 'Who am I to recommend the selection of a Sub-Contractor when the Chairman himself has taken the initiative to do so?' Of late, the EO had come to know about the secret deal of a lump sum and that had made him extra cautious not to be in such weighing down situations in future. He cursed those unseen mosquitoes of clogged drains for generating so much heat in the body politic of the NAC and declared a jihad to wipe out each one of them from Beethalgarh. Suddenly, like a plane, a mosquito zoomed past his ear and Das angrily slapped it, killing the insect on the spot and leaving a red mark on his cheek. The health inspector immediately inspected the corpse and shouted, 'Sir, anopheles.' Das literally cried out because of the pain he had inflicted on his own body and he barely heard the inspector's voice. The cashier of the NAC could be seen spraying something like insecticide in the meeting hall and everyone's attention was focused more on the EO than on the mosquitoes. He seemed to be keen to remain in the good books of the new officer. Everyone including the Chairman and the VC enjoyed watching the mosquitoes trying to escape through the windows.

7

THE RAILWAY COLONY situated on the other side of the town had virtually become a rendezvous for the mosquitoes. They were forced to decamp from the central NAC area on account of the relentless war waged against them by the NAC field staff under the direct command of the EO. Every family in the colony had fallen victim to the disease. Somen was no exception. The garbage had not been removed from the colony merely because the NAC couldn't exercise its supremacy here. The locality was still under the command of the railway authorities. Since there was no cross-drainage system, it had become a haven for mosquitoes. Somen and his father were victims of the fever. Lying slumped on their sickbeds, both kept yelling. Minati and her mum stood the test through their tireless nursing. Was it an easy task to attend to two malaria patients in the same house? Minati, in fact, ran from pillar to post. Her mind was full of morbid thoughts. Was life all about experiencing it in its anguished moments? The patients' temperatures suddenly rose above 102 °F. She immediately administered wet bandages on their foreheads. Whatever expertise Somen's mother had in handling symptoms of nausea and vertigo, he discounted. 'It is quackery, stop, Maa, please,' he cried out querulously. Frequent consumptions of quinine capsules weakened them both. To Somen, the world looked like a boiled apple. Nothing so attractive, eh! The mosquito nets hanging over their beds had several holes thus allowing the insects free access into the protected area. The mosquitoes could exercise their accomplishments freely. Somen brooded over these creatures that had existed for more than 260 million years unlike human civilization's four million years. Could malaria ever be eradicated? Could mosquitoes ever be tamed? Somen's mum went on massaging the aching bodies of both father and son.

'Maa! Your touch is so nice,' Somen said to conceal his earlier mood.

'Why don't you have a piece of apple, my dear?' she asked. Somen complied politely. So did his dad. Mrs Roy went on pushing some grapes into the mouths of her ailing son and husband.

'That is all, Mummy,' Somen shouted at his mother.

'One more,' she pleaded.

'No, Mummy please.'

Somen felt guilty about the sweetness as well as kindness that a mother had showered upon an unemployed son like him. It was so invigorating. Even during his illness, Somen couldn't stop condemning himself. 'Fie Somen! You are from among the vanquished lot,' but his mum interrupted him suddenly.

'Somen! My sweetheart!!'

'Maa.'

'Don't worry unnecessarily. The Almighty is there to pull us out unhurt. He will definitely listen to our woes one day.'

Somen wanted to extol his mum. So impeccable in her conduct! She didn't have an inch of dissatisfaction towards her son. She was yet to be tricked into speaking anything unnaturally. Somen slept rooted to the bed.

That was all. She switched off the light, and knelt before the supreme power offering a prayer to that unknown body with chiming bells and the flicker of a jyoti in both hands.

Mrs Roy stood all along with her natural affinity for Minati and her husband Roy. Her mind was exclusively a firm resolve of an affectionate circle incorporating these three dots. Like the saint poet Bhima Bhoi, her body was filled with sublime thought. 'Let me rot in hell but let the world be saved'.

Mrs Roy stood like a statue of primordial innocence defying all the shrewdness of a modern competitive world.

8

OUT OF ALL the people on earth, Pasayat, BDO, wanted to share his late evening gossip with Sub-Contractors, asbestos dealers, storage agents, etc., who would find easy access to his office chamber and occupy their respective chairs as if it was their prerogative. After

5 p.m., soon after the formal closure of office hours, the true functioning of the Block used to begin with usual vigour. The JEs returned to the office with the Sub-Contractors riding pillion on their motorbikes. Sometimes the positions were reversed and JEs Nanda and Rath could be seen as pillion riders on the vehicles of Patnaik and Mishra, Sub-Contractors of the block. Bhakta, the lone orderly, kept himself at the command of the BDO as he had proved to be trustworthy. Pasayat liked him because he never revealed the secrets of his office to the general public. The friendship between Nanda and Patnaik, the JE and Sub-Contractor, had become a deep done. So inseparable was their mobility that it was difficult to distinguish whose bike it was. At times, it was discovered that Nanda's motorcycle ran on the fuel supplied by Patnaik. When relatives arrived at the residence of Rath, another JE, Mishra, the Sub-Contractor, provided the entertainment packages. As soon as the office opened, Patnaik would arrive with folded hands to greet both Nanda and Rath.

'Yes…Patnaik.'

'Sir, namaste…, My bills, sir.'

'Not prepared yet, please come later.'

'Sir…I badly need the money to pay my labourers.'

'But the BDO is out of station.'

'No, but he is sure to return soon…Sir.'

'Oh! You are so bothersome, as always.'

'Sir please.'

Patnaik laid a packet of cigars on Nanda's table while suggesting the mode of preparation of the bill. Nanda, puffing a cigar from the pack, asked Patnaik to leave the room so that he could go ahead with the present task. Patnaik left immediately. Nanda once again shouted at him, 'Please ask for some coffee.'

Patnaik asked an attendant of the engineering section to follow him. Outside the office, he stood beside a coffee centre and found the man speaking against the staff. He narrated before the bystanders the percentage breakdown on the amount of their bills, for example, payment of 10 per cent to the JE, 5 per cent to BDO, 5 per cent to the head clerk, cashier and accounts section, and how in spite of this there was perpetual harassment and constant goading to get a bill passed. He was desperate for cash to meet demands like coffee, petrol, cigarettes and what not.

The coffee was ready. The peon carried a kettle and mounted his cycle. Someone from the public commented, 'The percentage rate is likely to increase in view of the spiralling price rise on all fronts. Maybe, this time the bribe-taker will be more stringent.'

Eh! If the situation continues like this the earthwork in rural ponds would take place only during the rainy season.

A majority of Block employees including the orderlies and drivers eyed the Sub-Contractors and watched out for the slightest movement of the Measurement Book and Case Records from one table to the next; the secret theory of giver and taker was being contemplated. This was examined time and again to justify the universal practice of greasing somebody's palm to receive something in return. Patnaik couldn't heave a sigh of relief. He cursed himself thoroughly for being in such an ignoble situation where he was forced to kneel before a JE just to live an ordinary life.

9

SHANTI HAD BEEN busy all morning applying mehndi on to the streaks of white hair on her head. Still wearing a nightie, she tilted her face in front of a giant mirror to separate the white from the black ringlets and kept massaging them. After that she washed her locks and dried them with a hairdryer. Her hair looked dishevelled as the ungentle breeze tossed it here and there. She did all these tasks herself because she wanted to look youthful. Looking at her husband she was eager to repeat the same with him.

'No, Shanti... Let it remain as it is,' he muttered.
'Why?'
'I wish to look the way I am.'
'But I don't like such ideas.'
'Young people will mock us.'

Shanti didn't like the note of dissent. She jumped to her feet to apply mehndi to the silvery portion of his head. Das, like a derailed engine, stood motionless. Shanti moved the tips of her fingers to his moustache. Das felt smothered. It was almost like an octopus embracing him.

'Oh! Shanti...leave me alone.'

'Don't be so silly.'

They heard someone entering the living room and moved apart at once. It was Banita their elder daughter, a first-year graduate student, returning from college after the morning session. She was followed by Sumita, the younger one, a plus two second year student. Banita was 21 while Sumita nineteen years old.

Das' two daughters were academically below average. They preferred an automatic two-wheeler to a bicycle to cover the distance from their residence to their college. Since the day they arrived in this town, they had been busy trying to consolidate their positions as if they were taking part in a beauty contest and were recognized to some extent as such. Whenever they were on the road, they switched over to their best clothes and always wanted to be on splendid terms with the self-styled Romeos of the town. They decked themselves up in Banarasi printed dress materials in brilliant colours and always remembered to match their kurtas with their salwars. With shampooed hair, lovely cream and wearing supple leather footwear, they would roam around the town like a couple of fairy queens descended from another planet. Many youngsters including a bachelor Councillor called Mohan used to knock at the door of the residence of the EO for some reason or the other. One day Mohan had come on a silly matter like his ward being inundated due to the seepage of water from the tube well provided by the NAC. The matter might have been flimsy but it gave Mohan an opportunity to sit with Shanti and at times exchange glances with her grown-up daughters. Shanti herself seemed to want to prolong the conversation on some pretext or the other.

'Mohan Babu, could you find a big grinder for us? Ours is a small one,' said Shanti.

'Oh! Why not? Our boys often visit Samastipur and someone could be sent to take care of this.'

'I have heard that your father was a great freedom fighter,' Shanti added.

'Yes Madam.'

'Kolkata is a beautiful city,' Banita interrupted.

'How many brothers and sisters do you have, Mohan Da?' Sunita joined in, not wanting to be left out of the dialogue.

The conversation was nothing but an attempt to deepen intimacy. Shanti, a lady who could hardly speak anything coherently, was enjoying the position of being able to command someone. She was entertaining a guy like Mohan so that her husband could be spared a lot of trouble.

10

YEARS OF TOIL, exciting competitions, the trauma of failure and fever had made Somen inconsolable. With every breath, he grew more disagreeable and was almost reduced to tears. He was recovering slowly from the dullness of fever. He looked through the window with a vacant gaze. Failure in finding a job had made him timorous and overtly self-conscious.

'Let us go out,' said Pradeep, his close friend in Beethalgarh.

'Why?'

'For a stroll...you are so weak!'

Somen hesitated, but agreed. It was about 5.30 p.m. He saw his dad returning home. Somen was fed up with this situation. He saw him struggling hard whereas he himself didn't. His idleness was an added source of irritation.

'Somen, please!' Pradeep wanted to break the monotony of silence with some juicy conversation. Instead, he feigned total calmness.

'It is hard labour indeed!' Pradeep said. 'There is a fresh advertisement in the newspaper today.'

Somen became attentive.

'What is it?'

'Company Executive. Karnataka Silk Factory in Bangalore invites applications from interested candidates having postgraduate degree in Chemistry'. Pradeep quoted.

'Nice idea! But what is the age limit?' queried Somen.

'Thirty years for a person who has opted for Polymer Science as one of his special papers in M.Sc.'

'Are you sure?' asked Somen.

'Yeh! I distinctly remember that,' replied Pradeep.

'For you, I went through the ad meticulously. In case someone gets selected, he will have to undergo a one-year probation period in textile dyeing and marketing at the company's cost.'

'Salary?'

'Quite attractive…there are other advantages as well. Spending life in a city, how many of us are favoured with such chances?' Pradeep said.

Somen's ambitions were suddenly recharged.

11

THE SMALL TOWN, Beethalgarh, started dancing to the tune of the evening tides like a garland frolicking around the neck of a drunkard. The rhymed steps of both Block and railway employees could be heard at Hotel Amar, where they had gathered after work to participate in its abundant gaiety. Ved Prakash, the owner, had all the pleasures at his disposal to quench the dry throats of his numerous visitors. Both the Block and Railway Colonies were the great thirst lands of deadened souls who resorted to the immortal pulsing of 'Amar' to add vitality to their life. After years of struggle the hotel was slowly gaining status. Pots of sweet-smelling plants and soft music wafting from the music system created a pleasant ambience. Ved Prakash, who had encroached upon half an acre of railway lands, had time and again contacted, and even entertained some of the officials who could easily pardon him for such an illegality. As a result, he had been let off the hook because 'Amar' had stood the test of time like an oasis in the vast expanse of a seemingly dry world.

The concept of honesty hardly mattered to anyone visiting the hotel. When the repair and maintenance of railway tracks was undertaken, the engineers in charge of supervising the work would go for unspecified items of materials. For example, the Sub-Contractor would collect hand-made aggregates from the local labour sardar, but on paper this would be shown as metals from stone crushers, thus computing a great difference between the pricing of the two. This went on in collections, too. Nowhere could the specified quantity be seen piling up. The Sub-Contractors deliberately aimed at collecting less than the stipulated amount but the entries in the Measurement Books, as made by the engineers, appeared to be inflated. The same was the case with earthwork, too. Some even hesitated to pay royalty to the State Government . Metals were deliberately stolen from nearby quarries and stored on the roadside under the cover of darkness. The railway tracks witnessed identical scenes. In the event of sporadic detections, the small-time revenue police personnel could easily be won over. It might so happen that the Tahsildar in one of his inspections would come across a crumbling granite hill without proportionate deposit of royalty in his office. Or he might notice a substantial stacking of timber, firewood on the side of the railway station with the male and female labourers loitering about, waiting for the next express to arrive. Surprisingly, the express trains that were not supposed to make a halt there invariably stopped. The logs of wood were packed inside the lavatories, in secret places of the compartments and even pushed into the railway engine and guard's cabin. The train ticket examiners fearlessly employed malpractices like allowing berths to passengers through gratification. In the process, the bona fide travellers became second benchers in spite of their loyalty to the Government dictum. The railway as such became a system within a system to patronize the cult of white-collar crimes.

These techniques were devised at Hotel Amar amidst frequent cocktails. The senior ticket examiners used to train their juniors on how to project artificial shortages of berths, etc. Corruption was conferred like a mass degree and 'Amar' stood like a small-scale convocation pandal where the voices of these acharyas had their greatest impact. Endowed with unquenchable thirst for such learning, the dark-robed juniors kept them contented for such ill-gotten counsel. What could gather greater alertness than this money raising theory? However, Roy and his two female colleagues were the glaring exceptions. The concept of kickbacks in booking and delivery of goods failed to rock their chairs. They were unaffected. Both Arati and Dolly in their delicate voices would present the latest rules with force without communicating false ideas to the consignors or consignees. They could substantially increase railway revenue, thus becoming bugbears for the unscrupulous elements in such racketeering. Their working grace, no doubt, brought enough relief to the commoners. The people paid them respect in return. Both ladies had overcome their earlier diffidence and were so down to earth! Roy guided them all along. Singularly, it was the only transparent segment within the whole set-up. It went on thriving like a small island in the sea of contamination. Any transgression of uprightness even in a hostile situation was beneath their dignity.

One day, Mohan, the young Councillor, wanted to book a pair of wooden beds to Cuttack. The EO, Das, desired their transportation to his in-laws there. The request came straight from Shanti. Mohan had nothing to do other than to comply with it. He came and peeped through the booking window. He wanted a discussion with Roy on this. On finding him absent, he addressed Arati, the lady assistant.

'Hello, Arati.'
'How dare you call me by my first name.'
'I am Mohan, Councillor of ward No. 17.'
'So what! Please don't address me in this way. It is not proper.'
'Then how should I address you?' asked Mohan.
'You should know.'
Mohan realized his lapse. He corrected himself at once.
'All right Madam, I need your help.'
'What for?'

'For sending something to Cuttack by train.'
'All right, stand in the queue, please.'
'But I am sending wooden furniture.'
'Let us see the permit.'

Mohan couldn't produce the travelling ticket permit from the forest department. Arati continued to insist on it. Seeing Mohan so desperate, she relented somewhat and asked for the cash memo in support of the materials. Again he couldn't provide it. Instead, he tried convincing Arati to write any name he could think of in the supplier's column. She flatly refused to do so. She commanded the coolies to unload the planks from the weighing machine and asked Mohan to take them back.

Mohan felt humiliated by the way Arati had conducted the whole show. As a card-bearer of the ruling party he wanted to take revenge on her for such an insult. After all, he was the representative of the local MP too. He felt like rebuking her right in front of the general public but the sudden entry of Roy cooled him down. Mohan sought Roy's help, but he repeated what Arati had said to him and insisted on a valid cash memo from a registered forest firm. Mohan was forced to return disappointed. Finally, he arranged for the papers the next day and the furniture could be sent to its destination, but only after such an exercise. He decided to teach the booking section a lesson.

The BDO and his staff specialized in making late night payments to the Sub-Contractors. That was purely with the intention of allowing their corrupt practices a free play. The Sub-Contractors brazenly wanted an arrangement to carry out their nefarious plans. This kind of thing was to cherish their nefarious means. While gratifying the BDO and his staff through hard cash, they never hesitated to renew their appeal for the next work order involving considerable profit. Pasayat, who was a great devotee of Mouni Baba, never forgot to light a lamp before the great saint after receiving kickbacks. While carefully overlooking such contradictions in his personal life, the BDO deliberately involved himself in the so-called social network and always tried to be gregarious. Kickbacks, devotion and hearty eating at Hotel Amar were all part of the same scheme. At dinner, people would notice his strange association with someone or the other at every occasion. He wanted to attain salvation through fried chicken and swigs of beer. People used to say that he was so large hearted that even strangers could approach his dining table and share his meal. Ved Prakash recorded these expenses and Pasayat came forward unhesitatingly to pay them. Pasayat was certainly a cult figure in the annals of Beethalgarh history, someone to be reckoned with.

12

THE RAIN THAT year wasn't as heavily as it usually was. The whole of Beethalgarh kept waiting for it. The paddy seeds lay scattered on the fields for days on end. Unable to sprout, they slowly disappeared into the dry soil. The farmers of the region sighed. A unique scene altogether. Everyone looked up at the sky. No sign of rain from anywhere. The sun rode through the clouds unchallenged. The dusty wind seemed to have gone crazy. The officials were quick to announce the advent of a drought. Soon, master plans were put in place in both official and non-official executing agencies to combat drought. More central grants were pumped into the state coffers. Intensive relief measures spread their golden wings over the whole of the Beethalgarh region. The khansama of Hotel Amar added more hot spices including chilli and turmeric to the chicken masala, a dish favoured by the officers engaged in drought work. With the arrival of different teams to the area to study the situation, Mohanty, the local Tahsildar, had already taken up crop cutting experiments in selective patches of different villages. He preserved such reports for the high-powered central teams too. Collector, Samastipur, ordered both the agriculture and rural engineering staff of the subdivision to assist the Sub-Collector, Beethalgarh, in preparing a comprehensive report on the drought situation of Beethalgarh tahsil area and district eyeing them up for the whole district. The foolproof measures were systematically recorded in it with alacrity; the petty officials set about arranging both food and accommodation for any number of higher teams visiting the area. Fleets of vehicles loaded with snacks and mineral water bottles were seen doing the rounds. Traditional food items like rice, dal, vegetable curry, etc., were prepared at the Public Works Department Inspection Bungalow but major dishes like chicken masala, prawn curry, fish fry, biriyani, egg fry and so many others were brought from Hotel Amar for entertaining the VIPs. Not that the members of the visiting teams didn't know what was going on, but many of them simply decided to enjoy themselves. These entertainments looked so bizarre before the hungry population of Beethalgarh! But for some officials, it was a means of rapport with senior bureaucrats and politicians at the cost of taxpayers. This, in turn, allowed them to continue in their present jobs.

It so happened that some officials came with dry lunch packets. They were moralists of a high order. They didn't want the petty officials to bother about them. They were quite aware that this spurt of activity exercised by these officials was to siphon off central funds. The spell of drought appeared like a boon to make fortunes out of the misfortunes of others. The local journalists published stories on the intimacy which had grown so suddenly between the local officials and the local businessmen and politicians. Some of them were even photographed holding glasses filled with Scotch whisky.

The pageantry associated with the visit of the central team to a particular area was a spectacular one. Uprooting dry grass from the broken soil in some places led to a theory of nature's initial support of the crops. The net result of the crop cutting experiments negated this. The yield was not even 50 per cent of the standard produce. The Government was tempted to declare the whole area drought prone. Officials went on a borewell installing spree. Hungry faces queued up for press photographers. Captions like the 'last stage of a starving man', 'a man without food for several days', etc., accompanied the photographs. The imagination was running wild!

13

THE EMPIRE OF Ved Prakash went on enlarging itself like white ants slowly taking over a molehill. It had become a canker inside the railway administration and the authorities frantically wanted to arrest his growing power in the railway colony. His high-handedness became the talk of the town. Ved fired his first salvo by installing a new stereo set and playing it maximum to attract more customers into his hotel. It was a nuisance to the students who lived nearby. The old people complained about the bizarre music as it disturbed their sleep. The worst problem was the free availability of liquor. The housewives failed to stop their husbands from frequenting the place. Quarrels arose everywhere, in many of the houses they became a routine.

Using every single skill to dominate the nocturnal proceedings, the players of 'running plus' would compete with one another to grab the amount. Cards were distributed among the players with minimum three as blind, three as seen and the rest three as pretty close to their chests. The competition went on and on, sometimes all through the night. People, in general, were outraged by this. They complained to the Senior Station Superintendent who, in turn, reported the fact to his higher-ups in Samastipur. The authorities prevailed upon the SSS to bring it to the knowledge of the Tahsildar, Beethalgarh. The SSS also consulted with Roy Babu and other senior members of the staff. They wanted to settle scores with Ved and therefore called for him. The latter refused point blank to turn up. Being aware of such high-handedness, the Senior Station Master wanted a dialogue with Mohanty, the Tahsildar, to find ways of evicting him from the land he had encroached upon. The news spread like wildfire as many office-goers were in the direct payroll of Ved. Immediately, he filed a writ before the Court of the Sub-Judge seeking injunction on the proceedings of the Tahsildar. The local lawyers within no time came to the rescue of Ved Prakash. Lawyers accustomed to frequent boozing at Hotel Amar declared their unconditional support for Ved against the railway authorities. They, in fact, had come with a brick in each hand to prepare for a victory stand. Ved was to gradually ascend, at any cost.

Mohanty proved to be a great scholar of revenue laws. He referred to certain sections of the Land Acquisition Act and insisted that if the requisitioning authority failed to utilize all of the acquired land for the purpose it was meant for, he would relinquish it to its previous right and titleholder. Incidentally, the Revenue Department would get back its own land. One court amin was deputed to measure details of the excess area including Ved Prakash's prized possessions. The Department hinted at the idea of deploying an Auxiliary Police Reserve Force with an Executive Magistrate and a gang of coolies to demolish the hotelier's structure but before that could be done, all papers must be ready or else Ved would sue them in all the appropriate courts.

Before Hotel Amar was established, the land was a grassy patch bordered by small bushes. All railway scrap materials were dumped in it. There was a natural water pool as the earth excavated from it was used for the construction of the road passing through the colony. The empty space appeared to be one of the best preserved corners. The wild forest growth of acacia prompted the children to play hide-and-seek there after school. Animals, including cattle and buffaloes, grazed freely there. The cattle would stay for days on end until their masters would come and identify them. The sluggish buffaloes relaxed there all day long, the butterflies would flutter around their necks and jousted with one another in mid-air skirmishes to establish aerial sovereignty. When the buffaloes left the place, herds of goats would move towards the small pool to quench their thirst. Ved Prakash, then a gang coolie from West Champaran district of Bihar, had cast his greedy eye on this unprotected plot and had started to encroach upon it. First he built a small cottage there. A cow entered but nobody claimed it, so Ved Prakash took the animal into his possession and declared himself as its prized owner. Since then, Ved had not looked back. In the small pool, lotuses sent delicate stalks spiralling up to the surface where the flowers would invite butterflies to sit on their soothing petals. A couple of swans and other aquatic creatures would glide across the water inviting the flying crane to stop there for a while like an ancient guest. But Ved, out of sheer malice and greed, destroyed such hospitality. He engaged fifteen to twenty labourers to drain out the pool and subsequently filled it with truckloads of soil and *moroom* to give shape to his lifelong dream, Hotel Amar.

Ved enrolled himself as a member of the local service cooperative society and manoeuvred to arrange a substantial loan in his favour. Since the land was not recorded in his name, the secretary of the society initially denied this favour to him. However, subsequently, under pressure, he passed the loan under the scheme 'small shop'. The amount was ultimately diverted towards the cause of the hotel, thereby opening the floodgates of prosperity for Prakash.

14

THE LONG-AWAITED DROUGHT finally arrived like the owl of Laxmi, the Goddess of Wealth. The central team, with a view to judging the scenario, left Delhi for Samastipur by air. The precious flight took off carrying all the great brains. Vested interests queued up in Samastipur's small airport with garlands in hand. The withering of flowers didn't pose a problem for them as such things had been arranged from distant places. After landing, the team wanted to do the field survey in its own way and a member went his way without adhering to the scheduled route chart prepared by the district administration. The motorcade was forced to change its route due to this spontaneous decision. As a result, the routine preparatory arrangements rolled away like wastewater. The Collector and many other senior officials tried convincing the team of the substandard conditions of the roads leading into interior pockets. But their objections were ignored. It so happened that one of the team members thought nothing of the privilege of travelling by car and climbed into a jeep. As a result, the Collector was compelled to sit in the back seat. It grievously injured his pride. He was not prepared to find himself in such a position. He could manage the situation, however. The SC, an expert in driving, wanted to be at the wheel, but as instructed by the Collector restrained himself and sat by his side. The driving was left to the seniormost driver. Others followed one by one. The route was a serpentine one and even the year's scanty rain had washed it out rendering it partially unfit for motoring. On the way, the BDO was seen jumping from his seat and dashing towards the first vehicle and this tremendous exercise had worn him out totally. The BDO wanted to be nearer the central team to give a detailed picture of the area, for example how the people of the neighbouring villages of Rampella, Katapali, Judabandh had been forced to sever links with Beethalgarh during the rainy season. But the Collector dissuaded him from such micro-projections particularly to the officers operating at the macro level. The BDO kept mum all through. Nevertheless, his facial expression was such that it seemed as if words were simmering inside his throat and were waiting to pour out at the slightest provocation.

One of the observers was heard making a remark with a wry smile, 'So, now we are all well connected.'

Ha...ha...ha...

Even the smile had to be rationed out in small doses. The team members were getting restless as the large potholes, about three to six inches deep in the middle of the road, were making it extremely difficult for the driver to negotiate the labyrinth of deep ruts and sandy ridges. The members could clearly see the hume pipes through sizeable *moroom* covering them and it appeared as if they were two inches thick rather than the stipulated six inches.

'What is the estimated cost of this road? the observer quipped.

The Collector looked at the BDO, who wanted to go through his personal diary to mention the exact amount, but the observer just wanted an approximate amount.

'Sir, one lakh thirty thousand,' he replied.

'Including masonry?'

'No Sir...only earthwork and moroom.'

'And the cost of hume pipes?'

'It is included in the estimate, Sir.'

'Then couldn't you make it at least jeepable? You people! Only want crores of rupees for your state in the name of droughts, floods but your standard of work is like this.'

Everyone kept quiet. Someone whispered, 'The observer is perhaps from a rural background, otherwise how could he be so knowledgeable.'

The observer quoted Cicero, 'You see... Literacy doesn't conduce necessarily to purity. Highly educated men are no more or no less virtuous than the untutored.'

The BDO wanted to tell the real story behind the work, how the brother of the local MLA forcibly took up the work order from his office along with an advance of 30,000 rupees and how thereafter he goaded the brother for months...but he couldn't dare say anything and his thoughts seemed to be cracking like falling trees. Someone echoed from inside, 'Espresso coffee and late night gossip with Sub-Contractors failed to bring him salvation in the end.' Inside the jeep, everyone felt like fish out of water due to the heat and dust. The jeep was stuffy and the dust had gathered in such a forceful manner it seemed as if there had been a bombardment in the nearby area. The travellers in the first jeep somehow managed, but the ones in the other vehicles were covered in a film of dust. They were transformed into dhulia babas, powdered monks. When they reached Jharghati, a group of villagers including women and children were waiting with bouquets in their hands. The observer was surprised by such a reception. Who was there to communicate this basic fact? The JE along with the road contractor had reached Jharghati earlier to alert the villagers on the issue. Was there a route other than the existing one between Jharghati and the main road leading to Beethalgarh? Someone hinted, 'Yes, there had been an ordinary road about two feet wide, created automatically by the pedestrians, and the scooter-riders were encouraged to use it sparingly.' People were used to this as the actual road, although maintained and repaired regularly, failed to satisfy the commuters. The story took a strange turn when it was discovered that the JE and the contractor rode their motorbikes through small lanes and paths avoiding the main route. How could the observers unveil a smokescreen of this kind, particularly at a time when the axe meant for weeding out poisonous plants was supported through a wood that was itself poisonous?

15

THE VILLAGERS STOOD in a group to welcome the stream of visitors to their village. The ladies, young and old, had decorated earthen pots with coconuts and the menfolks blew conches, the seashells. A young boy was seen sprinkling sandalwood paste at the crowd. The whole atmosphere seemed to have taken on a pious mood.

Mr Dave, the observer, asked, 'Are you okay?'

'Drought...Sir'

'Have you been destroyed or what?'

'No Sir... We are landless, we want to work but there's no work, Sir.'

'If we grant funds to your government, can you ensure proper farming next time?'

'Please speak.'

'Yes Sir.'

'Then how could there be a road like this?'

The observer obviously meant the road running nearby. Someone with a large moustache and a white kurta shouted out in his native dialect, 'Sir, this is a road on which lakhs of rupees are being squandered every year. There is a wider catchment and the velocity of rainwater is such that it will again wash out these hume pipes.'

Someone smoking a hookah interrupted, shouting 'Sahib, a total lie. He spits venom just because his men weren't selected as village leaders to assign contract work. Hence...'

'Okay, but stop smoking, please!'

Immediately one of the officials literally snatched the hookah away from his mouth. The first man became more furious and shouted, 'Sir, hang me if my proposition is proved incorrect. Please go through the office records if you think I am telling a lie.'

The battle lines were drawn. One rustic said loudly, 'Our pregnant ladies cannot even reach the Primary Health Centre.' The local officials including some elders tried to pacify both the groups. The JE and the contractor stood in a lonely corner as if to witness their little fiefdom melting away slowly.

The observer added, 'How can they commit such lapses?'

'I must look into that, Sir,' the Collector replied.

The ping-pong of allegations and counter-allegations came to a halt. A faint hope glimmered from within. The villagers desisted from further indulgence in politics.

A little schoolboy in the audience read out a memorandum in the local dialect. The essence of it was to depict their village as tribal and Harijan, with agriculture as their mainstay. Due to this year's inadequate rain, the kharif crop had failed. The underground aquifer had been receding rapidly making many lift irrigation points unworkable. Hence, he, on behalf of the villagers, was praying for the waiving of the crop loan and the implementation of immediate measures like labour-intensive works to combat the drought or else there would be starvation deaths.

Mr Dave, the observer, asked the boy a simple question: 'Could you tell us the quantum of loan availed by your father from the local service cooperative society?'

The boy started fumbling. The team members were ready to enter the paddy field for a crop cutting experiment but a couple of people with cold drinks tried to push the others away to reach the visitors.

'What is all this about?' queried the observer.

But nobody could identify the supplier of the cold drinks. Dave didn't relish such special treatment and politely declined the offer. Everyone made a rush for the nearby field. The crop-cutting experiment was carried out in the sweltering heat. The midday sun radiated heat and the temperature rose to around 38° Celsius. The central observers wondered how the earth could become like a frying pan in mid-September.

The spectre of drought was looming large as became evident from the crop-cutting experiment. Cultivators likely to gain 15 to 20 bags of paddy in an acre couldn't dream of getting even 5 bags. The small village was falling into an abyss of total despair. The prospect of having to struggle desperately in the days to come scared the villagers. There couldn't be any path-breaking solutions. Some small cultivators even broke down in front of the central team. This year, their rice bowls would be empty. The vast stretch of cropland surrounding the village lay parched. The central team entered a small cottage to examine if there was anything in store for the evening meal. To their shock, there was only a handful of rice and nothing else. Drought indeed, pronounced one of the team members.

All the vehicles including the first one took an about-turn. The team members picked up handkerchiefs to filter the dust. One blew away and the driver of the vehicle stopped and went off in pursuit of the same. It was found in the hand of a kid who was running behind the vehicle at top speed to hand the hanky to its owner.

The observer winced. He saw the boy giving him his missing handkerchief. Such an innocent chap! He took something from his wallet but the boy was reluctant to accept it. Dave pressed it into his palm.

The vehicles sped towards the main road. Dave was seen waving to the countless children trying frantically to race after the speeding vehicles. For some, it was a memorable sojourn, the first and the last in their career. The village stood motionless like a steel bird sitting under the endless sky.

16

AFTER APPLYING FOR the post of a company executive for a newly established silk yarn factory in Bangalore, Somen started concentrating on his studies again. The advertisement had said that age would be relaxed provided the candidate held a master's degree in chemistry with polymer science as a special paper. Experiences with regard to textile dyeing and bleaching would be extra qualifications. Both Somen and Pradeep tried frantically to obtain an experience certificate from the owner of a local power mill. After several approaches, the latter gave in and issued a certificate. Somen took care to send all his certificates and testimonials through Speed Post to Bangalore. Both worked very hard to equip themselves to answer each and every query contained in the proforma.

Somen's father had suffered a relapse. There was no substantial improvement in his health even after a week. Finally he was diagnosed with typhoid after a blood and urine test was done at a local pathology unit.

Somen dashed to the front door and saw a couple of young ladies peeping through the screen. Somen thought they were Arati and Dolly, his father's junior colleagues, and ushered them in.

'How is Roy Uncle?' Arati asked.

'Not well.'

'No remission of fever as yet?'

'No. The doctor has advised wet bandage on the forehead.'

'He is taking medicine as usual but he is not feeling better.' Somen left the living room to allow the ladies to talk freely with his parents. As such, the room was too small for five people.

Arati left a basket of fruits on the bed. She peeled an apple, cut it into small pieces and made Roy eat a piece. Roy who had lost his appetite succumbed to pressure from his two lady colleagues. Mrs Roy gave them silent moral support.

Arati was overenthusiastically pandering to the comforts of Roy. She wanted to apply balm to his aching legs but Roy politely dissuaded her saying, 'Arati, you are like my daughter. It would pain me to let you do this.' The illness had left Roy extremely weak.

Mrs Roy was busy preparing pakoras and aloo tikkis for the two girls who had never been to their residence before. Arati rushed to the kitchen to stop her from taking so much trouble on their account.

'Auntie, why do you worry about us when Uncle is so serious!'

'No matter...my darling! I must welcome you properly. After all, this is your first visit to our house.'

'So what...in no way should we be treated as guests.'

Arati took a good look at the kitchen. It was functional. She saw no trace of modernization anywhere. Roy, who spent almost everything he earned to help his son build his career, had forgotten all about his wife's small world. A small hearth with charcoal spouting fire and smoke in a corner, cheap silver colour utensils coated with black carbon, some old baby food tins as containers, bamboo baskets containing green vegetables, onions and potatoes, a bottle filled with mustard oil, garlic, turmeric, a tin can holding spices made up the little world of Mrs Roy's kitchen.

While gossiping, Mrs Roy noticed Arati's charming gestures. This reflected a sign of innocence. Even on her first visit, she drew everyone to her. This was in sharp contrast to the ways of modern girls. Her sobriety, a facet of genuineness, appealed to Mrs Roy the most. Arati had not applied any make-up. Her silky black hair fell over her shoulders and a hairband kept her well-groomed locks in place. For a while Mrs Roy, as she looked at her, forgot all about her husband's illness.

Mrs Roy considered both Arati and her son. In her mind's eye she saw them settling cosily into a flowery nest. Her heart warmed at the prospect of her son finding happiness after experiencing so many disappointments in life.

'Oh God! Please save us from uncertainties,' she cried out while praying for the speedy recovery of her husband.

17

A DISASTER LOOMED over the area. The official machinery easily welcomed the drought. With a hackneyed master plan in their hands, officials went around noting worn-out particles. They now decided to tackle the drought with the object of building their own fortunes out of the misfortunes of the people. Water became the most precious means to save the dying crops. Although rainfall was scanty, it certainly couldn't be the major reason for such a dismal scene. The fierce sun dried up the perennial stream. The entire surroundings resembled a parched desert. The ponds and tanks dried up. The Tahsildar and other revenue authorities were flooded with petitions pleading with them to cut embankments of several waterbodies. The farmers were all in a terrible dither. Villagers felt the noose slowly tightening around their necks. The sun-dried paddy crop put out the smiles from the faces of the farmers. Grains that were supposed to ripen remained dry. A quiver of helplessness ran through the farmers. Guardians were forced to recall their children from residential schools and college hostels. Nabanna, the day meant for partaking of new rice, turned into a cheerless event. For each family, the task was to survive the drought. The problem of bare survival demanded help in such a hopeless situation. Officials like Sub-District Magistrate, District Magistrate sat with their political masters and set up a crisis management team to work out a strategy for combating drought.

Floods and drought had been visiting Beethalgarh year after year. A pall of gloom hung over the fate of the farmers. They had to endure this disaster with inexhaustible patience. So much of pain without any healing touch. Often, the onset of the monsoon brought heavy rain but there was no appropriate mechanism to arrest the overflowing streams or rivers. Afterwards, the farmers were at the mercy of Indra, the rain god. Condemned to live in this manner for ages, they had no other way than to accept it as a curse from Indra for the sins they had committed earlier.

The cursed farmers were consumed with anxiety about the future. Their sweaty heads filled with worry. Who would extend a kerchief to wipe the sweat trickling down their faces? The emptying of their breadbaskets was nothing sort of nightmarish. They, en masse, looked like sinking in restlessness. The shadows of the afternoon looked sinister, threatening.

Some crooks with smiles on their faces waited for the situation to get worse. From the burnt earth, they started blossoming like jasmine. There might have been loud cries for water from every corner but these people would complacently move away. They would talk endlessly about drip irrigation, micro-sprinklers through computerized control systems and so on.

Soon after the central grants were released, the BDO started combating the drought by executing the special master plan and issuing work orders at full speed. In a majority of cases, advances were paid to the contractors and village leaders. The grants aimed at rapid labour-intensive works, which would provide full-time employment to the workers but where were they now? When they had found it too difficult to dig a pit in the hard laterite soil they went off in quest of less strenuous jobs. Sitting at home meant starvation. A soulless building like the Block office, its small-time cunning bureaucrats and Measurement Books had failed to stop them from migrating. They had fled to bigger places like Waltair, Raipur, in search of greener pastures and their bolted cottages looked like scarecrows. At every doorstep local-made locks could be seen hanging. Properties like earthen pots, broomsticks, tattered mats were visible through the chinks in the door. For any kind of survey, either the election or census, these empty houses didn't matter in the least to the officials. Passenger trains pulling into Beethalgarh were filled with this battered lot. Like migratory birds flocking together, they piled into one compartment, not looking for vacant spaces elsewhere in the train.

They did this out of fear of train ticket inspectors or the railway police. Being ticketless, they were frightened of such authorities. Their drooping moustaches were no match to those sported by the security guards. Collections were raised instantly from among themselves to pay for their unauthorized entry. Bargaining went on in whispers. Sometimes a constable would wield a stick and teach them a lesson. Another constable would grab a person's baggage and throw it outside. 'Let us collect more,' someone would shout. The villagers would find some ways of appeasing the new gods. Currency notes passed from one hand to the other. No one insisted on receipts. Being relieved of their initial fear they calmly looked out of the windows. Their piercing looks took in scenes of joy, of mango groves standing against the blue sky. Their own village receded into the distance.

Someone chanced upon discovering tall palm trees competing with the white Shiva temple in climbing towards the sky. Alas! The annual Shivratri fair had to be forgotten. Familiar sights faded from view. That was immensely saddening. How was it that their village wore such a desolate look? Did it resemble a cremation ground? So dim and listless! It looked like a dull ship on a dull sea.

The temple of Lord Shiva stood aloof. It was as if all his love for them had given way to a cruel expression of his fury. The drought was his heartless message. Something was eating into their vitals. Like animals they were going in search of greener pastures anywhere under the sky. Their native villages were like immortal music to their hearts. They glittered like the moon in their mind's sky.

To leave one's native place was indeed painful! The sprawling landscape both to the right and left of the railway track was receding away. In between, the train slowed down and stopped abruptly. Some curious passengers ventured out of the compartment. Anxiety was writ large upon their faces. Bloody bits of a calf's body lay scattered between the railway lines. They saw a villager running towards them at top speed. It had a dark dangling thread and scraps of corals that he had secured so dearly around its neck. He embraced the carcass and wept bitterly. Oh! The small bubble of the calf's life burst under the wheels of train. A collective pain echoed in the hearts of everyone present.

The train gave a long whistle and began to move slowly. *Jay Bam Bhole,* cried the seniormost among the labourers. 'Oh Lord Shiva, please spare us,' he said and promised to offer him a grand worship the next year. The temple disappeared into the distant horizon while the present occupied them as they waited for the unknown urban bliss.

Orange, groundnut and banana peels lay all over the floor of the compartment. The toilets packed with stolen woods were unfit for public use. No water in the tap. Fans and lights were out of order. The doorways were sealed with all kinds of heavy luggage. The compartment was totally in disarray. In spite of the breeze blowing in through the windows, the passengers kept sweating. Some sent little clouds of acrid smoke from the bidis they smoked. Like a group of frozen people the villagers lay quiet on their respective seats as the train relentlessly bore them towards an unknown horizon.

18

VERY FEW SONS of the soil stayed back in Beethalgarh to fight for its cause. Its nearby areas too wore a thin and pale look. NGOs and the Government machinery employed in test relief failed miserably to check such migration. To many, it usually came like a quiet tyrant with a sinister motive. The sun and the moon, two ancient friends, looked like following them to give company. The environment was a ghastly one, which fanned the greed of some people. Their family members began to look brighter than the brightest sky. Gossiping grew more frequent and more excited. The pain of serving in remote rural areas instantly metamorphosed into blessedness. The staff from the Rural Engineering Department including Block officials, like an orchestra, went on playing the symphony of drought. Dazzled by the glamour of easy earnings, the wives and children of officials engaged in test relief work weighed everything in terms of their gains. Although there were stipulated office hours, these officials preferred to overstay. So an office premises began to have nightlife. Dwellers of both the railway and the Block colonies made a foray into the town's different showrooms in search of the choicest goods. Washing machines, colour TVs, hairdryers, refrigerators, stereo systems, digital cameras all were lined up for inspection before them. These goods enlivened each day of their master's life. Familiar vehicles parked in front of the residences of the BDO, the JE and the Head Clerk gave rise to lingering whisperings. A wad of currency notes adorned a few hands while the majority of hands were empty. So much of money at one stroke! Gold chains glittered around the necks of the wives and daughters of these officials. TVs with multiple channels invaded the locality. From these they learnt the details of the inflow of central packages to Beethalgarh. A spirited mood sprang up in many on hearing this news. What a popular Government with such sanguine views! Hota, Inspector of Civil Supplies, along with Nanda, JE, went for a ride to the nearby Shiva temple for some kind of an offering. On entering the sanctum sanctorum, they folded their hands and offered prayers with deep reverence. 'Oh God,' the prayers went on in full swing. 'You have made us rich ignoring the rest. It speaks of your great love for us.'

Retailers and petty contractors assembled there like bees in a hive. As if Lord Shiva belonged only to them. Depriving every village of its usual quota of sugar and kerosene, tampering with stock and distribution ledgers, and the result looked spectacular! Lord Shiva was the biggest beneficiary. Copper plates were gifted, bearing the names of the two officials. What a generosity!

A somewhat painful conflict awaited most of the people of this locality. The burning sky threw away its rainbow into an unknown corner. The extreme heat wilted energy. Students' minds appeared disoriented. Teachers were appalled to see the low attendance rates. Master Babu picked up the attendance sheet on the table in Class fifth of Jharghati:

One
Two
Three
Four...Yes Sir
Five
Six...Yes sir
Seven...

The axe of his anger hacked away at the chalk, duster and the attendance register. Before his very eyes his green surroundings seemed to have been transformed into a dark spot. 'Let us go to your jhuggis,' he shouted at some of his pupils. Being afraid of his sudden outburst they followed him quietly. To his surprise, the cottages once teeming with so many lovely faces wore a forlorn look. Master Babu let out a yell while sitting on the earthen verandah of a cottage.

Mahesh!
Ramu!
Kripa!

'Hell with this,' he screamed at an empty cottage. He couldn't continue his search any further.

The village was covered in a shroud of silence. "Eh! What a desert?' Master Babu exclaimed. He couldn't endure the eerie loneliness and beat a hasty retreat. He asked the boys not to accompany him further. While returning, he talked to the guardians of some of the boys. He looked at the wall posters on joyful learning. So many messages, he wondered.

He felt a sudden stab of hunger. He opened his food packet with stiff fingers. On many occasions he had shared it with one or two of his hungry students. The wrinkle on his forehead grew deeper. He had not received his salary for the last three months. It was heart wrenching. He put some rice into his mouth but that was all. He washed his hand abruptly. Master Babu wanted to know where all these people had gone. 'Where are they now?'; 'No exact information,' came a sharp reply. Maybe Raipur, Waltair, or somewhere else. How to trace them in such a vast area? Master Babu looked perplexed. His little students, who he had nurtured so tenderly, had never faced such a harsh situation. How to endure such horror and such misfortune? So rare is the smell of rice. Where would they find shelter on this great earth? 'My boys,' he wailed silently. A sudden calm came over him. The children's memory pierced his heart like bullets. Until recently, the boys kept the tri-coloured flag afloat with the great patriotic song *Vande Mataram* on their quivering lips. Drought had ruined Beethalgarh. It had torn apart every heart. Greenery in the countryside had been pulverized by the scorching blow of the hot sun. Every field looked parched, brown and empty. The village stood stiff like a skeletal tree.

He gazed at the autumn sky where fleecy clouds were floating around in several directions. He saw the desiccated plants looking as if they had been burnt alive. The boys were taking loving care of them. But all efforts went in vain. The borewell in the school was out of order. It seemed everything had come to a gory end. Was it more akin to a seismic vibration? Not even a butterfly to represent the serene winsome mood of autumn. Master Babu looked at the school campus carefully. It was embarrassing to prolong one's stay there. It seemed so forlorn and empty!

Once again he looked at the sky. The hot sun had all the radiance to justify its sovereignty, and every single object was trying to escape from its cruel domination. Nowhere was there any sign of rain clouds. They failed miserably from streaming down from the vast sky to regenerate the greenness of the earth. Everything from a kitchen to a tree looked rusty. Master Babu shared the whole agony in utter disgust. 'Maa Durga,' he prayed spreading his arms. 'So magnificent are you! Please redeem us from this ghastly plot.'

He bolted the main gate with a strong wire and started cycling back to his house. The jangling sound of the chain and free wheel ruffled the calmness hanging over the village.

19

SOMEN, IN SPITE of his busy schedule, never failed to listen to the woes of the toiling masses. At times, the general public, that is, the rural folk were seen assembling outside his residence seeking advice from him on several matters. For them, he was their raison d'être. Bureaucratic apathy or harassment was on top of their agenda.

One such case came to him. Although he had played no decisive role in rural politics and was disenchanted by the practitioners of this art, the dwellers of Judabandh rushed to him for solace.

Judabandh, a small place twenty-five kilometres north-west of Beethalgarh, had been home to about two hundred families for more than thirty years. Although the area lay within a protected forest, the dwellers were certainly not in the category of wild animals. The small site of about two hundred fifty acres had been severed from the main revenue village, Bitabandh, and had shaped its own identity within the forest itself. A lush green valley with bountiful yields of paddy, the villagers never waited for clouds and showers since there were perennial streams nearby. The catchment area was around 65 per cent of the total reserved forest area. The network of rivulets acted as the water transport artery for the whole place. The villagers fished with the help of bamboo baskets and ate rice and fish as their staple food. It had a cool climate. The dwellers were strangers to politics. Far from the madding crowd, they were enclosed in their harmonious green world. Although not declared a revenue village, the dwellers had acquired two to three acres of land each by clearing the forest. The trees were felled. After such clearing operations, the dwellers settled there ignoring all the stringent laws governing forest and revenue administration.

The dwellers fell victim to the wrath of forest officials who considered the whole area as their *jagir*. Emboldened by an obsolete code and taking advantage of the villagers' desperation to continue with an assured living, the young Range Officer started throwing a dragnet to curb their movements inside their own living space. The forest guards, oblivious of the definition of a reserved forest, impounded the cattle, goats, poultry and all such domestic creatures grazing nearby. Even during harvesting, those whimsical guys would camp at the site waiting to let loose a reign of terror.

Self-styled representatives of the state, with an aim to drive out these humble rustics, would approach their threshing floors.

'Whose share of paddy is this?' thundered someone.

There was no reply.

A voice broke the eerie silence. 'We will seize everything here.'

And they did. Not even the kitchenware was spared.

The dwellers didn't have the courage to protest against the action of the officials. They were not conversant with the intricacies of the ruling system. So innocent were they! Before their very eyes, they saw carts being loaded with their own produce. The people in khaki had pocketed Laxmi, the Goddess of Wealth.

'Hajur!' An old fellow rushed up with folded hands. 'Please excuse our boys for any lapses!'

'We beg your pardon, Sir,' whimpered the others.

The guards, like ancient rulers, looked at them with contempt. They carried off the stock. Snatching had seemed so easy, more so when they saw it like a windfall! Not even an iota of investment. So luxurious a life! Both guards stood speechless honouring each other's flippant mood. They preferred to look grave. Never did they once look at those creatures again, they just confined themselves to collecting grain.

'What are we born for if not to die,' said someone in the valley.
'That concerns you,' came the sharp reply.

That was only the tip of the iceberg. The torment didn't end there. After the arrival of the Forester, the malignant motive was expressed more clearly. All atrocities took on a new dimension. The womenfolk were forced to prepare food and brew liquor for the so-called state agents. They behaved as if they were the government.

A fleeing chicken was pursued by a group of people. Malia rushed saying, 'Stop all this!'

'Why?'

'We live here. Nobody has the right to snatch our right to live.'

'What do you think of yourself?' shouted the Forester. The two forest guards pounced upon Malia. He was dragged, beaten up and called a scoundrel. Quickly the settlers positioned themselves to save Malia. It took no time to separate them. The Forester sent an SOS through VHF for special reinforcements. The RO responded at once. Within no time the whole area looked like an army camp.

The beating continued mercilessly. Malia became the target of the ego of a bunch of forest officials. 'Ooh...ooh...Bapa.'

His wife, mother and father cried out. 'Please save him...save him.' His wife raised herself just as a strong blow was being aimed at her husband. She fell down suddenly, her head bleeding. The blood covered her face. Malia's only child cried out in fear. His parents including hordes of dwellers let out a battle cry. Screams of protests filled the silent valley. Abuses mixed with local dialects were hurled at forest officials from all directions.

The RO arrested Malia, but it became impossible for him and his followers to lift the accused from the spot. It was a trying time for both. Although the armed force stood nearby, no firing could take place without an order from an EM. However, they resorted to blank firing. They were doubly cautious not to mention the incident in their office records.

The dwellers panicked at the sound of gunshots. They fled to hiding places in the valley carrying their children with them, but Malia's family stood there braving the bullets. They stood closer to him in a gesture of solidarity.

It was a well-thought-out plan to terrorize the whole valley. The hamlet was crushed by state power. The terror was to establish forest administration once and for all.

But the EM had a different view. He anticipated further danger from the furious mob. There might be a roadblock cutting off access to their retreat. Stones could fly from some unseen corner at them. The prospect scared him. He was not a professional warrior. A salaried employee like him was no good when it came to devising battle tactics.

They tried desperately to lift Malia from the unpaved spot. All of them were visibly vexed. Finally Malia gave up.

He was produced before the court of the Judicial Magistrate the next day.

Charged under several sections of the Odishsa Forest Act, Malia found it difficult to get someone to bail him out. Pradeep and Somen got involved in the situation because of their sympathy for the tribals. Somen became the bailer, producing a photocopy of the deed of a plot of land recorded in Somen's name. There were many hurdles to cross before Malia could be released. Someone offered a cigarette packet to the bench clerk who was to place the file before the Magistrate. 'Where is the matchbox?' he asked. Someone rushed to the roadside betel shop and brought a matchbox. 'Only the rich can withstand an onslaught by the state apparatus,' Pradeep muttered to somebody.

Malia was dressed in rags. As a result, the lawyers treated him with utter indifference. They had sensed that Malia would not be able to pay. So they quickly lost all interest in his case.

'Why is no one interested?' Somen asked in disgust.

'It is always like this,' replied a senior member of the Bar. He ridiculed the twosome for doing honorary service.

'Pradeep! Beware!! Do you want to starve?' voices cautioned them. To them this attitude seemed disgusting.

'Official gangsters!' Somen shouted at the forest officials standing nearby. Someone glanced at him out of the corner of his bulging eye. After a lot of hassles Malia was out on bail.

'Let us go.' Pradeep dragged Somen away. He didn't want to confront anyone there. They went outside. A group of tribals including women and children stood there holding bouquets to extend a warm welcome to their leader. They all took out a procession through the main street of the town. Somen, Malia and Pradeep walked at the head of the procession. The excited mob shouted abuses at the government. 'Down with the Forest Department.' The chorus grew louder and clearer. Placards adorned with cartoons of corrupt forest officials were waved by the protesters. Malia was in no mood to take on any kind of leadership. His only request was that Pradeep and Somen come to his hamlet and spend the night there among the villagers. They couldn't say no. Like a flaming rocket, slogans in praise of the trio soared into the sky.

Malia Zindabad
Somen Babu Zindabad
Pradeep Babu Zindabad
Long live our struggle

Somen and Pradeep decided to cycle to the obscure hamlet, Judabandh, to boost the morale of its settlers. The journey was arduous, more like an adventure. Parents in both houses had been informed. Their host Malia hinted at the type of hospitality likely to be extended in Judabandh. Somen and Pradeep would benefit from the unique experience of spending the night in the vicinity of a forest.

They left in the evening when it was not so hot. As they cycled they saw the sun setting in the western horizon. In the opposite direction, the moon showed its pale face. The surrounding forest was silent. Finally, after cycling for fifteen kilometres they reached their destination, Judabandh, where they were greeted with enthusiasm.

'How frank and open they are!' Somen thought. He observed Malia, their leader. His belligerence was writ large on his face. It exuded self-confidence. His brief utterances were nothing but a prelude to action. Malia had concealed his dreams under a tortoise-like veneer. 'The rule of the "khaki" uniform won't be tolerated any more,' he burst out.

'No respect will be shown to officers. The loudmouths are to be checked at any cost.' His followers repeated again and again.

Dinner arrangements had been made and several dishes prepared to accord a fitting reception to the guests. The whole valley was charged with a feeling of excitement. A wave of spontaneous enthusiasm swept through Judabandh.

A long discussion followed the dinner. What would be the next course of action? Both Somen and Pradeep strained every nerve to prepare a draft resolution declaring Judabandh a revenue village, and this would be forwarded to the government. This would bring an end to their bondage. 'The Government cannot close its eyes to their problems any more'. Why should the Government continue to be apathetic about their plight? Why should their road be blocked? Such questions were raised.

'Yeh! A well-pronounced judgement,' commented Malia.

'Yes,' came the reply from everyone. Like a heroic tale it got carried forward by collective excitement.

'Well,' Somen added, 'Judabandh fulfils all the criteria of a revenue village because it has a population of more than 150 and has been separated naturally from the main village. In case of rare provision, the Revenue Department should come forward to compensate the loss out of its own reserved lands. Only 250 acres.' The hamlet dwellers nodded to the proposal without any scrutiny. In an impassioned mood the dwellers were all determined to protest against the humiliation they had suffered at the hands of lawmakers. Were they thieves, criminals or swindlers?

Malia was in no mood to rejoice. How could he forget the memory of physical torture so quickly? His wife, sitting beside him, looked depressed. Despite her injury, she had not received any first-aid treatment except for a thin paste made from a medicinal herb. His mother's poor health did not deter her from looking after her grandchild. How does one cope with the heaviness of such inhuman savagery? How to protest against the attackers? The idea of revenge filled his mind.

However, the draft resolution took the form of a prayer petition. Copies of it were to reach the Collector, the SC and local MLA including the Tahsildar, who were to share the responsibility of delivering the same.

Like fading dreams regaining their lustre, the dwellers could forget their ignominy for a while and look forward to a brighter future. Judabandh now dreamt of electricity, borewells, primary schools and a black-topped road that would transform it beyond recognition. Gazing at one another the villagers dreamt the same dream. Judabandh wouldn't stay naked any more. That day certainly was not far off. Every mind got stirred again and again.

20

SOMEN AND PRADEEP spent a sleepless night in Judabandh. They were unable to cope with the lack of basic amenities like electricity. Was Judabandh worth fighting for? Somen had never been away from his house in this manner before. Being egalitarian didn't mean that one should plunge oneself into such a situation. Somen wished to get out of this dogmatic mood. He shouldn't sing such ideological songs any more. Under no circumstances should dissatisfaction cloud his life.

After the morning ablutions on the bank of the stream, he told Pradeep to say goodbye to the villagers. He wanted to go back to Beethalgarh.

A group of rustics, who looked like figures in a pantomime show, stood in front of him. They could sense Somen's disenchantment. His sullen face pricked them like thorns. Someone whispered something. He came to Somen and said in the local dialect, 'Somen Babu, what's troubling you? We won't let you return so soon.'

Somen replied coolly, 'I have a lot of things to do at home. I must go.'

'We beg you to stay a little longer, Somen Babu,' Malia pleaded. 'Who do our people have but the two of you.'

Somen stood motionless. So much of trust and love was being reposed in him. He couldn't push them aside so bluntly. In fact, they were nothing less than a sturdy shelter for Malia and the villagers.

Pradeep didn't wish to waste any more time. He was ready to leave. How does one live with poor, hungry rustics for days? He mentioned Roy, Somen's ailing father. The dwellers had absolutely no answer for this. They had come to understand the urgency of medical attention only recently. How different were the ways of celebrities coming from an urban set-up! Yes, they were all human beings, but what great differences in tastes and preferences! When each united in their innermost commitments nothing can subjugate their strength of will. People from nearby villages started arriving. Somen didn't want to display himself before the crowd like a showpiece in a museum.

Somen and Pradeep made their way back to Beethalgarh. They felt that their exertions could not heal people's wounds. They had to content themselves with such little actions. An agitation against state power was no dinner party or a stroll in the valley. One had to challenge the might of the state by singing a line from a rebel poet, 'What is the distance between violin and violence?' Their followers' loyalty couldn't be taken for granted, either. An outsider always remains an outsider.

Somen was not used to the rough life. He had never had any occasion to roam around freely in the green woods. Like a vast green mat, nature stretched endlessly to the horizon. Nothing here urged one to compete with other human beings. Yet they longed to leave Judabandh and return home.

No sooner had they left the village than the swinging leaves began to obstruct their path. The gentle flowers gently whipped them. Chirping birds performed aerial gymnastics in the distant sky. Somen watched the mid-air dancing of butterflies. The stream went rippling down the slopes. The never-ending song of crickets filled the bushes.

It is said that the bitterness of neem cannot be removed even if you bathe it with syrup a hundred times. So also outsiders like Somen and Pradeep who in spite of repeated requests didn't agree for their night stay in Judabandh.

At a nearby spot, Somen discovered a small masonry work, symbolizing the dwellers' unity and strength to create a channel for the rainwater. How could it be? 'Did you get any financial support from the government?'

'No, no,' shouted Malia

'How did you construct it then?' asked Somen

'Ours is a hamlet...not even a revenue village. How could we expect such a grant from the government? No road...school... nothing so far. Only a borewell and that too after a hectic parley between the local MLA, the Public Health Department and us. In office records, it has been shown elsewhere and not here. Our children are deprived of the facilities of normal schooling. As yet, not a single ration card so that we can purchase controlled commodities like sugar, kerosene, etc.,' said Malia.

'Yes, I know, but I didn't ask that.'

'I understand. We used our own labour. Frankly speaking, we stole timber from the forest and sold it to make money. A forest contractor helped us do this. He gave us some bags of cement too.'

'Oh! How nice. You were quite resourceful,' commented Pradeep. 'If there was such a consensus, then why not a full-fledged movement in support of our stand?'

Somen took careful stock of the work. 'What a nice arrangement for entering the village!' But Malia said, 'No...no, Sir, ours has not yet been declared a village.' Somen could sense that he felt hurt.

'What is this?'

'Something has been written in charcoal, hasn't it?' Somen added.

Mardingi Nallah

18/8 RCC

1 × 7.62 × 3.9 m

'Maybe the handiwork of a neo-literate,' Pradeep added.

All of them laughingly noticed a boy of around fifteen following them.

'Oh, I see, the boy wanted to demonstrate his command of arithmetic.'

'Look at his grammar,' said Pradeep. The boy bowed before the others. Comments came like muffled hits. He felt neither embarrassed nor elated. The learning potential of a rural boy without support from any teacher or learning material seemed astonishing. No one present could explain the reason for such a versatile mind.

'The boy is certainly in the wrong place,' said Somen. 'Unless he is taken care of, he will lose his talent.'

21

SOMEN AND PRADEEP did not want such a grand procession accompanying them home but Malia didn't want to leave them alone. 'Malia, please...Beethalgarh is not very far from here. We can certainly take care of ourselves,' Somen kept telling him.

Malia, however, smiled and said, 'Somen Babu, this area is full of wolves and bears. Even leopards cross the road sometimes. How can we let you travel alone?'

Somen didn't argue. In fact, the spectre of a leaping leopard flashed through his mind. The ghastly scene of a hunting predator sent a shudder down his spine. How concerned these people are about us, he thought. So much love for us. Somen felt something stirring within him. The same thought crossed Pradeep's mind.

Such a loving gesture had to be reciprocated. Somen didn't want to keep quiet, as it would mean indifference. At times the two of them tried to engage the villagers in small talk in order to break the monotony of the journey.

'Why are your people rarely seen in Beethalgarh?'

'Our people are afraid of your people, Somen Babu. Their attitude to us is painful.' He asked the people accompanying them to narrate experiences of their humiliation. But they would not oblige, maybe for fear of having to speak in unintelligible dialects. Many of them raised a shout, 'Speak...speak' but it failed to excite anyone. Malia took the lead and narrated one incident on their behalf.

'One of us had gone to Beethalgarh and seen a signboard there saying "Sarkar Clinic". He thought it distributed medicine free of cost. He entered because in local parlance "sarkar" means government. After a brief consultation, the doctor gave him some medicines but demanded a fixed amount in return. The patient was surprised at this because it was unbecoming on the part of a Government doctor to ask for money in a clinic.'

'Then?'

'Who told you this is a Government clinic?' the doctor asked angrily.

'Because the signboard says so.'

'What does it say?'

'Sarkar Clinic and sarkar means government.'

'Don't be stupid. Sarkar is my surname. This is a private clinic and you have to pay for the medicines.'

'Why use such a surname?'

'Don't be silly. Pay up.'

The poor villager paid the bill but rebuked himself for having committed such a mistake. He vowed never to pass through that route again.

Somen and Pradeep had a hearty laugh. The victim and the others took it in good spirit. Malia had narrated this ordinary tale merely to minimize the boredom of cycling.

Everyone had a story to tell. The duo had to lend their ears to many stories. They nodded, pretending to understand every word that was being uttered. Although ordinary, both enjoyed mixing, travelling with them.

'It was a case of extortion by rowdy elements of Beethalgarh. They demanded a substantial share from the sale of my cow at the weekly market. One gangster came forward to prove that it was a stolen cow.'

'Simple blackmailing,' added Pradeep.

'Finding no way out, I was compelled to part with half of the amount. Since then I have a lot of hatred for Beethalgarh,' said one villager.

'Strange,' replied Somen. He did not want to add to the discussion fearing that it might go on and on. 'The cause of servility is nothing but illiteracy. Some urbanites bank upon plundering and that makes them no different from a group like the Pindaris during the medieval period. How does one grapple with this?' Somen pondered over ways of easing social tension but now cycling kept him more occupied.

A sudden shout from Malia made everyone stop. He came forward and urged Somen and Pradeep to have a little rest. They sat under a mango tree.

The faces of both the guys had already turned red. Somen was panting heavily. Pradeep's condition was no better. They were breathless after riding up the hilly track and were sweating profusely. Their wet skins glistened. Malia wiped the sweat from Somen's body with his towel. Somen tried to dissuade him but Malia would not listen. After a while, they resumed their uphill journey. A boy came rushing up from behind, carrying a bag in his cycle. Everyone looked at him inquisitively. He brought out a hill mynah from his tattered bag. Malia snatched the bird from him and persuaded Somen to accept it as a souvenir. Somen looked perplexed. He wanted to refuse but restrained himself somehow. He couldn't bring himself to hurt the sentiments of the villagers. So he said he would accept the gift symbolically. He touched the bird and it was put back into the bag. The agitated bird started fluttering and Somen grabbed the bag with the intention of freeing it, but decided against it.

Everyone except Malia and a couple of others returned to the village from this point. Five cycles rolled up and down in a space of about three feet wide. Malia took the lead. Judabandh had an intricate topography of its own. It had both hills and plateaus. The road zigzagged and spiralled creating problems for amateur riders like Somen and Pradeep. The journey took a long time. Malia kept a watchful eye on their two guests. For a long time they skirted around the hilly terrain, at times losing the way. Malia prayed to Banadevi, whose shrine they had come across, seeking her blessings. It was against beliefs of both Somen and Pradeep but Malia's face glowed with devotion and for a moment he forgot all about his problems. Somen looked at him lying curled at the feet of Banadevi. He and Pradeep did the same. They all put vermilion on their foreheads and took prasad. This in a way energized them to resume their journey.

Gradually the forested terrain gave way to flat lush green fields near

Jharghati. Now their bicycles gathered speed. Beethalgarh stood about five kilometres from there. The sun was sinking slowly. The crimson horizon looked like a red fountain. A crescent moon appeared in the distant horizon. The lights of Beethalgarh beckoned from a distance. The landscape slowly darkened as evening fell. The starlit sky began to sparkle above the distant mountain. Their eyes filled with wonder. They could hear the fascinating sound of cymbals and the mridanga from a nearby dwelling. The rhythm was pleasant and brought them comfort. Malia suggested they take a little rest. Pradeep and Somen accepted the suggestion. They chose a lush green spot where a breeze caressed them. Malia now told them the story of his life.

'That was a very unfortunate night for my family and me. The forest officials came to our village in a jeep. Many of them were drunk. Before we could find out anything about them, they started ransacking our houses. They beat us mercilessly.'

'I think you have narrated this incident earlier.'

'No, the earlier one was to seize agricultural produce. This was for the timber, firewood, etc.'

'How many times did you face such atrocities?' Pradeep asked.

'On so many occasions that I have lost count of them.'

'They had nursed a grudge against my family and me for a long time. They were convinced that I was behind the theft of timber from the protected forest. Once, on the instruction of the RO, they tied me, beat me up mercilessly and threw me on the dusty road. Then one forest guard kicked me and urinated on me. My wife and family members rushed to save me from the attack. In the attempt, she received a flurry of blows in her abdomen and she bled profusely. She was pregnant then. Seeing her unconscious they arrested me and whisked me away in their office vehicle. The RO asked his subordinates to frame charges under a section of the Odisha Forest Rules and implicated me for contravention. The villagers requested them to spare me so that I could look after my wounded wife. They didn't listen. Nothing could melt their stony hearts. They were determined to prosecute me. I lay rotting in the hazat throughout the night. The next day I was produced before the JM for bail. It was granted at last.' Stories of cruelty had been heard often. They no longer excited Somen. They seemed to be the hard-luck story of an average rural Indian. It was as if fate had taken revenge on them.

'Then, what next?' Pradeep asked.

'Pradeep Babu, my wife regained her senses after several hours. She had bled profusely and lost consciousness again. We immediately shifted her to the nearby Primary Health Centre, but unfortunately the Government doctor was away attending to a private call. At the hospital, health care was available only to those who could pay. Initially, the midwives as well as the staff didn't look at her. They simply asked us to leave her on the floor. When they were given some money, they arranged a bed and came forward to help us. The nurse's idea of child delivery was absolutely funny. She simply looked at my wife as she cried bitterly. She applied a crude method of inserting her right hand into the uterus and administered three bottles of saline but nothing could stop the bleeding. She was again shifted to the Sub-Divisional Hospital, Beethalgarh, in a hired vehicle. No ambulance was available as it had taken the hospital staff to a picnic spot.'

'What happened next?'

'The doctor, nurse, technician asked us to get all kinds of tests done. My parents had never come across such greedy employees in their lifetime. The gynaecologist, even without looking at her, started haggling and charged an exorbitant amount as the case, according to him, had been mishandled by the Primary Health Centre staff. Even he became sceptical of her survival. Severe bleeding had drained away all her bodily strength and she was on the verge of collapsing. My father sold my mother's only gold chain and handed over the amount to the doctor. We succumbed to the pressure tactic of the hospital staff. Even a sweeper would not help a patient with a bedpan if not tipped properly.

'Oh! What a place the hospital is!' Somen burst out.

'Somebody's injury is their gain.'

'The doctor treated my wife as if she was an object. He inserted his hand and brought out a portion of the foetus from the uterus. Ultimately he removed the foetus and deprived us from having children forever. Our dreams including that of my parents were shattered,' Malia exclaimed.

'Bloody murderers.' Somen spat venom at those forest officials who had perpetrated such a crime.

'Do you still dream of becoming a father?' asked Pradeep.

Malia broke into tears. He was shocked by such a hard-hitting question. He became speechless. No one felt like asking him any further questions. They finally arrived at Beethalgarh. Somen stopped consoling Malia as it might be like rubbing salt into his wound. They came to a halt at Somen's residence. Somen could hear his father's ailing shouts. Somen formally asked Malia and the others to accept his hospitality for the night, but they politely refused. On seeing Mrs Roy, he requested politely for a small rope. He tied the hill mynah and handed it to her. Somen didn't want to part with Malia so soon. He offered them refreshments, but Malia wanted to return to his village immediately. Somen fed them at the nearby hotel. Malia and his companions reluctantly accepted his hospitality. They didn't like to burden him further. They chose the cheapest dishes. Malia, after washing his hands, even offered to pay for the meal, but the hotel owner on instruction from Somen refused to accept payment from him.

Somen stayed beside his ailing father to comfort him. It was strange, he was concentrating on affairs which had nothing to do with building his career. What really interests the ruling classes? Caring for a few and ignoring the rest? If so, a storm will blow in soon. 'What a strange world,' thought Somen to himself. Persons at the helm of affairs were always latched on to their fortunes.

22

THE DROUGHT CAME, saw and conquered the whole of Beethalgarh. For salaried people, the strain was less. Responsibilities increased manifold among the railway staff. But Roy Babu had yet to regain his normal physical strength. Arati, at times, rushed to the Roy residence on her own, without Dolly, to look after him. She was utterly selfless in her concern for the Roy family. Her growing zeal caused much speculation among the colony residents. Undaunted, Arati went on creating ripples in the whirlpool of Roy's family life. Both and Mrs Roy were careful not to hurt her sentiments, even though it had become more of a problem for them than the illness. It so happened that often, Mrs Roy and Minati had to accompany Arati to her residence at night. The high fever started reducing slowly.

However, there was a spontaneous opening up of the skies and thunderclouds dominated the distant horizons, bringing cheer to everyone's face. Tons of raindrops filled every pocket of the parched earth. The instant shower felt like the arrival of the rain queen with countless tubs to provide cooling baths for the frying living race. Some satanic creatures could not relish such a flow of compassion. They saw no personal benefit in it. The situation would be better if the shadow of drought culminated in famine! Let it first corrode the greenness of Mother Earth. Let it swallow every word from the dictionary except P...R...O...F...I...T. Every night it was the same dream, a dream that revolved around a theme called personal gain. Every dawn brought the usual sun of greed and every single word uttered was to do with bizarre grasping.

But for children, profit making was far from their minds. They were more interested in celebrating the worship of the 'frog king' since such scattered showers were not enough.

According to popular belief, frog worship brought plenty of rain, but this needed to be stopped at any cost. Those with vested interests wanted to poison the frog. They wanted to make a fast buck by taking advantage of drought. Renovation of tanks, repair of roads were like music to the hearts of those with vested interests. They started orbiting the circle of authorities to intensify labour-intensive work and so fixed their greedy eyes on earthwork.

A procession of children made its way down the dusty road. The frog king had been made up with touches of vermilion and collyrium around the eyes and was the focus of everyone's attention, except for a select few who were obsessed with percentage or PC. It became the fluttering banner for every repair or maintenance work that one came across in the area. They did not like shouts of the children welcoming the rain.

'What is the matter with you?' the assistant shouted at the boys. They ignored him and continued shouting.

Long live frog king!

No rain! No gain!

'What the hell,' the contractor burst out. He deputed another of his chums to give hot milk to the frog king. The latter poured the gift into an aluminium container. The tiny creature made a cracking sound and jumped out with a great leap and ran away. The children chased after it but the creature had disappeared.

'Revenge,' thundered the children. But how could it be? They were certainly no match for a mighty contractor. The kids knew their angry outbursts were futile. They were just pawns in the hands of a mighty contractor. Each child engaged in a silent protest in some form or other. They felt great hatred but it was of no use. The flavour of rain could not reach their tender lips. They dispersed with tears in their eyes. A shower was not enough for the plough to create furrows in the earth and this stood like a nagging pain for the cultivators. The boys had to hide themselves in the dim corners of their houses.

Misfortunes came down at a galloping speed to say hello to the majority of the dwellers. The subsidized rice meant for the poor found its way to the houses of the rich and millers only. Almost all the secretaries of the Gram Panchayats maintained lists of consumers without leaving any black spots on them. But in reality the open market bossed around the controlled market and fortune only smiled at these secretaries.

They swallowed every chargesheet from the court of the people like icing on the cake. Cartoons appeared on walls depicting these characters eating rice from jute bags, but these were dismissed as the envy of those who failed to gain anything out of the present system. They branded these elements as agents of Pakistan who had nothing to do other than outrage the modesty of Mother India.

A rational voice like Somen's felt alienated. It waited to be smothered by its worst enemies. 'The pain of living exceeded the pain of death.' In a living mechanism, delicate flowers gave way to thorns and the embers of a bonfire. 'Our main enemies are within us,' Somen pointed out. This penetrated deeply into the psyche of the common people. Somen could visualize something strange in the whole set-up. He discovered so many with syringes in their hands. Was it to administer intravenous fluid to an anemic? No, such large hearts had already fallen asleep. They were already locked from outside and could not step out any more.

The so-called nobles were like well-trained vultures. Was it their intention to keep the minimum amount of blood essential for survival and drain out the rest and then throw the body away like a dead monument?

Roy Babu like some others disliked corruption and the involvement of the local administration. The rumours of PC were also discussed by paan-eaters and tea-drinkers. It echoed continuously among the privileged and unprivileged and like an optical toy went on displaying its changing patterns of colours to a minor group of people leaving the rest of the human race to assess its importance.

23

ALTHOUGH PLENTY OF grants flowed into the Block office, the NAC could not snatch them away from them. This disturbed Das, the EO. He looked morose and did not like participating in official matters so wholeheartedly. Even the smile on his face became expressionless. He tried to find out the reason for such financial apathy. A self-styled person of super intelligence and exceptional ability, he decided to knock at the door of the Directorate of Municipal Administration at Bhubaneswar. Mohan, the Councillor-cum-VC, was to accompany him to expedite the whole affair. This had become necessary since the Chairman was indisposed. Like several others, the duo could be teamed up for negotiating a journey of about 400 kilometres to the state capital. Since the travelling allowance was meagre, they wanted an all-expenses-paid trip by the contractors. The office vehicle had been out of order for a long time. They hired a taxi owned by a NAC member through a benami transaction. By chance, the Under Secretary of the Directorate happened to be an erstwhile colleague of Das and he was very glad to see him. From him they gathered that the whole Department stood like the Vatican Hill of the minister's personal whims.

'In which way can the Minister be satisfied?' Das asked.

'That is known to everyone, replied the Under Secretary.

'Sir...please,' Mohan said.

'No please of any kind, please!' the Under Secretary added.

The Under Secretary looked as if he was bemoaning the loss of a fifty-paise coin. The state was perhaps nurturing him for beaming like an indifferent idol by fixing powerful specs to match his bald-headed domain where a bundle of files lay forgotten on the table. Like a piece of sculpture he sat on his chair from 10 a.m. to 5 p.m. every day so that worshippers like Das and Mohan could approach him. Both Das and the Under Secretary exchanged furtive glances like two members of an intelligence group. Their talks were conducted in monosyllables as if each was trying to get the better of the other. Could a drop of water pass through them?

'Would you like a cigarette?' Das offered him the packet.

'No, thank you. How long have you been smoking? I have never seen you with a cigarette before,' the Under Secretary recalled.

'Beethalgarh is such a dull place. A habit like this only rejuvenates me,' Das chuckled. The smoke from his cigarette rose as if taking a leaf from his ostensible ego with a note of caution to re-evaluate his status afresh.

The Under Secretary looked at his watch in a worried manner. Das could smell it. He asked, 'What is the matter with you?'

'I have to collect my grandson from the school.'

'What exactly do you require?' asked Das.

'A vehicle,' replied the Under Secretary.

'That could be arranged. Wait a bit.' Saying this, Das waved to his taxi driver.

The Under Secretary took the taxi to reach the nursery school, which was not so far away. Das and Mohan decided to go along with their dear friend.

On the way, they decided to seek an appointment with the Director. But they wanted to have the meeting behind closed doors. Das geared himself up to outdistance his counterparts at Beethalgarh. He went on conveying the sonorous music of material gain in a whispering tone inaudible even to the driver. Earlier, Das had found the opportunity to meet both the steno and the private secretary of the Director. Both had been tricked in the best possible manner. In a Shiva temple, the bull always makes a journey to the Lord and all the devout are eager to ride on this wave. Bureaucracy is no exception to this. The earlier apathetic mood had been slapped on its back assiduously. For the NAC, Beethalgarh, the flag of cooperation started fluttering in the office corridor of the Directorate.

'To each according to his status.'

A new official rhythm reverberated through the head office. Both Mohan and Das were able to play the tune perfectly like the music-makers in a melody.

They reached the school, picked up the child and left him at the residence of the Under Secretary. They wanted to have their lunch in a comparatively better hotel. Mohan wanted to do something grand and memorable so that it would resonate in the mind of the Under Secretary to the extent of not blocking the path of their files in the coming days. The Under Secretary sat calmly with them in a corner, defying all eagerness. With a creased dhoti drawn against his frail body, he looked out of place in such an environment, but was brave enough to face expensive food like soup, steaming biriyani, soft kebabs and fish cured in lime juice.

The duo had secured maximum proximity to the power blocks at Bhubaneswar. Both the Under Secretary and Das shared some final thoughts and then it was time to leave for Beethalgarh.

Their car like a swift-winged bird flew towards Beethalgarh and it was almost midnight when they reached their destination. The travellers carried with them the murmur of the grants and the hope of the fascinating percentage (PC). All along their thoughts concentrated on profit. The car made a screeching halt in front of the residence of the EO. Banita was still awake. On hearing the car stop, she, like a feathered queen, came flying out and unlocked the gate. She could sense her daddy's upbeat mood. Without waiting for anyone she lifted his baggage from the car and rushed back to their residence. The night watchman stood nearby, but could not match her enthusiasm. Nor could the driver. Banita could read the face of her daddy better than anyone else. The car left for Mohan's residence. Das stepped inside his house.

'Daddy...'

'Yes... my dear.'

'Please do me a little favour.'

'What is that, Maa?'

'Please swear...not to say "No."'

'Okay.'

'Please replace my moped with a Kinetic one.'

At once Shanti shouted at her husband, 'Don't let her rush you into making this commitment.' She looked at her daughter saying, 'Can't you wait, your daddy is yet to wash his face!'

'Mummy please... this is between Daddy and me,' said Banita.

'Eh! Shanti. Let her speak. She hasn't had a chance to speak to me for three days. Moreover, it is such a small matter,' Das announced like a victor from a war.

'Oh Daddy, you are so great!' Banita embraced her father enthusiastically. She went on and on passionately advocating the plus points of a Kinetic two-wheeler—its maximum mileage, automatic start, powerful headlight, stylish seat.

'What is there in a powerful headlight? Will you be going hunting or on a night-time raid?' Shanti snubbed her daughter.

'Oh Mummy! Don't always insult me,' Banita replied smilingly.

Das whispered to his daughter confidingly, 'The purchase will be made as soon as the Government releases the drought grants. Go and sleep comfortably.'

Banita mistook the grants for salary and went to her dad's office the next day to enquire about them. Finding her alone, Mohan invited her to the office chamber of the Chairman to have a good gossip. He asked far too many questions about her private life including the name of her boyfriend. Banita turned away from the rule of reason and the age-old inhibitions of a young girl and fell prey to the bawdy grins of a lech like Mohan. While replying, she expressed equal concern about Mohan's beloved, if he had one. Mohan was surprised by such a candid query from a teenager. Being caught in a slip-up, she forgot the real reason for her visit and allowed Mohan to focus his greedy eyes further on her glittering breast.

Banita and Mohan had nothing in common except that they were young.

Seeing the two of them alone, three unwanted youths entered the VC's chamber and sat down. They hurled several questions at Mohan that had no relevance to NAC administration.

'What do you want?' Mohan asked the boys sitting around.

'Drought,' came a reply.

'What drought?'

'People do not have any work. Why are you all keeping silent?' One of the threesome spoke out, looking at Banita.

'Well, that will be looked into. What next?' said Mohan.

'We are not interested in such VIP dialogues. Tell us what plans the NAC hopes to put into action,' commented another.

Mohan looked up and frowned at the boys. The idea of an immediate rebuff captured his mind. He restrained himself somehow. He tried to understand this aspect of democratic functioning. He thought ahead, perhaps he might need their help to retain his throne in the coming days. He minced his next words in support of his boiling mood. A politician's lifespan is uncertain and he must not annoy guys like these. Earlier, Mohan had propounded the theory of right to information on several platforms. Strangely enough, after occupying a small kingdom of power, he had started to ignore his earlier stand.

Mohan tried to give statistics on the deployment of the labour force in the NAC area. He hinted that as compared to the rural pockets their situation was not so alarming. But he restrained himself as not a single look was directed at him. Like vultures, they were eyeing Banita with rapacious glances.

But Banita appeared to be enjoying their attention. Vanity had already eaten up her conscience, and she mistook them to be her worshippers.

'Is there a drought?' she asked mockingly. 'Then why hasn't there been a single death yet? I do not like people brooding over such things.' Saying this, she laughed loudly. Her gawkiness seemed out of place in the whole atmosphere.

Her laughter embarrassed everyone. 'Is this really so amusing?' said one of them.

'No, I did not mean anything really,' replied Banita.

'You should go and look at the fields. The whole landscape is yellow in colour. It brilliantly matches your dress.'

'Eh, so a fine drought then! Yellow is my favourite colour,' Banita replied.

Banita couldn't bear to listen to such mundane talk any longer. She wanted to leave and indicated that they make way for her.

One of them obliged and Banita came out of the room.

For Mohan, there was nothing greater in public life than self-seeking. Selfishness was stealing a march on conscience. Did he have any interest in promoting anyone's cause other than his own? The reply would be 'No' in concrete terms. The dream of a palatial building to accentuate his personal charm, the soft glow of a lady like Banita to encircle his post-wedded image had already nestled within him. Once again, someone entered his room without permission. Of late, Mohan had developed an enormous wish to conduct himself like a bureaucrat. Although this was his aspiration, the majority of his visitors did not see him in such a position.

'Yes, Vasant.'

'I came just to meet you.'

'How strange! Did you forget to meet me after the final payment?' exclaimed Mohan.

'No...younger brother's illness. We had to urgently shift him to Burla Hospital,' Vasant said apologetically.

Mohan's eyes grew greedier as he waited for the next turn of events. Vasant extended his hand to part with the *percentage*. Mohan wanted this moment to eclipse all others. Both took extraordinary care to keep the deal a secret. The giver could not help expressing the amount that had been removed from the total profit. No doubt, PC was followed with a yard stick, a comparison to judge among the office staff like JE, EO, Head Clerk including non-officials like Chairman and VC. For a while both peeped through the screen for an outside view. They did not want to leave even a shred of evidence. The framed photograph of Mahatma Gandhi was fixed on the wall as if to emphasize evaporation of morality in public life.

Mohan gave a look of perfect elation. He expressed his all-time joy to prolong his relationship with Vasant. He wanted to return the favour to the giver in the form of a cup of tea. Vasant had nothing in his mind other than the next work order. Das, EO, joined them in due course and participated in the lively conversation. Both the JE and the HC were called for to find some kind of work that ideally suited Vasant. The estimated cost, geographical location, availability of manpower and raw materials appeared in their discussion. The volume of exchange seemed irrelevant to the others since nobody had anything to gain except the four.

Vasant couldn't escape the gimlet-eyed Sub-Contractors sitting side by side under the great banyan tree. It took them no time to smell the Vasant–Mohan nexus. How could they fall behind in such a race! They preferred the VC to the Chairman when seeking fresh favours from the newly established joint collaborating agency of Vasant, Mohan and Das.

24

DROUGHT RAISED ITS head like a dinosaur triggering off large-scale migration from almost all pockets of the Beethalgarh area. Since the fields had dried up, the people, particularly the working class, looked eagerly for alternative means of livelihood. Villagers frantically started migrating either to Waltair or Raipur. Some didn't even know which trains they were stepping into. The situation had worsened, but Pasayat, BDO, and his staff didn't wake up to their plight because of apparent obstinacy to accept the magnitude of such a crisis. The bureaucrats in general were fired with a common motto, 'stiffness of controlling reason'. They went through the motion of doing something to check the outflow, but stood motionless. They appeared to have few worries but in reality, their conscience dimmed. If someone from among the starved lot lodged a complaint on the non-availability of subsidized rice in the local Panchayat, the BDO instead of conducting an enquiry himself, deputed the village-level worker to look into the matter. The latter pulled himself out of the Block office and like an invader reached the spot in no time. There, he made his presence felt, which ultimately culminated in a grand lunch wherein the participants were the same people against whom the complaints had been lodged before the BDO.

This small-time mafia had ganged up and declared a soothing alliance between them. Ultimately the VLW declared in public, 'There is no such mismanagement.' An enquiry was conducted in such a manner that nothing could be used in evidence against the delinquent.

In case a tubewell was to be dug, its depth could safely be manipulated, including the utilization of the underground casing pipes. Nobody was going to unearth the pipes to check them and the entry in the Measurement Book was taken as sacred. In the case of earthwork and collection of moroom for repair and maintenance of rural roads, the Sub-Contractors exercised their hegemony over the Block administration. Advances in lakhs were released even before the work started. The BDO directed the Accountant to deduct a substantial amount from each advance. It was an administrative ploy to secure the amount as office expenses and the office had no voice of protest against such a malevolent action. Then there was the business of garlands for VIPs. Bhakta, the orderly, would pluck flowers from the courtyard, utilize needle and thread from the office, apply his labour but submit an exorbitant bill before the Accountant for instant payment. Once, in a vexatious mood, the latter queried the number of such garlands but Bhakta stood defiant in his reply, 'Eight.'

'How can there be eight when I marked only five.'

'Do you mean to say that I wore the rest myself?'

'Who said that?'

'Then why do you blame me so?'

Someone tried to produce the last remnants of the garlands as proof but desisted from doing so. The BDO didn't relish such an attempt. He insisted that all of them including Bhakta be high-minded. He prevailed upon the Accountant to collect such expenses from one of the bills of a Sub-Contractor. Thus, he wanted to have a bit of peace and quiet in the office.

Comparing the Case Records and Measurement Book with field-work could not be visualized through transparent glasses. The officials appeared to be safe against the ravages of time and space. Their material thirst defined them as people without pedigree.

That they had lost no material battle was reflected in the smiling, rejuvenated faces of their family members. The dance of greed had left no stone unturned. The mind looked sandwiched in between sin and virtue.

25

THE CENTRAL GOVERNMENT did not have a magic wand to stop the mass exodus of people in search of greener pastures. Its grants only favoured the implementing force within Beethalgarh, who otherwise preferred to desert it for longer vacations. Just like Banita's moped was to be replaced by a superior Kinetic, several drought-monitoring officials abandoned their personal goods on the plea that they were outdated. The selective, blessed people of various colonies bought the latest models of household items like colour TVs, washing machines, refrigerators, hairdryers, vacuum cleaners, etc. This mad race was nothing but the fallout of such massive grants. The acquisitive mind was the latest trendsetter that swept aside all other social values.

The special grant acted like an intravenous drip to enliven the dehydrated spirit of the NAC office. The grant-in-aid papers were placed with great care in the office drawer of the EO. Like a child, Das opened and closed the drawer intermittently to deepen his love of the grant. For long, the Accountant was not seen approaching the chamber of the EO because of an old feud. There was a reason for this. Das once had a formal get-together in his chamber after office hours and he tried to persuade the Accountant to pay for the expenses. The latter refused point blank. That was the end as well as the beginning of a new chapter in their relationship. But now they were ready to embrace each other by dumping the old arsenals into the unknown corners of their mind. For Das, the grant-in-aid file was like a mini-concert playing the perfect music to enthrall them all. They took it as fortune smiling upon them. Work orders could be seen all over the tables. Contractors who had been without contracts for long now looked cheerful. The whistle of engagement started blowing from all directions. The faces of the EO, JE and Head Clerk could be seen glittering like stars from the Block firmament. The office rooms wore illuminated looks even late at night. Their engagement schedule had been extended beyond measure. Vasant continued to loiter in the office premises like a member of the staff.

Like a beehive, the NAC office filled with contractors, Sub-Contractors and their followers.

One contractor was a party to such conversation. 'Really, the Government does not understand our plight, Sir,' he added immediately. 'Tomorrow is a public holiday and there will be no banking transactions. We will suffer the worst,' he continued.

'Of course, that is true,' said Das. He got off his chair and rushed to the Accountant to study the cash position directly. There he lingered over tea with the rest of his subordinates. He encountered the same lobbying there as well. Das' ultimate aim was to make payment in hard cash in direct contravention of Government policy. To do so, he wanted to pass a resolution at the next Councillors' meeting just to be on the safe side.

The EO's true state of mind could not be kept back from the others. Many of them, assembled there, were let into it. No one could resist the lure of PC. It was like the fresh breath of a triumphant life. After each payment, many waited in their office rooms for the arrival of the contractors. That was in spite of the fact that night had fallen. Das continued to cast his hidden glances all around. Each tried his best to conceal his motive from the others as the ultimate secret in life.

'Well, let us go one by one,' said a contractor to three others.
'When?'
'Right now.'

They did not want to postpone the payment to the next day since it would bring about further tension to trace the payee. The common practice was to receive it in seclusion. The bundle would be secreted either in a pocket or in a drawer, away from the public eye.

Meanwhile, Das talked to the BDO over the phone seeking clarification on the mode of payment. Such a post facto analysis was for nothing but to kill time in the office while waiting for the great PC. Pasayat quietly advised that they should obtain an undertaking from each contractor to say that they had no objection to such cash payment. The onus lay with them, said the BDO like a veteran bureaucrat. Das listened to such an advice carefully. Such an idea would not have occurred to his mind otherwise, he thought.

No evidence was left anywhere against such cash payments that would make Das accountable.

PC became the be-all and end-all of everything. It allowed the yoking of heterogeneous minds. Everyone aimed at grabbing the lion's share of the billing amount. The JE was skilful in this regard and could doctor the bill to inflate or reduce the amount.

'The bills are greatly exaggerated!' exclaimed someone from the contractor's side.

'That is to adjust unwarranted expenditure in connection with the visit of inspecting teams,' clarified the EO. The persons surrounding him took his words for granted.

The resources from PC proved enormous to all who were sharing it. The dark surroundings of the town glowed with its bright colour. It came like fresh air changing the colour of the lives of a few.

Beethalgarh as usual remained colourless. Any inspecting authority that visited Beethalgarh once in a while, were told such hackneyed stories about PC making.

So clever were they! They always concealed their personal assets, the by-product of state assets. There were no outward projections in case they might prove disproportionate to one's salary. Many of them exercised great care to keep such huge amounts safe. Some of them devised methods to show such assets as others through paperwork. What acting! The officers who did the verification were themselves originators of such theory. Like witches and wizards they used black magic to glorify fine living. For minds obsessed with consumerism even the moon seemed like an unattractive, older model.

26

IN JHARGHATI, A place near Beethalgarh, Master Babu asked the swelling crowd outside the school campus not to rush. They were waiting eagerly to have their share of the midday meal. Many appeared to be adults and were not eligible for the scheme, which was meant for children below eleven years of age. Some dropouts looking like freshers were trying to rush in. 'No, no,' Master Babu shouted at them, but then he recognized some of his old pupils and didn't have the heart to adhere to the rules. He withdrew from the spot and looked silently as they came in.

The monitoring agency could not provide necessary items like firewood, salt, onion, etc., to prepare the supplied rice and dal. Nor was the amount adequate for the same. Master Babu had to grapple with several obstacles to put the scheme into action. He had tried hard to find alternative means to check the rush but how could he?

The BDO, by chance, was passing through the route. On seeing the gathering, he asked his driver to stop and enquired about the situation. 'I am helpless, Sir,' replied Master Babu. He further pleaded his cause politely, 'The government's plan should be on par with the facilities.'

Pasayat, the BDO, looked annoyed. He looked at the teacher saying, 'Can't you exercise a little leadership to tackle the situation?'

'How can I? What resources are there at my command, Sir?' Master Babu replied submissively.

'Tactless,' Pasayat retorted. He asked for the stock ledger and daily register. Master Babu handed them over at once. The BDO told one of his assistants to verify it.

Master Babu didn't have much interest in maintaining the registers. He didn't have the time and energy for activities other than teaching the students.

'Some lapses,' whispered the clerk.

'Why this?' asked the BDO as if interrogating a thief in a police station.

'I don't know, Sir!'

'Why this discrepancy, then?'

'Maybe it was maintained by one of my ex-students.'

'Why?'

'I hardly get time during teaching hours.'

'How can you absolve yourself of the responsibility?'

'I do not deny it, Sir, but I have my own limitations.'

The BDO looked a bit aggressive. The small gathering started getting agitated. They wouldn't allow their beloved teacher to face any humiliation. For them, such lapses were baseless and had no strength at all. One of them said defiantly, 'How can a person suffering from ringworm sell ointment for the disease?' The comment was aimed at the BDO who in turn kept quiet. He took it otherwise and squarely held Master Babu responsible for his humiliation at the hands of the general public. He avoided further discussion and left the place immediately with an instruction to Master Babu to rectify the defects.

Master Babu was afraid of the BDO's vindictive mood. The BDO sadistically decided to teach Master Babu a lesson. He planned to transfer him suddenly to a comparatively remote place. But he didn't release the order because of the ban imposed by the Government on the employees engaged in drought work. However, the establishment head of his office in order to satisfy his boss deviously declared the order as a special case of administrative exigency. This was more so because Master Babu did not favour him with a bag of rice and dal out of his existing stock.

Finding no way out Master Babu knocked at the door of Somen. At once representations were forwarded to both the District Collector and Inspector of Schools with a request to cancel such an arbitrary order. Reasons like his only daughter's epilepsy and his ailing parents were cited accordingly. Subsequently, although the Inspector gave a patient hearing to Master Babu he didn't help in cancelling the transfer.

Even the clerk of the Inspector office didn't relent in any manner. Instead he shooed Master Babu off by saying 'Don't disturb me now! Come back later.' Knowing fully well the reason behind such utterances, Master Babu wanted to grease the palm of the assistant. In fact, he was willing to part with a larger amount of his salary component to cancel the order. After this, the Dealing Assistant himself took the same file to the Inspector but with a different spirit. Finally the order of the BDO was superseded by another order of the Inspector. However, the Inspector of Schools gave an order to the District Inspector of Schools, his junior, to seize the stock registers of midday meals from Jharghati's primary school. He prevailed upon him to send all such documents to him for his personal scrutiny. Master Babu heaved a sigh of relief. He didn't know what fate had in store for him. The commitment of a hard struggle stiffened his resolve.

Master Babu lost further interest in teaching. He didn't find his job satisfactory any more. He saw how backbenchers outshone the brilliant students in public life by choosing politics as their profession. The rise of lesser talents to overshadow genius seemed unethical to him. For him, there had been no respite from teaching and he wanted to take leave for at least a week. To stave off monotony, he left Beethalgarh for Visakhapatnam with a mission to flush out the students who fled from the school with their parents. He had never visited Visakhapatnam earlier. On reaching, he was amazed by the vastness of the city, the long coastline, the vibrant railway station with its several platforms, the wide, clean city roads and their flat dividers and the traffic lights. To him they were examples of perfect city planning. But where were Krishna and Subhas, his one-time favourite students?

They had left Jharghati a long time ago. Somebody had informed him that they were staying near a brick kiln on the outskirts of Visakhapatnam along with their parents. Master Babu exhausted himself by trying to find them in a large city like Visakhapatnam. It was such an alien place for him to find a person. He was not familiar with city life. He had the impression that children below twelve years of age couldn't be employed. But who cares about this? He roamed through the city for hours on end but had no luck. In the process he spent every pie of his pocket. But yet he didn't give up his quest. Despite the blaring horns and heavy traffic, sweet memories of the children's school days kept him going. 'Where are my students Krishna and Subhas? Where are they?' he asked the passers-by, the auto-drivers or any man or woman in his own dialect, but there was no response. He was hungry and exhausted and out of sheer helplessness he pleaded with an auto driver saying, 'For pity's sake, please help me.' However, he received a pitying look from him.

'Kiya Hua?'

And before Master Babu could say another word, the auto merged into the fleet of vehicles like twilight coalescing into the evening sky. As the evening drew nearer he began to feel nervous. He nearly lost his confidence and trudged on foot towards the outskirts of the city. He would very often strike up dialogues with pedestrians in broken Telugu. He felt disappointed but at no stage did he withdraw himself from the quest. The indifferent city could not deter him from abandoning his search. Master Babu looked at the city with repulsion, how unlike his small village it was.

No one, not even a schoolchild or an octogenarian going to the temple, could provide any information on the two students leave alone smile at him.

Where were Krishna, Subhas, then? Master Babu was yet to make his way to the brick kilns surrounding the city at a distance.

He wished to utter their names with full force. Although disturbed, his mind was not thrown out of gear.

Master Babu had left Jharghati relying on the vague information provided by somebody that the parents of both Krishna and Subhas were working in the brick kilns near Visakhapatnam. But was this information enough to find two families in a city like Visakhapatnam?

Throughout the day, Master Babu had squandered away his energy to trace his two students but all his efforts had been in vain. Being totally exhausted, he started grumbling, *Besharam... namak haraam*, but it was not certain who he was referring to.

Master Babu decided to spend the night at the railway station, away from the city. Completely exhausted, he had to walk all the way there. Terribly hungry, he ate something, spread his towel on the platform, lay his head on the bag and fell asleep.

27

EVERY DAY, THERE had been large-scale migrations from Beethalgarh. People usually travelled by train, as it was the cheapest of all. It was common for many not to book any tickets in advance. The Train Ticket Inspector would collect a small portion of the booking amount and allow the passenger to travel. In this way he would grab the largesse without reflecting the same in his receipt book. There had been a practice to carry passengers even inside and outside the railway engine.

The small-time PC makers from the NAC, Block and Railway offices gathered to greet one another at Hotel Amar under the stewardship of Ved Prakash. The cocktail parties there cut across departmental boundaries. The flow of music from the MP3 player enhanced the moods of Das, Mohan, Pasayat, Nanda, Rath and the others, and as the night stretched on they became more joyful. So bountiful despite the scarcity! The food and drink kept flowing, filling their bellies. The local VIPs had no immediate plan to return to their houses. The wives knew this and bowed to the wishes of their husbands. They were considered the epitome of rural power, the people who could throw their weight around and smash any protest if and when it rose. Ved Prakash was showered with thanks for providing such a life of pleasure; otherwise Beethalgarh would have been a desert. Each VIP had measured himself heroically as if to declare himself a local god. With no one to command them, they took the liberty of overpowering everything around them, even this small hotel. The smaller sahibs felt as if they were in a sanctuary and had the freedom to do as they willed.

Hotel Amar stood like the city centre of a metro and wore the status of a classless platform, where all officers irrespective of their grades would join hands for a common sharing of tables.

Ved Prakash, like a keen strategist or psychologist, knew the pulse of everyone around him. His mind was like an electronic gadget remembering everything that was useful. Contractors used to meet him to know about the fate of their tender papers or the mood and temperament of these small-time rulers. Similarly, the officers who wanted to know details about the comparatively higher payers made VP a tool in their hands.

Thus, Hotel Amar acted like a rural cybercafé to pass on information catering to someone's need. Was it then an interface between the past and present, earth and heaven, light and dark? Was it like a search engine, a rural information centre, a CCTV to record the movements of small-time administrators, politicians and businessmen?

'Ved Prakash, could you organize our food?' said Pasayat on behalf of Das and Mohanty.

'Yes Sir,' said Ved Prakash and within no time, the waiters sprang into action.

It was 11 p.m. The children were still at work, the pressure being such that there was no time to rest their frail bodies! In spite of having had a hard day, they were not being spared from working till late at night. Once Ved Prakash kicked a child for breaking a plate in his sleepiness. Such hotel boys couldn't sleep because of the shouts from drunkards. They had to work along with their parents to clean the utensils, fetch water from the nearby tube well, grind spices and throw away empty beer and rum bottles. They had to do such despicable tasks without food or rest. The boys slept in a dark corner, near the fireplace with its gunny bags full of coal brickets. It smelt of cooked food, edible oil and spices. Mosquitoes zoomed about like warplanes, irritating them with their noise and bites.

Ved Prakash had no knowledge of accountancy, but he had a cunning eye to inflate a bill and looked keenly at the payment. He appointed a young boy, a matriculate from the nearby colony, to discharge the duty of an accountant. After every sitting, Ved used to shout out the list of supplied items. The young one promptly added them on his calculator to announce the bill amount. Ved was only interested in the smell of cash and would keep the hotel open even for the whole night and day to earn more. With the night deepening further, the trio paid their bill and came out of the hotel. Ved went to the jeep to see them off. He talked to the driver with a smiling face. He was a middle-aged person who appeared as if he had zero interest in the personal doings of the officers. He started the vehicle and drove away. The trio sat in the vehicle as if like Brahma, Vishnu and Maheshwar, the whole world was at their command.

Ved took a whisky bottle in his hand, unscrewed it and started pouring peg after peg into a glass. While sipping his drink, he shouted at the boys to have their food. There was softness in his voice in contrast with his earlier mood.

The boys queued up before the chef to collect their share of the burnt breads and vegetable curry left in the dish.

'Eat your fill, you have worked for the whole day and night,' repeated Ved.

The boys were quiet as if aware of the degree of mercy in the voice of their boss. Their silence was the index of what was in their minds. 'Where there is enough…give them sufficient food,' Ved went on repeating the words to the chef, who replied: '*Saab… Haan… saab*'

The walls of Hotel Amar were hung with several posters of smiling national leaders. Some had come unstuck and were fluttering in the air. Had these cult figures heard the success stories of rural development from the group of officials who had sat there with glasses in hand?

The name Hotel Amar was flying high like a flag from the masthead of Beethalgarh as if sharing the deep-throated chorus of *Mera Bharat Mahan*...

28

THE DAS FAMILY had reached a particular standard of living in six months of their stay in Beethalgarh that they had failed to earn even in two decades. Das opened bank lockers secretly in Cuttack and Bhubaneswar in the names of his brothers-in-law. He booked an apartment in Bhubaneswar under the ownership of his wife.

Although Pasayat and Das had been together in Bhubaneswar, they hardly knew each other then. But now Beethalgarh brought a unique rapport between the two.

Mohan became the coordinator between Pasayat and Das. The trio had amassed great wealth within a short time raising doubts in others. It seemed incredible to many. In the NAC, Mohan had become the ultimate voice to assign contractual jobs. He had free access to the residence of Das and was treated like a family member. Both Banita and Shanti, the daughter and mother, were competing to earn his friendship. He used an intimate term like 'didi' while addressing Shanti. Das didn't mind. He spent most of his time confined to his office room and his only concern was PC. As a result, Shanti, Banita and Mohan got together very often for an evening gossip.

'Didi! What an innocent face you have!!'

'Mine?'

'Oh yes, so graceful and compassionate. God knows. No pimples, marks, nothing of the sort.'

'Stop flattering me.'

'I always say what I mean.'

'Aren't you calm and gentle?' Shanti asked.

Then they saw Banita looking bitter. Shanti realized that her daughter didn't like her talking to Mohan. She left the room in a hurry. Shanti came back after a while carrying plates of snacks that she left on the teapoy before going inside again. Silence prevailed for some time.

'How lovely your locks are.' Mohan praised Banita. 'Do you use a conditioner?'

'Oh, stop it please!' she barked at him.

Mohan lost the natural will to address Banita so affectionately. She still looked peeved. He felt embarrassed. Seeing no one around, Mohan came close to her and embraced her passionately. Banita tried her best to escape from his clutches. But…

Finding themselves alone made them greedy for each other's body. Banita found Mohan's skin hairy, while for Mohan she was both delicate and sweat-free. Intoxicated by the wine of love, she smiled at him. Mohan, like releasing the hand brake in a car, freed Banita gradually from his fold.

'Good heavens! I was afraid!' whispered Mohan.

'Should we go for an evening show?' he asked.

'No! Daddy will mind,' she replied.

Shanti returned again with cups of tea in her hands and as she was placing them on the teapoy, Mohan asked her if he could have a glass of water.

Shanti came back with a glass of water and handed it to Mohan. Shanti watched Mohan and her daughter and didn't want to sit with them like a quiet duck. She made an excuse and left for her kitchen.

Mohan took a sip of water. Both started whispering words of love.

The sudden return of Shanti compelled Banita to wriggle out of Mohan's arms. Banita pretended to behave as if nothing had happened. Shanti looked equally calm as if she had seen nothing objectionable. She put the water jar on the teapoy and offered the snacks and tea to Mohan. But Mohan wanted a smoke. Shanti graciously allowed him to do so. While sipping, both tried to read each other's faces. Mohan had to brush off the ash from his suit at times. While puffing, he saw a new set of jewellery adorning the neck and wrists of Shanti. For Banita, Mohan and her mummy stood like two indecipherable pieces of writings. She needed to be older and more mature to understand the psyche of her own mother. She, on the other hand, had no idea how to conceal the reddish glow of her cheek. It was a little spot in the middle of her right cheek that lay like a neatly drawn painting. Shanti was thrilled to see Mohan's passion for her daughter.

29

ALTHOUGH HE HAD crossed twenty-eight, Somen started preparing for the company executive post once again. His daddy warned him to study well. 'There should be minimum social services,' said he. Somen retorted saying, 'Baba, nothing becomes, everything comes.' They didn't want to prolong their battle of wits with such philosophical utterances. Somen couldn't relish remarks like 'Delhi boy tops', 'What is the secret of your success?', 'How did your parents contribute to your success?' And stock replies like 'God's blessings', 'family's grand wishes', 'years of hard labour', etc. What did these competition journals want? Did they seek educated mothers to propagate the glory of their successful children? In which way was one mother inferior to the other qualified mothers? Was it because she couldn't achieve higher degrees? Did she lack the effort or sincerity to promote her child or husband? Then, why?

Somen continued to reflect upon such matters. He remembered all his mummy's sacrifices for him. All her life she wore only cheap cotton saris. How she juggled her family's modest budget! Her only form of entertainment was to travel to Kolkata during puja to meet her parents. Slowly, that too had lessened. Somen's studies took priority over everything else. Notwithstanding her frequent complaints of muscular pain, sinusitis and bronchitis, she wouldn't go to a specialist for treatment but limited herself to ordinary over-the-counter pain-killers.

It so happened that one day, in the absence of Somen and the others, she consumed a pill meant for skin infection presuming that it was for amoebic dysentery. Roy Babu had repeatedly reprimanded her for such mistakes. Somen immediately contacted the railway physician and on his advice, administered a separate dose of medicine to neutralize the wrong one. Mrs Roy ignored her husband's anger but Somen didn't like his dad uttering vicious remarks like:

'I have never come across such an idiot...'

Usually Mrs Roy was tough enough to stand up to her husband. But now it dampened her spirit as she was at fault.

Somen began his preparatory study to appear for the interview for a textile executive. Both mother and sister prayed dutifully before the goddess to restore Somen's self-confidence.

Minati sang a long hymn with her mother at her side. Soon, she came out with a little prasad in hand and asked her mother to put it into her brother's mouth.

'Oh, Mama, prasad or what?' said Somen.

'Maa, don't you see, I am serious this time.'

'I think so, my dear,' she replied.

'Dada, you are concentrating on cotton dyeing. Is it relevant?' asked Minati.

'Of course.'

'But the interview is for a silk factory.'

Somen was surprised by her sister's intelligence. The management of a silk factory wouldn't like their executive to be a specialist in cotton dyeing. Somen asked his mother for a silk sari instead. Incidentally, Mrs Roy did have one as her prized possession since it was from her wedding day. The design of its embroidery was nearly thirty years old. There had been many changes in fashion since then. It sapped Somen's confidence. What could be the solution? Minati offered it. Both Arati and Dolly had two silk saris each that they had purchased from the Sambalpuri Handloom showroom in Samastipur. If Baba allowed it, Minati would borrow them for some time. Her mother took up the cause. Somen, in spite of his reluctance, didn't oppose the proposal. Minati and Mrs Roy met Dolly and Arati and communicated their request to them and then returned to their residence. Just then, as was normal in Beethalgarh, the lights went off. The whole house was plunged into darkness. Suddenly they heard unfamiliar voices from the gate. Minati went outside to see who was there. She immediately called out and Somen went outside. He looked at Arati directly and greeted her in a friendly manner. Dolly stood next to her. Was it to tie up loose ends? Arati, so long supra-orbital, was available so near. A hazy face close to her was that of Dolly's. Even in the darkness, Minati welcomed them both inside. They were both holding something that looked like saris in their hands. Arati narrated the art of silk dyeing even before Somen asked her any questions. 'I learnt it from one of my friends,' she said.

'Is your friend from a weaver's family?' Somen asked.

'Oh yes!'

'Then, please tell me in detail.'

'See, this silk yarn earlier contained both fibroin and sericin.'

'Please explain what fibroin and sericin are. See, Arati... I have been a student of Arts,' he said.

'Fibroin means real fibre and sericin means the silk gum. This silk gum needs to be separated from the silk yarn in order to bleach it.'

'Okay, carry on, please!'

'This operation is known as...as...as...' Arati suddenly forgot the technical term and looked at Dolly helplessly.

'Degumming,' supplemented Dolly at once. Somen gave her a small smile. He was concentrating on the facts.

'For removal of sericin, the best quality of soap is applied.'

'But is it in cold or boiling water?'

Both were in a fix to give the correct reply. However, Dolly at once said, 'Hot water...'

'Not hot but boiling water,' Arati added.

'What is the temperature?' asked Somen.

'Minimum 90–95° C,' replied Dolly.

'And the duration of boiling?'

'Minimum one hour.'

While conversing, Arati and Somen looked at each other appreciatively.

Arati, in her usual talkative manner, went into details like 'peroxide bleaching'. Both sat like teacher and pupil. They felt awkward to sit in such a position for long. They wanted to drift away to more private surroundings to declare their intentions. Arati couldn't reveal herself so openly in the presence of his parents. However, their subconscious minds were stimulated by their emotions; a thin film of sweat covered their faces in spite of the cool weather. Arati appeared breathless. Although not very house-proud, Somen wished his living room was more attractive. His own room looked messy. The chair and benches were rickety with legs missing somewhere. An old bedsheet was lying on the bed. Flashes of imagination lit up in everyone's mind. The dream that had captured Mrs Roy came alive. She was imagining the veiled face of Arati with a touch of vermilion on her forehead. Each family member kept thinking of Arati. 'Arati,' exclaimed Mrs Roy while stuffing a piece of apple into her mouth, 'don't you feel hungry?' Arati tried to chew the fruit. Mrs Roy gave another piece to Dolly. Seeing this, Somen sank into a queer mood. He flew off to his dreamland until the electricity was restored.

What would happen if he failed once again? 'No... never again,' he told himself and tried his best to put aside such silly thoughts. Once again he took his own stand to achieve what had not been achieved so far. He ran his fingers along the glossy silk saris, and minutely observed the weaving process, the proportionate intersecting of warp and weft and its effect on the surface of anchal and the exquisite tie-and-dye border.

30

THERE WERE PROVISIONS in the Odisha Mutation Rules to dispose off a case immediately by putting it up before the Tahsildar within fifteen days from the date of receipt of such an application. However, the tahsil administration in Beethalgarh would stretch the period for fifteen years and even more. Although Mohanty, the Tahsildar, looked like a giant-killer, he was seen twisting his tail before his higher-ups. He was submissive before any ordinary politician even for a small cause. Whenever he got down from his office jeep, he waved his hand like a king, forcing passers-by to listen to him carefully, otherwise he might damage anyone who did not do so.

One day his wife lost her temper with the Record Keeper of his office. One might be surprised at such an outburst since the man had done nothing that would cause Mrs Mohanty to hate him. 'Why should I know all this?' the Record Keeper growled before some of his colleagues.

It was a routine affair for the Record Keeper to provide either chicken or mutton to the residence of the Tahsildar every Sunday. Last time he neglected to do this probably because of his illness.

Mohanty's office vehicle bore the brunt of public fury and its new rexine torn in two confirmed it. However, he commanded one of his favourite staff members to replace the torn pieces before the return of RDC from tour. The garage owner acted promptly. Two or three garage boys dressed in tatters laboured at once to bring the vehicle to its perfect show. A skilled tailor was found to measure the size of the rexin that fitted closely to the seat. 'Oh, why this scratch? Are you blind or what?' The tahsil driver flew off the handle at one of the boys pointing his finger at the vehicle.

'We don't have polish,' he replied calmly.

'Why don't you bring it from the shop? Go immediately.'

'But I don't have money to buy it.'

'What do you say that for? Tell my name and bring it on credit,' the driver repeated.

The boys grumbled initially but didn't like to face the driver's ire. One of them, a little older, had to bring it from the shop on credit. As soon as the polish was applied, the vehicle started shining. After a few hours, Mohanty, the Tahsildar, was seen returning in the BDO's vehicle following the RDC and the Collector.

Soon after lunch, it was time for the officers to depart. The RDC left the Inspection Bungalow first, followed by the Collector and Additional District Magistrate. The chowkidar was seen locking up the VIP suite of the Inspection Bungalow. Once the same chowkidar with his drinking friend, the tahsil driver, had joined a party where the driver in a state of drunken rage created havoc. Like Lord Shiva, he undressed himself, waved his shirt as a trident and shouted about the integrity of the Tahsildar in a vulgar way.

The rural petitioners in the tahsil office were an ignorant lot, stamping their thumbs on a wakalatnama without being aware of the consequences. It was then the turn of a few of the advocates to harass them. The registered sale deed covering the land deal was cunningly collected from the purchaser of the land and was never returned to its owner. Cases were adjourned at their whim and the vested group went on exploiting the innocence of such office-goers. The drunkenness to exercise one's right, title and interest over a plot of land reached its height in the heart of a villager. The process server of the tahsil office while serving notices, the dealing assistant while putting up the case record before the Tahsildar, all had the eyes of sharks waiting for their dues. Neither the report from the revenue inspector nor documents from the Record Keeper were forwarded unless their palms were greased. Their irresistible impulse towards money had nothing to do with anyone's visit to the area.

'To hell with my luck,' shouted a villager.' If this practice continues in the tahsil office, we will be forced to bring it to the notice of the higher authorities.'

Somehow, the Tahsildar heard about the complainant through one of his subordinates. Although not afraid of anyone, he handled the matter intelligently. He took a reconciliatory approach with the gentleman. He called for the Nazir and whispered something intelligent to him. Soon, he lit a cigarette and blew the smoke into the air thereby giving the general public the impression that nothing as such had happened to him. A landless rural elevating himself to the status of a tenant was a matter of great joy. The Tahsildar could brighten up the gloomy fate of many such people of his area. Before the majority, he proved to be nicer. An average civilian embarking on any adventure couldn't antagonize the Tahsildar and that made his position secure. He also knew that any complaint against him was bound to be superfluous.

'I daresay that nobody can raise a finger at me,' said he emphatically. 'One mustn't think that I am a coward to face the authorities.'

Somen wanted to have a discussion with the Tahsildar on the issue of declaring Judabandh a revenue village. He had been to his office several times but found him either absent or busy. But soon, this began to anger Somen.

'What the hell is he doing every day?' Somen shouted at the office staff. He didn't wait for an explanation, but returned in the evening after office hours. The Tahsildar was present. Somen found him engaged in file work. 'Why are you not taking our appeal seriously?' Somen told Mohanty on entering the office room. The latter dismissed the idea of declaring Judabandh a revenue village as it came directly under the reserved forest area.

'How long will they rot like this?'

'Who?'

'The dwellers of Judabandh.'

'What can we do?' replied the Tahsildar. 'We don't have a map or Record of Rights on the reserved forest.'

'Damn it,' sweared Somen.

Mohanty lost his balance. 'Tell the Government to transfer me from here. I can't do something wrong,' said he.

'How many years will the people have to wait to see their problems solved?' Somen frowned. 'Let us all go to the MLA then.' Saying so, he left the office hurriedly.

Mohanty felt humiliated, but he didn't want to make a retaliatory move. His face became hot with shame but he tried his best to get rid of it. He along with one or two of his trusted employees went to meet the SC. They discussed the whole issue seriously and were determined to enforce the rule of law. 'The procedural formalities must be maintained,' said the SC like a final ruling. It might lead to clogging up but an official pattern loomed large in their mind.

'Is the Panchayat election drawing near?' asked Somen.

'Yes,' replied someone.

'Let this be made an issue then.'

'Unless Judabandh is granted the status of a revenue village, no MLA or MP would be allowed to enter their area,' shouted everyone in an agitated mood.

'H. u. r. r. a. h.!'

A huge group of people screamed louder and louder, the rebellious instinct sparkled with a vengeance radiating from each face.

31

MOHANTY WAS AN expert in survival skills and understood how to display apparent goodness before others. Though his real life was a contrast, he preferred to be a member of the local Radha–Krishna cult. The Bhagavad Gita brought solace to the Tahsildar and spent much time among the devotees. Here he was often surrounded by people for whom self-interest was the main motto. Although during office hours he crossed swords with revenue defaulters, he avoided such altercations here. Even the spectre of drought couldn't sap their devotion. Images of Radha and Krishna were placed in the mandap, from where the fragrance of incense and sandalwood obscured the smell of dry earth.

'No rest, drought all over. My body aches and pains,' said Pasayat.

'Sir, an email,' the receipt clerk told him. In a bit of a huff, Mr Pasayat asked for its contents.

'Rainfall report of the last week.'

'What! The same query again and again?' Pasayat burst out.

'Sir, another VHF,' said an office bearer. The messenger, a police constable, stood outside.

'Oh! Keep off, get away!' He sat in an armchair to relax.

Pasayat tore the letter open and went through it.

'Information on crop-cutting experiments required urgently, Collector.'

'Strange! The same information to be sent again and again.' He threw reproaches at the district administration for such irresponsible demands. One of his staff members came with some papers. It made him more disagreeable.

'What papers?'

'Monthly expenditure statements on labour-intensive works.'

'But we have already sent it to the district office.'

'No sir! Here is a telegram from the office of the Relief Commissioner. We have to comply with the information immediately.'

'Okay.'

He signed all the papers hurriedly at one stroke. There was an arithmetical error in the sheet under the heading 'Progressive expenditure' from the first of April onwards. No one could detect it. The dealing assistant said he had to go to the Radha-Krishna temple. Das and Pasayat and the other members of the cult too reached there late in the evening.

Sitting cross-legged before the idols with closed eyes was a scene to watch. Their devout poses seemed artificial. Such enthusiasts were only interested in having a good gossip with officials and sorting out official business.

The devotees including Das and Pasayat looked at the idols of Radha and Krishna on the pedestal with absolute devotion. Their demeanour was suitably quiet and grave.

'In this temple,' said a devotee, 'our VIPs forget official pressures by allowing their minds to become serene.'

But the people of Beethalgarh had altogether a different story to tell, more so the younger generation. 'What do these officers know other than to invent new methods of gratification? If there had been a research cell to find out new avenues for kickbacks, a thesis would have been prepared by these two in no time. When Das stands up to offer prayers, he will demand PC from God.' These conversations came to an end when both the officers left the temple in their jeeps.

Somen tried to meet Mohanty for the second time the next day. The people of Judabandh wanted to be introduced to the Tahsildar through a letter from the local MLA. Although he was from the Opposition, the feedback on him was positive. The Tahsildar didn't show any enthusiasim for the dwellers' demands. Like a seasoned officer he weighed everything on an official scale. Somen wanted to counter his apathetic mood and this made Mohanty furious.

Mohanty asked for the relevant file. The concerned clerk placed it on his table immediately. After closely examining it, he discovered the encroachment of vast tracts of forest land within the reserved area and instantly pounced upon the people who came to meet him.

'What right do you have to violate Government rules?' Mohanty declared in a loud tone. A strong-minded person like Somen couldn't take his words lightly. He didn't like to be at the mercy of Mohanty and tossed his head bitterly.

'Why are your laws against the poor? Can you snatch away their right to live? They have been occupying this land since the time of their forefathers, much before forest laws came into force,' he said in a sharp tongue.

Mohanty was not happy by this verbal assault. He considered it unlawful behaviour by the crowd. He summoned his assistants to find out the provisions in the Criminal Procedure Code for handling a situation of this kind.

He was showing his strength by calling for the law enforcing squad while the gathering stood quietly without misbehaving.

Somen looked at the Tahsildar and other Government officials bitterly. He didn't continue his fiery dialogues. He had realized that this was developing into a law and order situation. Mohanty had taken command of the whole situation.

'They have to vacate the encroached area and come out of the reserved zone. If necessary, our office will find an alternative arrangement for them.'

'All the dwellers here are landless and scheduled caste or scheduled tribe. When the Government introduces policy measures to rehabilitate weaker sections, you evict them. Where will they go after staying there for more than hundred years?' Somen argued.

Mohanty wanted to push such arguments away. Refusing to budge, he said emphatically, 'Don't try anything unlawful. Laws are well settled.'

Somen didn't relish the Tahsildar's sanctimonious attitude. He became excited and said, 'Mohantyji, you talk of law but people know how illegally caste and residential certificates are issued in the tahsil office.'

'Are you finding fault with my authority and office?' Mohanty retorted bluntly.

Without pointing out anything in particular, Somen fired his second salvo, saying, 'Your office is nothing but full of illegalities.'

'How?'

'You dispose of cases of your own interest within a month but others can linger on for years together.'

'All bunkum,' Mohanty retaliated.

Somen went near his followers to substantiate the charges. He wanted some of them to support him with material evidence. The people remained silent. Somen was appalled by their vacillation. He looked at the crowd apprehensively. Suddenly he saw Malia elbowing his way to the front line. In an instant, Somen wanted to take a giant swipe at Mohanty to quieten him at once but restrained himself somehow.

'Why do you speak like this? I command so much respect from the public but you just don't care about me,' complained the Tahsildar.

Meanwhile, Malia had taken position and began to speak: 'The village police was abolished thirty years ago but your office has been sitting on the Case Records till now. Your bench clerks have not yet given the date of the final settlement. They treat the chowkidars and village watchmen as their henchmen,' shouted Malia at the revenue personnel.

His words provoked Mohanty to react sharply. 'Those who live in glasshouses shouldn't throw stones at others. Being encroachers, how dare you say so! What I do is my own business and only my authorities can reprimand me. You accuse me without any veracity. Don't plead for these rural guys so hastily. You have little or no understanding of official formalities.'

Somen didn't relish such official clichés. He detested how small-time bureaucrats like Mohanty had used their power to subjugate the already deprived rural population. How power had blindfolded their conscience! He would persevere until victory was achieved. 'No question of surrender!' He promised that he would never give up and would continue with the struggle.

As the situation grew tenser, both Somen and Malia refrained from further arguments. Somen felt that his image before the officers was dwindling. Malia too smelled it and tried to banish the anger from his mind. Somen reined in his tongue and tried to think of his argument in a logical manner. His restless mood gradually cooled down.

The agitators had come in a procession like early birds. They held the tahsil office like a besieged fort. Displaying unconquerable will, they stood up for the fulfilment of their demands. Seeing their combined strength and marching feet Mohanty sought assistance from his staff and also from other departmental officers staying at Beethalgarh. The Forest Officer was one among them. His arrival at the tahsil office was in response to a telephonic direction from his immediate boss. He sat with Mohanty in his office chamber. It was as if the administration had changed its course. Behind the screen, the office became an incubator where plans were hatched to crush the people who were trying to defend their landed property rights. The Tahsildar sat in the tahsil chair, as if it was an offering from God, without ever thinking of leaving it in anyone else's hands. Undaunted, they were deeply involved in taking stock of the situation. In order to take steps against the inhabitants of Judabandh they invited a few of their lieutenants, like court amins and foresters, to evaluate their strategy. They moved fast in their attempts to teach the inhabitants a lesson. The subordinates stood around in huddles as if strengthening their historical pact to meet the growing challenges posed by Somen and others.

32

NEXT MORNING, SOMEN was woken up by the sudden touch of his mother. She was panting heavily, he couldn't understand why. Utterly speechless, she pointed at the window. Somen heard some sounds and he peeped out of the window to see what was happening. To his utter dismay, he discovered that a group of policemen and forest personnel had cordoned off his residence and were standing there with bayonets in their hands. Somen looked at his mother. She was in a state of panic and was trying hard to regain her breath. He consoled his mother, urging her to stop being frightened. Suddenly a group of villagers led by Mohan entered the house. Curious, the residents of the colony began to arrive as well. Looking at the increasing flow of outsiders, a police officer shouted at them to leave the place immediately. The slowly emerging crowd started melting away. The policemen had already taken their positions around the house. The Station House Officer present ordered Somen to come out of the house. 'You are under arrest... Here is the warrant from the Magistrate,' he shouted at him. Before Somen could speak out, he was whisked away to the nearest police station. But what was the ground of such an arrest?

Before Somen could find out the reason, they fired questions at him. Somen became excited. Someone from the crowd demanded, 'What distrust. How could police jeopardize someone's fundamental rights?' Somen too expressed his right to know the cause of his arrest. He was deeply shaken and wished to meet Pradeep, his lawyer friend. At least he could discuss everything with him.

Somen's father had not yet returned from his night duty. Minati rang him up to apprise him of the situation. He was surprised to know that Somen had already been taken to the police station. Just then, Pradeep called him and both went directly to the station. His father shouted at the officer-in-charge, 'Why did you arrest my son?' The OIC at once called one of his constables: 'Bring the seized plank!'

'What does it mean?' shouted Roy Babu.

'Be quiet. It is a piece of wood from the reserved forest that was found in your house,' said the OIC.

The RO intervened, 'It is direct stealing from the reserved forest. That is an offence under the Forest Act.'

'But why? We use it for firewood purposes,' said Roy Babu.

'The wood was seized from your residence,' replied a Forester.

'Then you arrest me, why my son? The house doesn't belong to him,' Roy protested vehemently. Pradeep had been waiting patiently till then to know what sections had been slapped on his friend. The OIC promised to give him a copy of the First Information Report.

No one took heed of Roy Babu's angry cries. The unrelenting police and forest troops had left the spot. This allowed Somen and his father to talk freely with Pradeep and the others who were standing around. Roy Babu was seen groaning with acute grief to find his son in such a helpless position. Just then Mrs Roy reached the police station with one or two political activists from the town.

Somen understood his mother's state of mind. It made him dispirited. Roy Babu tried his best to pacify her. She asked her husband if they knew any top-ranking police officer. Pradeep wanted to take her home, but Mrs Roy refused him outright.

'How can I leave my dearest in a place like a police station?' For her, life had taken a very inconvenient turn. Nervous at heart, she was unable to face the situation. She kept rushing up and down trying to catch a glimpse of her son. A policeman lost his temper. He started complaining about their gruelling early morning exercise saying, 'Had there been integrity, the forest area would not have suffered the loss of so many trees from the timber mafias.'

'Why is Beethalgarh so barren today?'

In tears, Mrs Roy caught hold of the iron railing of the *hazat*, drawing herself closer to her son. She was holding flowers in her frail palms.

'Babu, take this,' she said, her voice choked with emotion.

'Maa, what is this?'

'Flowers, a blessing from our family deity. They will keep you safe and secure. No harm will come to you at any point of time.'

They had no practical use for Somen. But he had to agree, keeping in mind the disturbed mood of his mother.

The gathering began to swell rapidly. The news of Somen's arrest had spread like wildfire. People from different corners started pouring into the police station. It was obvious that the majority of people admired him. People saw Mohan and Subhas coming towards the police station on their motorbikes. On reaching, they pleaded with the Inspector-in-Charge of the police station to spare Somen. The general public including Somen knew it was a ploy to hoodwink them.

Mrs Roy then started worrying about what her son would eat. There was nothing, no glass or anything. No filter water, leave alone decent food. How could a home's comforts be found in a *hazat*? Just then, Pradeep came with a container carrying some quality items of food. He requested the police to arrange a couple of plastic chairs for Somen to eat comfortably and within no time these were arranged.

The gradual flow of public into the police station made the officers including the SHO take Somen immediately to the court without any delay. The Assistant Conservator of Forests too arrived in a jeep. He looked quite adamant, as if determined to level the scores with Somen at any cost. The Tahsildar too reached there to discharge his role as an EM.

As an offender, Somen was booked under the Forest Act. The police officers wanted to parade him through the town in handcuffs. But Somen's followers protested vehemently. A youth shouted, 'If this happens, be prepared for bloodshed then!!' Somehow the Tahsildar and Assistant Conservator of Forest urged the mob to act cautiously.

'Am I a thief or what?' Somen angrily asked the constable who carried the handcuffs. Pradeep rushed to snatch them from him. 'You can't do this. Don't be silly. A man is handcuffed only when there is a chance of his slipping away. As a lawyer, I oppose this kind of barbarous act,' Pradeep thundered. Just then, the Deputy Superintendent of Police interrupted, 'Beware! He is from a respectable family. Don't do any thing that is contrary to the popular will of the public.' This scene inflicted great pain on Roy, as it seemed to be a crushing blow to his family status. He controlled his emotions somehow but felt utterly helpless. Somen was taken to a police van without any handcuffs. Mrs Roy ran to the vehicle but was restrained by Roy Babu and Pradeep.

All through the route, people waved out to Somen expressing

their solidarity for him. Soon Pradeep filed a bail petition in the court. Somen was released on bail late in the evening. A large gathering awaited him outside. Everyone including Mrs Roy, Arati and Dolly were there when he came out. An alert group took Somen in their arms. They garlanded him amidst the chanting of slogans condemning the civil administration.

Somen walked towards his parents with a rigid face and a little frown.

'My dear,' Mrs Roy embraced her son in full view of the public. Somen let his emotions flow out.

'Be aware, the Government has implicated me in a false case,' he cried out.

A car awaited Somen and his family members outside.

While leaving the court premises, slogans from the large crowd rent the air:

'*Somen Zindabad*'

'Long live the people's struggle'

'Tahsildar... OIC down down'

The court premises looked like a battleground. Everyone including Somen was stranded in their vehicles. They sat helplessly since the unruly crowd had blocked all exit points. They refused to disperse, ignoring repeated requests from senior members of the local Bar and other dignitaries of the town.

Somen detached himself from his supporters as their mood gradually began to cool down. He wondered why the Government was putting a check on a genuine demand of the villagers. Why a false case in his name, why? He returned to this thought again and again. He couldn't understand why he had become the villain. Why had he been shamed?

Neither war nor peace, he contradicted himself again and again. Someone opened the car door to garland him. 'Eh!' he shouted. 'Am I to become a leader or what?' But the situation didn't end there. Others rushed towards him. Garlands were thrown around his neck. Somen sat silently as the car began to move towards his residence.

33

THE NEWS OF Somen's arrest spread like wildfire. It ignited many rural youths who immediately became protesters and moved towards Beethalgarh to show their solidarity for Somen. Sensing trouble, the Sub-Divisional Magistrate, Beethalgarh, clamped down Section 144 of the CrPC on these disturbed villages. The Tahsildar, as a junior EM, tried to handle the situation in a self-styled manner. He acted so whimsically that the situation was likely to get aggravated. The local administration had invited spontaneous wrath from the general public because they had mishandled the situation.

Judabandh was filled with excitement. Each person in the hamlet, under the leadership of Malia, came out with their traditional weapons like sledgehammers, poniards, axes, etc., and waved them in the air. On seeing this, the Government employees like the forest guard, village-level worker planned to flee from the site out of fear.

'Stop,' shouted someone.

The little son of the worker panicked and started crying at once. As the opponents advanced, the wife of the Government servant became terrified. Her face was creased with fear and she was on the verge of fainting. The whole family was alarmed. Escape seemed to be their only redemption.

'Woman and child, let us save them,' shouted Malia from behind. He rushed to give them a protective covering. The excited mob retreated at once.

'Please save us,' the couple pleaded with folded hands.

'Don't worry, I am here,' Malia consoled.

The whole family was moved by the risk Malia was taking to ensure their safety.

All Government employees serving at the grassroots level abandoned their HQs forthwith. But to close one chapter and get out unscathed was nonetheless difficult.

To neutralize such an outbreak of violence was not easy. The youths protested against such restraints. But Malia stood firm.

The womenfolk couldn't stay behind their walls any longer. They raised an instant protest. They all stood in formidable groups, adding their support to Malia and his compatriots. The SDM saw the grave situation. A fresher in service, he immediately sought reinforcements from the Superintendent of Police, Samastipur. The Auxiliary Police Reserve force descended on the area. They pitched camps in the hilly terrain and kept themselves in prepared positions. A giant military-like arrangement embraced the area.

Although Malia had put his group into reverse gear, this was a sign for them to solidify their strength. The jungle was their own place. They knew all the shortest and hidden routes.

'I'll give them all a fitting reply,' Malia explained and commanded his people to defend themselves against the police. 'Go on, you have enough strength, this is your native place. Nobody will have the guts to drive you out from here.' His speeches provoked everyone including the youths who started blocking all entry points with huge boulders. Some of them cut down trees and blocked all passages leading to their hamlet.

The narrow path to Judabandh ran along a stony ridge, strewn with stones. They snaked up nettle vines at places. They dug secret ditches and packed leaves into them to teach the authorities a lesson. The village police somehow detected their tricks. The villagers pounced on him and produced him before Malia like a hostage. The latter asked that he be confined in the village. Everyone was thirsting to take revenge on him. Malia lashed out at him branding him a spy. He pleaded his innocence and swore with folded hands not to reveal these facts before the Station House Officer. He was asked to remain in Judabandh without going to Beethalgarh. The timid fellow agreed to this timorously like a rat.

The administrative trio, Mohanty, Pasayat and Das, prevailed upon their boss, the newly posted SC, to draw up battle lines with Somen's group. They projected him as a criminal. The SC listened to all such allegations with rapt attention and hinted at strategic devices to curb them. It so happened that in the flush of administrative zeal, he ordered the arrest of both Somen and Malia under the National Security Act.

However, both the Collector and SP advised him to exercise utmost restraint on the law and order front. The SC decided to display patience accordingly. There he was, the lone fish in the rural stream bearing the stamp of the Indian Administrative Service. But the petty officers like small fishes always hovered around him. He grumbled while listening to anyone speaking against somebody. A squeamish person like him was not interested in sharing plans with his subordinates. The villagers had support from Government employees serving at the grassroots and together they launched a campaign to fight for their cause.

After waiting for a few hours, the SC decided to snuff out the destructive mood of the agitators. As the mob started pelting stones at the police force, both the SC and DSP assessed the situation and clamped Section 144 of the CrPC around the area, which prevented people from assembling together.

'The mob is declared unlawful,' shouted the SC. Heedless of his command, the Circle Inspector didn't act upon his order at once. The SC lambasted him, 'What is this? Why such delay?'

The CI replied after a few minutes, 'How can I enforce it with such a small striking force, Sir? Please look at the strength of the unruly mob.'

'I am the Magistrate in charge of the striking force, I hereby order you to disperse the unlawful assembly.'

'Sir, but as a police officer I have to act according to the situation.'

'Do you mean to say that I am being unreasonable?'

'I don't mean so, Sir.'

'Go ahead, I say once again.'

The CI replied coolly, 'Unless there is adequate force. I can't... excuse me, Sir.' Just then the DSP was seen advising him on how to tackle the situation.

The SC paced up and down breathing heavily.

'Let me go, I can't work with a CI of this temperament.' The SC was seen rushing to the police van to use the VHF set for getting connected to the SP for further reinforcement.

'Hello! May I talk to the SP? There is an alarming law and order situation in Judabandh. The agitators are turning up in huge numbers. We need an additional contingent of two platoons of striking force, please.'

'There are no suitable officers at this moment,' replied the SP.

'But the situation has gone beyond control. Unless you arrange to send at least one platoon we will be in trouble,' he said putting down the phone.

After a few minutes, the VHF started to ring. The DSP rushed to respond. The CI was by his side.

'Who's speaking...over.'

'It's DSP Panda, Sir...over.'

'Yes...two platoons with officers will be reaching there very soon...Intimate the SC to recruit extra Magistrates. Keep me informed regularly,' said the officer-in-charge of the SP's control room.

'Yes Sir.'

Instantaneously, both the DSP and CI took their positions like commanders in a battlefield. Before giving the command to start operations, both requested the SC, Tahsildar, BDO and other EMs to wear helmets to protect themselves. Policemen with helmets and metal shields jumped into the crowd like roaring tigers, wielding their lathis. 'Stop the beating,' Malia shouted.

After some time, police vans could be seen arriving from a distance. The dazzling bayonets appeared like hanging masts to control the situation. The sight of the uniformed police force made the SC fly off the handle. The sergeant gave a long whistle. It instantly made everyone stand in a row. The publicity officer screamed loudly to again declare the assembly as unlawful. The crowd didn't disperse. Instead they bravely stood before the force. The entire contingent was ready to face a do-or-die situation.

Drim...Drim. Blank shots were fired, followed by shelling of tear gas and a lathi charge in sequential order.

'*Challo...aage badho...* Forward march,' shouted one of the sergeants taking the lead.

The force advanced towards the hamlet to flush out the unruly elements. Apprehensive of police excess, the SC and other Magistrates too joined the march like conscience keepers. The idea of revenge pushed the police forward with a determined spirit but the protesters were even more determined. Although the Magistrates had flattered themselves that they were the real controlling authorities of the force, the reality was something else. Catcalls, filthy abuses and stone throwing defiled the atmosphere. The protesters went on rampage. Malia took the lead and gave a battle cry to all of his compatriots. They stood as if to embrace the bullets like natural rain falling on human bodies.

Drim...Drim echoed both the first and second fire.

The frenzied mob mistook it as real and great commotion followed. People started fleeing from the spot in all directions with lightning speed.

The force took control of the area without much resistance. A serene valley witnessed a bloody fight that was unheard of before. There was a blast of fire in the jungle. No one knew who it was, but suddenly a tree caught fire and burning boughs started throwing fireballs in all directions singeing the lush greenery. The hot air blew all around. These arsonists were the same lot, the sons of the forest who grew up with the trees like twin brothers. The lush green canopy of flowering trees flew off in a wild cry of flames.

Nothing but the flaming leaves danced everywhere. Each page of the CrPC seemed to be burning with it. Judabandh stood like an impenetrable fort. In the process there were no rulers or ruled. The quiet environ was enveloped in millions of sparks of fire.

The SC stood like a victorious army general and so did his paramilitary group.

Malia and his group were deep in thought. Some looked worried. Anything would happen at any moment.

'Who is there?' shouted an ASI.

Someone was seen speeding away. The sharp focus from the searchlight concentrated on it. The ASI repeated, '*Kaun Hai*?'

No one replied. The police officer switched over to his third command. 'Hands up or I will fire.'

Still no one came forward. The nocturnal setting became more eerie. Without waiting any longer, he ordered, 'Fire!'

Bullets flew at the target at lightning speed.

'Doo...Doo...Doo...Doo.'

At once, they heard the wailing cry of an animal.

'Go and see,' the ASI commanded a constable.

The latter with one of his colleagues rushed to the spot. 'Sir, just a wolf,' the constable said. The carcass of the animal was lying in a pool of blood.

There were none to restrain the trigger-happy police officer.

Such mock-heroic warfare went on unabated. It was as if neither group had any fear of losing or hope of winning. The birds and crickets were disturbed; perhaps the atmosphere became uninviting for them. In one of the palm trees, a sparrow's nest was seen wearing a burning cap. The lifeless wolf was lying unattended as the bullets swallowed him up. Once again darkness descended bringing an end to the raid. The SC looked like a victor wanting to add 'His Highness' to his name, and so did the other members of the team.

34

BOTH SOMEN AND Pradeep were trying their best to provide clinical treatment to the wounded body of Judabandh. Strong groups of armed peasantry shielded the meeting spot. At night, one of the police armed guards entered stealthily. Many in the hamlet knew him as someone's father-in-law who lived in Judabandh once upon a time. He was taken aback by the warm welcome he received. He could be seen enjoying the status of a son-in-law and not a hated Government agent. He, in fact, told them about the differences between the SC and CI. The SP had no desire for such kind of an operation, said he.

'What is the matter then?' quipped Malia.

'The Tahsildar, BDO and EO are the real instigators. The SC being new to his job failed to foresee the aftermath of a lathi charge and blank fire,' he whispered.

'The RO is no less. He intentionally avoided coming to the front,' added another.

'Never rely on a Brahmin with dark complexion, he is one of them,' a villager said abruptly.

'Don't confuse human nature with a hackneyed adage,' cautioned Pradeep.

These officers in league with the RO were the fraternity group engaged in smuggling wood from the forest. Both the Collector and SP were aware of their clandestine trade. Now they instantly decided to let the SC become aware of the fact through an anonymous petition.

'Wood smuggling by officers? When the borders of a tilled field eat away their own standing crop, why am I being implicated under criminal charges?' Somen reacted sharply.

'Wood smuggling and Somen,' He brooded over this vilification campaign against him again and again. Out of wild fury, he beat his fists against the wall repeatedly. His eyes flashed like blazing fire and his teeth gnashed with fury. 'How can I forget the utter disregard,' he murmured.

After a marathon sitting, both Pradeep and Somen started to feel hungry. Two rural youths got up to arrange food for their leaders. Somen grabbed one of them and said, 'No special arrangements for us, first promise and then go.' All of a sudden, Malia intervened and Somen had to accept his comrade's words.

Just then another youth came in with freshly cooked chicken curry. Malia directed him to carry it to the anteroom.

'Well, Malia, I won't take such food from you,' said Somen.

'Somenji, what is cheaper and easily available other than this food?'

Somen, observing the others, didn't want to take his argument further. In the other room there was one earthen pot with molasses and liquid, a home-made brew from fermented mahua flowers that smelt repulsive. Somen felt like kicking everything. He didn't appreciate the innocent measures taken by the people to entertain him. They, on the other hand, thought that Somen would approve of such a hearty get-together. The gathering had noticed his tense mood and didn't want to push him. After a few had eaten and drunk, they once again sat together to scribble petitions against the 'trio', which they wanted to file before the authorities in the state capital. Somen gave a free flow to his mind for the draft. Top echelons in the Ministry of Forest were fed with detailed information exposing illegalities committed by the field staff at the grassroots level. The editor of the local Hindi weekly from Samastipur was also favoured with these facts.

'How strange! The editor seems close to them,' commented someone.

'Oh yes! These people supply him with wood to make furniture.'

Somen had seen the world around him and understood the never-ending result of such a war cry. Both the forest and media people were traumatizing him. He was trying hard to overcome this doleful mood. 'Face a problem only if you can resolve it,' shouted someone from within. He fortified himself to face any eventuality on earth.

In Judabandh, the rising darkness without any lights or electricity was allowing everyone to look at the bright faces of the stars. Perhaps one day, a rising star would smile upon this hamlet.

35

SOMEN AND PRADEEP returned to Beethalgarh the next day. Somen was dazed by the way people in the colony stared at him. Once a person goes to jail, he is looked down upon by society and that was true in Somen's case. Somen tried to take another route to avoid the staring faces, but this thought still hammered in his mind.

Without Pradeep, he didn't like to move anywhere within or beyond the town area. His friend thoughtfully accompanied Somen in spite of his busy schedule as a lawyer. Even on the street, Somen rarely talked to anyone or exchanged pleasantries. They usually went out late in the evening under the veil of darkness. He was keeping a low profile.

Somen was becoming like a wounded tiger. The humiliating treatment from police and forest people made him cry. He heard the greatest noise from within. A series of explosions with heated utterances burst out from him ever so often. The Roy family felt like fixing a tent somewhere between heaven and the earth and shifting there with bag and baggage to avoid public rumour of any kind. Their eyes scanned the colony with suspicion in case someone was whispering about them. Such suspicion was aimed at finding out if there was any conspiracy against the Roy family.

'Why did the police humiliate an intelligent youth like Somen,' lamented a lady while fetching water from the nearby tube well. Minati who was standing nearby kept mum. She saw the woman smiling slyly. Flattery seemed like a magic art many of the womenfolk had acquired. But their inner motives were kept hidden. The Roy family wanted them to reveal the true meaning of such looks.

Roy Babu was not bold enough to face reality. The plight of his unemployed son and unmarried daughter weighed heavily on his mind. It was as if his world had fallen into a ditch from where there was no way to escape. A quiet sorrow filled his thoughts.

Somen took a cup of tea and moved slowly towards an empty chair. Weakened as he was, he staggered slightly trying to support himself. He sat down and looked at the vacant sky.

The chair, finely chiselled and carved by a local carpenter, had survived the onslaught of time for many years.

His eyes turned towards Goddess Durga, decked with sandalwood paste, dry *tulsi* leaves and flowers, sitting on a small wooden throne. He reached towards her as if seeking consolation.

'A throne made only of paddy grains!' He looked carefully at its craftsmanship.

'Such a nice subtle design', he revealed further. 'What could be the price?'

'It's nothing but a family heirloom symbolizing artistic strength and dedication.

'No patronage by the Government to encourage such skills of the hands,' he wondered aloud. So exquisite a craft must have been the handiwork of an unemployed youth like him.

'Can't Durga shower a little of her benevolence on this poor artist?' he remarked.

'Babu!' His mother patted him on his back as she always did when he was lost in his own world. Holding incense sticks in her hand and with a wet sari draped around her body, she was advancing for her morning puja.

'Babu, my sweetheart.'

'Maa.'

'Let us pray before Maa Durga and Lord Shiva. They will certainly listen to our woes.'

'Maa! What a ridiculous idea,' he sneered at her in a hoarse voice.

'No my dearest...things are not favourable for us. Their blessings are the only options.'

Somen listened to his mother chanting mantras and ringing a bell. Faith entered his mind like a natural invader to cool his mind.

A flower got fixed on his right ear. Minati sipped a teaspoon of Lord Shiva's bathing water. Roy Babu took a little prasad in his folded hands. Everyone said a silent prayer. God was needed as some kind of a consolation. Somen sat transfixed as his family performed their worship.

He was constantly at odds with followers of God. Somen felt like assailing himself. His self-righteous mood refused everything. But where was the way to escape from such a bondage? There was no way to rescue oneself.

He was in despair and in some way insulted because of God. Morally he felt wounded.

The evening made its stylistic appearance stepping over the horizon. Twinkling stars were slowly making their presence felt in the marine blue sky. The clouds were galloping in the distance. The crescent moon was seen riding the waves of the eastern sky. The scent of sweet jasmine was struggling to defeat the unpleasant odour of the yellow grass. Herds of cattle were returning to their sheds with their bells tinkling and their hoofs raising a fine cloud of dust. Once in a while Somen peeped out of the window. He switched on the table lamp and plunged into the dry exercise of his last competitive battle.

36

THE HILL MYNAH presented by the people of Judabandh to Somen proved to be an excellent pupil. She imitated the human voice clearly and addressed 'Somen' and 'Mini' by their first names. She screeched for food whenever she caught sight of Mrs Roy or Minati but never in front of Somen or his dad. Mrs Roy secured a silver ring to ornament one of her feet and looked after the bird properly, including bathing and feeding her. Since her arrival, the Roy family granted the bird all privileges barring the day of Somen's arrest.

'Somen...Somen...Mini...Mini!'

On the day, while there had been a hullabaloo in the residence of Roy Babu, the bird couldn't see anything and looked perplexed. Her oft-repeated calls of 'Somen, Somen' went unnoticed. Supplication of 'Mini, Mini' too went unheard. Out of disgust one forest guard raised his fist at the bird. Somen was hurt by the attack on such a vulnerable creature. He retorted bluntly, 'Don't you feel ashamed of yourself?'

The mynah wanted to be totally loyal to her master but forced herself to keep quiet and became a nervous wreck instead.

Meanwhile, Roy Babu received a letter from Kolkata with a marriage proposal for Minati. The proposed bridegroom was Bengali, a little over thirty-five and an employee of the Kolkata Municipal Corporation. The old linkage between the two families ipso facto might have been the reason why the Roy family responded so quickly. It so happened a date was fixed for their upcoming trip to Beethalgarh. On being informed of the arrival, the whole family gave their house a good cleaning. Every household appliance was arranged with great care. Mrs Roy used a broomstick to clear the layers of dust and cobwebs. Somen had to pack up his scattered belongings. His had reverted to his earlier mood. He bought delicious eatables from the confectionery. Pradeep too helped in organizing many culinary delicacies from the neighbouring houses. Sen, his wife and their younger son reached Beethalgarh on the Kolkata-Chennai-Howrah-Express. Pradeep was waiting for them at the railway station and they arrived at Roy Babu's residence in a car.

The Roy family's only thought was that Minati should get married at any cost. Somen was waiting to see his parents' relaxed faces once the decision had been taken. As the day progressed, Somen and Pradeep intensified their activities, trying hard to keep the guests in a comfort zone. They continued to ask each of them what their food preferences were, what else they liked so that they could make every moment of their stay pleasant. Dressed stylishly and carefully made up, Minati appeared before the jury with a tray in her hands. With no tea stains on her clothes or any body odour, she was looking good in her silk sari, matching blouse and several ornaments. She looked so fresh as to carry the day with her! Was it Minati or somebody else? Why then did she look so formal and detached? She didn't look at the guests but confined herself to monosyllabic replies. The presence of her brother, daddy and mummy gave her the strength to control her fear. While walking out, the tray slipped from her hands. Mrs Sen made a quick dash to assist her. Both clasped each other and came closer. It was like a spontaneous caress to transmit an unspoken liking for a daughter-in-law.

The conversation went on in full swing. After a while, Mrs Sen went into the kitchen to gossip with Mrs Roy and Minati, who was intent on cooking the food. Sen, Roy Babu and the young boys were left alone in the drawing room to fend for themselves. Mrs Sen lingered in the kitchen, watching Minati closely. Her choice fell naturally on the young lady. Accepting Minati as her daughter-in-law was the only option left for Mrs Sen. Who would be more compatible with her son other than this one? Would she be missing an opportunity if she did not pick Minati as her daughter-in-law? Such a thought began to rule over Mrs Sen.

Roy Babu gave a warning shout for lunch. Both Somen and Pradeep wanted to know what was in the minds of the Sen family.

'Maa! What about their choice?' Somen asked.

'No hints as yet, my boy.'

'Why the silence?'

'Who knows? Let us try our luck.'

Somen decided not to ask any further questions.

They had their lunch in Somen's room. His reading table was converted into a dining table. The ladies from both the families served the men first and then they sat together comfortably in the kitchen to have their lunch. In the process, Minati picked up her brother's plate whereas both Mrs Roy and Mrs Sen ate their husbands' leftover food.

While looking lovingly at Minati, Mrs Sen expressed her happiness before the others. 'She will be ours,' she said. Mrs Roy at once responded with a smile. The Sen family's decision brought great joy to the Roy family but it also made them tight-lipped. Minati hid her delight.

'But...' Sen exclaimed abruptly.

All eyes concentrated on Sen's face.

'What on earth, things do not materialize so quickly,' Somen whispered to Pradeep.

'Marriages are made in heaven', replied Pradeep.

'Let us wait and see what the reason is,' Roy Babu told himself coolly.

Sen revealed what was on his mind. 'See, we have a daughter too. If you do not mind, let us come forward for an exchange marriage.'

Roy Babu took some time to understand what he was saying but Mrs Roy grasped its meaning at once.

Somen felt uneasy about such a proposal. 'Is he to act like a second string to Sen's bow?' he thought. It gave Mrs Roy an odd feeling. She wanted to bowl it over quietly as she didn't like to intervene in her only son's personal choice. The interplay between their benevolence and self-interest had taken her aback.

Roy couldn't decry the proposal outright. How to tackle a situation of this kind? He knew that in all matrimonial alliances there was a tug of war between the two families, but he didn't expect such unpleasantness. How were they to get over this hurdle? 'This is sheer hypocrisy,' Somen said audibly. Like a drowning man taking the help of a floating straw everyone looked at each other. 'What to do then?' was the common question in everyone's mind.

It was time for the guests to take the night train back to Kolkata. The Roy family, although dispirited, didn't fail in their duty to see their guests off.

Pradeep tried his best to diffuse the situation. 'It need not be so difficult,' he said, consoling. 'Let us take our guests to the station. We can discuss the matter freely after that.'

Roy Babu, Somen, Pradeep and the guests hurried to the railway station in two autorickshaws. The train was half an hour late. The earlier intimacy between the two families was lacking. While waiting for the train, the conversation between Roy Babu and Sen, leave alone Mrs Sen, was insipid. The night slowly began to open its wings enveloping the surroundings under its reign. It was as if to emphasize the loneliness everywhere.

37

THE ROMANCE BETWEEN Banita and Mohan had become the hot topic of discussion among the youngsters of the town. They, like a famous story, attracted the attention of both college-goers and dropouts. Their overt display was not approved of by the dwellers in the small town. The Das family was wholly accountable for such a premarital relationship. Comments were flung at them from every corner: 'Can a man who can't enforce discipline in his own family do so in his office?' Das incurred a bad name for spending office money irregularly with support from Mohan the VC, thus marginalizing the Chairman. All bills with respect to relief grants were passed with the countersignature of Mohan, overriding the Chairman who voiced his protest before the Collector against such impropriety. Das was crafty enough to submit a reply like 'The Chaiman hardly sits in the office. How can I get him to counter-sign?' Officially it appeared logical but in reality, it was the other way round. Mohan was the de facto executant for many labour-intensive works. The engineering section manipulated the Case Records and Measurement Books in order that profits could be maximized in his favour. For example, although moroom, the material used for road construction, was available nearby it was shown as being brought from a distance. Labourers were paid at a lesser rate than the prescribed norms. False entries were made in the Measurement Book allowing duplicity. Water sprinkling was shown deliberately to enhance the bill. A new intimacy had developed between Mohan and Das to cherish such aims. Mohan tried his best to gain the upper hand in all of Das' affairs. To elope with Banita became his ulterior motive. The Das couple had their own stimulus—the desire to earn more and more and to close their eyes against everything else.

Mohan had entered the Das family set-up concealing the looseness of his character. He was well dressed and had modulated his behavioural pattern on a Romeo, pretending to be heroic. He presented Banita with a set of pearl earrings and a necklace with a round locket with the tacit consent of her parents. She used to embellish her palms with henna, wore a gold hairband, and applied make-up. She would wear supple leather footwear presented by Mohan and the latest silk garments when they rode their bikes through the bylanes of the town. But such advancement in the field of love had nothing to do with the progress in her studies. She fared badly in every successive exam, winning a new degree from fellow mates who called her 'Miss Lilavati'. She was, according to her own opinion, the dazzling beauty queen of the area. Once, Mohan embraced her in the living room calling her 'My honey', in full view of Sunita, her sister.

'Such impudence!' Sunita looked gloomily at her sister and Mohan. Shanti was a curious enigma. How could a mother allow her daughter so much of freedom? So daring and shameless a spirit was not seen in traditional Indian society. Casting away all ethical norms, Mohan and Banita went hand in hand in a carefree manner justifying their flourishing romance. They were determined not to buckle under any known or unknown persons, no matter if they were older or younger than them.

38

STORM CLOUDS HAD started gathering over the Das family that played out in a horrific manner. A contingent of vigilance sleuths swirled around the house on charges of corruption that shocked the conscience of the small town. DSP, Anti-Corruption Cell, took up the lead. As usual, Das seemed unperturbed, and wanted to entertain the squad with refreshments. The offer was refused point blank. They raided the NAC office too. Measurement Books, Case Records, Hand Books were seized and handed over to a third party. Fieldwork was recorded in snapshots. Depositions were collected from public witnesses. Such a raid raised the fears of the office employees but Das advised everyone to have patience.

'Good God, how wealth accumulates so much!' shouted an official. Das failed to produce relevant documents in support of his earnings. He was exasperated and tried frantically to get rid of this prosecution. Some were cynical about the outcome.

'Very few vigilance cases have resulted in conviction,' opined a local press reporter standing nearby at the time of the raid.

Shanti tried her best to charm the enforcement squad but retreated.

'It's all a stage-managed drama,' shouted a local youth.

'Of course not,' said a vigilance official.

Das was trying to get his nerve back. He looked perplexed, nonetheless. 'I am clean,' he pleaded before the general public. 'We have fallen prey to a conspiracy,' added Shanti.

Both Shanti and Das stood together trying to sway the public opinion in their favour. Their two daughters were huddled in a corner. They were trying their best to come closer to the raiders.

The Deputy Superintendent of Police asked his subordinates to open the steel almirahs. One young constable rushed to comply with his order. Banita got nervous. She threw a pleading look requesting him to desist. 'A little bit of privacy, please!' Shanti pleaded for her daughters. While fiddling with her bangles she turned away dejected. The enforcement squad withdrew a little. A burning matchstick put out so suddenly!

'Go ahead,' the DSP barked at them.

Das broke the silence.

'Some touts have hatched a plan to harass us. I am sure they will never succeed. Am I corrupt? I have come to serve Beethalgarh. Let the Almighty decide,' said he.

'No disturbance, please,' thundered a sentry.

It was a blow to his status. 'A mere guard,' Das said.

One almirah was opened. Banita was flabbergasted. She made a dive to snatch something away. 'No jewellery...cash...nothing of the sort.' What then?

The enforcement squad moved away, allowing the young lady to come forward. In any case, touching her body would lead to further trouble. The DSP stepped forward. 'What nonsense!'

Banita with surprising strength and a steely hand snatched away some scraps of paper from the shelf.

An inspector shouted, 'Hand them over or face the worst.'

Banita pushed the papers under her skirt.

No one dared to pull them from her, as this could lead to the imposition of a vulnerable section of the CrPC for outraging the modesty of a young lady. It gave Banita an opportunity to prevent the materials from being seized.

'Love letters,' whispered someone.

'So many bottles of rum and whisky!'

It was an amazing discovery. Family photos, expensive saris, National Savings Certificates, bundles of currency notes, jewellery all sprang up at once!

'No!' shouted Shanti at the police. 'You can't seize all those, please stop.'

The police didn't bother and continued to go ahead with their task.

Das sounded incoherent. A marked sorrow glided over his face. It was as if the earth was slipping away from under his feet. He coughed out many sentences irritably.

The portrait of Gandhiji smiled from the wall, as if there was no choice.

The heat of seizure was radiating everywhere. Rural inquisitors who had gathered around Das' house started moving away slowly.

'You must have been hungry, Sir!' said Das.

The DSP didn't bother to reply. Das repeated his question. 'Mind your own business,' snubbed the police officer.

Das looked at him pathetically.

'Sir! You are also a family man. You know how difficult it is to maintain a family with a single income.'

'So your conscience has accepted this?'

Das felt unwanted. He went outside and gazed closely at the sky. While biting his lips he murmured, 'There can't be any reconciliation or back to the splendour of sweet official harmony.' The shrieking protests had quietened down. In life, perhaps it would have been better to choose a minimum needs corner. He pondered whether it would have been better to remain honest rather than undergo such trauma. A forced recluse even in one's own house. What a shame!'

'Where is the photographer? Let him take snaps,' shouted the DSP again and again. He perhaps wanted to showcase their efforts in apprehending an officer who enjoyed properties beyond the legal sources.

The camera flashed. Jewellery, National Savings Certificates, registered sale deeds, hard cash, four-wheelers, silk saris, everything was reduced to exhaustive photo shots. The DSP aimed at strengthening the case with sufficient evidence. There should be no comments from the Magistrate like benefit of doubt or facts…no clues, etc. The whole family was in a panic. His actions sent shivers down each member's spine.

'Let us go to the cowshed,' said a police officer.

The photographer ran immediately to the spot. There were three Jersey cows grazing at a distance. A boy with a stick stood nearby.

What would be the value of each one? One Sub-Inspector did an instant evaluation.

Shanti intervened. 'That's not black property. It was a present from my father to his son-in-law at the time of our wedding.' Such a statement made the police furious. 'Nothing to depose here, speak during the trial.'

'These are frogs in a well looking at a small part of the outside but taking it to be the whole world around them,' said Das excitedly.

The DSP heard this and immediately remarked, 'People in glasshouses shouldn't throw stones at others. It might put you in further trouble unnecessarily.'

Soon, a Government vehicle was seen approaching. The BDO Pasayat stepped down from it. He sat in his car and asked his driver to bring Das to him. Das had to seek permission from the DSP for such a meeting.

'What is wrong with us?' Pasayat consoled.

'God knows, they have been harassing me like anything,' said Das.

'Let me go and lodge a complaint before the Superintendent of Police.'

'Please! They are in an absolutely bizarre mood now.'

They huddled together for a long time, whispering into each other's ears. Das told him about the details of the police action. A policeman approached them.

'Why are you pursuing me so closely? Am I a criminal?' Das asked with disgust.

'Let us meet somewhere,' the BDO said. His friend was looking pale and sweaty. Pasayat wanted to leave the scene.

The road was bumpy and he found it difficult to drive on it. The engine stopped somewhere at a distance. No one stepped forward to help him. The BDO became aware of his unpopularity. He looked embarrassed.

The driver got down. He gave the vehicle a push with one hand while steering with the other. Pasayat was too aware of his power and position to do such manual labour. He preferred to keep himself away from any kind of physical exercise. The engine started abruptly after several splutterings. One police constable requested a lift. The BDO agreed to it.

39

IN WALTAIR, EVERY passing day was harrowing for Master Babu. His money was fast disappearing. He was forced to move around the city on foot. He was hungry and spoke in a feeble voice. His unkempt hair, torn pyjama and kurta made him look like a vagabond. His cerebellum seemed failing to house its usual memory. Waltair stood before him like a dark giant swallowing light before his eyes. He was smoking bidi after bidi, tossing them aside when they were over. Once, a lit stub hit a Honda rider who hurled all sorts of abuses at him. Master Babu had to tolerate him somehow. He had strained every nerve to trace his favourite student, Madhu, but to no effect. His existence began to blow with the air like ashes stockpiled somewhere in an ash pond.

It was a full moon night. Master Babu caught a swift glance of a young boy. Could it be Madhu or someone else? His attention was focused on a teenager who resembled Madhu lifting plates in a small dhaba. The place looked dirty with a low-watt bulb lighting the oily wooden bench. The same boy again appeared with glasses of water. Without looking at the customers sitting before him he put them on the table. He was dressed shabbily and looked unwell. His walk was slow like that of an ant. Master Babu looked at him and shouted piercingly, 'Madhu!'

The boy stopped his drudgery to glance at Master Babu. He did not speak. A wry smile appeared on his face. He recognized his teacher standing there without his usual weapons of chalk and duster in his hands.

'Madhu...my sweetheart,' Master Babu cried out. 'Where have you been for so long? How are you?' In his excitement he walked up to the boy and took hold of his wet fingers. They were cold beyond belief.

'Look, here I am, your Master Babu. Do you remember me?' Flashes of schooldays dazzled them. The flame of memory began to burn reaching its highest point. Master Babu wished to kiss the boy from tip to toe, but since it was a public place he embraced the boy tightly against his chest for a long time. The school premises, the dusty pavilion, jackfruit trees, riverbank, all filled their imagination. The boy good-naturedly responded but he was torn between affection and responsibility. The sudden call of duty stood like the sprinkling of dust on a polished white shirt. Master Babu understood the situation. The boy tore out of his arms shouting 'water' at the others. Master Babu grew silent and went outside. What could he do at this stage? Outside, the moon was steering across the sky. It looked busy playing hide-and-seek with the clouds. The clouds were floating like players running in the field. As yet, Madhu's position in the city was like a fish dangling its body in the water around a live bait. He was hopeful that he would be rid of the place. But ironically, Master Babu himself was missing the key of his own lock! Like insiders in a trojan horse, both decided to battle with the city for their safe exit.

The hotel owner shouted at the boy. When Master Babu saw this he came inside. 'Do you owe anything to the hotelier? If not, let us get going,' he said to Madhu in their native language. But the latter was too young to plan such an instantaneous exist. He could not exercise his superiority as a teacher in the classroom on him. Master Babu stood helpless like the hero of a flop show. No whipping cane in hand to swim across the air to reach its target. The onlookers were not his pupils but strangers in an alien land.

Suddenly, the boy had a vision of his long-time friends and the textbooks strewn around him. A searing pain blanketed his vision. He couldn't think further. 'Come here,' the hotelier yelled at him. Saying so, he raced across to catch the boy, his temper escalating. The boy tried to escape the anger of his boss. He jumped over a bench struggling frantically to remain at a safe distance from his master. The latter was spreading like boiled water. Madhu exercised every bit of his strength to diffuse the screaming scenario.

Master Babu was eager to say something to the hotelier, hoping to appeal to his kinder sense. But there was no such sign in him. He was shocked by his conduct. He had never experienced such a situation before. He stopped thinking, as it would lead him nowhere.

'The city is full of scarecrows,' Master Babu uttered angrily. The hotelier pushed himself forward aggressively. He looked furious. It was nothing but a ploy to flaunt his superiority. The occasion didn't demand such an action. The continuous abuse assaulted the ears of the poor teacher. Master Babu's mood was getting worse, but he was too weak to prolong his stand. He composed himself, sat on a chair and placed an order for something to satisfy his hunger. 'I doubt if you have anything in your pocket,' said the hotelier. Master Babu pulled off a gold ring from one of his fingers and placed it on the desk. The hotelier cast his greedy eyes on this small ornament and came forward to comply with the order. 'Sir,' shouted Madhu from a distance. The hotelier brought Master Babu some sweets from the glass almirah. 'Sir,' Madhu repeated again. He was trying to say something about the ring. Master Babu understood Madhu's anxiety. The hotelier grabbed Madhu and punched him so hard in the arm that he fell down. Like a monster, he jumped to hit him again. 'Don't be smart, rascal, I will finish you off.' The boy crawled painfully towards the feet of his lord.

'You fellow... What are you doing?' Master Babu rushed to save the boy. He couldn't control his tears. The blow made Madhu pant and he tried to dodge further punches. He embraced Master Babu convulsively to shield himself.

'Get out... It is me who gives you food to survive and now you betray my cause.'

Master Babu tried to face the situation. The thundering of the hotelier blew into his heart. He wanted to run away without bothering about his food order. But how could he leave Madhu, his much-loved student, in this cruel bondage?

Just then, the boy told him endearingly, 'Sir! How am I to stay here?' He looked as helpless as a candle flickering in a storm. His face was miserable as if dark clouds had enveloped it. Master Babu looked at Madhu sadly. He had to leave the place. He was not the same person he used to be, commanding respect from pupils, standing beside a blackboard like an army general. Finding no one to back him up, he came out of the hotel. The city appeared before him like a bandaged scar, a scene that disgusted him. He felt like a creature from another planet. He turned to the other side of the road and noticed a tap. His throat was parched and he felt an urge to drink water. He stretched his palms forward and drank deeply and then washed his face. The purity of water gave Master Babu another lease of life. His life's mission had not become fruitful and had to be forgotten for a while. Master Babu still failed to understand how people in a city could remain so indifferent to another's cause.

What he wanted was for people to show a little compassion, but wherever he went he was looked down upon. He unfastened the napkin from his waist and wiped his face. The tall mansions competing with the height of the sky, sprawling lawns, cars and autos dashing down the streets made no sense to him.

'To hell with the city,' he cried. He only wanted to go back to his native village at the earliest. Then all his worries would go away and life would be pleasant once again. He would meet his little boys and girls in their uniforms carrying school bags, the cowherds with their cattle, young girls standing by the side of tube wells and other such familiar scenes. His longing for his village was intense but it became difficult for him to immediately find a route that he would take to reach Beethalgarh. Master Babu recollected his immense nurturing spirit and his dedicated urge to implant knowledge into vacant heads.

Everyone has a way of interpreting things that happen around him or her. Master Babu was no exception. Had he been thrown into the midstream to face negative undercurrents, searching frantically for a breathing escape?

40

MOHAN AND BANITA managed to take a trip to Visakhapatnam. They went to a holiday resort and then visited a multiplex to watch a movie. Banita deeply felt the excitement of the escapade. Inside the hall, the cover of darkness gave her the confidence to surrender to Mohan's caresses. The storm of their passion had made them abandon all social conventions and they sat close together, touching each other, while watching the romantic pair on the screen.

'Why can't you sit properly?' snapped a middle-aged person from behind. Both were unprepared for such a reprimand. The words were sharper than a knife, making them realize that the hall didn't give them the privacy they sought. Mohan would have given a rude reply had it been in their native place. But who would save them here? They had to swallow the reprimand and behave themselves. The dullness of Beethalgarh was better. When the show was over they both stepped outside. They wanted to go all the way to the Shiva temple at Seemachalam but instead took an autorickshaw to the enchanting seashore. Banita remembered Yeats from her text syllabus, 'The land of fairy; where nobody gets old and godly and grave; where nobody gets old and crafty and wise; where nobody gets old and bitter of tongue.'

The scintillating view of the waves exhilarated their hearts. The gusts of wind were strong. Banita as a mark of tiredness closed her eyelids. Mohan had to find a suitable hotel on the shore to spend the night. After an hour or so of intense search, they found a place but only after showing their photo identities.

How good a time far from the heat and dust of Beethalgarh! Once inside the hotel room, tiredness began to swallow their bodies. The lights were switched off at once, barring a zero-power bulb that became a mute witness to their lovemaking.

A fine morning awaited them the next day. Mohan opened the windows and the room became light and airy. Both jumped up to glance at the distant horizon. They could see a ship in the distance. Banita gave a cry; this was the first time she had seen a ship.

After their morning rituals they hunted for a good breakfast. Later, they were both amused and amazed to see a dead submarine, abandoned in the naval yard. They decided to negotiate their way to Kailash Giri to experience its beauty. Banita looked smart and had managed to get Mohan to dress smartly as well. After reaching there, they thought the place was like an oscillating drop of water on the green surface of a banana leaf. The Bay of Bengal splashing the foot of the hill was such a wondrous sight!

'Look below, Mohan, What a marvellous sight!' she said excitedly. 'Oh! It's nice,' replied Mohan but in a colder manner. Over the vast blue expanse ships were sailing in a row in the distant horizon. Hundreds of visitors had gathered around the hill to have a darshan of the giant idols of Shiva and Parvati. They all stood closer to have a glimpse of such a winning attraction.

'So powerful the deities are here, let us extend our prayers to ward off evil,' said Banita.

'Of course.' Mohan threw away his mood with a note of consent. They held each other and pushed through the crowd. For Mohan, it was a ploy to caress her soft palm again and again. The air was cool, unlike the torrid heat of Beethalgarh. The whole setting strolled between hot and cold, shade and light. Those strange trees, fanned by the hilly breeze, were so grave and humble relaxing them both.

No whispering or eavesdropping either, again unlike Beethalgarh. The rhythm of life was sublimated to a new form. From a comparatively lonely corner, a man who looked like a priest gave a shout, 'Stop there!' He continued, 'How dare you leave the place without a grace.' Banita turned back. She looked frightened.

'Your husband!'

Mohan felt somehow embittered. He saw a bald-headed, saffron-clad man. His commanding presence was such that it was as if he had greater sovereignty than God. Both moved closer. A glimpse of apology could be marked in Banita. Mohan was in the reverse gear.

'Have this,' the priest said, offering a spoon of paduka to each. It smelled like coconut.

'What is this?' asked Mohan.

'Bathing water of the Lord,' replied the priest. Both took it calmly. 'Nothing to brood over, your problems will be solved in no time but...'

Banita stepped forward to give something monetary. Mohan

glanced up vacuously.

After receiving a fifty-rupee note from them, the priest gave his approval to the duo. The air was full of screechings made by anonymous creatures flying overhead. The aquatic birds faded slowly into the distant horizon only to descend once again on to the undulating thrones of sea waves.

Banita remembered her lacklustre past. Mohan was not interested in following this pattern of thought. Half of Banita's face was covered with joy and the other half with fear. 'Would Mohan betray her?' She was like a moth playing around the lamp of Mohan. She bent down before the almighty Kailash like the member of a small prayer group.

Banita wished to learn something beyond the physical aspect of their relationship. She didn't know Mohan's exact feelings for her. He was too young and immature to make any commitments beyond ravaging her body.

Mohan could smell Banita's disturbed thoughts and therefore asked, 'Are you upset about something?'

'No.'

'Then why are you looking so gloomy?' he retorted.

'I am thinking.'

'F...o...o, I pity you...come on...my sweetheart.' He pulled her hand aggressively.

Roaring waves lashed across the Bay of Bengal. Mohan leaned over Banita, adopting a Romeo-like pose. Banita was still in an introspective mood. Till date, her leisure hours had revolved around her family. This was the first time she was away from her parents.

The beach was full of romantic, amorous couples. The primordial urge kicked them both. The midday sun was at its height. A photographer popped out of somewhere and pleaded for a snap. Banita instantly agreed to get into a closer pose. But Mohan hesitated. The photographer repeated, 'Sir, Madam has agreed.'

'No...not now.'

Banita was shocked. What could be the reason? Perhaps Mohan wanted to suck honey like a bee buzzing from place to place and then abandon the flowers.

'Why do you say no?' she retorted.

'We are yet to be betrothed,' came his prompt reply.

On hearing this, Banita breathed heavily. She realized that her fortune would be all doom and gloom. She was irritated by such a breach of trust and felt like crying. The photographer could understand her state of mind and disappeared in pursuit of other clients.

'Come on...my sweetie.' Mohan picked her up in a ferocious way. Infuriated, Banita decided to resist his wanton attack. She wanted a permanent settlement. An assurance for life partnership. Mohan became furious. He dragged her stubbornly across the sand. Banita fought with utmost resistance, but Mohan was much stronger and pulled her violently.

'Okay, then let me quit.' Saying this Mohan walked away. Banita couldn't follow him initially. But after a little while she understood the motive of her paramour. 'So alone in Visakhapatnam,' she stammered and raced along the sandy beach. Seeing her following, Mohan halted, perhaps to provide a healing touch.

'Are you a human being or what?' Banita shouted. 'For this I left my family and everything. I can well imagine my future...Oh, too difficult to believe.' Banita hauled herself desperately. Tears welled up in her eyes.

Mohan suddenly became polite. He looked at Banita soberly, hoping to put her at ease. They wanted to move to a secluded corner to reveal what was in their minds. He smiled innocently like a child. They returned to their hotel via the ocean road for lunch and rest, observing the beauty of the sea. Banita's eyes soaked up the grandeur of the show. 'Oh! What a windy place! Let us marry and settle here for the rest of our life,' she said to Mohan.

Just then, the glass door of their hotel opened automatically and closed in the same way. Banita didn't ask why lest it would reveal her ignorance. Was it the magic of Disneyland or what!

41

MEMORIES OF BEETHALGARH haunted Banita's mind continuously. Whiling away time on the hotel balcony, she worried about leaving her home without informing her family members. What to do at present? She had relied upon a person, the champion of lewdness, and had run away from her house with him. Was such defiance justifiable? Out of all the people in the world, Banita couldn't remember anyone who was closer to her at this moment except Mohan. But that Mohan like a real crook even refused to get a photograph taken with her. Perhaps this was the dynamite in the undiscovered mine of love. As a teenager, to discover oneself as the rebel in the family life was awful. Instead of standing by her family she had preferred to go away with Mohan. But for how long could she keep herself away from her family and hometown? How long would the scenic vistas of the seashore attract her senses? Not wanting to stay with Mohan any longer, she started planning a quick return. The urge to separate filled her mind.

The fleeing pair, Banita and Mohan, had become the talk of the town. The Das family had launched a massive hunt for the duo. They with the help of their driver and two or three Councillors had searched the entire town as well as the nearby places but had failed to trace them. In order to remain incognito, Mohan had booked himself into the hotel under a false name. The receptionist was suspicious but kept quiet in case he was asked any questions.

But Das, acting on a tip-off, proceeded to Visakhapatnam in a private taxi. Somehow he managed to gather information on the hotel and the room number. He looked sleepy and excited when he arrived, and calmly asked the receptionist for the register. While ascertaining the room number and name of the occupant he gave the managerial staff an incredulous look. He was escorted to the room. He knocked at the door and Banita opened it.

'Papa!' she burst out and buried her face in his chest.

'You preferred Mohan,' Das exclaimed. 'Love has made you blind.'

He turned to Mohan, 'I believed in you, that is why you have given us this heartache.'

The young man didn't utter a word. He bowed before him like a criminal. However, the other two Councillors accompanying Das appeared quiet, despite the situation. Shanti too accompanied Das.

'Oh my God!' Das exploded helplessly. No doubt, the stupidity of his daughter had led to this acute state of depression.

His unhappiness seared Banita. 'Please, Daddy.' She collapsed at his feet and tearfully begged him to rescue her. A waiter who was standing on the threshold fetched her a glasss of water. With dull eyes, Mohan looked around rubbing his hands. For Das it was as if the floor was slipping away from under his feet. He was an emotional wreck. He saw his dearest child weeping pitifully to redeem herself from the debris of her smashed chastity.

'Daddy! I am shattered,' she spoke out simply. 'I know I shall be laughed at by everyone in Beethalgarh. I am gone…please save me.'

Das couldn't decide whether to vent his anger on his daughter or not. 'Is it right?' He thought carefully. The road to atonement was now totally blocked. Mohan, the so-called well-wisher of their family, was holding his breath. His daughter had been too naive to fathom out his evil heart.

'Okay, my dear…have guts. You want to have the whole of the sky at your command like a swift-winged lady. But how can you after your wings have been clipped?' Das admonished like a sage.

For the Das family, Mohan was now a total embarrassment. He had looted their pride. Was he worthy of being a son-in-law? Why had this happened? Because of the carelessness of Das himself! The lax family environment! Banita's growing awareness! 'Oh God, give me the strength to stand by the plight of my own child,' Das pleaded with the Almighty. At the same time, he argued with himself and cursed his daughter for jumping into a situation without judging the consequences.

'Let us go.' Das pulled Banita forcibly towards the door. He instructed the driver to collect and pack up all her belongings and lost no time in leaving the hotel. Although Banita knew that this would happen, she hadn't anticipated that it would be so soon. With the least resistance she let her dad take her away. With tearful eyes, she looked at Mohan for a while and then broke into incessant sobs.

Das had flexed his muscles and Mohan had no voice at all. He was aware of his limitations. Without waiting for the lift, Das dragged her down the staircase, which only added to the bitterness of the whole situation. Shanti, the two Councillors and the driver led them to the car. Das held his daughter tightly in the rear seat. Banita too surrendered herself. The whole situation was like the locking of a stable after the exit of the horse.

'Banita, don't go,' Mohan exclaimed following them to the car.

'What guarantee do you have for me?' Banita countered.

'You are my beloved!'

Das retorted, 'Who do you think you are? Damn you!'

Mohan realized that his relationship with the Das family was at stake, but he stood firm in his support of her. The other councillor sitting near the driver looked at Das perhaps waiting for his nod to leave.

Assuming the style of a Romeo, Mohan stood beside the window and fixed his eyes on Banita. Das gave a long sigh and asked the driver to start. Mohan was in a serious mood. Although devoid of any feeling, he felt guilty about betraying the trust of this family. He couldn't turn his head towards Das or the Councillors, leave alone make eye contact.

All of a sudden the driver started the car and turned in the direction of Vijayanagaram near the Andhra–Odisha border. Mohan returned to his hotel feeling hollow and ordered a few drinks. Waves of intoxication clouded his senses. It multiplied his anger. He came out of the room and went outside and tried to lash at a small statue on the lawn, thinking that it looked like Das.

Several people looked at him. 'Sir, please,' restrained the security guard. Mohan couldn't stand properly and the guard conducted him to his room calmly.

Mohan's voice of protest reverberated through the hotel. He felt as if he was in a vacuum.

The car carrying the five crossed the Andhra border. 'Let us get out of this Srikakulam-Koraput jungle area before midnight,' Das whispered to the driver.

'Why...for fear of terrorists?' mumbled one of the Councillors.

'No... not like that,' Das replied as he didn't like to buy instant stories on extremist activities.

There was nothing but darkness and fear around them. Both daybreak and Beethalgarh were far off. Tall trees, mountains and valleys stretched far and wide into the distant horizon. Their deep-seated fear was evident in their body language. The car sped through hilly terrain, over bridges and rivers on a single-lane road. The driver became cautious while negotiating curves and hairpin bends and undulating stretches. Das beseeched his family goddess to let them reach Beethalgarh safely. Was it proper to pass through this area at night? He interrogated himself. Both Shanti and Das through their silent prayers tried to invade the power of the night. Darkness coupled with the fear of an armed attack by hill rebels had frightened all of them. Das remembered lines from Rumi: 'In compassion and grace, be like the sun and in hiding other's blemishes, be like the night!'

'Bear!' shouted the Councillor from the front seat of the car just near the mountain tracks. The car headlights and the eyes of the passengers focused on a dark furry object. The driver while trying to speed up saw another bear looming out from the same direction. 'Perhaps a mating couple,' thought the driver but didn't want to share his idea with the others.

Wounded by the forced separation, Banita had been silent throughout. Her aggressive dad had been like an invader snatching her away from Mohan. She had to sit quietly in the car without even sharing her thoughts with her mum.

It had been a hectic day for everyone. For the Das family, it was neither a victory nor a defeat. It was almost midnight and the car had passed several district towns like Koraput, Nabrangpur, Kalahandi on the way to Beethalgarh. 'Now that we can have our food somewhere,' Das remarked. The driver stopped the car in front of a roadside dhaba. The Councillors and the driver stepped down and went ahead while Banita followed her parents like a lamb. The family members appeared calmer now.

Though no one had any appetite, they finished their dinner and got into the vehicle for their journey back to Beethalgarh. The fear of being exterminated by rebels had passed and they sat back and enjoyed the calm and cool night.

All through the journey Das was in a state of emotional disturbance. He wanted to share it with his wife but couldn't because of the two Councillors sitting nearby. Although Beethalgarh was not far off, Das wanted to reach there before dawn to escape the curious eyes of the onlookers.

Stepping down from the car with his wife and daughter, Das nodded his head heartily at both the Councillors. 'Oh, what a burden I have placed on you both. I am really grateful to you,' said he.

Leaving the Das family at their residence, the car moved ahead to drop the two Councillors at their houses.

42

MASTER BABU HAD stayed on in Visakhapatnam with the sole purpose of standing guard over Madhu should anything happen to him. The brutality of the hotelier had made him frantic with worry. Without any means of support, Master Babu was hampered by the lack of food and shelter. He wandered around almost like a beggar. He looked at alien faces, their robust bodies and obscure utterances. What could be the major aim of all such city dwellers? It was as if prosperity came into their lives without obstructions.

No doubt, the path of Master Babu was that of humiliation and fatigue. His stars were falling without any hope of striking a balance. He was like a rough fugitive driven by the force of uncertainty. The average city dweller was prone to treating all rural folk including Master Babu disdainfully. While passing by the window of a public school, he could partially hear the voice of a vernacular teacher praising this great country, its moonlit sky, verdant landscape, perennial rivers. This made Master Babu vexatious. Could such things alone permeate a teacher's vision? What prompted the poet not to discover the millions of hungry and thirsty people, the semi-nude existence of the downtrodden?

Master Babu's voice trailed away and became somewhat inaudible. His dirty clothes, worn-out chappals, unkempt beard made him look mysterious and naive. His body was crying out from sheer exhaustion. He preferred either a temple premises or a school verandah to rest his weary body.

Master Babu had to drive away a street dog in order to make a seat for himself on a cement bench. The sea wind soothed his bruises. He took a nap. Then he felt someone's presence.

'Madhu,' he shouted happily and grabbed his arm. 'My boy! How did you find me?' he looked at him questioningly.

Master Babu's blue-eyed boy stood near him. The boy knew that he had nothing substantial to receive from Master Babu. The latter knew he had nothing special to offer the boy. They knew the brutal tyranny of the hotelier and his fits of anger. Fear piled up in both of them. Their minds continued to ring with his curses. He would employ any means to snatch the boy from the clutches of Master Babu. Such a thought nestled in their minds with increasing concern. They stood helpless.

Oh! What an anxiety! Master Babu wanted to proceed towards the railway station but had no money in his pocket. It battered his spirit further. Fortunately, the boy had his earnings with him and they boarded a bus to take them to his parents. It was a dismal scene! Although the city was filled with light, this area looked distinctly gloomy. A thickly populated workers' zone spread before them.

'Papa...Papa,' shouted the boy.

A middle-aged man appeared. He was none other than the father of Madhu. 'Eh! Master Babu,' he said, greeting him with folded hands. He dragged a charpoy from behind a pile of bricks and politely requested Master Babu to sit down. A lady with a coarse Sambalpuri sari draped around her body appeared from a thatched cottage and bowed her head before him with utmost reverence.

'Maa,' said the boy to her. She looked pale and weatherbeaten and was astounded by the arrival of both Master Babu and her child. Before saying a word, she went back hurriedly into her cottage. Everyone could hear the rattle of cups and spoons.

She came out with thin slices of bread and red tea for all of them except herself. Madhu and Master Babu were both tired and hungry and consumed everything ravenously. Madhu's father brought out a couple of bidis and a matchbox from his waistband and offered one to Master Babu. Both lit them from the same stick. 'Don't you want your son to go to school? Do you want to keep him as foolish as you are?' Master Babu enquired, while drawing a long puff from his bidi.

What could be the other one's reply? He was glad that Master Babu had displayed an interest in his son's career and had come from such a long distance to meet an ordinary person like him.

'I have come here to seek permission from you to take Madhu back. Till all of you return, he can stay with me as a member of my family,' said Master Babu. It was a touching and loving moment for them despite their moneyless condition.

Both Master Babu and Madhu got ready for their return trip to Beethalgarh. They boarded a bus to reach the railway station. The Visakhapatnam-Raipur Express left the station on time. Master Babu had to strive hard to choose a safe corner in the train, lest the hotelier discover them. Fortunately there was nothing of that kind. The dreaded ruler had no occasion to stop a train that moved at such top speed.

43

THE PUBLIC FORUM in Beethalgarh with Somen as its kingpin was able to extend vital information to the vigilance sleuths on the recurring misdeeds of the BDO, Tahsildar, EO and the Forest Range Officer. As a result, their houses were raided. Somen wanted to ravenge his arrest by exposing the corrupt practices of all of them, including the BDO, Tahsildar and the Forest Officer. Malia and Pradeep, his trusted confidants, urged the whole town to stand together to depose against the four. The enthusiasm to punish them at any cost surged through the notified area. People had many doubts about the way forest checkposts were managed. The practice of checking was only in name. Gates had been put at the slightest pretext and the making of private deals became a routine affair. Seizures were enforced on small-time creatures like poor ladies entering the town carrying a little forest produce, whereas the timber mafia was protected under a defensive shield.

Roy Babu, however, was displeased by his son's involvement in such a public affair. The impatient father barked at Mrs Roy, telling her that Somen should be more involved with his studies. Somen, who had been diffident for a long time for want of a job of power and prestige, felt his stamina was being tested. A self-propelled zeal pushed him to navigate the sea of unemployment. His union activities appeared to be blocking his career plans. He didn't want to divert his mind any more. Although ideologically hostile to such a system, the silk factory at Bangalore with its well-organized executive chamber filled him with dreams. Even though Somen had plunged himself into the socio-political activities of the area, such an involvement was distasteful to him. He was not superstitious. But he couldn't show his rational outlook so openly because many of the villagers were superstitious and feared signs that seemed ominous. Had it been some other time, Somen's verbal artillery would have pulverized them. But now, he silently assumed the mantle of a dull bumpkin. Such humbug!

Somen's career occupied every little space in his brain. He went through the same old repetitive exercises to increase his knowledge. He despised such hardship and spat venom at the ruling class and their dexterous design to eliminate innumerable youths from qualifying for a job. A conscientious scholar like him was puzzled. He felt he had been thrown into an unfathomable well wherein his friends and peers were his competitors. Why was there such competition? He was aghast by the mighty battalion of contenders! So much effort to gain a foothold in the establishment! The red contoured bindings of competitive journals were beckoning him again and again. He pondered over the same question, 'Could he ever taste the fruit of success?'

Gradually he became a more self-assured person. It was a spring morning and a mellow sun winked at everyone from the sky. 'What to do?' he pondered. He kept moving to and fro perhaps in the excitement of things that awaited him. He leaned against a teak tree and fixed his eyes on the litter floating in the tank water, trying to find a reason for such defilement.

How to fit appropriately when the competition was always fluid?

Somen noticed that someone was standing behind the mango tree with a smile on his face. It was Malia. His presence didn't affect him any more. So like a commoner, almost non-interesting. No chitchat, hardly any discussion on police atrocity, or anything. How strange! Somen's strong cult had ended so soon!!

Malia was the product of a lost world. He had nothing further to lose. However, the abrupt changes in Somen made him unhappy. It seemed as if Somen exchanged lip pleasantries with the rural hero. It was neither a pleasant nor helpful meeting for both. Was it a fact that Somen's compassion had melted? Such questions puzzled everyone.

Malia gazed at the little house and its dwellers more closely than ever before. Feeling sentimental about the change in human courtesy, he perhaps pondered, 'Well, that is the reward you receive for making superior connections in a class-based fraternity.' But the Roy house, the meeting ground in Beethalgarh for Malia and others couldn't be avoided so easily. So, there was no goodbye, not even from Somen.

44

A LONG DRAFT addressed to the Revenue Minister was prepared covering all reasonable causes for declaring Judabandh a revenue village. The dwellers of the hamlet were signatories to it. They felt such a process could only establish their dignity and identity as a whole. However, till now, there had been no grant either for a school or post office leave alone hospital. There was no piped supply of drinking water, electricity or road connectivity unlike other improved villages. The earlier plan for a struggle was raised again. Like the twists and turns of a river, Somen changed his mind once again and came closer to their warpath.

'Why are you standing there? Come and put your thumb here,' Somen called out a person standing at a distance. Malia pushed the poor fellow forward. He had observed the marked change in Somen and without brooding too much accepted him as he was. The others followed Malia's example. Somen remembered a line from John Keats' *Endymion*: 'Pleasure is oft a visitant; but pain clings cruelly to us'. How long would the thought of a village rob them of their happiness on earth? The eyes of the protesters flickered for a virtual combat with the state apparatus. The dwellers vocalized their long-time demands in no uncertain terms. 'Be united under all circumstances,' thundered the leaders. 'Never let any Government agency know an inch of our plans.'

Notwithstanding his unsettled fortune, Somen wanted to organize the poor guys so that they could face all odds. 'There's nothing to keep them subjugated any longer. They will not grow like grass under the feet of the state, the roots must sprout with new leaves!' It was but natural to hope that the struggle would not be trampled upon for any reason. The people of Judabandh pledged to fight for their just cause. A spirit of revolt prowled through the whole area.

So many hands holding sickles and lathis were raised in the air. The womenfolk looked at their partners who were displaying a new aggression. The excitement was contagious. Sensing something unusual, the Forest Department had already thrown barbed wire around Judabandh to restrict them from further encroachment of the forest. In a sudden outburst, the agitators retaliated by uprooting the cement pillars. Like Pablo Neruda, they didn't like to say, 'I am a prisoner with the door open, with the world open'. After all it had been their land all along. The conflict was bound to flare up. Formidable challenges assailed them like a sweeping hurricane. Malia tried to reason with them through logic: 'Nothing is an achievement if the achievers are not there to enjoy the fruit.' His words came in the wake of a proposal by some to form a suicide squad.

Revenge blew out the lamp of tolerance but not of conscience. They defied the local administration's restrictive measures but never at the cost of ill-treating the administrators.

'The Forest Conservation Act doesn't mean harassing innocent people,' lambasted Somen. 'Even officers are subservient to the orders of the higher echelons.'

'Let them know that we can't even collect a handful of mahua flowers or a bunch of tendu leaves. The Government has denied us our ritual pleasures. Now, they must listen to us. We will not tolerate their suppression of our rights,' exclaimed Malia.

'We have been refused approach to our own houses. We are prisoners in our own territory,' Malia continued. 'Our oxcarts have been restricted by the forest guards and even our children, pregnant women, have no means of transport, endangering their lives'.

The crowds became uncontrollable. There was no one to pacify them. Old ladies, weak from starvation, queued up to lodge their protests. The enervated spirits of school-going boys and girls received a jolt of electricity. They forced their way forward, cut across the boundary line set up by the forest authority, uprooted the so-called checkpost and burnt the obstructing timber. The barrier between them and their neighbouring villages was removed.

Somen shouted at the forest guards, 'You khaki chaps! Where is your notification in the Odisha Gazette for a checkpost? Is your register legal? Let me have a look at it.' In defiance, this was not produced. There was a scuffle and Somen asked someone to snatch it from the person manning the checkpost.

'That is official, you are to suffer,' shouted a guard.

'Is that so? Why are you not granting a money receipt then?' Somen retorted.

Malia tried to grab the moneybag from one of the official heroes.

'This is illegal,' the guard yelled.

'My foot! When order is injustice, disorder is justice. You will face the consequences, not us,' Somen said with a frown.

'No Forest Act can ever give you, proper justice,' someone screamed. Others landed it unanimously. Some even took attempt to undress one of the forest guards.

'They are ordinary employees following the dictates of their masters. You needn't humiliate them.' Another fellow intervened to pacify the unruly crowd.

The khaki guards became aware of the opposition's strength and protested their innocence.

'We have been posted here very recently.'

'Don't plead your innocence,' Malia snubbed him. Everyone cheered lustily.

The villagers prepared for war. They swarmed forward and took up frontal positions for a showdown. Both Somen and Malia flagged off the march. It must have been a stunning sight, unprecedented. The procession made its way across valleys and hills and reached Beethalgarh. Some dragged their feet, but the majority became stronger as they entered the urban sphere for the first time. They felt like shouting, 'Just see…what we were, what we are and what we would like to become.'

◆

The Collector shouted from the IB, 'I am only concerned with the law and order situation. Matters should be sorted out peacefully, no matter what they are.'

The Inspector-in-charge of the police station and the DSP watched the procession from a close angle. Although they were less comfortable, they could not suppress their revengeful motives. Regardless of the consequence, the administrative set-up was prepared for a strong blowout. Suite No. 1 in the Inspection Bungalow welcomed all the precious bodies of the district to discuss the law and order situation.

The Collector, the man of weight and power, along with the Tahsildar, EO, BDO and an EM began to put together a plan that could be executed if the mob turned violent. Cashew nuts, pistas and hot coffee were served. The peons had brought everything in advance since they didn't want to push through the agitators.

'Where the hell is the Nazir?' shouted the Tahsildar. A timid fellow rushed up to him.

'Where are the Bisleri water, imported cigarettes, mosquito repellent, newspapers, and TV for the sahib?' thundered Mohanty.

Within no time the men were provided with their requirements. The special food items from Hotel Amar came in an official jeep. Containers were carried into the VIP suite through the back entry. The police contingent was taken care of as well.

Outside, the EO was busy networking, praising the lovable aspects of the Collector's personality before a group of sycophants.

'How generous he is! He placed an order for a wooden bed and sheets with so much of reluctance. Not at all conscious about his status, and that is very rare in his cadre.'

Who were those rapt listeners? A group of defeated Councillors, job seekers for centrally sponsored schemes, aspiring retailers under the public distribution system formed a thick circle around him.

◆

Malia's legions hovered around chanting slogans that invaded the ears of the people.

'*Inquilab Zindabad!*'
'Declare Judabandh a revenue village!'
'Long live the people's struggle!'
'Long live, long live...'

The ultraists' slogans hounded the custodians of law and order. The officers tried projecting that the situation was 'under control'. However, the Collector wanted to examine the enemy's strength by coming outside personally. It was as if to state: 'Who can beat me, my chair?'

The SHO sought an explicit order from his boss to arrest the leaders in order to give them a dose of police medicine. In turn, the Collector told the DSP to exercise restraint. The agitators were quite orderly and the followers no doubt were loyal to the maximum.

The APR force didn't have the matching zeal to confront the crowd. 'Well, let them come.' The Collector wanted to make way for the agitators. He studied their body language and evaluated the situation. The police contingent stood like idols in a pantomime show. 'I am afraid there may be a clash,' the EO exclaimed with a prickle of fear. 'Eh! What courage they have,' shouted another.

Everybody had a difficult time judging the situation. The multitudes of agitators didn't make any wrong moves.

The procession slackened when they saw the officers standing nearby. Malia, with a petition in hand, moved towards the Collector. One or two persons followed. The DSP shouted at them, 'Who is that fellow?' The Tahsildar added, 'A fool without study or mind.'

But the young Collector welcomed them with a cheerful smile. Malia with folded hands handed a copy of the memorandum to this custodian of administration. But the latter was reluctant to take it from him. Instead, he instructed the SC to receive it on his behalf. The entire gamut of exercise, from writing to handing it over, stood before them like a pillar of great achievement.

Both Somen and Pradeep watched the proceedings intently from a distance. Somen felt angry and wanted to break the Tahsildar's legs. The torture of his arrest was perhaps still fresh in his mind.

All of a sudden, two armed policemen appeared on the scene and stood near the Collector like escorts. The DSP was anxious that the Collector say adieu to the general public. 'Finish your job and go... go,' the DSP repeated himself.

'Yes Sir,' Malia replied.

'Then back to your queue,' the DSP ordered the agitators including Malia.

'What the bloody hell are they going to do with this petition' exclaimed Pradeep.

'Fie on them!' Somen said to Pradeep and both tried to leave the spot. However, Mohanty, the Tahsildar, saw them and said, 'Hello Somen Babu.'

'Yes, but my discussion is with your boss and not you.'

'Please have patience.'

'Don't try to advise me,' Somen replied defiantly.

'Eh! Please, you are intelligent and dynamic, you shouldn't lose your cool,' retorted Mohanty.

'Enough of your sermons ... You are a wretch,' Somen said.

The SC tried to pacify Somen but failed. Yes, that failure proved to be a mistake.

'Get away, please!' Somen reiterated. There was wild applause for Somen. His penetrating voice drowned the voice of the officers. Like a bomber fighter plane Somen pulverized the fabric of the local ruling fort. The SC looked an amateur trying to tackle the situation.

They all wanted to control the gathering but there was an impasse. Sensing the mood, the SC deviated from the path of the DSP and asked a couple of leaders to have further discourse with the Collector inside the suite. But Somen outright rejected the proposal saying, 'No. I think not. It would make people suspicious of us.' 'Yes, yes,' screamed the group with inflamed passion. Although the Tahsildar insisted on a dialogue with the administration, he couldn't tell the public directly about this. He distanced himself and stood like a dormant volcano. The agitated crowd started swelling on all fronts. The SC and others scampered away to the VIP suite and the Collector, no doubt overwhelmed by the protesters, made a move to follow. The Inspector in Charge blew the whistle and the armed force trooped to the gate for a showdown. In the melee, Somen fell down which caused a severe pain in his head. His breath became hotly and voice louder, 'Bloody hell! We won't spare anyone.' He felt he had been humiliated in front of his own people.

Tensions were building up. The scorching heat made everyone sweat profusely. The wild mob straightened themselves, drops of sweat falling from their bodies. Everyone including the police rushed to find shade from the hot sun. But where were the trees or buildings? As their throats dried, the thirst for water began to haunt everyone. Some went to a nearby well and drank soiled water from it. Their demand seemed to have temporarily vanished from their minds. Their need for food and water made them bad-tempered.

'Eh! How tired you all are. Won't you get up to fight against the enemy,' Malia shouted. 'How could you be worn out so quickly?' Malia looked dishevelled and tense. The atmosphere was strained. Eventually all agreed upon sending both Somen and Pradeep to suite No. 1 for a dialogue with the Collector. The latter was puffing a cigar and looked reticent. On seeing the duo, he came out and asked, 'What is your problem?' Somen was appalled to hear this. The great District Magistrate was yet to take stock of the situation. 'The dwellers of Judabandh demand village status for their hamlet, Sir,' Somen said.

'How?'

'You have the key, Sir. A report from the Collector to the state authorities will resolve the problem at once,' Pradeep supplemented. Somen tried his best to explain the genuineness of their cause. The officer rejected outright the logic of such an argument. The Collector told them, 'See! There have been restrictions on the use of forest land for non-forest purposes and such impositions are directly from the central government. Even the State Government has little say in it.'

'But there are always alternatives,' said Pradeep.

'Oh, you speak of compensatory afforestation. An equal share of forest land shall be taken from the revenue to convert it for forest purposes. But that is a remote possibility.'

'But if the Collector speaks this line!'

'No...I don't speak...the law itself speaks of it. The Central Government guidelines are very clear. There would be an advisory committee for looking into the matter.'

Somen said in a polite voice, 'Look, Sir, the dwellers have been subjected to all types of harassment. The forest authorities are flexing their muscles at them. You should rescue the innocents.' The Collector replied promptly, 'Who are the innocents in today's world?'

The Collector, as the district chief, had already learned the technique of a patient hearing. Holding a public chair, he didn't want to create fear through dialogue. But a word of negotiation is rare in the dictionary of administration. His subordinates wanted to whisk him away. But they were helpless.

The Collector leaned back on the sofa, giving the impression that he was sympathetic to their cause. Was it a mask or what?

'What crime does a man commit if he utilizes something that is nature's gift as a means of livelihood?' Pradeep burst out philosophically.

The Collector did not want any further conversation. He wished to give vent to his irritation but suppressed it somehow. 'You are all smart enough to take leadership, but the rule of law doesn't allow a person to enter a reserved forest area. If they leave the area, they will be rewarded with fully subsidized houses.'

'But how can they? They are permanent settlers of the area. Even their ancestors have tilled the fallow land. They have inhaled the primordial scent of Mother Earth. Rich harvests have made their life smooth and now you wish to divest them of their rice bowl. Are they second-class citizens who will not be provided with a roof over their heads?'

The Collector had nothing to say. He felt embarrassed by such a public relations activity amidst a law and order situation. The war of wits seemed endless. Slowly his eyes floated over his opponents with ferocity. The police officers understood the change. A bayonet was raised high. Rattles sprouted from the body of every rifle. The sergent grunted, 'Get ready...'

The atmosphere tensed up once again. It was enough to provoke the BDO, Tahsildar and FRO for a showdown. The earlier thought of reconciliation began to melt away. Further slogans were raised. Like empty pots filled up with rainwater energetic voices rent the air. They started pursuing revenge too closely.

The officers became tormented by the prolonged slogans like 'People of Judabandh Zindabad', 'Long live our struggle', etc., that rocked the Inspection Bungalow. There was no respite from them. 'Oh bloody hell!' The Collector closed his eyes and instructed the police-in-charge to remove the whole lot from the place.

The continuous shouts began to wane because of the police's countermeasures. The grand voice of the Collector moved in a rhythmic manner. It suppressed all the impulses of the other officers just because they were inferior in status. They had to dance to the rhythm of his all-knowing dialogue. He said, 'Had there been no forest department, the jungle wouldn't have been denuded as it is today.' The officers nodded subserviently. Everyone looked subdued as if nothing existed in front of a real administrator. The trio had to look at each other to save themselves from the wild eyes of the young Collector. Like acolytes they revolved around him like satellites. His commanding position had made him superior enough not to consider anyone else's views but his own.

'Mohanty!'

'Sir!'

'What about the Record-of-Rights of Judabandh?'

'We don't have it, Sir.'

'How come?'

'That is not a revenue village, Sir! The area comes under the forest reserve. So, the map might be available with the forest department.'

'Bring it immediately. Prepare a fresh proceeding for effecting changes in the boundary line. Let us recommend it to the Government for granting it village status or else we would be remiss in doing so. Okay?'

'Sir! But that comes under the reserved forest. Even a minor settlement would be objected to by the forest authorities,' said the Tahsildar.

'What are the ways then?'

'We may have to carve out a matching area from our revenue land. Preferably *abad yogya anabadi* or *abdi* and hand it over to the Forest Department as a compensatory measure. The Government of India is stringent about not utilizing forest land for non-forest purpose. A de-reservation proceeding is a must, Sir.'

'Before that, study the hamlet closely. List out the names of the genuine occupants, their caste and the extent of land held by each family. You may count the total acreage including homesteads and threshing floors. We may initiate dialogues with the Divisional Forest Officer afterwards to compensate the whole area.'

'But, Sir, they are in the middle of a reserve forest. It will lead to a lot of administrative inconvenience if Judabandh gets the status of a revenue village,' said the Tahsildar.

Both Malia and Somen mustered their strength to battle with the misgivings of the Tahsildar. 'These officers are experts in hiding their motives under the veneer of a smile,' they spoke out candidly before the Collector.

'Don't be fallacious, Mohanty, a forest can be created but not a hearth. The Government will find it more difficult to house such a large number of people.' The Collector sneered at the Tahsildar. The SC, a fresher from the All India Administrative Service, found such exchanges a little unintelligible. What were those boundary changes? De-reservation, after all? He was yet to understand revenue laws. But since he was superior in hiearchy, he was unwilling to learn anything from his subordinates. Although from the same All India Service, the Collector preferred to discuss matters relating to revenue law with the Tahsildar instead of the Sub-Collector and the reason was obvious. 'It is a well-known paradox in the official system,' Somen murmured to himself.

The Collector followed up. 'See! In every village there are communal lands to meet the demands of the people. This stipulation gives 5 per cent for *gochar*, I mean for cattle grazing, and 10 per cent for *gram jungle* to meet the requirement of firewood. But actually reserve lands are in excess in many villages. We have to build up a case on this and then de-reservation proceedings may be initiated accordingly.'

'But, Sir, we have analysed the situation, there is no excess land in our tahsil,' replied the Tahsildar.

The Collector looked visibly agitated. 'I think you all have been misinformed by your staff. You should have some regard for the cause of poor people. I have my own information. Even the rice millers have encroached upon Government lands but hardly any cases have been booked against them.'

The Tahsildar couldn't reclaim his position of defence. 'We have booked a number of such cases, Sir.'

'Have you actually evicted anyone?'

'Sir, those cases are all locked up on appeal.'

'Don't be so sanctimonious. Forget it! Look at this problem now,' the Collector censured him.

The Tahsildar didn't want to further his argument. His bristling moustache failed to wave so freely. He didn't want to displease the Collector further. His grasp of revenue laws was locked away.

The subordinates listened with smiles fading from their faces.

The declaration of Judabandh as a revenue village would be their nemesis. Unless the trio got into the process of streamlining it officially the hamlet might turn into a snake and eat them all like mouse. The Collector's decision made the agitators and their leaders jubilant. What could be a greater joy than this?

The midday sun was beating down heavily. Somen tried to share some of his thoughts with the officers.

'Sir, the Indian Forest Act is quite funny to interpret.'

'How?' asked the Collector.

'In it, elephants, tigers are also treated like cattle.'

'Is that so?' The SC joined in.

'A stream is counted as a river. A cane is defined as a tree. So when a small brushwood or cane is seized, it gains entry into the register as a tree,' said Somen smilingly.

Everyone laughed at the way Government laws were interpreted.

Outside, the wings of the procession looked like they were being clipped. The participants were dreaming of things to come. They were so gratified by the behaviour of the local administrators including the police that they abandoned their war cry. A spontaneous optimism arose in the hope of their desired goal. They started leaving in a relaxed mood, dancing joyfully on the road. Happiness was etched in each person's face. Their leaders insisted that the Collector speak a few words to them directly but the latter sent his SC instead to tell them about the positive view of the administration.

The disturbance had died down and the bayonet-wielding forces had no relevance to the scene. The people of Judabandh were united by the single ambition of seeing their hamlet as a revenue village. Eyeing the officers, they raised slogans like:

'Inquilab…Zindabad!'

'Collector Sahib…Zindabad!'
'Long live our leaders Somen, Malia, Pradeep… Long live!'
The police who looked tough earlier now seemed benign. One of the constables asked a villager for a bidi. Malia saw it and rushed up with a pack of cigars.

45

MOHAN'S BEHAVIOUR TOWARDS Banita was a shock to the Das family, and they grew wild with the idea of taking revenge on the seducer. Banita was condemned to sit alone, like a prisoner.

Das dragged Shanti to the dock. He squarely fingered her for their misfortune. Was there any way to retrieve their lost prestige? They had to hold on to whatever was left of their reputation. It was as if the family was searching for its lost glory and giving vent to their bleeding souls with faces out of focus. The moral code as prescribed for a family had given them irresistible blows. In a way, it had stiffened their conscience.

Ah! Those forlorn moments and adverse awakenings! Each in a melancholy mood had no voice to share with the other. The family members, although living under the same roof, looked as if they were merely surviving.

Mohan should be taught a lesson. 'Revenge.' Banita sighed. She paced up and down searching for ideas. In total desolation, she heard the walls speak, 'Don't you know that you have lost your virginity to Mohan?'

Banita with dishevelled hair twirled barefoot in continual pain. Wallowing in self-pity, she recollected scene after scene, the delicate warmth of Mohan's body, his affable kisses and tender clasp beside the coastline of Visakhapatnam. But his hypocritical voice haunted her, beset her mindset like a sin. Such thoughts made her despise all lovers on earth. She couldn't think further. For many days her room was in a mess. No one came in to clean or tidy up, not even her family members. Except for one or two lizards on the wall and a stray rat, her room stood desolate in testimony to her memories. Her days in the marine city imprisoned her and she felt nauseated. Mohan, like a vulture, hovered over her and she needed someone to dress her wounds. How long?

The family, except for Sunita, made no attempt to come near her. From time to time, Sunita would come and stand beside her didi, sweeping the floor, removing cobwebs and picking up the garments that were strewn around.

She wanted to urge her didi not to be bullied by this lone factor in life but to gird up her loins and fight back. She wanted to embolden her but was reluctant about challenging her parents. But how? She couldn't allow such thoughts to develop since she was seized by terrible conservatism.

'Didi! You haven't eaten anything since morning. Please...'

She picked up a sweet and stuffed it into her mouth. Banita hesitated. She looked at her sister closely keeping the sweet in her mouth. 'Oh Didi! Please don't do that,' Sunita blurted out trying to quieten her turbulent mood.

Banita ate the sweet but tears filled her eyes. So too Sunita's. Banita embraced her younger sister.

'Sunita, my dear, I am finished. Why didn't it strike me earlier? Now I am bewildered. How can I find a way to atone? How can I mend my ruptured character?' Banita cried out.

Banita sobbed endlessly. In order to avoid such embarrassing moments, Sunita patted her again and again to soothe her. It was a real proof of her mettle. Never in the past had there been a situation that demanded such close bonding. Ultimately both burst into tears. They were really at a loss at what to do next and sank deeper into the complexities of the world.

Banita's unkempt locks, pale cheeks, swollen eyes made her look decrepit. The darkness of the room had become like an alien zone for the sisters. The rays of the sun couldn't make their entry through the closed window in spite of trying. The fresh air with a thirst to purify her had to prolong its wait outside. Who could offer her a new way of living? Would there be an auspicious ray of light to guide her towards a virtuous path?

Banita had cast aside all happiness. The sense of disquiet was so great that she was yet to regain her normalcy. Not being one to complain, she simmered. 'What a nasty person Mohan is! What a mean person indeed! Oh such a sinner!' It was as if she had made a resolution to take revenge, to engage *supari* killers to eliminate Mohan from the world!

'Didi! Would you like to meet Somen?' Sunita asked.

'Why?'

'At least for help.'

'What kind of help?'

'You will only know that afterwards. Would you?'

So now she had to bend herself before a common person like Somen? Would he support her for such wrongdoings? What would be the outcome of such a meeting? She was undecided.

The stench of betrayal nauseated her. Her face curled up with bitterness. She saw the watch Mohan had presented her lying on the table. She threw it on the floor in a fit of anger. Sunita lost the desire to dissuade her from doing so. Perhaps she wanted to extinguish all evidence of their relationship.

Finally they opened the door and the maid entered with cups of tea and biscuits on a tray. She was eager to serve her dearest mistress. Soon Shanti tiptoed into the room.

'Won't you eat something, darling Bani?' Shanti asked her daughter with utmost tenderness. She herself had brought all of her choicest snacks like brinjal pakoras, samosas and aloo-chop. Patting her lovingly on the back, she consoled her to forget everything like a nightmare.

Banita decided to meet Somen, but she didn't know whether he would respond to her properly or not. Moreover who would escort her to his residence other than Sunita? She agreed because she understood how her family's reputation had suffered in the marriage market. What was there to keep her spirit alive after this? Both Maa and Sunita could feel the trauma she was going through and tried everything to restore her happiness. If her parents had told her to be circumspect in her dealings with a boyfriend, this disgrace would never have happened. The heat of anguish tormented them so much that they all sat together like imbeciles. The fear of public criticism ate their minds. Shanti visualized young vagabonds in Beethalgarh carrying placards depicting her daughter's relationship with Mohan. Mother and her two daughters sat together amidst the loneliness of their residence, lost in their own thoughts. As if they were rummaging round in a burning ghat for a blade of grass. As if their breaths had been crushed and smothered violently.

'Please, Bani, my dear.' Shanti roused herself and tried to feed a samosa to Banita.

Shanti continued, 'See, in our life, we have always gone through rough times but your Baba and I have struggled to overcome them. Come what may, we have aways confronted hostile situations with courage. It is the only script written in our luck, my dear, and nothing else. Can we chop off Mohan's head? No, not at all. The Almighty is there to judge us. He may escape from us, but not from him. If you will not eat or sleep and just shed tears, take it granted nothing will be solved.'

The aggressive feeding made Banita cough irritably. She was seized by a fit of nausea. Looking at her condition Shanti whipped the plate away from her sight.

Banita was in no mood to tolerate anyone further. Her misfortune had depressed her and she wanted to be alone for the rest of the day. Any advice damaged her eardrums. Somehow, she went outside and looked at the road morosely. Pale-eyed and haggard, she imagined a hail of abuses from both known and unknown corners. Pangs of guilt tormented her. How to resist this headlong fall? Who could redeem her from such a breakdown? Like the blind, she had lost her way in the labyrinth of life. Was she at a point beyond redemption? She washed her face, changed her dress, combed her hair and took out her moped to go to Somen's house.

'I don't understand how you can go. Are you okay to ride in a two-wheeler?' Shanti hastened from the kitchen to ask her. Sunita rushed to give her company.

The sisters brought their scooty to a screeching halt before Somen's house and waited at the gate for a green signal. Somen had heard about the whole affair earlier. Both Pradeep and Malia were beside him. They had not been introduced formally. Initially she hesitated from entering. She made an innocent gesture introducing herself and her sister. This brought a flush to Somen's face. He kept himself away from everyone in the house and talked to the sisters outside.

'Tell Mohan that he has spoiled you. Now he must not evade responsibility and as an eligible bachelor, he should marry you outright.'

Banita replied, 'Somen Babu! I have come to meet you against my parents' wishes. I am in the abyss of sin. Please save me.' Saying so, she started crying like a child.

Pradeep and Malia urged Somen to be careful about a shrewd girl like Banita. They made sharp remarks against her. 'A girl without a shred of morality,' said Pradeep and cautioned Somen that people would feel that such help was beneath their status. 'The Das family doesn't deserve any respect, nor does Mohan.'

Somen paused to give his *fatwa* that since Banita had surrendered at his feet, there was no point in denying a favour to her.

However, Mohan's debauchery came under severe scrutiny. He was looked upon as a persona non grata.

Finally a consensus was arrived at. They decided to force Mohan to accept Banita as his life partner. An appropriate warning from them would certainly take root, they thought.

The assurance given by Somen encouraged Banita. She became determined to carry forward her mission neutralizing the negative thoughts swirling around her mind. She wouldn't buckle under injustice and preferred to carry on her struggle at any cost.

46

IT WAS NORMAL for the townsmen to quarrel on the slightest pretext. This time they woke up to the cause of the Das family. Athough they were outsiders, they gained instant sympathy because the fate of a girl was involved.

A quiet mood hovered over Mohan's conscience. His eyes ran fiercely towards the activities of the citizens' meet. He had hung himself like a pathetic banner and was feeling frightened. He had laid himself open to being humiliated by the guardians of daughters.

'What the hell are you talking about?' The town's jury snubbed his oral testimony.

Mohan had no penchant for the authoritarian voice of the gathering. His position as VC was at stake and he didn't want to lose his power and prestige. But he felt that the public would evaluate his actions His prophetic zeal towards social service and all his work would be questioned. A moral undertone played in his conscience amidst regrets. Being on the razor's edge, he didn't break in spite of all the accusations and heckling.

'Do you consider me a maniac?' Mohan burst out in one of the citizens' meets.

'You fellow, don't argue like that, we have seen many leaders like you,' someone shouted from the crowd. Another added: 'A lover's eyes will gaze an eagle blind, a lover's ear will hear the lowest sound'. Can Shakespeare ever become obsolete?' Mohan's opponents were more vocal than his army of supporters. The jury passed their verdict. They forced him to accept Banita at any cost.

Mohan's throat was dry. He couldn't think of any ideas. Chewing something, he shot up suddenly. 'Who are you to confer on me a marital status?' Saying this, he made a face and got up ready to leave.

'Stop there! What do you think of yourself? Because of you the whole town has been put to shame,' a bystander yelled. The whole atmosphere became as thrilling as a reality show.

Mohan was terrified. He struggled to handle the scene but he was forced to surrender before the chorus of vitriolic calls. A pandemonium broke out. The unruly supporters of the jury insisted that he accept Banita. It was obvious that Mohan had to retreat or else he would lose face before everyone. How could he be let off? Snatching away a young girl was not a whim. The jury demanded an undertaking in writing from Mohan. This irritated him further.

Such a promissory note weighed heavily on him. He turned on his protest tap and opposed the proposal outright.

The confrontation became more spirited. Some of Mohan's supporters tried to defend him but their voices got drowned. The opposite group insisted, 'A slippery fish, like Mohan, must not be allowed to escape.' But Mohan looked defiant. 'Did I do anything without her consent?' he shot back. 'Let us see what happens next.' Perhaps he wanted to study mob psyche. He was a public figure and recognized many people in the crowd. Mohan appeared confident.

The crowd became more rowdy. They insisted that a *fatwa* be issued to excommunicate Mohan and his family members from society. The family was to be deprived of the services of the town's barber, washerman and milkman. Mohan received a sudden jolt and he started sweating profusely. One family versus the rest, the spectre haunted him. He tried to cope with the aggravation but couldn't salvage his influence over the people of his town. He couldn't understand why he had failed to do so.

Was there some kind of an emergency being clamped down on the state of affairs? It would further alienate his family from the mainstream of public life. The situation was graver than he had thought it would be. For Mohan's parents, their son was always the trump card. Such a dictum would downsize their prestige further. What a blow. It was only through social contact that one could establish a status in public life. This was more so in a village. Such a decision would push them back into a corner. The injury to their reputation would be beyond any healing touch.

Mohan was now given his turn. He stood like an unwilling ox before a stony patch, expressing its inability to plough further. The crowd was getting more strident. Mohan grew more and more apprehensive.

Das, although an outsider, could muster enough strength in favour of his daughter. Beethalgarh backed him solidly. It was Mohan's family who faced the public ire. The village Panchayat ordered that there would be a perpetual vigilance on the family. The meeting wound up with a definite plan of action. Unless Mohan agreed to the decision and married Banita, the whole town would continue to ostracize them. Mohan, still adamant about his stand, left in a disagreeable mood. So bullish indeed! The spirit of revenge began to crystallize in both camps.

As a result, Mohan's mother was restricted from entering the local temple to offer prayers. It gave her a severe shock. She cried out, 'Oh God! You have snuffed out the flame of devotion from my heart. My family suffers so much at your command. I cannot show my face to people.'

Mohan looked at his mother and called out, 'What is this, Maa? Have patience. Everything will be all right.' His father nodded.

'Incense sticks, prasad and matchbox, my usual stock gets exhausted. My God must have been hungry.' Tears welled up in her eyes.

'How does one overcome this?' Mohan's father looked at his wife seeking some kind of a solution. 'The family honour has gone,' he lambasted his son.

Mohan's younger brother had just returned from college. None of his classmates had spoken to him. The young boy was visibly upset. His eyelids were wet tears dwindled to trickles of tears.

'What an unusual scene! Even my classmates avoided me.' He stood blankly like a statue.

'Why don't you talk to your principal or adviser of the college union?' His father admonished him in a stern voice. The boy kept mum about what he had experienced in college. Did he have the courage to face the principal or the adviser? 'Oh bloody hell! The students are making the college a platform for politics,' said Mohan, frowning. He grimaced. An angry atmosphere prevailed within the house. Mohan thought he would never forgive the college authorities for this. 'What the hell have you done!' Mohan's father said to him.

'You have cut off my nose. I can't show my face to the public.' Mohan didn't reply.

The family tried to overcome the hostile situation they found themselves in. Their story had became common knowledge among most of the dwellers of Beethalgarh. The youngsters of the town would stand at the roadsides, around the paan shops, culverts and chatter unendingly about the matter. Would they ever be able to perform the purificatory rites to wash away the sin of the elder son? But how?

In a way, the dirty linen remained as it was without being washed.

47

THE ASSEMBLED CITIZENS of Beethalgarh laid down a diktat that Mohan could not attend the executive body meeting of the NAC. It aimed at debarring him from town politics by disqualifying him for being absent for three consecutive times. On the other hand, Das was forced to go to the police station to lodge an FIR against Mohan under Section 375 of the Indian Penal Code, claiming that the whole incident carried the overtone of rape without consent.

The SHO wanted a detailed description from the rape victim herself. Moreover, witnesses were to be examined to learn the true details of the incident. Das opposed it. 'Oh, Das Babu, listen,' the SHO said, 'In a police station, everything is recorded in terms of evidence only. Where is the proof unless the rape victim expresses it herself?' This was due to the fact that Mohan, as VC of the Block, commanded a special status. In the police station, Das was not even offered a chair. Suddenly, his head reeled and he felt like collapsing. Scarcely able to stand up, he searched for a vacant chair. A constable, by chance, came to his rescue. He led him to a chair and fetched a glass of water. Das reflected upon such happenings inside a police station. So merciless indeed! It was perhaps the real place to meet his Waterloo. His family members were informed of the situation over the phone. Shanti and Banita rushed to the police station.

The light in the police station was very dim. Gazing vacantly at the ceiling, Das mopped his sweating body with his handkerchief. He felt a thorough distaste for his surroundings. Abandoned by everyone, he sat there alone.

One Councillor, perhaps a novice, went to his residence on some pretext. Finding him pliable, he said, 'Why can't you try to remove

Mohan from the post of VC? You are fit enough to hold the chair provided you really want it.' The latter, more of an ambitious mind, listened to him in a hearty manner. But he had no standing in rural politics and couldn't venture further on the mere lip support of the EO. Das was open-mouthed, this could be his revenge.

Mohan was forced to rethink the situation. His family too couldn't escape this. They had realized that antagonizing the world around them would lead to further hardships. Estranged from society, his position would deteriorate inviting hostility from all corners. It would jeopardize his family's existence. Mohan, therefore, rethought the situation and applied every tactic to convince his family members to accept the proposal. They would have to be less rigid and arrogant.

Mohan urged his family to go for an early settlement. He decided not to choose any other life partner but Banita. The long hours and days of tensions had to be buried somehow.

The parents decided not to proceed immediately, even after their son's consent. They studied the proposal carefully, held lengthy debates with their friends and relatives before they said 'yes'. Finally, the family had to let go of their rigid stance on the caste factor. But then something occurred to Mohan's father. 'Oh! Listen,' he told everyone present there, 'I'll allow my son to marry Banita only if the marriage is conducted through our rituals.'

The imposition didn't hinder the settlement. All ears were tuned towards Banita and her parents for their final word.

The Das family received the message. On hearing it, Banita felt strangely rebellious. Das, however, ran in from the town lobby, sprouting a smile on his face and enjoined his wife to convince Banita on the issue.

'Mummy! Don't force me; don't put me to further hardship!'

'No...no, my dear, be happy. Although without a permanent job, Mohan comes from a rich family. They have considerable status.'

'How can you say this, Maa? How can I, an officer's daughter, marry a person from his background? Can't you find me a white-collar professional like Baba?'

'Bani, my darling! Don't you know the amount of wealth that

family has accumulated! They can command many officers like me. Once you marry, the advantages will be enormous. So many housemaids and servants at your command. You won't have to worry about housekeeping. You will have a comfortable life.'

'No, Baba, I won't!' Banita looked defiant. 'I don't want to rot in Beethalgarh for my whole life. Please think sensibly. All my friends want to marry and settle in metros, enjoying their husbands' fat pay packets, huge bank balances, cars, apartments and you want to abandon me in this mofussil town forever.'

Das clutched her hands and covered his face with them. 'Don't embarrass me further! Don't you know that I will be by your side till the end of my life? Who will enjoy my pension? I have no son and heir. All my properties will be yours and Sunita's.' Das embraced his daughter imploringly. Banita thought his act was unbecoming. She saw her father's disturbed mood. Shanti stood nearby, looking unforgiving. 'What is the point of all this?' She looked at her accusingly.

'She doesn't deserve such cajoling!' She wanted her daughter to be aware that her Baba and Maa would become the scapegoats.

Sensing her Maa's mood, Banita started fidgeting.

'All right, let her choose her own husband then!' Shanti spoke out.

'Yes, Maa,' Banita said defiantly, but with a hint of diffidence.

'Yeah! Fine. Let us see then!' Sunita sneaked up and cautioned her to keep within limits.

Although Banita spoke abruptly, her mother's reply swept through her ears like a whirlwind. She knew her reply would make her parents more unsympathetic. She felt crestfallen.

Looking at her, she said, 'Maa, you have told me time and again how you and Baba pulled through all the vicissitudes in life. What is the harm, Maa, if at all I dream of my rosy future? Will you not feel elated if your daughter comes out like a lotus from the dirt of a pond and keeps up her position in society? After all, I am your daughter. I have come from your womb and from nowhere else. Now my mind is absolutely clear and I have no hesitation in accepting Mohan as my life partner. If my parents give me their blessings, I won't bother about anything else in life.'

'Oh Bani! My sweetheart.' Shanti pulled her daughter closer into her arms and wailed like a child.

48

ALTHOUGH SHE HAD agreed, Banita was a bit nervous. All she wanted from Mohan's family was a little bit of assurance on her safety and security. But her face didn't reflect her inner turmoil. In spite of her consent, her Baba asked, 'Okay Maa, should I go ahead with the negotiation then?'

'I don't want to wait until she finishes her studies. Let us start the preparations,' Das said.

Banita was glad to keep the discussion on her marriage alive and was keen to fix a date. After a long time, the neighbours could feel the flood of cordiality within the family set-up of Das. Banita found that she could leave her residence without the earlier distress. Now she felt more in accordance with Mohan's family and not the earlier jangling conflict. She felt more mature. Her bankrupt face began to smile with the flood of cheques. After a long time, the house seemed calm and content. As if all the problems had disappeared. The sorrows of the vigilance raid and Banita's elopement became a thing of the past.

Das stepped outside, looking for someone. His face was filled with happiness. He smiled at someone, presumably a person from his office. The latter reciprocated gratefully. In an elated mood he sent a message to Mohan's family through him. The latter complied and got into the NAC jeep.

'No...no, not you alone,' shouted Das. 'Take as many people as you like but don't go alone.' Then he looked around to find other close associates. He talked to some people over the phone and waited for their arrival. He stood there looking down the road. Within no time, sounds of two-wheelers could be heard in front of his residence. He briefed them on the dialogues to be exchanged with Mohan's family.

The office vehicle got overloaded looking like a private carrier. Das closed his eyes in consecration to his family's happiness.

The jeep stopped in front of Mohan's residence. The family members received the whole group with utmost respect. Mohan's father and relatives and neighbours came to the gate to give them a hearty welcome. 'Please have a seat,' said he while commanding the others to bring an array of delectable snacks.

The whole lot, while stuffing their mouths, didn't forget to convey Das' consent for a negotiation. Mohan's father demonstrated his family's pedigree whenever he spoke. He opined at length, 'We too agree, but let Das Babu grant us sufficient time so that we can inform our relations who live far away.' Everyone glared. A prompt reply came from someone, 'Of course, marriage is not child's play, after all!' Everyone seemed to agree with the comment. Mohan's family seemed well disposed to the whole affair.

After receiving the confirmation, they all returned to the Das residence. Shanti, Das and the others awaited them in their drawing room. While the jeep was parked in front, the whole lot came in jubilantly to convey the result of their visit.

The message was clear to Shanti and Das. Their dreams had become reality. Shanti was overwhelmed and brought out a deluge of sweets. The fridge became empty within no time. Das waved his teacup and told the gathering, 'Yes, I would like to make the marriage of my daughter an event people will remember for all time to come.' Shanti like a smart wife came closer to him unlike any other time in her life. Soon, a lunch of delectable dishes was consumed even after the amounts they had eaten at Mohan's house. The celebration didn't look as if it would end. Like the family, the outsiders enjoyed sharing their domestic talks.

A real happiness seized every cell of his body. In sheer humility, he folded his hands even to youngsters. In total absorption, he bade farewell to the party raising his hand pleasantly at everyone. The whole scenario filled him with pride. He had discovered that this large group was like members of his family.

The house floated with happiness. On finding Shanti lonely, Das observed, 'See, our first problem is over now. We should think of the next after some time, isn't it?' Shanti answered in a calm way: 'Oh, what a dreary moment that was. I wish it would never happen again.'

'Yeah,' said Das. 'Perhaps it is God's wish too.'

49

NOVEMBER 15 WAS the scheduled date of the interview fixed by the management of the silk yarn factory. After receiving the letter, he deliberated vigorously as he didn't want to miss this opportunity. He pondered: if by chance there was a repetition of his failure, it would be his ultimate crash. Hence, he decided not to lose anything this time. He began to prepare for the interview. He started sorting out question papers in textile technology. The well-tended notes were reopened. All books, note sheets that were not of direct benefit were heaped in a corner. It so happened that his Maa and at times the maidservant found it a problem to clean the floor. He meandered around the little room, sometimes lying on the cot and at other times on the mat. His mind began to simmer with the heat of knowledge. He had a practice of trying for his own cause like keeping himself away from the threat of non-engagement and adopting a path, however hard it might prove. How could he overcome his present helplessness? How could he climb the victory stand? How to celebrate life through collective clapping? Like a sage, his eyes rolled over all his collections that would ultimately inspire him to earn siddhis but first he was to complete his ultimate penance in life.

'Fierce competitors like the sons and daughters of aristocrats would certainly bowl out this chap this time also,' whispered the neighbours. Despite overhearing these words, Somen was determined not to stop his hard toil.

Periodically, his mother came in with snacks and tea, which she stuffed into Somen's mouth with loving care. Her interest in Somen was like a mother for a small child. He proved absent-minded, resting his eyes fully on a book. He even had to be reminded to drink a glass of water to quench his thirst. Somen had few words to say. He switched over to the cult of silence so much so that it was difficult to know if he was in the house. His mother and Minati acted untiringly to straighten up his room.

While studying, if by chance Malia or any of his compatriots came to meet him, he told them gently, 'Please, spare me this time.' He was so absorbed in his work that he didn't have time for the people's front. He couldn't act like a boatman looking one way and rowing another. But Malia wanted a favour from Somen—a draft in the form of an ultimatum to be addressed to the Collector. Burdened by work, Somen didn't want to drag himself down the old path. He didn't want anything to wreck his ambition. But he had to pacify such outbursts. He had to maintain his usual composure.

'I fully understand your tension, Somen Babu,' Malia said, 'but we have no way other than this. Our entire struggles have been futile. Each failure appears more dismal than the previous one. We are almost paralysed with the discharge of the battery of knowledge.'

'Do you need my help right now?' Somen asked Malia indignantly. Somen asked Malia to sit and drafted a petition requesting the Collector, Samastipur, to depute his field staff for the demarcation of the boundaries of Judabandh. He emphasized that either a Chief Survey Officer or a Settlement Officer be posted for this. Somen and Malia together decided not to drag local revenue officials like the Tahsildar and SC as they were busy tackling the drought. Soon, with petition in hand the group walked hurriedly out of the house. They didn't want to steal away the valuable time of Somen. The latter gave them an obstinate look as if to say let's close the chapter for good. Somen had a premonition of their failure. Who knew, like innumerable applications pouring into the Collectorate every day, this might be added to their rubbish dump.

'What an excellent mind Somen has!' Malia told his companions and they nodded in agreement.

50

THE DATE FOR the interview was approaching fast. Somen had to assimilate as much information as he could on important national and international events. Like the processor speed of a superior megabyte he had to convert his mind to a hard disk capacitor surpassing others. The burgeoning pile of books and periodicals were garrisoned his bed and table almost like soldiers around a fort.

Duty-bound, Somen made a last-ditch effort to salvage his prestige before the public. He moved like a grief-stricken father, who even after losing his child was forced to report for duty. Every job interview he had been for so far had been unsuccessful. It might be the same this time also. In his desire for success, he once again plunged into the current of competitive flow knowing full well that his expectations could well be dashed as in the past. He looked like being drugged up to the eyeballs with book and journal pills.

Looking at her only son's overstrained state, Mrs Roy couldn't help but keep pouring water over the head of Lord Mahadev and placing lotuses at his feet. Minati too joined her with folded hands praying, 'Oh God! Please be merciful to my brother!' Mrs Roy added, 'What a gruesome ordeal you have placed before my child. Don't create bumps, this time at least! I absolutely long for your mercy and certainly shall offer you 108 bel leaves as a token of naivedya.' The voice of Roy too blended with the major currents of both mother and daughter. Their eyes were half-closed, their minds fully concentrating on the redemption of the gem of their souls, Somen.

With every dawn came the cry of devotion as if pleading before the Almighty, 'Let darkness be withered from the life of Somen. Let his miseries be eased out.' Mrs Roy advanced a step further. She also wished for a good bridegroom for Minati and who could gratify such a demand except the Lord of the Universe. In a way, she solicited the restoration of good luck for her small family. The prayers ultimately circulated among all the deities of the small town. Every Tuesday evening they offered prayers to the Goddess Ghanteswari along with innumerable other ladies. The tinkling bells and flickers of arati made this the grandest show of a magnificent worship.

Both Minati and her Maa became the most active devotees, staying longer in the temple than anyone else. The inside of the temple had no window and the rows of ghee lamps emitted both light and trails of smoke that were enough to deoxygenate a person. Such devotion was a common phenomenon and the Roy family was no exception. But for them, there was a deeper reason, that of mobilizing the priest's mind exclusively for pronouncing a special benediction on Somen. Somen queried this repeatedly at his residence and Mrs Roy had no qualms about revealing the fact.

'Minati, how much do you spend in the temple?' enquired Somen.'

'That is none of your business. Bother about your studies only,' replied Maa at once.

'Very bad, I don't like this,' Somen said defiantly.

Mr Roy took out a little vermilion from a half-burnt mango leaf and drew a blessed line in the middle of his son's forehead. Somen could not oppose it. Minati was surprised. The atmosphere pulsated with spirituality. Somen stretched his palms over the flickering flames of the arati. Together, both ladies approached him and sprinkled sacred rice over his head to bless him. They wanted to flush the agnosticism out of Somen. The latter pressed his palms over his head in response to the sacred mood.

That night, Somen boarded the Bokaro-Chennai Express perhaps to appear for his last interview. Pradeep, Malia, his father and another close friend were there to see him off. Someone tried to find Somen's name on the bulletin board but Roy refrained from doing so since he was the officer for the allotment of the quotas. A problem was discovered when the train arrived. A businessman from the earlier station, being deprived of a berth, was occupying that of Somen's.

Soon after Beethalgarh, he used his heavy luggage as an excuse and requested that they exchange their berths. Somen agreed even though he knew it was a pretext to grab his berth. He had no idea about how to deal with the mischief of a co-traveller. After some time the original occupier came and told Somen to vacate the seat. Somen was compelled to shrink himself into a corner but was ready to get into a scuffle with the businessman. Looking at his frowning face, the latter settled the problem before the arrival of the ticket collector.

Somen arrived in Chennai the following day. The express drew into Egmore and made a screeching halt. He had never been to the city earlier. After alighting from the train, he tried to locate the cloakroom to deposit his luggage. He was catching the night express to Bangalore and so decided to explore the city. He didn't like to miss this rare chance to discover the magnificent bazaars and historic places of Chennai.

'Where is Marina?' Somen asked a khaki-clad constable who gave him the number of the bus that would take him there. On reaching the beach, he asked a person standing nearby, 'Whose statue is this?'

'Anna's.'

Somen didn't want to reveal his ignorance about Chennai any further. Instead he walked into the sea. Sandy water lapped his feet and the sea breeze caressed his face. There were others who were enjoying the beach. Could it be that they were also unemployed? He looked at the distant horizon and all he could see were the rising waves. The external setting of the blue expanse relaxed him.

The beach was lined with commercial buildings. But Somen could only hear the tinkling of the anklets of several south Indian ladies and see the vast expanse of the ocean in front of him. He could visualize countless boats sailing in close harmony with the blue water. The dividing line between the sky and sea was so sparse, Somen pondered a little. Boats were appearing and disappearing like an artery in the struggling hands of a cardiologist. He saw one of the boats struggling to reach the shore. In spite of the turbulent waves, more boats were nearing the shore. But were there smiles on the faces of the fishermen? Yes, without even a flash of fear. Each one conquered the aquatic conflict with determination and skill. They all landed ashore with their catch of fish. What a great lesson for the inexperienced heart of Somen and his philosophy behind a struggle.

Now that Somen was in Chennai away from his native land he brazenly celebrated his youthful impulse of looking at young ladies. So many tall, good-looking ladies! Even some of the old ladies had not forgotten their make-up, adding a touch of glamour to the scene. Kids were mostly snivelling for balloons, toys or potato chips. Somen found that he was totally unknown here. As a result, he looked at everyone straight in the eye.

Although his maiden visit to Marina sent Somen into raptures, it was time to make his way back to the railway station to catch his train to Bangalore. But something struck him at once! Eight to ten fishermen wearing loincloths were engaged in a Herculean task, dragging a huge net filled with fish from the deep recesses of the sea. A lot of marine species like dog-face puffer fish, moon jellyfish, and blotchy fish with green emerald eyes could be seen nearing the end of their lives. Suddenly the spot became crowded. 'So many prized fish,' one of them exclaimed in Tamil.

He took an autorickshaw to the railway station and was caught up in the evening rush hour.

A little embittered, he read the election posters, advertisements and such other commercial propaganda. The posters portraying overpowering villains seemed as if they were displaying the soul of soulless films that proved insipid to his eyes. The autorickshaw dropped him off at Egmore station. He went to the cloakroom and collected his luggage.

Beethalgarh at night was in total contrast with the bright lights of this great city. The rugged scenario of his small native town had been blown away by the attractions of the city. The stylish displays of the shopping complexes, their fabulous merchandising eclipsed his disapproving look. Unlike his sluggish birthplace, Chennai was seductive. The majestic flyovers, the galaxy of apartments, glittering showrooms garlanded the city with their magnificent glow. For a while, Somen wanted to throw the bitter frustrations of his life into cold storage. Chennai appeared before him like a golden lining ridding the dark clouds of his mind, unlike the partial gloom of Beethalgarh. A sleepy, dusty mofussil town with commonplace dwellings couldn't compete with the fluorescent wonders of a city.

Somen arrived at platform No. 3 and boarded the train after confirming his berth from the chart. The train left at 1 a.m. for

Bangalore and was soon plunged into a hallucinogenic dark world. In the train the mood was nothing but of ample tiredness. He knew no one and that gave him the chance to withdraw into himself. Somen opened the container and carefully brought out the food packs. In no time he finished off his meal, put on his pyjamas and peeped outside the window. Somen lay on the berth to sleep, but at times was woken up by the jarring sound of tracks as the train approached several railway stations. He saw passengers either descending or ascending, some running from one corner to the other searching for a berth. He quietly listened to the various voices and accents and the shouts of the railway constables disturbing the sleep of passengers. A gust of wind came through the window, which was suddenly closed by a passenger. He was compelled to open it again. The passing skyscrapers alerted Somen by their dazzling lights and he discovered many prosperous areas through the veil of night, adding to his new experiences of life. Streets lit with halogen and mercury bulbs looked like they were offering a guard of honour to a new visitor.

51

SOMEN WOKE UP to the ambient noise of the railway platforms of Bangalore, the software city. He disgorged himself from the overcrowded compartment elbowing his way frantically through the crowd of passengers. As soon as he came out of the platform, he started enjoying the sprawling garden city in its morning hues. Indolence fell from his eyes and a spontaneous happiness gripped his mind. The city appeared to be glowing in an atmosphere that was perfect for the upkeep of its lush foliage. He was to appear before the interview board the next day. Somen hired an autorickshaw to take him to an affordable hotel on MG Road. He entered his room and lay down on the bed to rest for a while. The bedsheet seemed unclean and the hotel boy entered with a fresh one. He requested Somen to get up so that he could change the sheets and freshen up the room. Somen unpacked his belongings and went through his morning rituals before ordering breakfast and settling down to his revision study. This time, he would try his best to accomplish his ambition. He didn't want to leave anything to chance. In spite of his tiredness, he started his feverish preparation to combat all questions in the interview board.

In the evening, he enquired at the reception counter about the location of the Karnataka Silk Factory. The receptionist kept mum as he didn't know where it was. So Somen had to ask the same question to a person standing nearby. '*Aap Jaante Hain*, I mean the Karnataka Silk Factory.' 'So many silk factories in Bangalore itself, which one do you want?' the person concerned replied gazing deep into his face.

Finally, he went to his room and came back with his call letter. He showed it to the hotel manager. 'Oh! I see…a joint sector undertaking.' The manager said it was 18 kilometres from Bangalore city near Devanahalli. But the interview was to take place in their office at Richmond Town.

Luckily he came across another candidate, a Patna-born Maharashtrian, staying next door. The latter had already appeared for both the written and viva the previous day. Somen immediately asked, 'Ah brother, why didn't we meet earlier? What were the types of questions? Who were there at the viva?' The latter calmly narrated the key questions he was supposed to have remembered about textile technology.

'What are the ingredients to remove stains from silk fabrics?'

'Yes, for grease and oil, it is either benzin or petrol.'

'For varnish?'

'Methylated spirit.'

'For others?'

'For tea and coffee…potassium permanganate solution.'

He thanked the stranger for revealing such vital facts that provided an insight into the interview. This short conversation raised his self-confidence a little. It filled him with zeal to make his position stronger before the interviewers. He didn't want to spare even a second and asked another set of questions that had been overlooked.

'Tell me the ways for dry cleaning woollen garments.'

'Same like motor spirit, petrol, benzin, etc.' The other one replied more like a minicomputer. Somen felt a little confused.

'But why are they asking questions about woollen goods? After all, it is an executive job in a silk factory.'

'That is true...but not very true,' replied the other in a shrill manner.

Somen didn't add to it.

'What yaar! They may put questions from any corner. After all, they have to screen out people like us,' he replied with a tone of detachment.

52

THE INTERVIEW BEGAN on time the next day. Both the written and viva tests went as smoothly as he wished they would. He gave his best performance because he had come prepared. The earnest longing for finding a prestigious job compelled him to make the maximum effort. Frequent appearances for written tests gave him the strength not to leave anything unanswered. One of them asked:

'You are Somen Roy.'

'Yes Sir.'

'Are you a Bengali?'

'Yes Sir.'

'But it is mentioned that you are from Odisha. How come?'

'Although I am a Bengali, my parents left Bengal a long time ago.'

'Why?'

'My father is an employee of the South-Eastern Railway based in Odisha.'

'So you are a Bengali and an Odia both,' the other board member intervened.

'Can you say something about Odisha? I mean, why is Odisha famous?'

'For Sambalpuri saris and the Odissi dance, Sir.'

'Give details.'

'The art of tie and dye is mainly the hereditary profession of handloom weavers in the western belt of Odisha. They produce Sambalpuri saris that are unique in our country.'

'And the other one?'

'Odissi, the most artistic and graceful dance form of Odisha, maybe at par with Bharatnatyam.' Suddenly one member gave up questioning allowing the other one to intervene.

'How many colours does the rainbow have?'

'Sir…seven.'

'What are they?'

'Sir…violet, indigo, blue, green, yellow, orange and red.'

'What are the primary ones?'

'Blue…red and yellow.'

'And, secondary?'

'Orange…green and violet.'

'What are the constituents of these colours?'

'Orange is a mixture of red and yellow, green a blend of yellow and blue, and violet of red and blue both.'

Another member after a long spell of silence asked a sudden question:

'What are the names of two famous Odia and Kannada medieval poets?'

'Sir, Sarala Das and Sarvajna.'

The board members asked several questions. At the same time, he was to be envied. Why? For the promptness and dazzle of his answering style. Further questions were shot at him in quick succession. The members could read his face; there was no turmoil of any kind. Replies came as naturally as goats leaving their sheds to follow a common route in a village.

Somen left the place soon after the interview. Exhausted, he leaned against the seat of a city bus and brooded over his performance. Never did he express himself so satisfactorily in an interview. It was so swift and pleasant. He was neither weighing himself like Narcissus nor slaving before the factory management to crown him with a career. After the hectic day, he took a joyride around the city. Strands of electric lights had garlanded the city. It looked as if it was boasting its affluence to envelop Somen within its net. Although he had lived in the world for several years, everything he had seen before looked dim and dull.

He felt like safeguarding himself against being swept away by an urban deluge. Somen had not imagined how swiftly the city had developed over these years. The shining boom of software in the form of digital technology was everywhere. While passing through Keonic City, he could feel the electronic throb. From crèche to health club, swimming pool to supermarket, high-tech computer centre to children's park—every spot looked sophisticated from top to bottom. Somen could smell the differences between Beethalgarh and Bangalore—the superhighway information network drawing inspiration from high-tech electronic gadgets and devices whereas his small town still banked on its old and dilapidated past.

But who would listen to his piteous cry for social justice? It was natural that this would be unanswered in Asia's Silicon Valley. Every situation seemed geared up for trade and nothing else. What a glory to revere a faceless human deal! As if the whole world was tipped to be a market and the entire population either in the camp of sellers or purchasers. Dish antennas were found hanging here and there like the round skulls of dead human beings.

Somen didn't have much time to linger. He had to pack his luggage and return home. Under no circumstances could he stay on even though he wanted to spend more time at the International Technology Park near Whitefield.

He went to his hotel, paid his bills and proceeded to the railway station to board the Chennai-bound Express. His first step was to arrange a berth for himself.

The Train Ticket Inspector came up to Somen and asked if he had a berth. Instead, Somen requested for a berth up to Chennai. The TTI pointed to several passengers who were already waiting in the queue. Somen looked in the corner and saw a group of passengers, most probably non-ticket-holders, who were whispering for berths.

It seemed as if they were puzzling about what they were going to do. One or two of them were hobnobbing with the TTI and the reason was obvious. He overheard the TTI telling others, 'See, limited berths, you have to vacate for the genuine allottees.'

What could one do to appease a TTI? Many passengers didn't become impatient... Instead they looked relaxed after the TTI favoured them with a small glance. Somen seemed to be an exception. But what course of action should he take?

He was opposed to the idea of tipping the TTI for a berth. The body language of the latter seemed greedy. He was interacting with the onlookers while concealing his real motive. Somen was seized with the idea of plucking off his official mask or should he compromise? Perhaps, for a little comfort he should put aside his moral values, but what would his comrades think of him when they heard this? Thus, a nerve-racking battle was taking place within him.

Was there no way but to succumb? To give in to such dishonest practices would undermine his integrity. The TTI was behaving like a king who considered the whole train as a part of his *jagir*. 'I feel like a lone fighter. No one is even looking at me, leave alone supporting my views.' Somen heaved a sigh.

'What are you thinking about?' someone shouted from within. He looked scared. His defiance would be nightmarish and would lead him nowhere. Without a berth he would have a most unhappy journey. He decided to make this sacrifice rather than tread on the rotten path of corruption. The other passengers had no such scruples and were moving towards their berths triumphantly. He divided the whole lot of travellers into the privileged and unprivileged, those like Somen who had to stand all night listening to the snores of the other passengers. But everyone didn't appear so cruel. One allowed Somen to occupy a little space on his berth. Somen's legs wobbled, he wished for a little comfort but sat in a cramped position. Finally he unfastened his luggage and spread it out on the dirty floor and stretched out. He preferred not to worry about the lack of cleanliness.

Somen reached Chennai the next morning. From there he boarded the Chennai-Bokaro Express for Beethalgarh. Even though the train was two hours behind schedule, Pradeep and his dad were at the station to receive him.

When they arrived at their residence, both his mother and Minati were there to welcome Somen with beaming smiles. Nothing had changed—the dusty backyard, the water supplier carrying tins of water on his shoulder, the betel and tea stalls and the bald-headed tutor surrounded by inattentive students. The comparatively hackneyed scene was no match for the festive garden city. Such a languorous scene disheartened Somen, who was still preoccupied with Bangalore.

53

THE BRIDAL KNOT between Banita and Mohan was tied in a fit of festivity. The wedding took place in mid-December when the weather was cool but pleasant. It was an inter-caste marriage and both sides made great efforts to honour each other's rituals. Although the parents of the groom had the ultimate say in the planning, the bride's family wanted to exercise some control. Finally, both the Tahsildar and BDO became the joint arbiters to find out details to strike a balance between the two families. The Das residence became the meeting point of many elated youngsters asking both relevant and irrelevant questions. Their repeated visits was to gather marriage intelligence on several matters. Many of them happened to be friends of either Banita or Sunita. Sitting under an appliquéd canopy, rows of guests found time to listen to an excellent music system having stereophonic sound effects. Both Shanti and Das received guests with open arms. Flowers and buntings interspersed with mango leaves hung all around the altar. Although Das was a tainted officer, he had tried to enlarge his public network. The gathering drew its strength mainly from different employees and small-time contractors including fortune-seekers. Both Shanti and Das had their eyes fixed upon the guests, more so the VIPs, including the Collector, Samastipur. The eagerness for a VIP was visible from Das' face.

'Did you make all the arrangements in suite No. 1? See, the Collector is very punctual,' he said. Simultaneously he kept his ear to the cellphone. Das eagerly waited for his VIP guest no. 1 to arrive at the venue of his daughter's marriage. He nursed a great desire for him to grace his residence so as to immortalize the occasion. But there was no sign of his arrival so far. His eagerness was not so much for the son-in-law as it was for the DM. 'Collector!' the shrill voice chanted time and again like a mantra. Without the presence of this great man, the event would be eventless! Without the arrival of his majesty the Collector, how futile would be the ardour of celebration. The faces of the Das couple looked cheerless and their voices dull.

'Please tell me the exact time of the Collector's arrival here?' he asked the latter's Private Secretary on the phone but there was no satisfactory reply from the other side. As understood, both the Collector and SC were away visiting a drought-stricken area. Das, after ascertaining the fact, looked so dry, but knowingly concealed the fact. Such a VIP should have arrived at his residence instead.

The sad truth was that the bright plumage of celebration did not attract the Collector and SC. They had definite information that Das' performance as an officer was not up to standard. His official conduct had generated enough enemies both inside and outside the town. Hence, in order to avoid him the SC had drawn up a tour programme and got it endorsed by the Collector.

'Why are you so absent-minded? You should get ready to receive the bridegroom and baraat party,' Shanti ordered her husband.

Das looked at his watch and got to his feet. He had to reconcile with the fact and keep himself alive to the occasion.

Both the senior officers wanted to tour the drought area. The train of events had motivated them to start labour-intensive work in right earnest. It might check the outflow of labour to distant places.

But how to endure the absence of Mohanty and Pasayat who were accompanying their bosses in the field? Unless they were relieved of the duty they couldn't come to the wedding. Such close friends should participate in an occasion of this kind.

'Eh! Great people from All India Services,' Das said to himself. He had never imagined that a situation of this kind would happen at all.

Just then someone came running. '*Baraat...baraat!*' he shouted. The procession was drawing nearer. All of a sudden the Das family focused on the arrival of the baraat. Curious onlookers rushed from all directions to witness the show. In the front were enthusiastic teenagers and groups of dancers surrounded by elders. The atmosphere was made more thrilling by the exploding firecrackers and rockets brightening up the sky. The procession had already blocked the road causing problems to the passers-by. Many of them were gyrating to the beat of the drums much to the delight of the onlookers. The groom was being escorted by youths in high spirits and some were even performing acrobatics. Mohan sat with his father in his decorated car. The festivities looked never-ending. The bride's side waited to receive the groom. The gathering was huge and the fleet of vehicles stretched as far as the eye could see. Such an exhibit had no direct utility. However, in a semi-rural set-up this could be seen as a status symbol. It would convince the people of the family's aristocratic background.

Das in his white dhoti, kurta and Sambalpuri napkin, Shanti in her best embroidered silk sari stood at the gate along with guests and relatives to receive the groom. The sound of music and the stream of lights were drawing closer. Green coconuts placed on mango leaves on top of earthenware pots were being carried by heavily veiled ladies to signify the auspiciousness of the occasion, while the bursting crackers added to the festive mood.

The procession seemed like the mother of all such shows that the town had seen in the past. Some of the richer folk envied the extravagance of the baraat. The expensive decorations, the lines of luxury vehicles emphasized the wealth and status of Mohan's family.

The bridegroom got off from the car looking fresh. The waiting ladies welcomed him in the traditional manner. Das bathed the dyed feet of his son-in-law and then wiped them with his napkin. Shanti offered him a paan to chew and Das escorted him to the altar, accompanied by relatives and close friends. Many elders and other guests were gathered around to get a closer view of the rituals that would be conducted by priests from both the sides.

Maids of honour and female relatives accompanied the bride to the altar. She had covered her head with the pallu of her costly sari. The crowd around the altar was getting thicker and Shanti kept requesting the wives of several officials and non-officials to stay until the chanting of the mantras from the Rig Veda was over. Ladies present complied with her command attentively. With potatoes and mung dal in steel trays they wended their way to the marriage home. They were following a rich tradition. One of the family members placed such offers in a corner of the storeroom against the wishes of Shanti. She was hesitant to accept such gifts more because of lack of space. But Das had no such hesitation and gratefully acknowledged the offerings with folded hands. The families of Mohanty and Pasayat made up for the absence of their menfolk by supporting Shanti and Das and helping them with various tasks.

However, both the Tahsildar and BDO did manage to reach the venue much later, and the trio as usual discussed the officers and office work despite the festive occasion. Reassured that their bosses were not coming, they exchanged random views on information gathered on the tour.

'I have first-hand information that even the SC runs after vitamin M.'

'Vitamin M?'

'Yes…money.'

'So early, from the first year of his service?'

'Might be his extreme love for Goddess Laxmi.'

'But how are they untouched by any anti-corruption sleuths?'

'Just because he belongs to the superior grade of All India Services.'

'But is it myth or what?'

'As you may infer.'

Such light-hearted talk cheered them up. Suddenly one of them quipped, 'Let us not waste time any more. Look after the guests.'

'Don't worry. Volunteers are looking after the arrangements,' said Das.

'Well, but we shouldn't leave everything in the hands of young chaps. Are they sufficient in numbers?' Mohanty asked.

'I can't give the exact count. Our tax collectors are very much on the job.'

Mohan looked majestic seated on the altar. Many guests lacked the table manners for a buffet. They ran back and forth elbowing frantically to join the queue at the serving platform. It was a chaotic scene as they tried to grab plates of mutton curry and shrimp fry. The ladies and children stood helpless, unable to cope with such muscular strength.

Soon, the service was at its height. The caterers ran here and there serving the food at the numerous tables. The supply was plentiful. But the people from the baraat surprised the hosts with undignified manners. In their eagerness, they even ransacked the restricted cooking area in their quest for mutton. 'I don't think there's enough food,' exclaimed a guest. One of the caterers brought a full container of mutton curry, saying, 'Please don't think otherwise. I won't let any guest be dissatisfied. Take as much as you like.' Saying so he went on filling up the guest's plate.

After dinner, the rituals began and the priest began his invocation of mantras—*Om Namo Ganesha Bighnesha Girija Nandan Prabho*. The vibration of the slokas restored the tranquil state of the night. It somehow brought a kind of automatic retreat for the persons in quest of food. Although such disgruntled elements had no fear of seniors or the officers, they now took their respective positions.

Now all the senior members from both sides started gathering around the altar to closely watch the marriage ceremony. The Chairman of the NAC, a middle-aged sleek aristocrat, sat in the front row drawing special attention from the crowd. Many, out of reverence, stood at a reasonable distance to have a few words with him. Being the prime political magnate of the town, he attracted both officials and non-officials.

Although Mohan was not new to the Das family, his sherwani with a silk dhoti and ethnic turban elevated him to a different level. Both ladies and teenagers displayed a special longing to have a look at him, a wish to stand beside the new couple in order to derive a special pleasure. Everyone looked jubilant. Sunita introduced a group of friends to her new brother-in-law. Mohan responded with a smile. It was as if the unruly tiger had been tamed at the altar.

Banita cast a magnetic smile at her sister's team. Her transparent veil studded with radiant *chumki* added a new banner of the wedded state to her personality. The round vermilion dot on her forehead enhanced the look. Her face was glowing with the thought of being both a daughter and daughter-in-law.

Both the videographer and still-photographer were busy taking snaps or video coverage of the events, obliging the desires of family members as well as the groom's side.

While the celebration was at its peak, some outsiders, maybe small-time contractors, gathered near the sets of furniture that were supposed to go along with the bride. The dining table, sofa set, dressing mirror, marriage bed and other wooden items were packed carefully to avoid damage during transportation. Although the distance was less than a kilometre, such packages needed full protection. Briefcases, steel almirahs, LCD TV and several other articles were loaded a carriage for safe delivery to Mohan's house.

Engagement of petty contractors was the focal point of Das' circuit. This was a by-product of the extra earnings over and above the official salary that were part and parcel of the construction world. Das knew it would stir up a scandal but he was governed by his role as a father.

Das also went ahead and invited Somen and many of his friends to the function. Although they didn't appear to be fitting in with the occasion, it seemed expedient to extend a hand of friendship to them. Like making a pact with those rebels who very often passed critical remarks about them. The trio spoke to the group members freely, allowing them to pass time in a good way.

Dressed up in an exquisite sari studded with mirror work and embroidery Banita was escorted from her green room to the altar by her near and dear.

Banita's swaying body was covered with ornaments from head to toe. She had adorned herself with gold bangles of the latest designs and there were rings on each of her fingers. On her head she wore a golden hairband and strands of perfumed jasmine.

Das in dhoti and sherwani sat on the altar totally engrossed in the rituals. The timing for the *hastabandhan* drew nearer. The priest heightened his recitation of the Vedic chants—*Om Agnaye Namah, Abahayami, Sthapayami, Dhyaami, Ehaagachha Ehatistha*, and pushed holy wood into the fire that leapt higher perhaps to chase the evil spirits away from the couple. Now, every senior assembled near the altar to bless them both through gifts in cash or kind. Both the hands came closer and were tied together lording over each other's world for good.

After the holy fire came the pushpanjali. The priest completed the other rites and then sprinkled holy water on those sitting around him. The priest too was in a hurry to finish. *Om Shanti…Shanti*, he said at length with a tired tongue.

Soon after the bandhan, Banita and her parents became quiet and contemplative. When Banita exchanged glances with her parents, there were hints of tears in their eyes. Their daughter would now belong to another family. Such an unexplored intimacy with a strange family suddenly seemed frightening. Banita hadn't as yet thought about moving away from her home. What guarantee was there that her entry into the new premises would be as rosy? Banita went on thinking and arguing with herself, advocating the plus points in a marriage that was the inevitable fate for every lady. Once again the priest started chanting from the Rig Veda: *Om Madhu Ksharante Sindhabaa…*

The night was deepening further. The SC finally reached the venue after his day-long tour. The trio sprang to their feet when they saw the jeep coming in. They were all prepared to welcome the smaller prince. So when he arrived, they greeted him with toothy smiles.

'Oh! Such a busy life,' exclaimed the subdivisional chief while getting down from the vehicle. Das looked extremely delighted, almost as if Krishna himself had alighted from the chariot. He had brought some kind of a gift, which he presented before the onlookers. Das had been waiting for this blissful moment. He was overwhelmed and commanded everyone in sight to arrange food for the sahib and his driver. He was escorted to the altar to exchange pleasantries with the new pair. Some elders including the father of Mohan joined together to share this moment of glory with the young IAS officer.

The conch shells blew loud and the ululations from ladies rent the air. The couple exchanged garlands and stretched their hands to be joined together. This lovely moment was enthusiastically recorded by the photographers.

'Is everything fine?' the Sub-Collector asked as if he was really concerned. 'Yes Sir, things went off very smoothly,' replied the Tahsildar. Das nodded, endorsing the view of his friend.

The Tahsildar and BDO extended the same courtesy to the driver of the SC, almost as if he was like Brishava, the bull who attracted the attention of devotees even before Lord Shiva. The duo ran from pillar to post in search of non-vegetarian items and sweets to satisfy the driver. Superior items such as mutton, shrimp fry, porridge, sweets, etc. had already been finished off, but rice, dal, mixed curry and some other dishes were available in plenty. With a tired hand, one of the servers tried to search for a piece of mutton but his attentive eyes could not find the fruit.

Shanti rushed to their rescue and platters of mutton and porridge were brought from the kitchen. Both Shanti and her husband stood beside the SC for closely monitoring the service.

'Okay, take care of my driver,' the SC told Das in a commanding voice.

The SC finished his meal, thanked his hosts and left.

Das and Shanti looked in the direction of their family members. It was their earnest longing to come closer to their daughter. Time was approaching to see the new couple off. Das tried to find Shanti and saw her with their daughter shedding tears and embracing each other in a corner. Das couldn't bear the sight and looked sadly at them. He slipped the veil off Banita's head and laid his soothing palms on both her cheeks.

Shanti had to prepare for the parting. She fixed an earthen pot at the doorstep to soothe the departure. The couple Banita and Mohan wore a turban and crown on their respective heads.

The priest chanted mantras unceasingly that warmed up an otherwise solemn scenario. He sprinkled scented rice and fresh petals over the couple to bless them for a prosperous life ahead. Slowly dawn was breaking in the eastern sky striking a new chord. Das, Mohanty and Pasayat sat together looking exhausted. The house of Das was slipping back into its cocoon.

Das looked back at his past years. He depended on Banita for every personal matter. Whenever he returned to his house, it was Banita who took care of his rumpled clothes, made tea for him and his friends. Similarly, whenever he left for his office, Banita would help him find his hanky, wristwatch, cellphone and even his wallet. Once again, his heart sank into the recesses of sorrow. To whom could he convey the agony of his heart? Unseen tears misted his eyes. Bidding farewell to a daughter was certainly not one's cup of tea.

The well-decorated car appeared at the flower-bedecked gate. The family members and near relatives gazed intently at the couple when they stepped into the car. As the driver was about to start, someone prompted him to back a little before driving off, probably to avoid a passing cat, considered a bad omen. He did exactly that before moving down the road. An unknown fear gripped Banita once again. It was Mohan's turn now to console her, as neither her mother nor father had a role to play. Banita bowed before her ultimate fate, thus presuming it to be inevitable. She brooded: was this the same village route she had taken so often? Then why did she feel like she was trudging up a hill? Why?

54

MOHAN'S HOUSE WAS eager to welcome the couple. Although it was early dawn, the people of the locality, particularly the ladies, had all gathered there. Sounds from conch shells and ululations filled the air. Firecrackers were burst, twinkling and exploding in mid-air. The thrill of the hour held sway over a group of people from tiny tots to octogenarians who danced before the car, their movements matching the tunes played by the band. For elders, the show was like a walk down the memory lane, reminding them of their own marriages.

Banita and Mohan stepped down from the car, moved ahead at a leisurely pace to allow the ladies to receive them. The breaking dawn brought freshness to the air. The *purnakumbha* was tucked with leaves of mango and a green coconut on it. The doorstep glinted with lit lamps. Hordes of ladies from Mohan's family holding betel leaves transmitted symbolically the heat from the flickering *arati* and caressed the cheeks of Banita with it. After that, Lali, the younger sister of Mohan, came forward and asked, 'Where is my gift, otherwise I won't allow Bhabhi to enter.' Obedient to the command someone lifted an attaché from the car and handed it instantly to her.

It was of course a chance for her to interact with her Bhabhi. She smilingly grabbed her hand and made way for the couple to go inside. She heralded them in and Banita followed with Mohan behind her. Now, they would permanently stay together under the same roof. The high ritual journey had come to an end for the time being.

Banita was chilled to see the house that would become her shelter for the rest of her life. She felt that the surrounding looked alien. She was overwhelmed by the strangeness in everything. How could one adjust to this? What was the testing ground to know the other one? Her sister-in-law Lali escorted her to a corner room designed specially for them. Mohan had no immediate thought on how to soothe her shimmering shock. He understood her sickness and told his sister to look after her. Lali and two of her friends sat together with visible happiness in their hearts. They spent their time gossiping with Banita as the passive listener. All of a sudden, Mohan's mother shouted at her to have her morning bath. Immediately she was provided with clothes, bathing soap, etc. and Lali accompanied her to the bathroom in the backyard. Banita reluctantly entered, she was afraid of everything but forced herself to overcome her awkwardness.

Mohan had taken the initial sickness of Banita for granted, as it was usual on the part of a newlywed. In the absence of near and dear ones, everything felt strange.

Banita felt the room was a little hot. She did not want to wear harsh silk on her body and picked a Sambalpuri cotton sari and a semi-cotton blouse to put on. The heavy gold ornaments annoyed her. But she was helpless. Of course, he wouldn't let his family dictate on how she should look. It was okay.

Through the door, Banita opened her eyes to a peculiar scene. Two old persons were puffing a chillum making the smoke blow out like steam from an old railway engine. They looked joyous! The smell reached her nostrils. As such, Banita was drooping with tiredness and her head was aching because of the smoke from the puja rituals. Unlike her house, she couldn't have a little nap. She had to sit tight in spite of the uneasiness. Banita thought for a while. Was this the end result of her fleeing to Vizag with a young man like Mohan?

'Who is that old man?' Banita asked Lali, pointing at the person with the chillum in his hand.

'Oh! He is our uncle,' Lali replied casually.

'That means...'

'Elder brother to my mummy.'

'What is he?'

'A simple cultivator. He stays in the nearby village. We will go there. My aunty has already extended her invitation to you through Mohan Dada,' replied Lali.

Before saying anything further, Banita saw a horde of women coming towards her. One of them, an old lady, pulled the veil over her wet hair perhaps to study her looks.

'Oh! So good-looking. I couldn't imagine her beauty. I have always seen her rushing down the road, talking either to a classmate or someone else. Frankly speaking, I was afraid of her smartness. But what a grace! As if she's Laxmi in her true form,' she shouted to Mohan's mother appreciatively.

Banita was puzzled by the lady's sharp tongue. Who wanted to wound someone through such unrelenting shots? Banita had heard of such formidable beings and their commanding status in a village but had never experienced such remarks so far. She desperately tried to ease herself out of the old lady's clutches and to keep a safe distance from her.

'What do you think of Mohan?' the other one asked with a wry smile.

Banita's facial expression revealed that she was unhappy by the question. But the lady repeated her words. Banita looked perturbed but kept her cool and replied, 'Of course, he is my husband and naturally I hold him in high esteem.'

'What is your preference for your first child? Son or daughter?' another one asked.

This annoyed Banita. She felt as if they were deliberately upsetting her through such silly interrogations. 'Please don't ask me such awkward questions,' Banita said in a firm but polite voice.

'Banita, it is a common thing to ask any new bride. Moreover, there is pride in replying to a question of this kind,' the middle-aged lady said.

Both Lali and her mother could see the signs of bitterness in Banita. They knew that if Mohan could hear this, he wouldn't spare them too. A sudden idea struck them. Mohan's mother gazed at her, saying, 'Maa! Could you prepare some cups of tea for us all... It would be so nice to have it from you for the first time.'

Banita had wanted this opportunity. She immediately left the room and entered the kitchen with Lali. It was a comparatively smaller set-up without any outlet for the smoke. Also, it seemed inadequately equipped. Mohan's mother came and wiped the gas chullah with a cloth. She showed her where the tea dust, milk and sugar were kept and then she and Lali left. Banita found the surroundings depressing but she didn't have a choice. After a while, Banita entered with the tea. Without uttering anything, she put the tray on the floor. Her mother-in-law added, 'Have some tea. You must have my daughter-in-law's mithailadoo.'

'Oh! Don't think your daughter-in-law will serve us. We will help ourselves,' said one of the guests.

Both Lali and Banita slipped away to bring the sweets. One of the guests followed them silently. Her eyes gleamed while stuffing a laddoo into her mouth. 'Oh! What a taste!' she complimented.

Banita's mother-in-law gave the lady a hearty smile. It made the atmosphere more cordial.

'Okay. We have a number of domestic chores to do. Let your son's married life be happy and prosperous,' said and the guests left the house.

'Why don't you come to our house with your son and daughter-in-law one day,' someone piped up with an invitation before leaving.

Mohan's mother graciously replied, 'Certainly, we will try.'

Banita asked Lali to help her find her suitcase. On finding it, Banita opened it, searching for something eagerly.

'Where is my hairdryer?'

Both looked here and there but couldn't find it. 'Eh! Not here. Let us open your brother's attaché,' said Banita.

Banita immersed herself in putting her possessions in their proper places. The phone rang again and again and every time it was either a friend or a relative on the other side.

'Who is that?' her mother-in-law asked.

'One of my friends...Maa.'

'But they should know that you are now in your father-in-law's house,' she reminded her.

Her mother-in-law's words stung her. She replied abruptly: 'I am aware of it, Maa.'

'Banita, hang your wet clothes in the sun,' she instructed her further.

Banita was unprepared for this sudden jolt. Had it been her house someone would have done the task for her.

'Banita, where is your bindiya? Put vermilion on your forehead.'

Banita thought of her parents and how soothing their voices were. How to make anyone understand her inner feelings, the carefree life she had led so far?

Suddenly, a bespectacled old man entered with the help of a stick. In a frail voice he asked to meet the bride. 'Dada, please come here and sit down,' Mohan's father said, welcoming him.

The old man looked around with a vacant gaze. Mohan's mother came and touched his feet. '*Ayusmati bhabah*,' came the blessing from him.

'Where is your daughter-in-law? I must have a look at her,' said the old one.

The family members summoned Banita. She too sank to her knees as a mark of respect. 'He is my elder cousin,' Bishnu, Mohan's dad, introduced him.

The old man stood up from the chair to bless her. His face was brimming over with happiness.

'Just like my youngest daughter-in-law. You know Maa... my son who lives in Jabalpur. He teaches in a school of business administration. His wife, my daughter-in-law, is also a teacher there in a convent school. You look exactly like her.'

Getting no chance to leave, Banita stood there patiently listening to his praises of his daughter-in-law. It was fairly boring paying attention to this garrulous old man.

'Dada, what would you like to have?' said Bishnu.

'Sorry Bishnu, my health doesn't permit me to take anything from outside. That is kind of you.' But Bishnu persisted. He asked his daughter-in-law to bring a glass of lassi.

Banita became frightened of such domestic chores. As if her workload had multiplied.

Finding the old man alone, Bishnu talked to him candidly. 'Doesn't your elder daughter-in-law come to your help when you need medical attention?'

'Bishnu, she has to support her big family. Three children and of course, my son, who at times loses control of himself. She has great stamina and looks after the domestic cows and oxen, providing them fodder and at times gruel and bran as well as attending to domestic chores. In fact, she doesn't have a free moment even late at night. So how can she take care of me?'

Banita adjusted her slipping veil and went out with the glass on a tray.

'Why so much of trouble?' the old man asked in a sympathetic voice. 'Since the marriage is just over, many people would come to see her. Does it mean that she will hang around the kitchen all the time?' he asked while lifting the glass from the tray.

'Eh, this is very tasty, thanks for the preparation.' His praises became louder. 'Your daughter-in-law's lassi is perfect.'

A small smile appeared on Banita's face that could not be hidden from Lali.

55

ONCE THE WEDDING was over, Das, like a free bird, flew about in a relaxed mood. His friend Pasayat had cautioned him. 'Unless there is a grand get-together in Hotel Amar, we are not going to spare you any longer.' 'Well, I am not scared of running away from your proposal,' said Das. After such a triumphant success why would he retreat from such a small commitment? He alerted his friends to ready themselves for the party at night. Das felt himself inferior in status as the other two belonged to the state civil service, a comparatively higher stream than his own of a clerical cadre. He therefore wished to assume the mantle of an officer that would in a way conceal his past identity. He got in touch with Ved Prakash and informed him about their plan to visit his hotel the next day. It became a chance for Ved to plan his two-pronged strategy, first to earn through higher billing and secondly to convince the Tahsildar, Mohanty, to mutate the hotel land in his favour. People in the line could understand his toadying zeal. Although the right and title of the plot was recorded in the name of the railway department, Ved wanted to snatch it away from them. He talked to Das: 'Sir, please come on time. It may rain.'

'Thank you! I am already tired and this will be a respite for me and my friends,' replied Das.

'Sir, you will be toasted with bottles of the finest drinks. I have kept these for a long time only for you.' Ved flattered Das with very many dialogues, in a way laced with cunning asides.

The evocative memory of the hotel dragged the trio there at

about 8.30 p.m. the next day. They wanted to be free from all official bugs and switched off connections to the various Government departments. They sat together in a wooden cubicle feeling very light-hearted. Perhaps such a session was the by-product for gilding the pill of drought created through the magic wand of PC. Ved planted himself before the trio with a smile.

'Sir! May I know your choice?'

'Please show us your menu.'

'It would be better if you order without looking at the chart,' Ved said while suggesting salad, papad and soup. Das, in a fit of generosity, indicated that money was not an issue. Both the Tahsildar and BDO looked at each other enjoying Das' carefree words.

Slowly the cabin became alive with the tinkling of glasses as the trio, in a flush of gaiety, downed several pegs until the glasses and bottles became empty.

They became uproarious, swapping jokes with each other.

'The SC was damn pleased with your party,' said Mohanty.

'I feel so,' replied Das.

'Without these higher-ups, the atmosphere would have been lacklustre,' added Pasayat.

'See...for the Additional District Magistrate's daughter's wedding, the SC didn't turn up whereas in my case, he came without any hesitation,' Das said proudly.

'He is from an All India Service. Naturally has less warmth for officers of the state cadre.'

'However, mine was an exception,' Das said smugly.

'At your family event, the SC wanted some curd. I tried to search for it everywhere including the fridge. Do you know what the storm of words from him was? He said that Tahsildars have enough expertise to arrange things,' said Mohanty. 'But you are not up to expectation. His words came like an explosion.'

'Is that so? I didn't know this,' exclaimed Das.

Ved laboured hard to satisfy the trio. The tandoori chicken freshly roasted in a brick oven came in plates. But the khansama followed this with other delectable dishes like chicken pakoras, biriyani, parathas, colourful drinks and so on. With such irresistible food items all around, they were galloping through a food valley.

Before they left, Ved thought it proper to mention his ultimate goal. He came running with plates of sweets like jalebis, rasgullas, etc., and literally stuffed them into their mouths.

'Let us go!' said Mohanty. 'We will have some paan and a smoke outside.'

'No Sir, let me bring them for you.'

'Well', said Das, 'but be quick.'

Within no time he brought a bundle and said, 'Here is everything you want but I have a request.'

The hotelier continued, 'The hotel is yours. I would be nothing without your help. You are all well respected. Sir, I deem it a privilege to host a small party like this. Please don't ask me for the bill. But I have my own grievance to put forth.'

'We will certainly listen to you, but not before payment of the bill,' Mohanty said emphatically.

'Sir, I don't deny accepting payment. But please mutate this land in my name.'

'But this land comes under railway property,' Mohanty remarked.

'In the records it is in the possession of the railways but physically I have occupied it for a long time,' replied Ved.

'How long?'

'Almost twenty years, maybe more than that.'

'But in case the railway authorities don't require this land, it will revert in favour of the original owner. I mean the revenue department.'

'Sir, it all depends on your report. I beg this from you. Please understand…it is my bread and butter.' Ved went ahead to narrate how his name found a place as an adverse possessor in the remarks column of the settlement record.

Das asked for the bill. Ved mentioned an amount that seemed so small! Das brought out his wallet to pay. 'Sir please! You are not leaving us so quickly,' Ved pleaded submissively.

The trio looked a bit hesitant as the code of conduct was hanging over their heads like the sword of Damocles.

However, Das paid for the food while sharing pleasantries with Ved Prakash. Such a gesture was perhaps because the amount was not a burden on the purse.

The hotelier conducted the trio to the jeep. It was midnight and they should have been at their houses. Ved had persistently pleaded his case. It was such an intensely interesting night. It had made the trio closer friends. They finally made their way back to their homes.

56

THE NEXT MORNING people saw Ved Prakash emerging out of the residence of the Tahsildar. A letter had been dispatched to the Revenue Inspector giving details of the encroachment of the plot on which the hotel was built. The RI requested a meeting with the Tahsildar at his residence, saying, 'Sir, which piece of land?'

'What a question? Don't you know the plot of land on which Hotel Amar stands?'

'But Sir, that comes under railway property.'

'Look, refer to the Record of Rights of Beethalgarh in the computer,' said the Tahsildar. 'As I understand, there was no formal transfer of the holding from revenue to railways. Don't reveal this to anyone and keep the matter to yourself,' he reiterated.

'Sir! This hotel was built recently. There has to be an uninterrupted possession for a minimum period of twelve years,' the RI repeated.

'How do you get such laws? Can't you have this small twist to help the cause of a needy person?'

The Tahsildar indicated to the RI to come closer. He whispered something to him. Might be to entice him to relook at his stance on the issue.

All at once the RI turned gloomy and looked questioningly for a second clarification. Now, the Tahsildar decided to provide him with clues to excuse the encroachment. But the RI had serious objections to settle the land in favour of the encroacher. He mustered further courage to face his immediate boss. 'Sir, Ved's wife.'

'Again the same question. Do you mean to say that I should be there to enquire about his family history?' the Tahsildar said in an aggressive tone.

'No Sir, it is not like that. People say Ved has three wives. One is in her native place in Bihar and the other two are here.'

'What do you say!' Mohanty exclaimed. Both then sat down on a bench to decide the further course of action. After pondering for a moment, the Tahsildar stood up and advised the RI to collect an affidavit from Ved on the issue of not having more than one wife. The onus would be on him to prove the same before any court of law divesting them of their responsibility.

Like a rotating leaf in a whirlwind his mind began to face severe blows. The RI felt a bit perplexed.

'What are you thinking of?' asked the Tahsildar commandingly.

'Sir, Ved Prakash practises dirty tricks but never shows the same to officers like you. He has turned many young members into drunkards offering free parties at his hotel. They move from office to office at odd hours and pressurize many to do wrong things. Otherwise they pick up quarrels and are abusive even to the extent of manhandling the clerks,' said the RI in a scared tone.

'But nobody has yet reported this fact to me,' said the Tahsildar in a tone of surprise.

'Sir, only out of fear.'

'Okay, I shall look into the matter in greater detail but take my instruction seriously.'

The RI didn't say anything further. He decided to take one or two of his staff to book the case. He begged leave of his boss and headed for his destination. As he was leaving, the RI felt as if his conscience was almost falling out. He came out of the residence of the Tahsildar as fast as he could.

57

THE COMMAND FROM the Tahsildar gave the RI an immediate surge of strength to book an encroachment case in the name of the first wife of Ved Prakash. There was no immediate necessity to secure an affidavit from the hotelier. The clerk-in-charge of the section was alerted to put up the same on priority. The other such cases were bundled out to come in a phased manner. 'Listen, Peshkar Babu,' the Tahsildar told the bench clerk, 'this case record should match up to your smartness.'

'Yes Sir,' the BC said promptly. 'Sir, should I date it in a camp court or Lok Adalat?'

'No, you keep it for a disposal in office.' The court patwari was sent to verify the spot by means of the trace map. The Record Keeper was told to carefully examine the issue, taking help from the RI. Once reassured, the Tahsildar asked his Revenue Supervisor to have a sarjamin enquiry of the spot. The man who was on the verge of retirement didn't show much enthusiasm but his boss soon persuaded him to do so. He dispassionately collected details. Ved Prakash tried hard to minimize the gap between the RS and his obstinacy. The initial report showed the hotelier as a landless person and as per the rule the encroachment case was to be converted to a lease case in order to settle the land in favour of the encroacher.

Senior advocates, Councillors and other such officials visited the tahsil office very often to espouse the cause of the hotelier. The Tahsildar praised them for taking a personal interest in the case. He had a keen perception to discern human psychology. Sitting over his morning cup of tea, he gave his darshan to the local sarpanch who had his eye on a piece of land owned by his neighbour, a widow. He kept his rapport with such a vulture but continued to display his humility before the general public. Always surrounded by a group of sycophants, his thoughts about warming his pocket hardly pricked his conscience. His outward mask of calmness had nothing to do with his rummaging about in the office for cash. On weekly market days when villagers from far-off places made a beeline for his record room for certified copies of their records, a look of pleasure peeped through his face.

Rushing away from his office chamber, he sat tight in the record room to sign the copies and the reason was obvious. Such a turnout of villagers from smaller pockets on the plea of marketing and to collect official copies of their landholdings was like steady drops of water for the thirsty lips of the tahsil staff. From peons to the seniors, they tossed eagerly in their chairs even beyond office hours to facilitate the copy seekers. They no doubt yielded themselves up to this greed. Some young advocates fitted them cunningly into the whole affair. A man like the Tahsildar, tricky to the backbone, used to console them, 'Don't worry. I am at your service. Just wait a little longer.' But people knew such waiting could be endless.

Nevertheless, the advocates in court uniform used to stand before him and address him as 'your honour'! He nodded graciously while flicking his eyes all around perhaps to confirm once again how every item of official work was clearly priced. He quite believed that no one had discovered his bribe-taking so far. The praises from the public suited him admirably.

At times, Mohanty was prompt to convert encroachment into lease cases, through his manoeuvring skill and sending them to the SC for confirmation. Contrary to all norms, persons owning lands were treated like the landless and proposals were mooted to settle encroached lands in their favour. Such cases were examined meticulously, and placed in his confidential file describing him as a cunning officer trying to mislead his bosses.

He had made a loud fuss about such remarks and appealed before the appropriate authority to expunge them from the roll. He was perturbed at such an official stigma and became doubly vigilant. He frowned at those who relayed the secrets of his office to higher-ups. He fixed his eyes intently upon the encroachment cases and scrutinized them thoroughly before converting them to lease proceedings.

His wife Sabitri was not exactly aware of the rank and status of her husband and often complained. 'Look at how privileged the families of officers-in-charge of the Forest Range and police station are.' Mohanty feigned ignorance but recalled an earlier fact that the FRO had offered a wooden sofa set to the SDO, telephone, in exchange for a broadband 3G net connection at his residence.

Sabitri had no basic idea of governance. She understood very little of any administrative theory. Any lacuna in housekeeping she attributed to her husband's incompetence. Jealous of the neighbouring officials, she grumbled at both the Government and her husband. Mohanty took several gambles in order to prove himself as a loyal husband. He had found a piece of Government land somewhere in the town for the maidservant of the SDO. Settling such a plot in anyone's favour should essentially fulfil the mandatory criterion of the lessee's landless status. Taking the land as a kind of permanent asset, the SDO extorted manual work from the maidservant. Soon, in exchange, Mohanty was facilitated with a land phone at his residence. The SDO, telephone, went out of the way to help the cause of Mohanty, the Tahsildar.

'You are so nice...lovely,' Sabitri told her husband.

'Just wait and see how speedily I can pull you through the road of prosperity.'

'You are so sure ... I believe it too.'

'Yes Sabitri. All you have to do is to hang out here and see what happens next.'

Sabitri's face instantly lit up with an amorous glow in anticipation of such a fortune. She switched on her cellphone to call her younger brother at Kolkata.

'Hello Babu, it is me...your Didi from Beethalgarh.'

'Hello Didi... Namaste... How are you?'

Sabitri had no idea of saying 'fine'. She went on and on talking loudly about her husband's cold and fever, how she could only enter the sanctum sanctorum of the Vindhyabasini temple because she was the wife of the Tahsildar. She had no clue of the cost of such frequent calls and never realized that the amount was almost half the monthly pay of her husband! Leave alone Mohanty Babu, even her own children reprimanded her.

Sabitri had no argument in her defence and decided to cut down on her calls. Mohanty looked at his wife's glum face and agreed to foot the phone bill if she never repeated this mistake again. Sabitri enquired about the mode of payment.

'Don't worry,' he soothed her. 'The local Revenue Inspector is there to look after it.'

58

LIKE BEETHALGARH WINNING its ultimate soul, Somen was successful in the interview. His selection as an executive in a silk factory in Karnataka made Somen the local intellectual hero. His family, which had been forgotten like a worn-out fabric, regained their lustre. His success story would now flow from ear to ear like an inspiring nugget of local news. Roy Babu ensconced himself as the guardian of an achiever. The rural folk who had hitherto made comments on his son's failures now acknowledged his talent. So, in a nutshell, Somen became the family's lucky mascot and in a way would lead them forward.

'What about sweets?' shouted one of Roy's colleagues.

'Whenever you say,' replied Roy.

'Your son is really lucky,' commented another. 'The image of a father is enhanced by his son's success. After all, he's an executive in a high-flying corporate house—dream of a lifetime,' was the thought that passed by many of Roy's colleagues.

Roy was elated. He strolled around proudly, sipping tea and puffing cigarettes. He wished to settle the problem of his daughter's marriage next. In a determined effort, he decided to throw away his old ways and seize upon the hassle-free years ahead. His voice grew louder with the lofty affability of a dignified man. He could now talk about his daughter's goodness to anyone. Many suggested offering prayers before Goddess Mauleswari. Somen didn't respond to this devotional impulse nor did he resist it. The spiritual urge of Minati and her father tried to find an outlet in Pradeep, Somen's friend, since he listened to them with more patience and equanimity. He also knew that Somen didn't undermine the status of God.

They all arrived in the temple. Each one bowed before the idol, which glowed amidst burning candles and the aromatic smell of incense sticks. Somen left the sanctum perhaps to allow his mother and sister to offer puja. Mrs Roy promised to hold a continuous three-day prayer session if she was successful in finding a good bridegroom for her daughter. Both intently gazed upon the idol with devotion and extreme piety. No one knew if the goddess was appeased, but the family continued to beseech her. So deep was their faith in the deity.

59

THE CONTINUING TUSSLE between the local administration and the people of Judabandh took a new turn once the Revenue Minister extended his support to their demands. However, now that he had been selected for a job, Somen knew that his stay in Beethalgarh was limited. Before leaving, he wanted to be certain about Judabandh's future. Even though the Government had apparent sympathy for their cause, he brought up the matter again before the higher-ups.

On hearing that the Secretary, Revenue, and Minister, were at Samastipur, the trio met them in the Inspection Bungalow for a long discussion. Although they had decided to declare Judabandh a revenue village, there were some complications on the legal front since the area came under the reserved forest. Arguments continued for many hours. The local MLA too joined them. The people who had gathered there took the help of the Tahsildar, Revenue Inspector and FRO. The dispensers of justice looked at both the SC and Collector who were present as a part of protocol. Malia would relax, even smile, at the thought of a solution. He was overwhelmed to see the state power at his doorstep.

However, the revenue machinery at the grassroots was not ready with the statistical data computing the *gram jungle* and *goachar* land of the main village. In the presence of the Minister everyone became alive to the interest of the hamlet dwellers and keenly attended to the task of creating the new village. For this the minimum requirement was 5 per cent *goachar* land for cattle grazing and 10 per cent as *gram jungle* to meet the firewood demands of the people. This total area was to be taken from the reserved forest without decreasing its status. Since the Government had strict rules protecting the forest, the arable land of the existing village was to compensate for the same. That would be the boundary of the new village of Judabandh. 'This is to be followed in letter and spirit,' said the Collector emphatically. 'Central laws have to be acted upon,' added an officer sitting nearby. The Tahsildar was told once again to be meticulous in order to make the process smooth. He stood before the bosses looking humble. In no time Malia sensed the immediacy of the problem. He rushed to a nearby village where a retired amin lived. And before he knew anything, Malia dragged him away with his kit containing instruments for survey like scale, maps, Record of Rights, cone, divider. When they reached the VIPs, he opened a booklet entitled 'The Odisha Survey and Settlement Code, 1962'. It looked tattered and damaged but the old man proved himself useful to both the RI and Tahsildar. The Collector and SC didn't want to tear themselves away from their gossip to interact with the old one. They preferred to be in close contact with the Minister inside the VIP suite. They didn't want to speak to the old amin as it would belittle them before a higher authority like the minister. A few onlookers made some sharp comments. 'Why was this amin not consulted before? Was it because he held a small job? The old fellow untied the knot and came out with a detailed plan of the arable lands of the whole tahsil and computed the required area for *gram jungle*. As such, there would have been ample Government lands for allocation under the gram jungle.'

Judabandh did have the minimum acreage and its status could easily be upgraded from a hamlet to a village. This gave a clear signal to diffuse the prolonged crisis. Malia and a few others from Judabandh smiled after listening carefully to the whole process. Now the Collectorate could move ahead in right earnest. Some were apprehensive of the clerical negligence. It might be unpleasant but it was everybody's concern to get on with the task without dilly-dallying. Each one present displayed enthusiasm for this common cause. One of the villagers murmured, 'Maybe the Collectorate or tahsil staff won't do anything unless their palms are greased.' The Tahsildar overheard this and quipped, 'I will have it done. Only allow me some more time.' The SC, an apparent novice, told the Tahsildar, 'See, we are not overburdened with revenue collection now. We have to comply with the task lying on our heads.'

The Tahsildar then questioned the authenticity of the amin's information.

'Sir, here is my chart,' replied the old one. He looked confident in spite of his lanky physique. His face came alive with conviction.

'Be serious,' the Tahsildar thundered. 'The calculation sheet will be tabled before both the Minister and Commissioner.'

Then the Collector intervened, 'Okay, Mohanty, give us the exact date of compliance. The Hon'ble Minister can't wait any longer, he may have to face the wrath of the opposition party in the Assembly.'

'Sir! At the earliest,' came the reply. Everyone wanted to show the Collector how efficient the staff at the grassroots was.

'I have strained every nerve, Sir,' the old amin told the Collector politely.

'Hmm.' The voice of the Collector grew louder. He wanted to ascertain from both the SC and Tahsildar if the amin had sufficient expertise to calculate on his own.

The Tahsildar asked for his RI's feedback. He too quickly presented the facts, might be due to pressure from his superiors.

'Okay, Mohanty! Come to the Minister's chamber for a discussion,' the Collector said.

'Yes Sir,' said the Tahsildar, not happy to be at the receiving end. He didn't relish frequent commands from an amateur like the SC but had little choice. He looked at his subordinates standing here and there. It made him tired. It would be a grave mistake to give any wrong data to the Minister or Secretary.

He turned to the amin to ascertain the relevant facts. The old man's cone, divider and maps seemed like tools that could save his chair. He tried to recollect a phrase from his college days: 'Man is not made for defeat. A man can be destroyed but not defeated.'

Both the Tahsildar and Revenue Supervisor entered the suite to place the information sheet before the Minister. The Commissioner, Collector and SC were sitting around him in a semi-circle.

'Oh nice!' said the Minister and looked at the papers before him. He wanted to hear his officers' views so that there was no secrecy. More like a sthitapragnya, almost without any attachment or detachment, he wanted to prove that he had received the people of Judabandh with open arms to award them the status of villagers.

The Tahsildar preferred to stand before his bosses. So also the RS. They stared at the Minister sitting like a demigod. He handed over the papers to the Collector, saying, 'Take care of the papers and send me the report at the earliest through the Commissioner.'

'Yes Sir,' the Collector said.

The Secretary, Revenue Commissioner and the Minister looked at one another. Although the Revenue Supervisor and RI had the relevant papers, they were unable to express themselves fluently. The Collector came to their rescue and presented the gist of their ideas succinctly. 'Sir!' There won't be any problem to declare Judabandh a revenue village,' he said emphatically and looked around to ensure that his subordinates shared the same view. The RS let out a quick reply falteringly, 'Yes Sir...Judabandh, revenue village, Sir.'

'I am not satisfied with you. You apply your mind properly or else keep quiet,' the Minister upbraided the duo. Both the Commissioner and Collector pounced upon the Tahsildar and RS. They looked at each other nervously while he hurled his verbal artillery at them. But somehow they recovered and bowed slightly to give detailed analysis of their study. 'Wait, let me speak.' The Minister wanted to know in concrete terms that the government's order would not be taken lightly by anyone to delay the process.

'It is our submission before the Hon'ble Minister that there won't be any laxity at any stage in giving effect to the Government order,' the Collector said firmly. The Minister wanted to involve the Secretary, Revenue, as the prime mover to deal with the matter. He wanted him to have a joint say with the Collector and Revenue Divisional Commissioner so that he could instantly communicate the order before the general public waiting outside. 'Sir, you can tell the public as I find no difficulty in the paperwork,' said the Secretary.

'Let me go and tell it to the people then,' said the Minister. Seeing him, the onlookers rushed forward and bustled about to get a glimpse of the VIP.

'Let me tell you all in the presence of Secretary, Revenue, Commissioner, Collector, SC and Tahsildar that Judabandh, your hamlet, from henceforth would gain the status of a revenue village.'

'Long live the Minister, Long live the Secretary, Revenue, Long live the Commissioner, Long live the Collector, Long live the Tahsildar!'

'Hold on, please,' the Minister calmed them. 'It is your struggle, and the credit goes to your leaders Somen and Malia and no one else.'

The small group of people were jubilant. They all guffawed at each other to display their joy and excitement. Their dreams would be translated into reality. Their slender hamlet would be honoured with the status of a village. They all felt a sense of security. Their daughters-in-law or daughters would not be subjected to humiliation any more. They would not be discriminated against or face further humiliation. They would not need to challenge the mighty administration of the state. 'All help from our side,' the Collector assured them before the Minister and other functionaries.

After the Minister and other VIPs left, Malia turned to Somen and said in a quivering voice, 'Somen Babu, it is you who did everything for us. You pursued the matter wholeheartedly and now you are going to leave us. It will be painful to blot you out from our hearts.' The other villagers stepped around both and joined Malia to express their gratitude to Somen. It was like a passionate evocation from their hearts.

'Malia, I am pained as well. But I will surely not forget any of you,' Somen said with emotion.

'Get married soon, Somen Babu! May you climb higher and be mightier in the public field. You gave us the strength to live with dignity, the ultimate crutch to stand up with. Please do remember us at times. Maybe we are not rich or powerful but we are certainly from the human species.'

Saying so they left the place en masse cheering as they moved away. Every one of them picked up a cycle with minimum three riders on each. Malia directed them to check the tyre pressures. He allowed no one to ride unless the checking was done.

As the sun was setting, they entered the quiet forest area. Malia as the last rider gave a shout to the others to move ahead carefully looking on either side of the hilly path. He focused his dynamo torch to show them the way, repeating his command again and again: 'Look straight! Don't lose your grip of the handles.' His voice like a loving general warmed everyone. A new map showing Judabandh began to nestle in everyone's mind. In some including Malia it began to dazzle like a page from the children's geography book showing details of their living facts. Judabandh looked like being put into the row of a growth centre with school, factory, hospital and so many attractive structures all around.

60

THE DEGREE OF happiness shown by Somen's family was shared by Arati, their neighbour and Roy Babu's colleague. However, she didn't think it wise to reveal her joy even to her closest colleague Dolly. She was keen to go to the residence of Roy Babu to congratulate his son but restrained herself somehow. One day, as the sun dimmed in the western sky, Arati was seen strolling in her family's kitchen garden, where varieties of vegetables and fruits like tomato, cauliflower, pumpkin, onion were growing. But due to the lack of water they looked dry. The earlier greenness was a story of the past. Arati and her parents used to fetch buckets of water from the nearby tube well to water the backyard but it was really a trying time to conserve the flora. All attempts to maintain the green vegetables were laid to waste. All gardening work like sowing, manuring, weeding had to be stalled for a while. So Arati and her mother concentrated on the flower garden but on a smaller scale. Arati used her creative skill to keep the house in an orderly fashion. She embroidered many covers for the TV, fridge, table, etc. Pink was her favourite colour. Her artistry really enhanced the beauty of the house.

Arati was 26 and had been working for three years. Although a postgraduate in sociology from Sambalpur University, she couldn't find a place in the Department and instead had to appear for a recruitment test of the Railway Board.

Arati nurtured her fondness for Somen like a lovebird cooing somewhere from within her heart. Her heart quivered excitedly for this handsome young man! Just like the flower arrows exchanged between Kandarpa and Rati, legendary lovers from Indian mythology. Both the families had known each other for the last decade. They were both Bengalis from the same caste and stationed in a place far away from their native province of West Bengal. This perhaps fanned their inexpressible love for each other.

Somen fairly endowed with a compassionate heart and sincere nature had enough to attract the fair sex. Arati heard a voice from within encouraging her not to lose heart but to extend her hand towards Somen's.

Arati found it uncomfortable being in the same office as Roy Babu. She was uncomfortable sitting beside him. Her thoughts and desires for Somen made her nervous just to look at him. He could feel it easily. He probably thought, 'This young girl, why not take her for my dearest son to brighten our home.'

On seeing her, Roy Babu gave her an affectionate look.

'Arati!'

'Ji.'

'How are you?'

'Fine.'

Her sweet reply charmed Roy Babu further. But he became conscious of not exceeding the limit since she was his junior colleague.

Arati left her office before closing time. As a senior, Roy Babu allowed her to do so. Everything looked peaceful and silent as she walked home. Her house looked the same and so did Roy Babu's. The afternoon shadows had created an aura of loneliness. The dwellers in both the houses were to be credited for such silent settings. Chasing her tumultuous mind, Arati entered Roy Babu's residence as if her dreams had guided her.

Somen was inside. On seeing Arati, a storm of excitement engulfed him. A kind of love blossomed in a corner of his heart. He came out wearing a lungi and kameez and welcomed Arati and asked her to come in. There was no one inside except the two of them. Who would start to talk? Perhaps, the same thought occupied them both. How to make the most of this meeting? The current of love began to flow intensely between them. They were like Romeo and Juliet and other such immortal pairs caught in the throes of love.

They wanted to speak but couldn't find the words to express their emotion.

Then Arati asked, 'Where is Aunty?' But Somen did not reply, so she repeated, 'Aunty?'

'Temple,' sharp came the reply from Somen. Arati paused a little and then looked at a photograph hanging on the wall.

'Is that your photo when you were a teenager?'

'Yes, Arati, it is me,' said Somen.

'What an innocent look!'

'At that age, perhaps everyone looks like this. Anyway, I didn't need to be deceptive then,' Somen said with a small laugh.

They talked to each other as if they were spending their most important moments in life. Every minute started falling away like drops of water from a thirsty lips. During their conversation each word had a deeper, more passionate meaning behind it. It represented the inner feelings of two young hearts.

Somen became aware that he had forgotten to ask Arati to sit down. 'Arati, please take a seat,' he said at once. For Arati, such words vibrated like a swarm of bees buzzing around a lotus flower.

Then she asked, 'When will Mummy return?'

'Maybe within half an hour.'
'Where is Minati?'
'She is with Mummy.'

Arati couldn't think of what else to say. They sat in silence, looking at each other, the unasked questions lingering around them. It was almost as if they were conversing through their eyes.

Somen once again waved his hand at a chair asking Arati to take a seat. Arati just stared at Somen unblinkingly. Both looked at each other. From the window it appeared as if it was going to be a beautiful evening. The gold rings on Arati's fingers dazzled Somen's eyes. So did the gold chain around her neck. Like Trishanku, the middle heaven, the earthly duo stood like they had the chance of becoming its citizens. Arati broke the silence, 'When are you joining work?'

'After a fortnight.'

Both stood straight as if they would not let anything detract from their conversations. Was it to speak the unspeakable? The maidservant could be seen struggling to open the gate while carrying one metallic container of water on her head and the other on her waist. She was coming from the tube well and water was spilling out drenching her sari and body with each step she took. Her wet blouse revealed the contours of her swelling breasts moving rhythmically for want of a bra. Suddenly both woke up to reality and Arati wanted to run away. She didn't want to belittle herself before the colony people. She became scared of her presence in Somen's house. Her intended strategy was perhaps to lure Somen, but how?

In fact, what was her intention? Why did Arati walk all the way here? She didn't want to be a victim of her impulsive love any more. Even walls had ears. She decided to leave Somen's house immediately, one of the reasons being the fear of public rumours. 'Oh heavens, how did I dare to enter someone's house and be alone with a bachelor son? Is it just the call of passion or something else?' she wondered.

'Let me leave… I will come when Mummy and Minati are here,' said Arati to Somen.

The main door stood open and Somen escorted her out.

The evening sky was clear. A row of birds were flapping their wings in mid-air, perhaps to find a safe place to nestle down for the night. Arati felt like melting and flowing down quietly somewhere. Maybe like the quiet flow of a small river waiting for the support of the sea to take care of it. She walked home as if in a dream, her mind resting uninterruptedly on Somen and his natural courtesy. Her walking was like Gajagamini's, the slow move of an elephant so that the neighbours did not put her under the radar of their surveillance.

While stepping into her house, her mother said, 'Maa! Where have you been for so long? Your food is getting cold. I will have to heat it up again.'

Arati kept quiet. Perhaps this was the kind of situation she had expected. Although she didn't repeat herself, her tone alerted Arati. She went into the drawing room where her mother was moving plates around keeping pace with the music of her mind.

61

THE WOES AND uneasiness of the people of Judabandh could finally be buried. The hard labour of Malia and Somen would bear fruit at last. Judabandh became a revenue *mouza* in exercise of the powers under the Odisha Survey and Settlement Act conferred on the State Government. On the strength of a special notification of the Revenue Department, the Tahsildar of Beethalgarh was empowered to start proceedings for effecting changes in the boundaries of Judabandh. From the tahsil office a special messenger was deputed to this tiny habitation to hand over a copy of the Government notification for the general information of its inhabitants. The Tahsildar accordingly served a notice in the village in the form of a show cause inviting objections, if any, to this kind of an operation for a new village. The villagers, as yet wedded to their non-status, gave an overwhelming reception to the messenger. They physically lifted him high into the air, cheering and clapping hysterically. A huge sunrise of hope and joy appeared on the horizon of Judabandh.

In the evening, the villagers decided to celebrate. Their percussion instruments along with clarinets enthralled the valley. *Nishan* and *tasa* were played delighting everyone's ears. The men, women and children held each other's waists and danced with joy to the tune of the musical instruments. Their jubilant mood united them under the tree called kalpavriksha where the flow of toddy liquor and mutton was plentiful. The kitchen fire leapt higher as the chullahs were fed with more wood. It was as if the rural goddess had come alive with human spirit and blood. Her vermilion and red garments defied even the purple-hued setting sun. 'Why not dhunkel?[*] What a freshness it provides! What a fool you are!' Malia shouted at someone. Many of them rushed in several directions searching for the instrument and its player. 'The show of drums is the drummer,' some elderly man said in a sharp tone. One young chap quipped smilingly, 'Really, I don't know at all.' But such exchanges led to further toning up. The villagers shouted together: 'More, more.' The dhunkel player turned up with a bamboo winnowing basket and a stick to play the music. The flow of song and dance went on unabated capturing each one's ears and eyes. They danced without any hurry, as the day turned into the night. So open-hearted and thrilled, their dancing reflected their rapture.

'Such an occasion should continue for some more time,' yelled an old man from the audience. Malia didn't object. For all, it was a sleepless night with the earth more vibrant and colourful than usual.

'Let me ask all of you again and again,' Malia shouted.' Are you really afraid of a forest officer now?'

'No...not at all,' yelled one young lad at his side. Others joined in.

'Yes, I want my village to get rid of all fearers,' Malia continued.

A great happiness captured his heart. For Malia and others, it was the mother of all their experiences in life. For all, nothing looked greater than this bliss.

However, some young fellows with weapons in hand guarded the area against wild creatures. Might be reptiles under someone's

---

[*]A musical instrument made of bamboo

feet but none were seen. The hot blood of Malia cried out once again, 'Cast off your past. Forget the days of fear and disgrace. No Government official can now show red eyes at us.'

The revelry continued until the late hours of the night. There was no electricity or gaslights so the villagers took the help of those who carried lanterns. Mothers picked up their sleepy babies in their arms under the flickering light. Being free of the long trauma, Malia made his way home, smiling goodbye to everyone including his comrades-in-arms.

'Ah me! I am deep-rooted here. Can't you recognize me? How many times I have come here to meet my relations. Today I am eager to watch your success.'

As the stranger spoke, one or two tried to identify him. Someone prompted, 'It seems he is a relation of one of us. But why is he in a khaki uniform? He is certainly not a service holder either from the Police or Forest Department.'

'Police,' shouted a little boy.

'Don't be afraid, my dear! I am not a police officer. My clothes are few and unclean. So I have to wear my son's attire,' he explained with a big laugh.

'Your son is a policeman then?'

'Yes. Otherwise who would eat *ilis* (hilsa fish),' joked someone. Everyone laughed. They wanted to entertain him like a guest. Some damsels standing nearby jumped forward to join the band of singers to entertain their new guest. Talking proudly about his son's police job, he was whisked to the village by the jubilant lads. With *tashas* fastened to their waists, the beating continued with a masculine spirit. Judabandh once again turned into a valley of singing and dancing.

'It is so exciting to hear the trumpeting of *tasha*,' the newcomer said with an elated mood. *Dhol, nishan* added piquancy. With the horns of a stag fixed to the percussion instrument the players went on demonstrating acrobatics in their valorous mood. The players of the *nishan* jazzed up the different tunes by blowing air into the instruments. Their sounds assaulted everyone's ears. Then someone came forward to recite his own composition.

> Behold the police of the town
> His moustache is his pride
> And the truncheon, his ultimate strength
> He is omniscient.... omnipotent
> Let us all be at his royal feet
> Oh Police...Oh Police...

A cartoon of a police was sketched in charcoal on an earthen pot abandoned nearby. Everyone shared the joke.

The jubilant gathering moved along the path to their dinner field. While walking, they were thrilled to enjoy the night beauty surrounding their village. No more unrecognized! Like a sunflower, Judabandh had to keep its tryst with tomorrow's sunrise.

A grand dinner had been arranged and the dusty ground had to be prepared for the rural banquet. Malia set about organizing the collection of utensils and kitchenware from each house as well as vegetables, rice, dal and other cooking ingredients. In no time dry logs were cut into pieces for firewood. Young volunteers went to distant and near villages to arrange for gaslights. Simultaneously, a group of youths swept all the dry leaves from the spot and removed the dirt. While doing so a thought arose in many of them, is this the same forest that terrorized us for so long?

'Water!' Malia shouted and a group of idlers leapt into action. Soon, water flowed in buckets. The field looked bare. It was covered with community carpets.

The diners waited eagerly for the dinner. Many took off their shirts, hung them on the nearby branches, tightened napkins around their waists and started cooking. The ladies winnowed the rice to remove the chaff. Not being content with mutton curry, some went to the nearby stream to fish. Each wholeheartedly worked to create a delectable dinner. Two young boys set off to collect banana leaves to use them as plates. Just then, a hornet stung one boy and he screamed in pain. The rest started crossing swords with the virulent wasps. This alerted a group who flew to the spot with flame jets in their hands. They went on a killing spree shaking the burning torches and within no time the ground was heaped with the charred bodies of the wasps. One took off the clothes of the wounded boy and shook them. Red scars ran all over his body. 'Help...help,' he cried loudly. The leaves of bisalyakarani, a medicinal herb, were mashed into a paste and applied all over his body. Malia too rushed to the person on a rescue mission. Turning a deaf ear to the cries of pain, he took the boy to a nearby peepul tree to offer his prayers for immediate relief. Then to a nearby *amla* tree. '*Om Jagadatri*,' Malia chanted a mantra with closed eyes and poured water at its root. He asked the sufferer to do the same. This was characteristic of the worship of the tree god, said to be residing in its boughs. The victim helplessly followed him without any instant relief.

All at once, a dry twig fell from the tree. It fell to the ground so suddenly that nobody noticed it. It was sheer good luck that no child was under the tree when the wind moved the leaves otherwise the situation would have become a cruel joke of fate on the villagers.

The whole village waited with bated breath as the boy started showing signs of recovery. For the dwellers of Judabandh, this misfortune too seemed to have been overcome. It was time to return to their celebrations. Endowed with a fresh liberty, Judabandh could now inhale the free air that it had been deprived of so far! The ray of freedom was falling upon each face making everyone optimistic to the core.

62

THEREAFTER, THE DWELLERS of Judabandh became a part of the mainstream of Indian life. For the first time they wanted to celebrate 26 January, India's Republic Day. Malia planned to invite Somen, Pradeep, the BDO, Tahsildar and SC from Beethalgarh to grace the occasion. But the Government officials didn't have the prerogative to leave Headquarters en masse on such a pretext. Moreover, there was no decent route from Beethalgarh to Judabandh. But some young guys at Malia's command came forward with axes and spades to remove the clumpy shrubs and the tightly knitted creepers. After widening the width, they dressed up the surface by breaking rocks on the ridges. It was hard work but for Malia and the others it was all for the good cause of their tiny village. Something of a community development at public expense and labour. Malia shouted, 'Please don't disgrace Judabandh; after all, the first impression lasts the longest.' Malia kept cycling around arranging food and water and motivating the workers. A combined zeal overpowered all impossibilities. The continuous digging of dry soil, filled the air with dust.

Imbued with a rare zeal, Malia scanned each spot to check if a vehicle could enter their village.

'Such huge rocks and boulders,' Malia said dragging someone to the spot. 'Come on, bend a little and lift them.' Both with their strong hands picked them up and placed them on the side. A big rock could not be moved and had to be smashed into pieces. In the process someone was injured and drops of blood began to flow. 'Are you a fool or what? Didn't you see the pointed bits?' Malia yelled in fury. A boy came to the rescue. Instantly he brought out a little antiseptic powder and cotton from his pocket, applied them on the wound and bandaged it with a handkerchief. The injured one smiled while Malia tightened the bandage.

'So tight, I can't even walk,' he said light-heartedly.

'Sit here until I tell you to stand,' Malia said in a commanding tone.

The injured looked at his steward devoutly, perhaps measuring his warm-hearted spirit.

A forest guard who was passing by objected to the removal of branches from the trees. As always, they were never good to these dwellers. Some onlookers felt like bulldozing him but left the matter to Malia. 'What makes you speak like this? Don't you know that VIPs are coming to our village.'

'Since how long is yours a village?' asked the guard.

Malia replied quietly, 'Please check with your higher-ups. Don't talk like a great maharaj.'

'You lawbreaker... Don't touch even a leaf! It violates forest rules,' the guard shouted. Malia with a typical flush of wrath raised his fist at the guard.

The guard looked panicky. He looked around uneasily to see if any of his colleagues would come to his rescue. The village guys immediately made their way to the spot and swarmed around the timid guard but found that Malia had the matter under control. Sensing something had changed, the guard looked at the gathering as if he wanted to assert his authority. But the sudden crumbling of the bastion of power left him exhausted and he speedily disappeared.

Malia took the help of the old amin to identify the route. They both surveyed the track.

'Let me tell you, Malia, there are obstacles from some privately owned plots of land,' the amin said.

'Malia, it would be good if you could spare some of our plots. A small bit will do,' an old man standing nearby said politely.

'Is it so, Mausa? Don't worry then. I am there to compensate your loss,' Malia whispered in his ear. The old one didn't argue any further.

Some landowners who had hitherto been deprived would now be able to walk on a proper road. A four-wheeler and a heavy vehicle could reach their village directly. The road, even if it lacked the polished surface of a national highway, would make the village accessible.

Malia walked with the amin to observe the survey work. A little more eager than before, he kept scrutinizing the road plan. In order to relax, he took out a packet of bidis from his pocket and passed it around. While puffing, he said, 'Amin Babu! Please demarcate both Government and private plots.'

'Certainly,' the old one said, who was well aware of his responsibility.

Fixing a pencil on his right ear, he wrinkled up his face while glancing through the torn map. On it they could see a way to establish surface linkage between Judabandh and the nearby GP Road. Malia could visualize what the road would look like. Enthusiastically, they all drew closer to find out the edges of the path. From the amin's facial expression it appeared as if the possibility of finding a connecting link if not primrose was certainly not rocky and thorny. In the distance, the road stretched into the horizon, which made everyone hazy about its course in concrete terms. Malia felt his spirits rising. The thought of a road hit his mind like an incessant shower. 'If we stand here, nothing will happen,' he said to the old one. 'Let's proceed further until we find a small passage.' They negotiated a distant ground that covered the vast *goachar* of a nearby village that had not even a blade of grass for the cattle to browse. The stretch of land was filled with *opuntia* and such other weeds. They both trampled upon the thorns and rough patches of the abandoned land and asked the others to follow. They wandered slowly towards the nearby GP Road.

The amin grew tired since the road survey was too big a task for his old body. After embracing Malia he decided leave.

From here, Malia and the other two left for Beethalgarh on cycles. There he met Somen once again. Matters concerning printing of cards, making of banners, hiring of chairs from the local tent house, photography, arrangement for the microphone set and refreshments were discussed threadbare. They wanted to prevent any lapses that might occur. Malia went in search of the VIPs. With the help of Somen, he met the SC, Tahsildar, BDO and invited them to Judabandh for the Republic Day celebrations. Although the SC found it hard to accept, he couldn't say 'no'. Both the Tahsildar and BDO were reluctant initially but couldn't refuse because their boss had consented.

What a wonderful achievement that was! Malia thought to himself. They all returned to Judabandh to work wholeheartedly to achieve their mission. Malia roused each one of them. 'Come on, it is for our prestige, the prestige of the village,' he shouted. Happily they all jumped to shoulder different duties. Patches and potholes were filled up. The forest route was levelled out so that the official vehicles of the SC, BDO and Tahsildar should reach their village with fewer hurdles. While clearing up the forest route, they became overzealous and began to cut the delicate branches of the trees.

On receiving information, more and more forest staff including the Assistant Conservator and RO gathered from all corners. Their faces appeared stubborn. However, they dared not seize the cutting tools. 'Stop it, don't go ahead,' shouted an officer standing nearby.

Malia came forward to meet the challenge. He looked furious. 'I will teach them for the first time at least,' he burst out. Looking at him, all his compatriots swung into instant action.

The forest officers faced the angry protesters with courage. Behind their apparent boldness, they were really frightened. They acted as if they were hiding behind branches and falling back slowly at times. Malia confronted the officials again and again. His indomitable valour inspired the mob wonderfully. The Government servants were too selfish a group and were only concerned with their own interests. They lacked the commitment so the commands from the administration fell on deaf ears. Seeing their reaction, the agitated villagers relaxed. 'Continue with the construction. After all, a road to one's habitation is a minimum need,' said one forest officer employing a cunning device to neutralize the anger of the whole lot. Such a sympathetic sentence turned the tide of the whole situation.

Malia in his usual humble way ran forward to pay his respects to the officer. 'Come on, let us shake hands, please,' the officer shouted in an attempt to bring peace to their warring minds.

What could have been an explosive situation metamorphosed into an abode of peace like a hermit's selective spot. The forest laws had vaguely peeped out from the printed pages of a law book. Its strings and arrows wouldn't pierce into the heart of Judabandh any more. The forest staff had to disperse ultimately.

Once they were sure that the administration wouldn't come and prevent them, the villagers started collecting firewood to make a bonfire at night. With the advent of darkness, the search for firewood accelerated. Finally the dry logs collected were piled up and set on fire. The wind-whipped flames leapt up into the starry sky. It had been a tiring day and they wanted to relax and enjoy the thrill of free living. Constructing the road had exhausted them. Their bodies were streaked with sweat despite the wintry night and many had badly bruised their palms. But no one complained, instead they collected more dead leaves strewn around to keep the fire burning. The flames streaked across the sky of Judabandh upholding the jubilant mood of the whole group. The birds on the trees flew off their nests in several directions. The fire showed no sign of burning out and a relative fear hung around the gathering. Malia ordered buckets of water, but the flames slowly started to die out. Their mood became tranquil yet again. Somewhere in the sky, the crescent moon rose out of the cloud like a light to strip away the veil of gloom.

Ruefully Malia commanded them to walk back. The fire had receded substantially. Many of them squatted against the small bushes sharing tobacco powder like the victorious soldiers of Alexander the Great. A few loin-clothed, half-drowsy men drew close together discovering for the first time the free courtyard of living.

There was shouting and clapping to debate the glorious fortune of Judabandh. In the excitement, some wished to rekindle the fire. 'Let the flame of Judabandh be taller than any campfires in the surrounding,' someone shouted. The gathering went from place to place in the jungle and piled the dead wood in one area. There, the second fire was lit. They threw pieces of dry leaves into the flames. The spiralling fire licked up the total dryness of the spot apprehending burning of a vast area. The drifting flame alarmed the forest watchers who took no time to reach the spot.

The joy of the villagers was hateful to them. Although they shrieked scornfully at their laughing and dancing they couldn't stop them. They stood for a while and left the place attributing everything to Malia as the conscience keeper. Just then a peculiar fire-fever was running through each one's body.

'Don't worry, Sir! I am here,' Malia said repeatedly. One of the watchers murmured, 'Bloody rural louts.'

After having food in the field some of them preferred to spread their napkins on the dust-encrusted ground to welcome the Goddess of Sleep while gazing at the starry sky.

'Get up, you idle fellows. Let us finish off the unfinished,' Malia shouted at everyone.

63

THE VILLAGERS IN the neighboured of Judabandh were equally jubilant when they heard the news. They all wanted to celebrate 26 January in a true republican spirit. Filled with joy the ladies in Judabandh fetched flowers of all hues to decorate the portals of the houses. Leafy banners were hung on both sides of the road. On the outskirts of the village, a platform was built in the style of the Jagannath temple at Puri with twenty-two steps leading up to the podium. In every kitchen, food for the guests was lovingly prepared. The villagers had joined together to arrange a luncheon party for about two thousand persons. Children scampered around with flavoured drinks made of coconut, banana, cheese and candy. Large brick chullahs were erected for the preparation of food on a greater scale. The ladies sat together peeling potatoes and other green vegetables.

The guests were mainly wearing white dhotis and kameezes. The old and new sarpanches representing their villages were offered chairs whereas the *aam aadmi* shared the carpeted floor. They were all waiting to welcome the VIPs. Some young girls had cleaned the premises of the houses and decorated them with linear drawings. Paintings were done near the raised platform. The patterns made with diluted rice powder shone brightly. Cowdung proportionately mixed with water was poured on the ground to keep the surface dust-free. Malia supervised all the arrangements so that the village looked neat and clean. Hawkers from distant places seized upon such an opportunity and arrived with toys and fruits to sale.

In the forenoon, the first vehicle of the Field Publicity Department drove to the meeting spot. The cheering villagers were relieved that their new road had made the journey possible.

Some curious villagers particularly the children wandered on to the newly constructed road. Some of them had never come across a four-wheeler earlier.

Just then, three vehicles could be seen approaching at moderate speed. Malia commanded the band to start playing music. The girls were waiting to start their welcome song as soon as the blowing of conch shells was over. One group played on the mridanga to the accompaniment of the metallic clashing of cymbals. Malia roused everyone, 'Get ready, they are reaching here,' as if their future hinged on how perfectly they received the VIPs. Young girls with matching saris stood in a row with garlands in their hands. The three vehicles came to a screeching halt. The village priest started chanting Vedic mantras in fulsome praise of the rural goddess. The SC and his personal staff alighted from the first vehicle, the Tahsildar and Additional Tahsildar from the second and the BDO and Revenue Officer from the last one. Simultaneously, Pradeep and Somen were seen approaching on a two-wheeler. Within no time, there appeared a number of motorcycles one after another. The villagers gave a rousing welcome to each one of them. It seemed that Judabandh's past emptiness wouldn't show its ugly teeth any more.

After exchanging formal pleasantries, the invitees was conducted to the meeting venue.

'Please Sir! Wait for a while,' said Malia.

'Why?' asked one officer.

'We have a custom of our own. Please allow us to honour our guests.'

'But... We are Government servants governed by our own official conduct rules,' said the SC.

'We the villagers wish to welcome you, Sir, in our own way,' said one standing close to Malia. The officers smiled.

Malia and others started performing some local rituals at a quicker pace. The ladies came forward to clean the feet of the guests and wiped off drops of water and dust with their saris. Somen and Pradeep looked disapprovingly but maintained silence.

The VIPs although embarrassed didn't comment in case it hurt the sentiments of the villagers. The SC was requested to hoist the national flag. In a formal speech, he assured all official help to the gathering by virtue of them joining the national mainstream. His speech was greeted with a big round of applause. The young SC flushed with happiness. He looked at the gathering and saw the same jollity in their faces. 'Are you all happy now?' he said, adding further, 'I can definitely read it from your faces.'

'See...the heart of a young administrator...so fine indeed.' Somen waved his hand praising the SC before the rapt listeners.

'Isn't it a fact that he pursued and spoke for us before the Government again and again,' he added further. 'As an officer, he has shared the aspirations and feelings of rural folk, which is why he is regarded with such high esteem.' Somen prevailed upon the villagers to follow such examples to lead a meaningful life with dignity. He, however, requested the hosts to remain friendlier with the people. Pradeep repeated the same words.

After the flag hoisting, the formal meeting began on time.

The meeting came to an end at about 2 p.m. A luncheon party awaited all of them, but the guests including Somen and Pradeep stood by the respective vehicles, ready to leave. Many youngsters followed, entreating them to join their celebratory meal.

The SC was about to decline politely but the other officers gazed at him intently, hoping that he would agree to stay on for lunch. Gradually, he gave in to the requests from the grey-haired elders who thought he looked so young. The young administrator perhaps thought that such leniency wouldn't cripple his ethical principles for all time to come. Without any ado, he followed Malia to the nearby dining space. He walked ahead, with the remaining officers, staff and other people following closely behind.

The village banquet area soon became crowded and many of them had to find a comparatively quiet corner. At once a reed mat was spread over the ground. Malia cautioned his rural compatriots to wipe the dust from their feet before coming in for food. All the officers, Somen, Pradeep and some local political heads sat in a row. Some leaders were keen to sit near the officers but Malia wanted to square it with the small-time staff members of the officers first. One of such persons agreed amicably. 'Let us go from here', he told his friends and left to sit somewhere else.

Malia beamed with a smiling face and went off to see the arrangements for the lunch of the dignitaries.

Malia rushed to the cooking shed becoming increasingly restless as he watched the time crossing 2 p.m. Looking at his face, the whole contingent plunged into immediate services.

As such the SC was off his food. He was only seized by the hospitable minds of these people. Almost like a prisoner of his own gentility, he had no clue on how to transgress the bounds of social etiquette.

'No sign of drought anywhere in the village.' The SC broke his silence.

'They had a bumper harvest this year also. Plenty of rice in each family to tackle any drought situation,' replied the Tahsildar.

Food items were served to the VIPs with an uninterrupted flow. The head cook had applied all his experience to prepare a seasonal menu. Fresh vegetables were carefully handled with all culinary zeal and an assortment of dishes appeared one after the other. The villagers didn't want the food to run short in case the pens of these officers would strike Judabandh out from the map of the district. Other people from the same sitting waited for the guests to be served despite being hungry.

The officers finished at the earliest. Without waiting for anyone, the SC came out to wash his hands. As night follows day, the Tahsildar and the rest followed him. Somen, Pradeep and the other members of the contingent expressed formal admiration for the arrangement and took their lunch collectively.

The drivers were hungry but had to keep a balance between food and their duties. They had no option but to leave when the officers were ready to depart. Malia came running back and with folded hands urged the charioteers to have something to eat, but they didn't comply. For them, the subordinates have limited choice.

The volunteers in spite of being quiet were hungry too. Malia took up their cause. Looking at the insufficient rice he immediately whipped up the ladies of the village to keep the hearths burning. Malia wanted to get rid of such an unpleasant situation as quickly as possible.

Malia, his volunteers and the women engaged in cooking became tired and flustered. The sun was slowly sinking deep into the west. One of them tore newspapers for people to sit on, while the ladies filled leafy banana trays with cooked items.

'So Malia, let's see if we can cross the jungle before night falls,' said Pradeep.

The villagers flanked them, not wanting them to leave alone. They were concerned about their security. But Somen didn't want to burden the villagers and said they would speed up the motorbike to cross the forest area before evening. Just then the setting sun looked magnificent in the twilight sky.

Before leaving Somen told the gathered public, 'Brothers, we wish all of you a perfect life that matches your spirited growth. Let no state ever snatch away happiness from you and your family. Let your children be endowed with adequate talents in keeping with the children of other developed areas. Let no one injure your pride any more on the plea of a so-called superior status.'

Night was falling rapidly. Pradeep looked into the petrol tank to ascertain the quantity of fuel.

The desire to return invaded their spirits.

'It's been quite enjoyable to spend such a good deal of time with you all,' Pradeep said starting his bike.

'Namaskar…see you again,' said Somen before occupying his seat as the pillion rider.

'Make way for the vehicle to move,' Malia told the small crowd.

Pradeep drove slowly while Somen waved his hand. He threw a last glance before the vehicle picked up speed. The approaching night as if like streaks of darkness was climbing over the cloud-castles at a leisurely pace.

Judabandh was gradually moving out of sight slipping into the recesses of darkness.

64

LIKE A SECRET agent sniffing for vital information, Roy Babu nosed around for a suitable bridegroom for Minati, his only daughter. She was already twenty-nine and had past the usual marriageable age. This worried the family. Recently a family had come all the way from Kolkata for the first round of negotiations. The guy looked smart and was working in the corporate sector. But after their departure, the matter seemed to be in cold storage. 'Well...then, what next?' Mrs Roy asked her husband to contact that family in Kolkata for an opinion. 'It has been more than two months since they came here. If they are interested, why can't they phone or send a mail. They know my email id. As father of a daughter, see, it is not decent for me to pursue this. Let us try somewhere else,' said Roy Babu. Mrs Roy had no words to say further.

The whole situation disturbed the peace of the family. They were like a ship sailing through stormy waters.

However, to their surprise, Sengupta, the head of the family, resumed contact over the phone to keep the proposal alive for some more time. Roy Babu said: 'That is nice Sengupta but how long can I wait? I would prefer a reply, either yes or no. Frankly speaking, my daughter is already twenty-nine. My son's marriage is also due. You can understand my state of mind, can't you?' The next day, after Roy returned from office, he received a phone call from Sengupta. 'See, we have agreed to accept Minati as our daughter-in-law. But please allow me at least a month's time for the marriage celebration.' One month is reasonable period, can't we wait till then? Ray Babu said to his wife who accepted it beamingly. This assurance was a signal that there were better days ahead for the Roy family.

Thereafter, all queries were sorted out over the phone. The Sengupta family moved in a positive direction for the marriage of their son Ajay with Minati. The wedding was to be solemnized on a particular date at an auspicious moment. The Roy family already knew that Sengupta's daughter, Kokila, was Minati's age and was yet to get married. But now a bridegroom had been found for her. One day Sengupta told Roy Babu over phone, 'I want to solemnize both the marriages of my son and daughter at one stroke.' That meant he wanted to kill two birds with one stone. He was opposed to the idea of spending money twice to entertain the guests. So he desired to have both the marriages at the same time. Roy Babu could not disagree. He immediately communicated the willing support of his family. Of course, Sengupta Babu imposed a set of conditions. He demanded some hard cash in the form of dowry perhaps with a view to diverting the same to his daughter's cause.

'Who the hell is he?' Minati cried out angrily.

'Don't worry. I am here to look after everything,' Roy Babu said soothingly.

'Am I somebody to sell at an auction?' she said.

'Didi! Don't worry. We can't be at life's losing end all the time,' Somen pleaded.

All the family members discussed the matter to solve the problem. It became a real headache for Minati. She feared that her marriage properties would be diverted to the cause of her would-be sister-in-law. Her heady days of married life would be diminished. This thought occupied her mind for long. It made her low. 'Better the devil you know, than the devil you don't,' she pondered. Growing older before parents' eyes and turning into a chronic headache for them. 'You silly cunning fox,' she cursed her would-be father-in-law. She ran to her Daddy in fury, 'Daddy! Why are you so eager? Am I a burden on you or old enough to be disposed of at any cost?'

'No...my ladli...certainly not. What made you think in this way?' Roy Babu said to his daughter.

'Then why can't you search for another instead of this one?'

'Maa, be practical,' he said patting her back. 'What exactly is wrong with this proposal?' Roy Babu asked.

'He will take away my belongings and hand them to his daughter,' Minati told her father.

'Why on earth do you fear that?' Roy said.

Somen could hear his daddy consoling his elder sister. He could sense his uneasiness and rushed to them.

'Didi! It is not good to speculate anything beforehand. It is time to put all swords in their sheaths. Can't you imagine the tensions of both Mummy and Daddy?' Somen spoke out standing between the two.

'What are your apprehensions?' Somen asked his sister.

'Because they are planning two marrages in one stroke. I know that they don't have sufficient means. That is why they are doing it this way,' Minati told her brother.

'But it seems unbelievable!' said Somen.

'Somu! My dear...my heart says this...but I have my life to live. Why should someone grab my valuables?' Minati added further.

'We also agree with what you say, but time does not favour what we think,' said Roy Babu.

Although Minati was defiant, she knew the consequence of such a denial. For every such sowing the parents would have to reap the harvest. Marriage appeared before her like a mirage. She felt she was facing the toughest challenge of her life. She questioned herself. 'And this is the fate you have waited so long for. Well, you will be leaving your parental house to spend the rest of your life with these people. Do they or your ornaments matter to you? Are they really fond of you to make you a member of their family?'

Seeing her daughter's changing mood Mrs Roy strolled over to them.

'Well, Maa.' Mrs Roy put her arm around her daughter's neck affectionately. 'So long as we are alive, no harm will come your way,' she said trying to suppress her daughter's fear.

65

ALTHOUGH A WORKING lady, Arati had the rare quality of a daughter-in-law, a quality that had been observed over the years by both Minati and her mother. Roy Babu too shared this opinion. Discussions on the nature and behaviour of the bride always took place whenever there was an outside proposal for Somen. Roy Babu was reluctant to reveal his mind to his son mainly because Somen would not appreciate it. Perhaps his wife could find out what was in their son's mind. Mrs Roy promptly agreed to communicate their choice. Minati too backed her on this.

Mrs Roy entered Somen's room with a cup of tea. 'Babu, since the problem of your job is over, would you mind if we concentrate on your marriage?' she asked him affectionately.

'Maa, please, not now,' he replied politely.

'Why?'

'We have to settle ourselves comfortably first. Moreover the marriage of Didi is our priority.'

Mrs Roy spoke to her son in a slow, unhurried voice. 'But such worrying is unnecessary. Your dad is there to look after everything.'

'We don't have the space to accommodate another person here!'

'I think we could spare our bedroom for you. We could partition the verandah and easily accommodate ourselves there. Moreover, after Minati's marriage, we won't face a problem of this kind any more,' said Mrs Ray.

'Maa! Why now? Is it that urgent?'

'Look Babu, my dear! We are all right when we have a proper plan. I can't really bear to see you a bachelor any more. Moreover...'

'But Maa! Tell me frankly. Do you have anyone in particular for me?'

'No, our choice may not be of great help to you. She should be compatible with you only.'

'Okay! If you are so confident, then tell me her name.'

'What to speak of Somen's choice right now! Tell me frankly whether you would be happy to get her as your daughter-in-law or not.'

Mrs Roy had no stock reply to give. Several questions whispered within her. She was confident that all of them would scrutinize her choice together. She had to decide upon her only son's life partner, one who would enrich his domestic world.

'What makes you to think so long? Tell me,' repeated Roy Babu.

'Let me talk to my child, and then I will tell you,' added Mrs Roy.

'How much time will you take on this?'

'Stop worrying me with such questions. After all, it is a question of one's life.'

'Useless!'

Mrs Roy was used to her husband's sharp tongue. She shrugged him away calmly.

Although not named, their discussion revolved around Arati, her beauty, intelligence and over the family status. Someone praised her nature whereas the other one condemned her gait. Likewise they pored over their selection process. The choice became a selector's dilemma. Roy Babu said bluntly, 'Sober and good-looking no doubt but her job commands little respect, clerical after all.' Roy Babu was immediately contradicted by his wife and Minati. To them, goodness was enough for a daughter-in-law. Any evildoing would rock their family boat. They didn't want anyone to scratch a hole in it.

Mrs Roy looked forward to a quieter time at their residence to study her son's mind. During the week, her husband would be at office so perhaps such a time would be better to talk about this.

The next day, Mrs Roy asked her son frankly, 'Somu! You must have noticed that all our talks lingered on Arati, our neighbour's daughter. Do you have any other in mind so far?'

'Hey Maa! You are yet to study your son then.'

'No... my dear! I know...that is why I ask you.' 'Now I have to share my choice with you,' said Mrs Roy. A meek smile flickered on her face. Looking at her son's affable glance she blurted out, 'Would Arati be your choice as my daughter-in-law?' Somen was ready for such an interrogation. To him, it was a good mix of his own desire. Somen didn't fight shy of her proposal. In spite of his joining the corporate field, he didn't want to denigrate the choice of his parents. He replied coolly, 'Maa... as you like.'

A strange delight lorded over the mind of Mrs Roy. The imaginary pair of Arati–Somen danced before her eyes. That they would be the ultimate refuge in the last days of her life made her very happy. She would tend their offspring with all the love and affection of a true grandma. Her old days would be spent in their sweet company. The cloud of uncertainty that surfaced in her mind's sky began to disappear slowly.

Within no time the clouds of doubt were removed from the minds of Minati and Roy Babu. Pradeep too felt relaxed. Roy Babu wanted to bring the matter up with the parents of Arati. After all, it was they who would choose their son-in-law. As the father of a young executive, he had the confidence to put things forward. It was obvious, in such a situation, the side of the bridegroom stood mostly at the receiving end.

The Roy family wanted to avoid any fake superiority and decided to make an appointment to call on Arati's parents. Therefore they consulted their family astrologer for an auspicious day. He asked for the young one's horoscope and *nakshatra*, and then calculated the auspicious day and time after drawing puzzles with his chalk on the ground. The date, time and purpose of the visit were communicated to Arati's parents through Pradeep within no time.

On her parents' advice Arati had to take leave from her office on that day. She had to wear a Sambalpuri sari and matching blouse to fit her slim body.

'Jagdev Babu...Namaskar.'

Mr and Mrs Jagdev were happy to welcome the Roy couple and Minati. They greeted each other with utmost cordiality. The guests were led to the drawing room. Without any prelude, Roy Babu started: 'Jagdev Babu! We have something important to talk about.'

'First let us congratulate Somen through you both for his success.'

'Okay, fine. Thank you,' said Roy Babu. 'You must be imagining the reason for our visit. Pradeep must have told you about this.'

'It was nice of him...' said Jagdev. Immediately he lowered his voice at his wife indicating that she leave. But Mrs Roy forced her back. Roy Babu requested Jagdev to be comfortable. He repeated his words.

'Let us open up. We are looking for a daughter-in-law. On this, we want something concrete from you.'

'See...that is also our family concern. We are frantically in search of a bridegroom for our daughter,' said Jagdev.

'Do you have anyone in mind for her so far?'

'Some stray proposals from here and there but nothing suitable.'

'No finalization then.'

'No...nothing of that sort.'

'We have brought a proposal for Arati, as you can imagine, for our son Somen.'

'That is okay, Roy Babu... You have voiced our own thoughts.'

It was a moment of great joy for Jagdev. Was it real or mere talk? He chose to hide his surge of middle-class ecstasy about the marriage of his daughter. Mrs Sen, wife of Jagdev, couldn't conceal her excitement. That such a dignified and intelligent person like Somen had chosen Arati, her daughter, as his life partner, filled her heart with pride. A sweet smile crept into her eyes. How could she ever forget such a precious moment?

Just then Arati appeared with cold drinks on a tray, eyes cast demurely downwards. Although she was Roy Babu's colleague, he didn't allow himself to be conscious of her beauty. She quietly put the tray on the teapoy, bowed her head before all and then started handing over the glasses one after another. At once Roy Babu asked her to take a seat. Arati took one of the cane chairs to a corner and sat there with a beaming face.

In the kitchen, the gas chullah was burning. Arati and her mother were preparing pakoras, vegetable chops, chutney and a few such other items. A hissing noise came from the kitchen. Jagdev exclaimed with satisfaction, 'I think, it is ready now.'

The whole family helped to serve the dishes to their guests. There were trays full of subtly flavoured items. The Roy couple had no appetite and sat there almost helplessly. Minati, as the youngest, ate everything happily. On friendly pressure Mrs Roy took a little on her plate but Roy Babu had to content himself with a cup of tea only despite repeated requests. However, all heaped praises on Arati and her mummy for their caring way.

The family members took leave of each one with the robust hope that their son and daughter would be betrothed. They decided not to reveal the news just yet to ward off envious eyes. The situation was delightfully acceptable to both families.

66

SOMEN HAD RECEIVED both an email and a telegram to join his new job at Bangalore. With a radiant smile he showed his mother the appointment letter, 'Maa! See this. I have to pack my luggage...' Saying so, he handed the telegram to Minati, standing nearby.

Such an assignment for a young one like Somen was perfectly all right. But his mummy's response was a little unfavourable. She didn't want her dearest son to move so far away. She said abrupty, 'Somu! Can't you find a job somewhere here!' Somen merely laughed.

Mrs Roy said, 'This house will soon become deserted. Oh! How terrible it would be!! Your daddy will be away at the railway station and I'll be alone here. Could you ever imagine the loneliness?'

'Mummy! The TV and radio will become your best friends,' Minati spoke in a lighter mood.

'Oh! I would simply lose my mind. Nowadays, the serials are so boring. Only ladies doubting ladies and nothing else,' Mrs Roy burst out spiritedly.

'Mummy! Some classical novels, travelogues and comics would best suit your urge,' added Minati.

Somen had to leave Beethalgarh, his dearest land, cutting off his all-time attachment for it. When the train crossed Rangei hill, he stood for a prayer of apology and became deeply sentimental. Barren fields and sombre trees of the verdant jungle stretched out on both sides. The meandering river Vel faded away into the distant horizon. From the window he could see thatched cottages and ploughed fields; it was as if they were bidding farewell to their dearest friend. Somen was almost racked with sobs to leave behind his treasured happy days. No doubt, the prospect of a job and earning money stimulated his spirit, but to give up one's own land for a handful of rupees made him emotional.

Slowly the land, his familiar people and their habitat stood far behind. Passengers with hardcore Deccan accents got into the train. The tea being sold in plastic cups by the vendors became less enjoyable when contrasted with his home brew.

After stepping down from the Super-Fast Express at Bangalore, Somen moved outside the railway station with his luggage. For some time he couldn't see anyone coming to his help. He had been told that a company car would be there to pick him up, but how could he find the right one? A little worried, he looked around again and again but no one could be seen anywhere. What to do then? In a perturbed mood Somen looked around once again. Just then, he saw a white car with a logo in small red letters: 'KSF'. The driver perhaps stood nearby like a maverick hero who hadn't noticed his arrival.

'Are you from the Karnatak Silk Factory?' Somen asked.

'Yes saab.'

'Are you here to pick up anybody?'

'Yes, Somen Babu from Odisha.'

'Yes, that is me... Hum hain,' Somen spoke in a mixture of Hindi and English.

'Yes sir...Namaste.' The driver raised his right hand with a sudden show of alertness. Then, he turned his mind to Somen's luggage. He snatched the luggage from him and kept it in the dicky of the car. He opened the door and Somen got inside. The seats were of red velvet and the car was well maintained and had power brakes and AC.

'Sorry Sir, I didn't recognize you,' he apologized.

'No matter. I'm glad I found you otherwise I would have had a problem.'

The driver nodded politely.

The car started moving. Although Somen was sleepy, he was excited to discover a new city. The driver gave monosyllabic answers to any questions he asked. He looked out of the window at the fleet of vehicles and fast swelling crowd. There was a kind of vibrancy about the beautifully designed apartments, cafés and landscaped gardens. was this city mainly for connoisseurs? So magnificent really! He dragged his mind to the cause of his mother and of course his sister and father. How would he spend his days in a faraway city leaving behind his little town?

The car reached the silk factory's residential complex after a short pebbled drive. It then proceeded to a corner, to a semi-circular industrial structure. 'Sir, guest house,' said the driver and parked the vehicle in the portico. 'Take the luggage', he instructed an old man in a superior voice. 'Saab.' He came rushing to the car. 'Please call me whenever you feel necessary and this is my cell number.'

'Okay,' said Somen.

The old man was dressed in a white uniform with a Gandhi cap on his head—he looked like an archetypal khadi hero. After paying due respects to Somen, he lifted his suitcase and walked towards a room He unlocked the door and went inside, straight to the closed window and opened it to allow fresh air and sunshine to come in. Somen looked out on to the field and saw some boys playing cricket. The stumps and bats were the same but the shouts were in the local language.

Somen's new assignment made him incapable to reason out the process of labour. He scarcely did justice to his own conscience. He went near the dressing table and looked at his own reflection. He felt as if he stood there headless. Both the attendant and the khansama had to spend hours worshipping idols like him but conversely he had to switch off his own conscience for them. He slammed the door of his room and reclined on the sofa to read the newspaper. Just then someone knocked and Somen went to open the door.

'Good evening Somen Babu. I am Banerjee, officer-in-charge of the guest house.'

'Hello Banerjee… Good evening,' said Somen extending his hand with a warm smile.

Both conversed politely. There was an instant connection between them. Both had their roots in Bengal and were meeting each other in a far-off place. Banerjee repeated himself, 'Do you find anything lacking here. I mean in the services of the staff?'

'No… I am absolutely fine. The staff members are very caring.'

But Banerjee warned him, 'See…these people are too cunning. You have to whip them like oxen to plod along.' Gradually their discourse centred on their tradition. They discussed the poems of Rabindranath Tagore and paintings by Nandalal Bose and his last days spent in Kolkata. It slowly moved to the soccer matches of

Mohan Bagan vs East Bengal. Somen, though absolutely new to the set-up, participated in a reverent manner so as to not hurt the other one at any point. He had to develop a personality that was suitable for the corporate world. Suddenly the lights of the suite went off. Banerjee shouted for a candle but no one responded.

'Where are these idiotic chaps,' shouted Banerjee.

He appeared visibly tense and went out of the room, shouting again and again. It was only 9.15. He groped around for a candle or an emergency light. However, the electricity was restored automatically and both heaved a sigh of relief. Banerjee noticed that the attendant's room was bolted from outside.

'Somen Babu! Did they seek your permission to leave?'

'No, nothing like that,' Somen replied coolly.

'What then?'

Somen mildly tried to make excuses on their behalf. The OIC burst out, 'Being new, you do not know them. These two guys are habitual cinegoers. I hardly see them after 9 p.m. They take advantage of the simplicity of guests like you, and now they will only return late at night.'

Somen didn't want this kind of tension to spoil the first night of his executive life. What was the crime if someone wanted to relax by seeing a movie after a long working day? Why be so touchy even if someone bunks duty a mere half an hour before closing time?

Banerjee guessed that his new colleague didn't share his grievance against the staff. Somen wasn't pleased to breathe the air of hatred for the low wage earners. Somen wasn't interested in worrying about such a commonplace occurrence. However, neither did he want to confront the so-called superior position of those in power.

They resumed their conversation, discussing the present cost of fish in Bangalore and their respective native places and comparing the quality of sweets in the garden city and Kolkata. Banerjee talked at length about what he had done for the company all these long years. Somen listened patiently. Finally, Banerjee looked at his watch and ended their session. Before leaving, he invited Somen to his residence.

Somen bolted the door of his room from inside. He switched

off all the lights except the dim one. He was very tired and thought lovingly of Maa, Dad and Minati. But it was Arati who occupied his mind the most and as he lay in bed, images of her flashed before his tired eyes.

Next morning, a sudden knock on the door woke up Somen. 'Saab...tea.'

From his window he could see the rising sun showing its glowing face. What a spectacular sunrise! For all these years, he had mostly experienced the hot sun of Beethalgarh. He looked at Gopal's face but it didn't seem to be lacking in innocence. He had nothing to wonder. While lifting the teacup from the tray for a sip, he looked at Gopal saying, 'Are you okay?'

67

SOMEN WENT TO the administrative Block of KSF the next day and submitted his joining letter before the Chief Personnel Manager. He had carried all the required testimonials with him. The company car with a liaison officer from the Human Resource wing conducted him to the chamber of the Chief Personnel Manager. He sat on his executive chair, assuming himself to be a little bigger than usual. A few staff members and their sectional head came to welcome him carrying bouquets. Somen stood up and shook hands warmly with each one of them. He felt a thrill of excitement. He had to identify with the spirit of corporate life, to put down his roots and share both pleasure and pain with these chaps. He made a courtesy call on the Executive Director, General Manager and other senior members of the administrative staff. Somen was keen to know his young colleagues. He didn't want to be misunderstood either by higher-ups or by the employees below him. Somen saw young boys and girls sitting in their cubicles, looking like a picture of young India. He visited the call centre and shared experiences with the staff members there to explore various ways leading to their marketing strategy. One senior executive from the managerial group, Rodrigues, outlined his training programme:

'Mr Roy, we would like you to be perfect in everything.'

'I would like to meet your expectation, Sir.'

At once, the officer personally accompanied him to the computer cell of the building where he saw a broad expanse of computers with trained personnel from the IT sector. Somen saw young developers with animation-rich websites to analyse the colour and brightness of different yarn patterns. He could observe promptitude towards delivery of services. Somen knew that the backbone of the Internet connection was through free space optics. The connecting data was like the health card of each employee and service particulars such as year of birth, date of entry into company service, etc., were transmitted at high speed through laser beams. The bandwidth requirement of the factory was well supported by high-tech installations on the top floor terrace of the building. Somen had no first-hand knowledge about the financial health of the company but it sounded good! Somehow, Somen felt encouraged and moved like a disciple to the evocative beckoning of the set up. He looked at the modern gadgetry. He along with a couple of operators became engaged in finding out several graphics on the screen for redefining the motifs on the different coloured yarn. They moved to the pallu and played around with the mouse to experiment with different gilded spires. Flashes of feminine images appeared on the screen recurrently and the computer lady downloaded rarer designs from the net to encash her professional expertise. One young boy sitting beside her helped to balance the intricacies behind such vivid attempts. Somen was pleased with the working environment, it all looked very exciting.

He peered all around to take stock of the sincerity of the workforce. Technicians were engaged with robust whole-heartedness to help the cause of the organization. The commercial overtures gave him the idea of an upswing management and he became optimistic of the company's foot on the digital pedal. The business front of the portal was being taken care of properly.

Neither was Somen the sole authority nor the computer cell the sole centre to answer all the dreams of a corporate world. Could it be possible to ascertain time by simply watching the second hand of a clock? The computer cell couldn't be the be-all and end-all of everything.

They then met a group in another corner of the hall. The developer introduced Somen to them: 'This is Somen Roy, our new executive.' The three stood up respectfully and introduced themselves with glittering eyes:

'I am Dilip Bhatt.'

'I am R. Ramesh.'

'I am Chitra Piramal.'

'Where do you come from?' asked Somen.

'We are all from Karnataka,' Dilip replied.

'What are you observing?' Somen queried.

'Just our usual job chart, Sir. We like adding glamour to our silk designs.'

'How is the media campaign of our product?' Somen asked further.

'Sir... Ours is excellent... Would you like to see, Sir?' asked Chitra.

'But your efforts should aim at understanding the requirements of the commoners. You have so many high-tech terminals. Why not get all of them to find out what the consumers think of our product? Our marketing people should remain alert until the last email is received even if it's from somewhere beyond the globe.' Saying so, Somen looked at them and gave a hearty laugh. The others joined him instantly.

'Do you have a data bank with the birthdays of all front-ranking ladies of our country?' Somen asked one of the data operators standing nearby. The lady operator kept mum as she had no such information either in her data bank or in the whole cell.

'See, you may forget your own birthday but not the birthdays of silk wearers. You should know their *nakshatras* and choice of colour, only then would the computer cell prove to be worthwhile.'

Meanwhile, the three laboured hard in quest of eye-catching images. The Public Relations Officer arrived and introduced himself to Somen. He wanted to talk about commercial aesthetics. He inserted a CD into the computer and opened the file. At once a lady holding a coconut appeared on the desktop. Suddenly a gust of wind blew a luminous silk sari that wrapped itself around her body.

'Oh! Excellent!' Somen shouted. But the trio didn't want to show their enthusiasm as did the probationary officer.

Somen felt like ushering in a new era against the backdrop of graphic design. However, his mind was at war between establishment and anti-establishment. He wished to bottle up his true voice but trained his tongue to superficially join the chorus of 'bytes and brains'.

There was no other way but to embrace the corporate wilderness and to balance his mind between temptation and detachment. To cash in on the software field, he had to be fast paced. All whizz-kids, and e-commerce as if it was a buzzword of the latest market drive. He was to be trained to make every fashion-conscious lady want to embellish her beauty with a silk sari, but the idea repelled him. What actually would it earn him or society if every lady on earth did wear the KSF brand?

Somen felt annoyed. The profit monster would devour him. He had to be motivated by targets. All his committed values would be crushed. He would be just one component in a large apparatus, a pointer on a PC screen to explore the unexplored. He would become almost like a robot. Somen had to be cautious and not allow the silk market to melt down at any point of time. He had to become rough and tough to expand the venture entrusted to him. Business is so addictive, in a way like a Disney product attracting an insect like him into the flaming wheel of marketing.

Somen wanted to have a smoke, but he was in an air-conditioned sphere. His memory flew back to the past. Pradeep, Minati and others in faraway places like Beethalgarh and Judabandh, the happy spirits dancing across the pleasant earth. Would he ever go there again? Somen now had to reinvent himself to meet the demands of his new job and life. It was a new experience.

68

SOMEN PUSHED HIMSELF forward to understand the demands of his job. He had been provided with a cubicle in the shape of a semicircle within the same computer complex. A curtain separated his office chamber from the rest. There were desktop and laptop computers, a printer, an intercom, a separate telephone line and a TV set in his office room. A red carpet was also spread on the floor. He had to take on partial responsibilities from both production and marketing to gain ideas. He was to be alert to find out petty disorders in any sphere and bring them to the knowledge of the bosses. He found it convenient to administer, raising a lensman's eye at everything happening around him. He had to exercise maximum vigilance in all matters, which wasn't exactly easy. He kept a close watch at both the punctuality and efficiency of the staff. Whether or not the bosses actually witnessed Somen's work, they were at least aware of his commitment to his new assignment. Looking at his zeal, the ED allowed him to play the big brother and that naturally bred envy among senior colleagues.

Somen was told to inspect both stock and stores of raw materials and finished products. He was to keep a close account of the same. Several accountants including accounts officers switched to a whispered campaign. They had to become extremely mindful to put all accounting procedures in order. With the help of a junior technician and a production assistant, Somen verified the large quantity of silk yarn. The finished products like silk saris were also counted in minute details. The storekeeper cried aloud:

'Oh Sir! Please spare us the details.'

'Why?'

'Here, the ongoing practice is terrible. Truckloads of material and their stock entries, horrible!' said the storekeeper.

'But everything is to be recorded first. There must be a stock entry for each item. Otherwise how can one's integrity be judged?' said Somen.

'I don't dispute this, Sir... Only permit us some more time,' replied one of the storekeepers. The store superintendent, his boss, joined him at once.

Somen went to the vast agricultural land adjacent to the factory where he saw the rearing of silkworms and the growth of cocoons. Earlier, he didn't have any basic idea about the production of silk yarn. The field stretched across more than five hundred acres and was dense with mulberry plants, the leaves of which were food for the caterpillars. The qualification for harvest could suitably be discovered through routine inspection. Labourers had been there since morning channelizing watercourses, upturning the soil and generally keeping a close eye on the health of the plants. Somen went up to them. Just then, they were busy cutting leaves into smaller pieces for easy feeding of these tiny creatures. A small group of genetic engineers tried briefing him while examining the whole process with a magnifying glass. Some labourers chopped off dry portions of the plants with sickles. Somen couldn't keep himself restricted. Without any formal introduction, he talked to them freely.

'What about this cocoon cultivation?' Somen wanted some basic ideas about the production cycle.

Both the men stared at each other probably waiting for the other to reply. Then Somen had a better idea. 'Let us go to the processing unit. I should get a better idea of the style of production.'

The young executive was still ignorant of his authority of command. Could he prevail upon the genetic engineers? In an absolute sense it was 'No' but in a relative sense 'Yes'. However, looking at his high speed mind, the young engineers, at least for courtesy's sake strode down the field.

Somen persisted at a throbbing speed but had to slow down to match with the rest. He was naturally thrilled to reach the unit. One of the Assistant Managers of the production unit greeted him with a handshake and offered him a chair. He was a north Indian, a youngster of around thirty-five. He explained the entire process to Somen including the freezing and steam drying of cocoons and how delayed storage of cocoons could cause stains on the silk. He held a cocoon in his hand, identified the regular filament on it and unfolded the same while reeling it on his fingertips.

No doubt the conversation was technical and Somen wondered what questions he should ask without showing his ignorance. 'Yes, the great vacuity that may sweep a subordinate off his mind and retain the usual glory of superiority,' Somen brooded.

Tonal variations! Others could ascribe his body movement as a sign of inferiority. Did he have to shoot words like arrows to show his command?

'Tough, no doubt?'

Somen was faced with a dilemma. What should a soft-spoken person like him do? He became passionately desirous to rebuke someone. If he had to survive in the corporate sector he had to be authoritative.

'Show me the details of your work chart,' Somen ordered the Assistant Manager. The latter half-bowed taking long breaths. He grappled for the right kind of words and tried his best not to appear incompetent.

'Please be quick,' Somen commanded, as the administrative spirit caught hold of him. A terrifying vanity seemed to have entered his mind.

'It is time for us to return,' said one of the men accompanying him. The other one looked at the watch and said, 'It is half past twelve. Oh, we have an important task ahead! Our boss will tear us apart. Let us go.'

Somen was appalled by such insubordination. Why were they hesitating to show any respect for him?

'You may go. I have to spend some more time here,' he retorted. The men left at once. He reanalysed himself. He had to go a long way to understand the commanding structure of the unit. Such a lesson was yet to begin.

Finding Somen alone, the Assistant Manager wished to entertain him over a cup of tea. Somen hesitated for a moment but then agreed. Encouraged, the employee bustled around his heater to make the tea. A short silence prevailed while Somen thought about how to deal with the existing power structure. Would the authorities approve of his taking tea with a junior employee? The socialist in him disapproved of such man-made hierarchies. He retrieved the situation by taking a cup of tea.

He wanted to clarify some occupational doubts and put several questions to this north Indian employee:

'Yes, Mr...'

'Saxena, Sir.'

'Yes... Yes. What is the quantity of mulberry leaves a caterpillar consumes for one kilogram of cocoon?'

'Thirty kilos, Sir.'

'What is the average number of mulberry plants in an acre of land?'

'Five hundred.'

'What is the average yield of a good cocoon?'

'Around 900 feet, Sir.'

Before leaving, some of the guys had furnished vague data in a light-hearted manner, so Somen was eager to extract further information. He wanted to discover the hidden mystery at the egg stage.

'The caterpillar constitutes the larva period. Then comes the chrysalis or the pupa stage when the caterpillars are sufficiently mature to release a thread-like filament, which when blended with saliva forms an egg-shaped cocoon that confines the chrysalis within it,' Saxena explained.

Saxena's explanations were lively and interesting but Somen didn't have sufficient time to listen to him. He advised him to improve the quality aspect of the whole process. 'All we wish is that the caterpillars should be properly fed so that the quantity of silk doesn't go down.'

Somen asked another question, 'What are the major obstacles in producing good silk?'

'So many, Sir. For example, the chrysalis shouldn't break out of the cocoon to emerge as a butterfly. In such cases, they should be picked up earlier. Damaged cocoons yield inferior variety of silk.'

'Do they have any other use?'

'Coarse variety of winter cover, *kantia*, is made out of it.'

Somen stopped asking further questions. He raced through some registers and documents. Saxena could dispel so many doubts from his mind, but for how long could he make the other employees wait for him? He popped out of the cubicle and proceeded towards his office room. Saxena accompanied Somen to the main block.

'Saxena, do you find the job interesting?'

'It is tough. One has to face a lot of hurdles. There is hardly any time left for relaxation, Sir.'

'Are you married?'

'Yes Sir... Two kids also. One is a son and the other a daughter. The elder one is in standard three. The younger is just a beginner.'

'Did you find any language problem here?'

'Both are picking up Kannada. But in our house we talk in Hindi only.'

The Junior Technician and Personal Assistant following closely behind watched the two deeply engrossed in conversation. The classless fraternity of their new boss diminished their enthusiasm. Would this be the end of administration, then?

Somen entered his room, but just then a couple of young officers came in. In fact, the company had engaged them to be of some assistance to the new executive but...

They were shirkers and didn't want to be dictated by a young probationer like him. Their prime concern was to run away from any command. Somen smelled their attitude but couldn't reason with their motive. Asking them to sit down, he merely glanced at their faces. They looked proud and egotistical.

Why did they exhibit their disdain for him? Why were they judging him? Why, then, had they come to sit before him? Somen thought again and again.

'Sir, may we go now,' said one of them to Somen.

Somen noticed that Saxena and the two didn't interact. Had they met earlier today? They didn't even look at one another. It was as if one had a grudge against the other.

From there Saxena returned to his office after offering due regard to Somen. Soon after, the two officers railed against Saxena branding him a union leader. 'He condemns us saying we are agents of the management,' said one of them

'But he is sincere in his duties,' replied Somen.

'Maybe, but he is too junior to offer you a cup of tea, Sir.'

Somen turned on the two with an air of calmness. Gravity was writ large on his face. Although severely dissatisfied, he didn't like to reveal his true spirit. He restrained himself and asked the duo to wait outside.

The day appeared colourless before Somen. He took no pleasure in looking for warmth in the faces of his colleagues. Like broken hairpins they carried sharpness with them. There was envy 'in every heart and jealousy in every eye'. Within a fraction of a second a wall would fall like a screen in a theatre partitioning two hearts. Would the feet and hands of his conscience go the same way with a chain around them?

It was time for lunch. Somen came out of his chamber on his way to the guest house. As usual, he maintained his calmness. But the rebel in him got provoked. Looking at the two waiting outside, he went closer to them. On hearing him, the two looked awkward. They didn't expect such a pro-worker attitude from a fresh company executive. Somen said, 'Look! I propose to update communication templates to remove such suspicions from our mindset. The company's own Twitter-Instagram would allow all of us to exchange our views and thoughts in more detail.'

Somen walked towards the guest house. The two didn't even say goodbye. Somen failed to understand whether they were traditionally unsolicitous or not.

While passing by the cosy bungalows and green lawns, Somen tried to compare his birthplace with Bangalore. There was a glaring mismatch between the two.

Somen was steeped in introspection. Was he born to buckle under the scurrying dark clouds of the corporate sky? What about his valued freedom? The stormy thoughts blew through his mind from all directions. Could he retrive his state of mind?

Somen told himself, 'My dear revolutionary, how cunningly you have embraced the establishment.' Was he fleeing away from the war zone? He didn't like to think about his jobless days. 'No further grieving.' No, he couldn't forget the trauma that he had experienced during those struggling years.

'I exist,' his conscience flashed once again. 'Yes, of course! I need to exist, at whatever cost it might be.'

There would be no chance to be misled in any manner. It was certain; he wouldn't join any losing war in life. Come what may! He fixed himself on the shoulder of KSF with a secured arm round its neck.

'Sir, I am waiting for you,' a voice came from a little distance. It was Gopal, the khansama. Somen gave a little smile and moved towards the dining hall.

He washed his hands and took a seat there. He looked at the quick-eyed boy putting plates and dishes with great efficiency. Although neither mother nor sister were nearby, Somen could feel the delicacies of cooked items, of course with their south Indian flavours. He spoke to himself, 'The economic pot is always on the boil. What cooks is value.' The dynamics of the workforce recognizes neither the cooking style of a mother nor the loving service of a sister standing face to face with her brother. The boy's hand lifted the ladle time and again perhaps not to undermine a paid professional hand, which, at times, might jump to the level of intimacy.

69

THE JOB OF a company executive brought both prestige and wealth for Somen to navigate his way smoothly across the mundane sea. Now, the family budget turned surplus, making for cosy comfortable living. Gradually the pressure of the job clipped his free wings. He hardly found any time for leisure. After office hours, he was mostly confined to the guest house, watching TV and reading newspapers and sitting before the company's laptop. Once in a while, he had to call on his senior colleagues in the evening. Very often his colleagues asked him sharp questions like. 'Did you meet the ED?', 'Do you know the choice of his brand, quantum of pegs, etc.?' Somen had little interest in such stereotype conversations with his staff members. Their spouses mostly repeated conventional phrases like, 'Do you have any idea of the colour choice of the sari of the MD's wife?' 'Do you know her favourite TV serial?', 'Do you know her preferred goddess?' It seemed such playing and replaying of records was only to ensure that their husbands remained in the MD's good book. Whenever Somen visited anyone's residence, the housewife would display her purchases from big bazaars or exhibitions. The talk would concentrate on each one's shopping ability like how she found the last piece and what a shocking design, etc.

Then it would be the turn for snacks. Once again, there would be the same boastful look on her face and the expectation of praise for the types of pickles prepared by her. 'How is the taste?' Thereafter, photo albums would be produced and he would be shown pictures of her children winning prizes. Somen had to bear with all this. He smiled at their routine, stereotype lives and interests. Their environment was limited and they saw no need to cross anyone, leave alone the wives of neighbours and colleagues. If the child were at home he/she would be asked to sing or play a tune on his/her musical instrument. As a visitor Somen had to listen to everything. Apart from blowing one's own trumpet, the talks concentrated on known and unknown personalities. It made no difference to Somen.

It so happened, on any courtesy call, the other one preferred to talk about himself and his family only. There was little or no interest to know about the guest or his background. At times, the gossip went sharply against any union activities. Such collective condemnation was everywhere and their leaders were laughed at. It seemed that this whispering was a by-product of the privileged class. It was sheer foolishness to open one's heart before such fence sitters and Somen knew that their rank opportunism would lead him nowhere.

The hyperactive campus besides including the factory had roads, apartments, a club, auditorium, gym, playground and other such facilities. Despite the magnificence of its set-up, the atmosphere heavy with suspicion, distrust and mutual jealousies among the divided groups of employees debilitated him.

KSF on its way to modernization wanted to raise its production capacity greatly. The MD engaged Somen to make this happen. Although a fresher, Somen had the requisite zeal and drive for hard work. He came up like a big player but decided to play cautiously. He consulted experts in the line, particularly several marketing groups, to prepare a project report on this. Some specialists who hadn't been consulted huddled in corners voicing their criticism. But Somen didn't allow their whispers to distract him and remained steadfast in his approach. It was such a hard task! Within the four walls of his chamber, Somen busied himself without allowing his energy to fritter away. Sniffing at every minute detail, he went through the balance sheet of yesteryears. Searching old files from different racks and jotting down notes from them took much of his time. His work engrossed him so much that it invaded even the late hours of the night.

Reports were prepared for both short- and medium-term loans. Prior to this, it was to establish before the financing institutions KSF's non-defaulting status, sufficient profit margins, declaration of dividends on equity shares, etc., catering to the Company's Act. The employees meanwhile staged a silent protest for an increase in the bonus equivalent to their salary for three months. The management after hectic parleys with union office bearers only agreed for one month. The employees didn't withdraw their demand so easily. 'What a protest,' shouted one of the union leaders in excitement. 'See! They don't have any sympathy for our cause. They only know how to lead a life of luxury. Making frequent trips outside, staying in five-star hotels, enjoying cocktail parties at company's cost whereas we rot here.' Other workers joined in perhaps to teach the whole establishment a lesson. Saxena could be seen in the front clenching his fists in fury. Bitterly disappointed, the officers including Somen looked at the angry protesters.

The management succumbed to the pressure tactics of the protest march. It sanctioned two months' salary in the form of bonus. The strike ended and both the groups heaved a sigh of relief. One from the melting crowd spoke loudly, 'We'll refashion life on Earth.' Now experts from several fields came forward to tackle the project report. Endowed with team vigour, they wanted to make the report flawless. Each person from stenos to the statistical assistants and accounting staff got on with the task diligently. Somen took the lead and announced a special package for each enthusiast.

A group of specialists, executives including chartered accountants, gave the best of their minds and settled down to the responsibility of preparing the PR. The modalities detailing the acquisition of capital goods, both indigenous and imported, along with the addresses of foreign suppliers were shown on it. The whole process needed strong competence and Somen's determined zeal was a motivating factor. He along with his core group carried out this heavy task clinging firmly to their respective chairs. Somen picked further hard-working staff for this time-bound project. He had been alert ever since he was asked to supervise the project. This team exercise could ultimately yield spectacular results. One of the lady typists was driven to protest. 'Hopeless! Would you kill us!' Somen at first contemplated imposing a minor penalty on her for such insubordination but controlled himself somehow. He diverted some of her burden to the other table. 'See, Sir! My workload,' the programmer shouted in a high pitch. 'All right, do this only, I believe in your capacity,' said Somen cajolingly. Such complaints were common but he tried to neutralize them with humour.

'One clip,' a junior asked a bald-headed senior.

'How dare you ask me for a clip!'

'Sorry! Please don't mind,' said the young assistant, suddenly contrite. Somen smilingly went to the old assistant and took a clip from his table and handed it over to the young one. Everyone smiled.

'Here is something for all of you,' Somen told his team. One of the bearers swiftly put a packet of food on each table.

'Please finish eating,' Somen told everyone with heavy eyes. 'Our bosses will be shown how we have laboured for the PR.' Saying this he returned to his office chamber.

After all the hard labour the project report was finally ready. After handing it for printing and binding, Somen heaved a sigh of relief. He thanked everyone needed for the purpose.

The PR was to be tabled before the meeting of the board of Directors for their scrutiny and approval.

'Who has prepared this report? It is excellent. Must have taken enough time and energy,' commented one of the directors. Both the MD and GM gave a detailed personality account about Somen before the Board. That was certainly not on the agenda. Like 'jealousy, thy name is colleague' the young group envied Somen as they were not interested in hearing the top bosses praise him. They were certain that a greenhorn like Somen would get a lucrative raise bypassing them all. Somen could smell the bitterness of their talks. He had not received any cooperation from these gossip-mongers but that didn't mean that they should appreciate what he had done. Why should he refuse when the company wanted to utilize his brains for its own growth? The MD with an aim to praise Somen, made a rare visit to the junior's chamber.

'Somenji.'

'Yes Sir.' Somen stood up at once.

'The PR is excellent. Everyone in the Board has appreciated it.'

'Thank you, Sir.'

'Here is a little gift from the company to you.' Saying so, the MD kept a wad of currency notes on the table. Somen couldn't decline such an offer. 'But you have to liaison for the sanction of a loan for KSF with the office of the Industrial Development Corporation,' the MD said in a slightly overbearing tone.

'Excuse me Sir! I am ready to do anything assigned by you and for the cause of KSF but...'

'What is your problem then?'

'To my little mind, Sir, such liasing should be done by experienced seniors.'

'Why are you hesitant, Somenji? The Board has enough confidence in you for carrying out the job. Everything would be fine.' Saying so, the MD got up and extended his hand to Somen with a smile. 'Good luck,' he uttered and Somen politely replied, 'Thank you, Sir.'

Somen came out of his room. While he was going down the stairs, he met a couple of trade unionists. One of them quipped, 'Will you lead KSF superseding all seniors?'

Somen looked at them gravely, nonplussed at such an insulting remark. 'Somen can't be persuaded by anyone on earth other than his own conscience,' he thought and excused himself.

At once, his team members rushed to him to know what the MD had said. They enthusiastically congratulated Somen, after all who made it possible? Somen!

Somen gave a brief account of the talk between the MD and him. It excited the whole lot. He then handed over the packet to one of the guys. He opened it and saw a bundle of notes. Somen wanted to arrange a party for everyone with it. But a few opposed the proposal.

'It is a gift exclusively for you.'

'So what?'

'No, we shouldn't spend it.'

'Why? You have every right to this,' said Somen.

He was determined not to take a single rupee for himself from the gift packet. Looking at his firm face, nobody argued further.

Somen leaned back in his chair and looked at files. He then collected all the relevant papers, the office laptop, the PR and headed for his mission. A slight look of perplexity crossed his face. A sense of seriousness dwelt upon his mind whipping his conscience repeatedly. How could a committed comrade succumb to the allures of KSF?

Now Somen had to become extra cautious to pursue the interests of KSF. As a result, his erstwhile struggle to fight against social injustice became a thing of the past.

Although Somen couldn't say 'no' to his boss, his staff didn't want him to be labelled by the authorities as a yes man. They yelled at him to flatly refuse such a command.

'But why,' Somen retorted. He had to share his thoughts with his colleagues to know the reason behind their unwillingness.

'This is because nothing moves in the Industrial Development Corporation without greasing somebody's palm. The occupant of every chair sits like a devil. Anyone coming in meets their greedy eyes. Generally the chaprasi doesn't grant entry to anyone without his fixed quota. Similarly the liftman stands with a begging palm before any visitor known or unknown. The atmosphere looks irremediable,' said one of the staff members.

Somen knew there had been a sinister design behind choosing him. He had been chosen by some mid-rank officer, who had deliberately entrusted him with this heavy task of loan processing in an alien environment over which he had no control. But nothing could bring him down. But Somen had to go for a meeting with the MD to reiterate his stand on this.

'I am afraid, Sir, I can't shoulder such a task,' said Somen quietly.

'Why? What for?' the MD looked like he was speaking purely from a bureaucratic angle.

'I have yet to gain the expertise to convince senior officials,' he replied softly.

'Don't judge yourself like that. Leave it to be decided by us.'

The MD urged him to go ahead with the assigned task. He spoke assertively. 'As a young executive, you have miles to go and this experience will help you.'

Somen stood unmoved like an electric post. He looked at the MD discouragingly. Then all of a sudden, he turned and left his office without bothering whether the MD wanted him to leave or not. He swiftly crossed the VIP corridor lest any further arrows be hurled at him in the form of advice.

70

THE TOGETHERNESS IN Roy Babu's family had come to a sudden halt. Minati's betrothal and now Somen's engagement to Arati meant that the Roy family would soon start preparing for the marriages.

It was a time of jubilation for all of them, something they hadn't experienced before. and Mrs Roy were filled with joy at the idea of spending days in Bangalore city with their son.

Roy Babu had not availed of his leave travel concession earlier but now wanted to do so. They wished to visit Bangalore before the celebrations. and Mrs Roy with Minati reached the city by train. Somen was at the platform to receive them. The very appearance of Somen came like a feast for the greedy eyes of his mummy. Her heart was filled with great happiness. 'Hey Mummy, how come you got down here at Bangalore station?' Somen said to his mother just for fun. Mrs Roy merely smiled.

He took them all in the staff car and reached his allotted flat. After settling their luggage Minati and her mummy entered the kitchen. It was in complete disorder! The saucepan with dregs of tea dust was dumped in the basin. The soap powder was there in a red pot but without a cotton rag. The pressure cooker and frying pan hadn't been washed for a long time. Immediately they gave the utensils a thorough cleaning to make them retrieve their earlier shine. It was a real hassle to clean the floor. Although the kitchen was airy and received sunlight, they seemed to be locked up somewhere.

In the bedroom, the bedsheet and pillowcases were creased and dirty. Minati whisked away all the untidy covers and replaced them with clean ones.

Mrs Roy, although tired, wanted to prepare all her son's favourite dishes. Minati went to her assistance. Their faces glowed with undying love as they went about the preparation. With gutka in his hand Roy Babu looked cheerful while he leafed through a Bengali newspaper.

'Somen,' he shouted uneasily. 'Babu, where am I to spit?'

'In the basin, Baba,' Somen replied.

But Roy didn't want to in case it left a stain, but Somen told him not to worry. When a news item flashed on the TV, he sat closer to the set and looked at the screen intently. He couldn't keep quiet and insisted upon relaying the news to anyone sitting nearby.

Mrs Roy had been accustomed to a traditional life pattern and her cooking was typically Bengali. Accordingly, she poured hot spices but less of chilli powder in the curry. Somen had purchased the vegetables the family liked from the local market and these were stored in the fridge. Mrs Roy stood beside the window quietly enjoying the cool air and wiped the beads of sweat from her body. The surroundings were in sharp contrast to her place. Apartments rose skyward and little children came out smiling unlike the dull and dry faces in Beethalgarh. Mrs Roy imagined for a while her own grandchild, who one day she would clasp to her breast.

71

THE INDUSTRIAL DEVELOPMENT Corporation was the premier organization in Karnataka that provided loans to outfits that required them. Although not his choice, Somen entered its campus in his staff car looking like a tormented soul. From beginning to end, Somen had to dance to its tune through various means of indirect bargaining. There, the officers made him the scapegoat, breaking his neck with various objections. Like playing the same CD over and over again, their diktats became monotonous. It seemed as if IDC was holding the reins of KSF between its teeth and taking it for a ride. Somen narrated all these facts to his dad who had encouraged him to shoulder all burdens of the company.

'It is your probation period, take everything as a challenge,' said his daddy.

'But, Dad, this bargaining is awful. It holds me down,' Somen told his father.

There was absolutely no respite from this Herculean task. However, his father's advice acted like an instant relief on his pain-wrecked body. Earlier, there was no one to look after his tired body. Now, the presence of his family members brought him strength. Any shout from disgruntled employees could be put aside easily due to the moral support from his family members. They had enclosed him within a protective boundary.

He leaned back on the company's strength calling upon services from hired hands. While walking along the pathways and lawns of the KSF campus, Somen planned out new methods to get the company's work done with IDC.

Roy Babu had some cash in hand from his provident fund. He withdrew the same as non-refundable. He enjoyed such an entitlement because his service had spanned a period of more than two decades. In the evening, they all decided to go shopping for the forthcoming weddings. Ready-made garments, saris in bulk, LCD TV, fridge, clothes for the groom and suchlike were listed in order of priority. Before they left their residence, Somen requested them all to be cautious while dealing with the shopkeepers. 'There should be no bargaining unless you are too sure of the purchase,' Somen repeated.

Soon, they arrived in the city and entered a shop. Mrs Roy looked all around—it was the biggest showroom she had ever come across in her life. Somen realized that the use of a mirrored wall made the carpet area appear much larger. It was in a way to hoodwink a customer into presuming the shop was a superior one. Mrs Roy while moving across the shop dashed against the glass inadvertently. Roy Babu looked frowningly at her saying, 'You should not have gone so near that!' Minati and Somen and one of the salesmen came to her rescue immediately. At once Mrs Roy decided not to venture near the glass.

Mrs Roy relapsed into her usual way of bargaining much to the chagrin of her family members. 'Hey Mummy, don't talk like that. They are not the hawkers of Beethalgarh,' Minati whispered to her mother but Somen was not at all downhearted. He took his mother's ways jovially. He was proud to see his parents and sister in an AC complex in the garden city, away from the withered kitchen of Beethalgarh! No more like a bronze statue with a ladle in hand to take care of the growing hunger of a family.

Roy Babu looked at something in the showcase. They were silver toe-rings. Mrs Roy and Somen ran to him to know what it was. 'Toe-rings,' said Mrs Roy. It was like a *mangalsutra*, and mostly sought after in a marriage. She said, 'Let us find out its price then.' Soon the salesman came and tapped his finger on the price tag.

'Oh! No...so costly,' shouted Mrs Roy.

'Oh! Mummy... please,' Minati implored.

Mrs Roy persisted in her attempt to reduce the price. She repeated her urge. The shopkeeper said in a flat voice, 'No bargaining please!'

It was embarrassing to bargain in such a big shop in a metro. Everyone including Mrs Roy looked helpless She kept trying to convince the salesman in chaste Bengali that such an item was necessary in a marriage. The salesman only nodded with a smile without responding to her request. He could well imagine her rusticity. Mrs Roy looked at her husband. It was to be finalized somehow. Roy Babu talked maturely. 'Is there scope to bring down the price?'

'Mummy, here the rates are fixed', Somen said quietly to his mother. Mrs Roy glanced up at Minati. She confirmed the rate. Mrs Roy now had no other plea to avoid the deal. The purchasing mood ran ahead of all other considerations. Very cautiously, she crept off to a corner to avoid public view and brought out her money purse from the waist. A bundle of currency notes was stored within. She handed Minati the purse to count the exact amount. But the well-dressed salesman insisted that payment must be made at the counter only.

On the way home, Roy Babu brought up the subject of their return to Beethalgarh. At once Somen turned hostile to the idea. He burst out: 'Dad, what is so fascinating there right now? Send a medical certificate to your authority. No question of going back so soon!'

The Roy couple knew that Somen would not let them leave so soon. But several problems swept through their thoughts. Who would water the plants, they must have dried. Feeding and raising the calf, that is another headache. The person in charge of watching the house would soon leave for his village. Roy Babu didn't want to reveal such worries to his son.

Once they reached home, Somen had to take the help of the driver and some others to unload the packages from the car.

Mrs Roy came and stood nearby watching the persons carrying the goods into their residence. She looked at them sympathetically.

Soon she came out with platefuls of snacks for all. Minati too brought tea and glasses of water. Somen had no objection to the driver and his helpers occupying cushions in the drawing room and drinking tea with him. 'Thanks', he told them at last.

'How to part with Mummy and Daddy so soon and embrace loneliness once again after long office hours,' Somen brooded. The enjoyable mocking between Maa and Baba would come to a halt. Because of Mummy there were pleasant Bengali dishes. Life had passed smoothly. Once his parents and Minati left, life would become lonely again.

A week rolled by. Mrs Roy's heart began to beat faster. She knew she had to leave her son soon. How could she reveal the intensity of her mind? Her bloodshot eyes became the index of her suppressed feelings. Sorrow glowed uninterruptedly defying all outward happiness.

On the eve of their departure, Mrs Roy and Minati prepared some snacks that could be stored. Somen opposed it saying who was there to eat them.

'Don't you know, *beta*, outside food is not good for your health,' Mrs Roy told her son.

Observing his mother's spirit he didn't object further. Both mother and daughter were busy chopping vegetables and frying them in hot oil. Somen watched them with minute attention, helping them by bringing the pepper, cumin, coriander, etc. from the cupboard.

Despite the heat of the kitchen, they were completely occupied in their task. Roy Babu entered the kitchen to see what was happening but made a quick exit unable to relish the heat. However, the aroma of spring rolls, hot *gaja* and tomato chutney made everyone's mouths water. They would keep Somen happy for a few days.

Finally the three had to leave Bangalore for Chennai in a night-bound express. The staff car took them to the station. Mrs Roy appeared a little upset. Somen accompanied his parents to the platform. In between he opened up himself.

'Maa! You don't feel happy, it seems!'

'No Babu! I am just thinking about you. I will be relieved once my daughter-in-law comes to shoulder your responsibility.' Somen gave his mummy a little smile. All of her emotions were aimed at pushing Somen into marriage.

The train started leaving the station slowly. The parting was difficult for all of them.

Mrs Roy's thoughts speeded with the speeding train as if in a parallel spirit. The face of her son dazzled in her mind, with no scope of deserting her at all. Why had she left Bangalore?

Somen managed to get down from the running train that was gradually gaining speed. Mrs Roy nervously watched her son elbowing others frantically to step on to the platform. She looked scared and couldn't utter anything other than to shout in panic: 'Babu...Babu.' Roy Babu peeped through the window trying to keep Somen in sight. 'Yes', shouted Roy Babu at his wife. 'I can clearly see him. Now take your seat comfortably. I will look after the luggage.'

'Well, let us go back to office,' Somen told the driver. He peeped out of the window uninterested in what he was seeing. Perhaps he could find something of interest in Bangalore in the absence of his family members.

Silence once more! Could Somen wriggle himself out from the KSF net pitch? Was there any escape route leading to any hidden corner? It appeared as if the whole earth was nothing but a cage! And he of course was the fluttering bird inside.

72

FINALLY THE TIME arrived for the dazzling marriages of both Somen and his sister Minati. The walls, both inside and outside of Roy Babu's residence, were painted white. The doors and windows had also been freshly painted. Ladies from the neighbourhood had drawn different motifs on the walls including wheels and banana plants. It was a sure sign of closeness with the family. As a part of the marriage ritual, iron ladles were dipped into coloured water and then stuck on walls, a country ritual in Odisha. These mute motifs looked as if they telling everyone about the forthcoming event.

Somen had taken leave for two weeks for this momentous occasion. Two young executives and a junior typist travelled all the way from Bangalore to Beethalgarh as representatives from KSF. Somen and his parents showered extraordinary care on them.

The guests' south Indian accent made the children outside curious. The guests listened to their exclamations attentively. It was a way to bridge the gap between the native and exotic cultures, the differences between the east and the south. Out of wonder, ladies and children peeped through the curtains of their homes to watch the guests. Their style of taking food and eating behaviour was totally in contrast with the local manner. Looking at them, the children couldn't suppress their laughter. The elders got annoyed with their kids. It so happened that their quirky sense of conversation was mimicked more in a clownish spirit. It was unsavoury, Somen thought, like reaching the bitter end of a civilization. Rubbish! He got ruffled and shouted rudely, 'Get out from here!' Instantly two or three of his friends chased the loin-clothed children away.

Soon after the lunch hour, they got ready to receive the *baraat* party from Kolkata.

Around a hundred persons, including women and children, alighted from the Howrah-Chennai Express as members of the group. The host contingent was there both at the station and guest houses to receive them. Most of them were from Kolkata city and thus walked around with an air of subtle superiority. A fleet of vehicles waited outside the platform to pick them up. Young boys with Somen and Pradeep as their leaders rushed up to transport them to the guest house. The groom, his father, uncle and the priest were taken in a luxury car to the nearby Hotel Bholaram where two AC rooms had been reserved for them.

Roy Babu noticed the sincerity with which his son's friends made an effort to combat all constraints. The aggressiveness of the *baraat* group had to be tolerated by the bride's side. The guests appeared too fastidious. Their persistent cravings for odd items made many of them tense. Despite the elaborate preparations, some shouted, let loose abuses at the organizers: 'Hell with such food. You should have specialized items like fish.' The hosts had no option but to digest such unpalatable demands calmly. They had to wait for the auspicious moment of *hastabandhan* after which the tying of hands would be strengthened for good.

The *baraat* party found Beethalgarh too uninspiring. Here, everything big or small looked dusty and rickety. Dust was everywhere, on the windowsills, rooftops, leaves and branches of the trees and streets. Even the stray animals looked dusty. Malia walked around with a kettle and some paper cups to serve tea.

Someone from the *baraat* team shouted:

'What is that?'

'Tea ... Sir.'

'Looks so dirty.'

'Hi...hi... Hi...'

'Oh! Why so little milk? Have the cows died or do we have to teach our children that the colour of tea is black...not brown,' blurted another. Somen heard such piercing comments and wanted to pay them back in the same coin. But everyone present there told him to suppress his fury as it would harm his own sister. But such sharp words stabbed the heart! How were the preparations to go in a better way than this? What made them downplay someone's labour so harshly? Why? Despite their tension, the Roy family and their close associates handled the guests with ample patience and good humour.

Even though pressed with sterner responsibilities, Somen found time to ponder over the situation. What kind of social system was this that didn't give due weightage to the bride's family? Was it their prerogative to throw themselves like bombs to splinter the bride's party? Why did one inherit a system where the bride's camp had to suffer the ignominy of a low price before the increasing value of its counterpart?

But it would be rude to raise a voice against the *baraat* members in case it would have an adverse effect on Minati's wedded life. Malia like a good comrade went to the kitchen to supervise the making of tea. He personally measured out larger proportions of milk, sugar and standard tea dust to give the brew a good taste. He sat attentively near the burning chullah and left nothing to chance.

With kettles in both hands, Malia rushed out of the kitchen to serve hot tea to the *baraat* party.

'Oh! Fine,' said someone smilingly to Malia.

Malia made a positive response and said politely, 'So Sir, now the children can be taught that the colour of tea is white.'

Everyone laughed and the tension in the air suddenly vanished. 'Such a witty reply!' a guest said. There was a sudden respite from their angry rigidness. 'What an innocent entertainer!' commented another.

The Kolkatans felt let down and in a sense out of tune with the surroundings. Every spot was like sitting upon a chair of dust. The heaps of garbage lying around sickened them. Above all was the stench, not only of rotting waste but also from the public toilets. They carried a poor opinion of this small town.

A small hill, standing on the outskirts of the town, draped in a green veil attracted many *baraat* members and they were eager to climb it. But many from the locality dissuaded these strangers from doing so. Why? 'No one goes there after the evening falls,' replied someone.

'But why?'

'A phantom lives there,' he added.

'But how can he stay without a house? Does he stand on the sloping hill?' a teenager from the *baraat* group queried.

'I can't say for certain,' said the same one. He was embarrassed and didn't know what explanation to give. He didn't want to sound ignorant before a city dweller.

The zeal to climb the hill stimulated the teenagers. The elders too felt the same thrill. The fragrance from unknown herbs made them wild. What would be the contrast between the ground and the top? In spite of a word of warning, they started their ascent. Hearing their footsteps, the unseen birds flew off in several directions. The countless blooms of nameless flowers from variegated bushes brought the scent of freshness to their urban nostrils.

'It's so peaceful up here,' exclaimed a climber.

Just then, some dragonflies made an abrupt escape into the air. This made the children fidgety. As they climbed higher, every step became difficult. The small kids began to complain and the elders felt they could not advance further. How to return? 'Do you need any assistance?' a villager shouted from below. Finding him a stranger, no one responded. Just then Malia and his group passed by on their cycles. They saw the stranded climbers and went up to them. They caught hold of the children and helped them go up the hill. They were familiar with every step of the route and their presence was a support to the climbers. As they ascended, the sky began to darken as evening set in. The orange glow of the setting sun stirred the mind of every onlooker. Doves cooed and birds flapped their wings. The beauties of nature enchanted the city dwellers. 'Let's carry sufficient *amla* fruits, it is dearer in Kolkata,' said someone. 'Sure, I have never seen so many of them before. Let us carry as much as we like.' It was getting late. Malia gazed at the distant sky and discovered one or two stars appearing slowly overhead. It was time to leave but the group's excitement had yet to wane. Malia had to find a way to convince them to return. Finally he used the threat of monkeys and their bite to frighten them. It acted wonderfully. Everyone including the elders wanted to descend immediately. They made their way down with utmost care, supporting each other across the rocky path. When they reached the bottom, their other party members, who had been watching their ascent, greeted them joyfully as if they had just scaled Mount Everest. They all laughed and thanked Malia profusely for their safe return.

A Bengali gentleman picked up his son saying, 'Oh! Avinash … my dear…'

'Dad!'

'Must be feeling like Tenzing Norgay. Isn't it?'

'Dad! Climbing up a hill is so exciting!!'

'And Malia uncle?'

'Oh Dad, he is so nice really. We must take him to Kolkata,' said a child endearingly.

'Of course,' joined another from the party.

Just then, the moment of benediction arrived and people began to gather near the altar. Immediately the relatives particularly the ladies rushed to witness this fascinating sight. They sought their male counterparts and collected the usual gifts both in cash and kind to offer the new couple at the peak moment of *hastabandhan*. The blowing of conch shells rent the air. Knots were tied between the ends of the dhoti and the sari and the pair circled around the holy fire. They offered flowers, sacred rice and ghee into the burning wood to satisfy all the the *navagrahas*. The *baraat* group was in a hurry to witness the last scene at the altar. The cameramen and videographers from both sides took up their strategic stand to record the whole event from different angles. Suddenly the MP3 played an old film song, 'Babul pyare', that perfectly matched the parting moment. The priests chanted mantras loudly perhaps to appease the devtas. The rituals finally came to an end, and the time of separation drew nearer. Tears started orbiting around the eyes of both mother and daughter. Somen and his father felt their hearts grow heavier. Minati, wearing a costly Banarasi sari and bedecked with gold jewellery and fragrant flowers, looked like a lovely queen. A well-decorated car waited outside. The party had to reach the railway station for boarding the Kolkata-bound night express. It was as if the night had woken up to give Minati a hearty send-off. Plants in the courtyard, as if with tears in their serene eyes, recollected the sweet memories of her watering them with her delicate hands. The priests recited scriptures like *Yatha Ravanasya Mandodhari, Yatha Ramasya Sitah…* and sprinkled fragrant rice over the couple's heads showering blessings on them. A clay figurine set on a pedestal kept near the holy fire was an icon of the ancestors. The priest told the pair to fold their hands before it to seek blessings from the deceased. Both were asked to name their lineage for ancestor worship and bow in homage to their forefathers. Ladies stood at the entrance holding lamps in their hands. The *purnakumbha* was placed at the auspicious point. After the *kanyadaan*, each person's sentiment rose to the peak. Tears streamed down the cheeks of several ladies. Roy Babu clasped his daughter in a deep embrace and cried out, 'Maa! May you have your own world.' He was too grief-stricken to say more; the pain of the *bidai* was difficult to cope with. Mrs Roy broke down but somehow clutched her daughter's arm to speak tearfully, 'Maa, how nice… how lucky you are to have your new home.' Saying so, she moved her fingers over her daughter's face to wipe away her tears.

Minati's friends started falling back slowly. The parting moment had brought anguish to everyone's hearts.

Pradeep, Malia and Somen supervised the luggage.

One of the elders intervened. 'Let us carry all the luggage to the platform immediately.' The couple bowed before all seniors, seeking their final blessings, and entered the car. It then proceeded slowly towards the railway station.

Before leaving for the platform, Sengupta hugged his *samudi* and said, 'Okay, Roy Babu, I would naturally expect both of you at our residence in Kolkata at any time. Now it is your daughter's house. I needn't have to tell you this.' Roy Babu tried to say something in reply, but he was too emotional about parting from his dearest daughter. However, he folded his hands at Sengupta saying inaudibly, '*Samudi!* Please forgive me for any lapses in the arrangement.' 'Oh, *samudi*, what is this thought? Everything went off fine. All credit goes to you,' said Sengupta wholeheartedly. Others silently listened to their mutually cordial views.

The *baraat* members reached the station in other vehicles. The express train arrived on time. Although Somen was to accompany his sister to Kolkata as part of the marriage ritual, he couldn't because his marriage was to take place the next day. Hence a cousin of Somen was chosen for the task.

73

THE DAY OF Somen's marriage arrived and the house began to sparkle with happiness. The festive spirit that had closed its heart due to the absence of Minati returned. Minati's marriage and Somen's job were a great source of relief for the Roy family. Their previous burdens, anxieties and frustrations could no longer show their ugly teeth. The unprivileged rural community who yearned for Somen's help no longer had easy access to their house. What had haunted his mind for several years could no more stir his heart. Now that he had a company job, he would not have the time or opportunity to indulge in his craze for social service.

Roy Babu shouted at his wife while pulling out a number of carry bags hanging on the wall. He was in a hurry to get to the market before the other customers to purchase large quantities of vegetables and bring them back in an autorickshaw. The family had to make adequate arrangements for a number of guests for both lunch and dinner.

'Where is the list?' Roy Babu yelled at his wife, trying to assert his authority.

'Why do you ask me the same question again and again? If you can't remember a few items like potatoes, tomatoes, brinjal, cauliflower and cabbage, then what can I do?' Mrs Roy retorted.

'See...I have to get ready for the auspicious time when the conventional ritual like the *mangala* begins. Babu has bathed already,' added Mrs Roy. Without waiting for anyone Roy Babu left for the weekly market.

Soon after the *mangala*, Somen had put on his bridegroom's attire. No problems like Minati's marriage or his own job were there to deter him, so naturally there was jubilation in his heart. The rhythm of life was harmonious! In the courtyard of the Roy house, a silk appliqué hanging gave the space a festive look. Somen had to wait for the ladies to finish applying collyrium in his eyes. A mark of vermilion and sandalwood paste had been applied on his forehead. He was dressed in a sherwani and churidars and a turban was wrapped tightly around his head. The ladies worshipped 'the sacred lamp' and sprinkled scented rice on the bridegroom. Then, holding a coconut and fresh lotus in his hands, Somen proceeded to the nearby temple to offer prayers. Just then, the band party started playing the *mangala-badya*, and the priest spread a mat before the goddess asking Somen to sit on it. He bowed down before the deity seeking her blessings.

After the purchase of essential vegetables and a few other items, Roy Babu hurried home as the *baraat* time was approaching. At the same time he didn't forget to purchase the essential perfume spray to sprinkle on the *baraat* party. Somen had reminded his daddy that the *baraat* members were arriving. Soon they all swelled to about two hundred. Das, Pasayat and Mohanty all came in a group to join the *baraat*. The SC initially didn't want to take part but subsequently changed his mind. He didn't forget to send congratulatory messages from the Collector and Additional Collector of Samastipur to Somen as a token of courtesy and rushed to join the *baraat*.

The officers and the public had forgotten the conflict and strife that had existed between them in the past. For the first time on this festive occasion they came together to embrace each other. The cooing of doves and the voice of the falcon were heard from the same branch of the tree. A tumultuous welcome was extended to all by the Roy family. Such a get-together was marked by pleasure on every face. The *baraat* members were filled with cheer. Somen made a handsome bridegroom. He had returned from the temple with the spirit of a devoutly religious young man. Before the start of the wedding procession, Mrs Roy brought out her necklace to garland her son and pushed a ring on to his middle finger. Then the procession started in time led by the director of the band party. The light carriers fell in to line, among old ladies and small children. Somen was in the car with the priest and other elders of their family. Although the destination was not far off, the procession moved in a roundabout way so that the *aam aadmi* could enjoy the show. The onlookers, especially the women and children from different houses, kept their eyes glued on Somen. As the night deepened, the crackers burst across the vast sky. The officers were drawn to the front, joined in a group, and took the lead guiding the whole show. Once, the *baraat* came into sight, Sen, Mrs Sen and their near and dear ones came out to the front of their houses to welcome the groom's party. The youngsters from both sides got to their feet and began to dance exuberantly. Sparklers and fireworks lit the air. Even though they were nearing their destination, the younger generation didn't want to stop dancing. In fact, a group of enthusiasts made everyone including the bridegroom move slowly. However, looking at the target drawing nearer, the pulse energy of the majority, including the drummers, moved at high velocity. With so many people from several directions, the procession began to swell while approaching the front gate of the Sen family. The crowds were great and it was difficult for the members to stand freely as the space appeared inadequate. Leave alone the cavalcade of the *baraat* members, the bridegroom's vehicle found no way to reach the entry point of the main gate of Sen's house.

But Somen managed to descend from the car and received a tumultuous welcome from the female members of Sen's family. Mrs Sen applied a mark of vermilion on his forehead and stuffed a betel nut into his mouth. Then Sen, although elderly, washed his feet in keeping with the ritual and led him to the altar. Somen looked at his leather sandals that played hide-and-seek with the scarlet border of *alta* on both his feet. He was ashamed of himself but had no words to utter. So many cameras clicked from several directions. The variety of fireworks caught the eyes while moving across the distant sky. They wrapped around the body of the night like a dazzling shawl.

The bride's side received their guests with warm-hearted cordiality. Before settling them into chairs, each one was offered a rose, the sprinkling of essence over the whole body, and fresh sandalwood paste on the forehead. Ladies with auspicious lamps in their hands stood at the altar as if receiving their own sons. Could there be a dividing line between son and son-in-law! The conch shells blew again and again in close proximity expressing the time of the *muhurat*. The old and young ladies wearing colourful silk saris advanced to the altar to attend to the needs of the bridegroom.

Within no time, the guests were being served.

'Cigarette please.'

Malia smiled and picked five instead of one to give to each of his compatriots who were sitting nearby. Someone censured such an oddity but Malia stood as if nothing had happened.

The eyes of the caterers wandered from guest to guest serving them with great care. The host party had pulled all its strength to appease their needs. Even the tea served had a unique flavour. Somen's ideological link with the oppressed community had brought many of them to this celebration. But the majority were onlookers. They split into several directions and loitered around noisily. The officers like leopards didn't change their spots and stuck to their respective chairs. The Tahsildar, EO, BDO and other officials had formed a semi-circle around the SC, as if competing with each other on who would come closer to him. Like a segregated group, they didn't like to mingle with the others lest their status be diluted. Their conversation lacked variety and they mainly talked about promotions and increments, as if there was nothing else in life other than this. The talks between the SC and his colleagues didn't appear to be on an effective scale as no one talked to his boss in his natural way. Even though he was younger than all of them, his words were taken to be the voice of a mini-prophet. Officers, no matter how authoritative they were for the common public, were subdued before their higher authorities and were lavishing flattery on them. It was as if caught in a spider web, the victim had no chance of relieving oneself of one's own servility.

'Namaste...Saab.' A young man dressed in a blue suit offered his respects to them.

'Who is he?' queried the SC.

'A social worker, Sir,' replied the BDO.

'I have seen him loitering near my office claiming payment at times,' the SC added.

'Right Sir, he is an NAC contractor,' quipped the Tahsildar.

'But a contractor can be a social worker too,' the SC added amusingly. The person was not close to the group to hear what was being said about him. It could be seen that the SC had the intention of introducing a contractor as a social worker. The officers chattered among themselves while the drums started beating to announce the hour of benediction. The blowing of conches reverberated through the air. Ululations went on uninterrupted.

The priest and others waited for the auspicious moment of *lagna* to solemnize the *hastabandhan*. The priest was preoccupied with sticking to the exact time. Arati sat quietly at the altar with a glowing smile. Surrounded by relatives and friends, she emerged time and again to cope with different stages of the ritual. Sometimes alone and sometimes with the groom. Some of the elderly persons from the *baraat* encircled the altar to participate in the rituals.

Dressed in a *bankei* silk sari that flowed from her waist downwards and a separate one wrapped around her head, Arati was the focus of all attention. She peeped out from behind the veil like the face of a full moon coming out of a host of clouds. Decked out in gold bangles and other jewellery, she looked beautiful. It was as if a bright star had dropped out of the sky and fallen on the earth to show its lustrous form.

Soon after, the guests started dispersing in all directions. The auspicious moment of moving around the nuptial fire arrived. Somen appeared on the altar with the ever-winning pride of a maverick hero. With flowers in hand, both he and Arati stood up in a composed manner. The two hearts that had hitherto continued to keep apart had come together. Arati looked proud that she had found a life partner like Somen.

Arati with her golden necklace, gem-studded earrings, sparkling bangles and shining rings and multicoloured silk sari looked slow-paced. Her body language adequately expressed her jolly mood. It became the searching point for all staring eyes. Ahead of the altar was a small pavilion bedecked with colourful flowers. Four plaintain trees had been arranged in a quadrangle for the *sampradana*, the ritual that would solemnize the bride's handing over to the bridegroom. Arati's dad, Sen, came with a pair of new garments for his son-in-law and offered them to Somen as a token of *kanyadaan*. On the altar, both appeared like a king and queen peeping out from the pages of a fairy tale.

The onlookers watched the newlyweds performing the *saptapadi goman*, jointly taking seven steps together. Both, voiceless, mechanically gazed at the polestar Dhruba and its adjacent Arundhati on the distant horizon. They too were made to climb a flat stone to undertake *silarohan* without questioning anything whether it came under Vedic or folk rituals.

Gradually darkness spread across the whole sky. The deep silence drowned all other voices except some crickets and stray dogs barking here and there. Somewhere a municipality tap was leaking. Just then, a small fish appeared in a water pot standing in a corner of the marriage altar perhaps discharging its ultimate duty to prove its auspiciousness before the new couple. The *baraat* party had dispersed by now, paving the way for the couple to return home.

74

AS IS USUAL in the life of any newly-wed pair, the long-cherished honeymoon arrived. Both seemed drowning in colourful dreams trying hard to locate the bank for a support. The god of imagination reigned supreme over both hearts. The couple seemed to be flying in a chariot drawn by horses in the air. It was no doubt a journey to an unknown land.

'Today is the honeymoon day of our marriage. Both your *sasur* and *sasudi* wait for the Bou-anno. When are you going to do the same?' Somen said to Arati.

Arati gave a wholehearted smile. Somen looked at Arati's face waiting for a reply. But no words crossed her lips. Somen enjoyed confronting such a situation. He caressed her chin and gradually his fingers strayed across her body. He picked her up in his arms. Arati made no protest. She meekly surrendered to the wishes of her husband. Both had to play the game as Cupid had designed. Passion joined them together soundlessly. Both delved deeper into the preciousness of the hour. The small love plant that had been grafted many years before could now blossom. Like the string of a lyre, Arati could be stirred into an ecstatic tune. Like a bee flying straight into the trap of a rose, Arati submissively yielded to Somen's clasp. Kandarpa, the God of Love, invited the immortal pair Radha and Krishna to share the shade of the *kadamba*. Arati, more like Radha, might be compared to the face of the moon and her physique was both graceful and lyrical like that of a creeper. Her starry eyes could be equated with those of a deer, both swift and captivating. Somen, like Krishna, was transformed into a handsome hero, his complexion more akin to dark clouds. With their bodily quest for each other, they splashed like waves in a tiny pot. They had the pleasure to harmonize into one mood and one soul.

To them the night became incredibly short. The clock struck 2 a.m. Somen and Arati went near the pedestal on which sat their family goddess. She poured some ghee into the lamp. Then Somen took a little vermilion on his fingertip and applied it in the parting of the hair on Arati's forehead.

'Arati...'

'Now my duty of *sindur-daan* is over,' said Somen in a charged tone.

'We have certainly accepted each other till our last breath,' added Arati in an equally choked voice. Although Somen had no devotional fervour, he had to honour the wishes of his Maa and Baba. Arati followed her husband and both bowed before the goddess. Suddenly Somen's cellphone rang, surprising them both. The number reflected on the screen suggested an overseas call. Somen answered but the call got disconnected.

'Leave it,' said Arati. 'Might be a ghost call or from some international call centre.' In response, Somen switched off the phone. They turned to one another, but again were disturbed by a child's shrill cry. Somen broke away from the embrace and perspired with bitterness. The guests who had turned up for the marriage were yet to leave. The child might be looking for her mother. What a scene! Somen thought. 'Who knows that a mother could be so careless,' he said, somewhat irritated, and took Arati in his arms.

An erotic storm swept both their minds and bodies to subdue every other human sense. Their passion for each other was unquenchable and burnt every sensitive spot of their bodies. Both their eyes were robbed of sleep and they had exhausted most of the night. Flowers on the nuptial bed and the sacred lamp stood like mute witnesses to the whole spectacle.

There wouldn't be any exchange of dialogue any more. Such an ending appeared like a beginning.

Everyone else in the house was asleep except the duo. Both tried to invite sleep by simultaneously stuffing a sweet into each other's mouth. With closed eyes, Arati got up to fetch a blanket to cover his body. He had fallen into deep sleep. The whole room and its eerie silence gave her a peculiar feeling.

Arati got up next morning before sunrise. She got out of bed and opened the window for a while. The star of the dawn was grinning through the lattice window. Somen was still sleeping soundly. Resting her face against the railings she looked out of the window. The colony wore a deserted look. In the distance, a goods train rumbled past. The tinkling of a lady's bangles and the squeak of a hand pump came from nearby. Arati wished for a good sleep, but how? She was not a daughter but a daughter-in-law. She wouldn't have the freedom that she had had in her own home. As a daughter-in-law rising early was part of her ritual, otherwise her mother-in-law would complain. All of a sudden, someone knocked at the door. Before opening, she had to imagine who it was. But first, she tidied herself and Somen up. When she unbolted the door she saw a middle-aged lady smiling at her. She urged Arati to get ready for her morning bath. Although she didn't like a cold bath on a winter morning, she couldn't refuse. Obediently, she followed the lady to a bathing space built nearby. She pushed the wooden door shut. Although roofless, its red brick walls barricaded the space, allowing a person some privacy. Shampoo, bathing soap, hair oil, etc., were arranged on a shelf.

She cleaned her teeth with a new toothbrush. The lady brought some turmeric paste and applied it on her back. Arati appeared reluctant but had to concede meekly. She shrank to take her bath with water from the well. Although freshly drawn, it was comparatively a little warmer. After her bath, she had to change out of her wet clothes in the open. This worried her. What if someone saw her? Of course, the middle-aged lady was standing at a distance like a protective shield between her and some passers-by. The old lady held some of the wet clothes and made her run around in circles to find a spot to keep them. Before that Arati had been briefed about the sun-beaten spot and the timing of sunlight. The old lady murmured, 'During my young days, I used to know all such things. The daughter-in-law has to carry every minute idea in her head. She can't do anything wrong.' The lady continued to talk while she helped Arati apply cosmetics and get dressed.

Arati usually had breakfast before she left for office, but now she had to abide by the time schedule of the Roy family. Mrs Roy took her to the storeroom to brief her about the policy of the house. She was given all the keys and asked to keep vigil on each item. Mrs Roy showed her all the rations like rice, dal, oil, sugar, etc. Arati had to listen to her mother-in-law's words and followed her here and there, conscious of her new responsibility. 'Maa Arati, take care of your veil, it is slipping off your head,' Mrs Roy warned. At once both her hands covered her head with the *pallu* of her sari. Arati, till date, had been a free bird who enjoyed her parents' support and had no kind of household responsibility. However, as daughter-in-law, a new chapter had begun in her life and she couldn't go back to retrieve her past freedom ignoring the new challenges of her in-laws' house.

75

SOMEN RECEIVED A message to return to work forthwith. He took this as a part of corporate shrewdness.

'Frankly speaking, I don't like your company's overbearing attitude. At least they should have allowed you a minimum of a week's leave,' commented Arati. This denial of leave made Somen remember his mental distaste for a company job.

'Why this bloody message? Will they not allow me to marry even?' Somen told his family members excitedly.

'It would have been nice to leave Beethalgarh together,' Arati repeated.

'But how?' Somen queried.

The spectre of separation convulsed both of their minds. Arati couldn't join him in Bangalore just yet. Could she leave a permanent job so easily to join her husband in Bangalore? Moreover, they still had to make a proper living arrangement in the garden city. Could he ignore this message? 'No, not possible,' he soliloquized at once. The corporate world was a hard taskmaster. Somen's private life did not matter to them to grant him even the minimum leave.

For Arati, the thought of Somen leaving was a great wrench. For a newlywed bride, spending time in her in-laws' house without the husband would no doubt be monotonous. She could live her days in this new environment because of Somen's company but in his absence how could she spend her time? Just remaining behind curtains in a scantily aired room waiting for calls from her in-laws. Oh! Horrible!! Arati retreated to the kitchen, followed by Somen. Prior to this, Somen had no real idea of how hot and stuffy it was. His sympathy for Arati deepened. Who would rescue her from such an airless place? He looked at her. Drops of sweat trickled down her neck.

Reality returned to their minds. Wrinkles surfaced on both their foreheads. Somen had to leave Beethalgarh at once! Arati's face was pale with nervousness. Pangs of separation began to burn desperately in both. Somen had no alternative other than to leave and board the Chennai-bound night express.

The news of Somen's depature plunged the Roy family into despair. The jubilant house came to a standstill. Before leaving, he promised Arati and his parents that he would return soon. But she could not accept such a conjecture. The irony lay in the fact that although her parents lived barely a stone's throw from this house, her life without Somen seemed impossible. Somen's absence would fill her life with boredom. Her father-in-law, although a colleague, had the status of a father-in-law. She couldn't converse with him in a normal manner.

Mrs Roy being a lady noticed her sullen face but her sympathy was of no use. She tried her best to remove Arati's gloom but in vain. Like stray clippings, memories of the pleasant days with Somen flashed through her mind even though the spectre of parting loomed ahead.

Arati went out quietly to collect Somen's clothes from the clothes line and packed them with great care. Somen advised her to continue with her job for the time being. But Arati knew that zonal transfers were a Herculean task. Authorities of both the zones would have to be contacted, cajoled, and flattered before the transfer could happen.

Somen brought a sheet of paper and told Arati to sign on it. It was a request for a zonal transfer from the East Coast Railway Zone to South Western Railway Zone. Somen was determined that Arati's transfer should happen as soon as possible.

Arati was afraid of Bangalore's cosmopolitan lifestyle, particularly the liberated ladies working in corporate houses. She had seen how they hooked their bosses on TV. Being a working lady herself she was aware of how her sex behaved. Such an apprehension reverberated through her mind again and again and she wished that Somen wouldn't go back to that city without her. But both she and her father-in-law had to earn to meet their monthly expenditure, so such an option didn't exist yet. This unknown fear obsessed Arati and she tried her best to conceal it. Finding Somen alone for a little while, she buttoned up his shirt and implored, 'Take care of your health first!'

Somen, too, felt that he was not like he was earlier. Being married, he now had to consider his dearest half. He took the least interest in his baggage and packets of food. 'Oh! Lots of bundles,' cried out Somen. He cast a fleeting glance at the mounting pile of eatables from pickles to *badi*.* The auto driver lifted everything one by one and put it in the rickshaw in an orderly fashion. The parting now became really intense. Arati became so anguished that she had to confine herself to the bedroom, but Mrs Roy promptly brought her out of the house to see Somen off. He trudged up to the rickshaw. Arati and Mrs Roy went near Somen looking anguished.

---

*A food item, taken fried, made of *bidi* paste

After touching his mother's feet, he instructed the auto driver to take him to the railway station. Mrs Roy patted her son and struggled to check her rolling tears. Arati couldn't bear to see her husband leave and looked in the other direction. Roy Babu followed his son on a cycle so that he could return home without anyone's help.

Arati peeped out of the window, watching the auto and cycle slowly disappear. Her blurred eyes couldn't distinguish anything so she closed the window and let her loneliness enclose her.

After some time, she heard a long whistle from a distance. It further enhanced Arati and her mother-in-law's grief. Both lay on the bed waiting for the arrival of Roy Babu from the railway station.

The sound of the cycle broke the silence. Roy Babu came in saying, 'The train was late by half an hour and the air-conditioned coach was just in front of our house.'

Arati had no earlier experience of how this house operated without Somen. On seeing Roy Babu, she felt like dissolving into tears. Perhaps this would reduce the distance between a father and a father-in-law. The three of them hoped that their shared sorrow over Somen's departure would draw them closer together. But the night had its own demands and they made their way to their respective beds.

76

SOON AFTER HIS return to Bangalore, professional worries pushed Somen down to hard work. There were frequent calls from the MD on some matter or other. The usual courtesy like congratulating a junior on his marriage even took a back seat in his mind due to work pressure. Innumerable files and records dampened the romantic mood of Somen. Assignments, unattended so far, kept on bowling him over. Somen came across one of the directors who alerted him, 'Somenji! Now that you are married and definitely happy, please make us happier through your sincerity. Our Board desires a solid initiative from you in the loan matter. Please carry on.'

Somen got into his earlier job like an ascetic concentrating on meditation. He would carry on working long after the office closed, studying the data structure of loan components to upgrade them, or searching the Internet for leading textile units of the world to know about their production and marketing strategies.

But something distracted Somen and often Arati's face would flash across the screen of the computer obscuring the columns of data. It started surfacing and resurfacing again and again from the screen saver. In a way her smiling face enveloped the whole screen. He frantically wished to refresh his mind with her bright face and pleasing looks. Arati's photos were everywhere, not just the TV, but also the cellphone and such other gadgets.

But whenever they talked, Arati would grumble, 'You are busy there working wholeheartedly on your job. But how can I spend my days in Beethalgarh. I feel so useless here!'

Such friction was bound to take place when a busy husband appeared like neglecting his wife, deserting her in a remote corner of a mofussil town. More so, when a husband was in a metro, surrounded by young female colleagues, she would naturally feel jealous.

But Somen's work pressure was increasing. 'Look Somen!' The Vice-President nagged him over the intercom. 'The IDC guys are super intelligent. You have to deal with them cautiously otherwise our front-end papers would go to back-ends.'

Somen kept mum and resigned himself to the next course of strategy with IDC.

What were these sahibs? Neither friend nor enemy, Somen detested their bossiness. He soliloquized, 'You better watch my performance. Don't break my eardrums with piercing shots.' The bald-headed VP didn't want to be appreciated. He was cold and condescending to everyone below him. His image at KSF was of a tough officer who never spared anyone.

Somen acknowledged his loyalty and listened to every word from his multiple masters. 'Okay, get on with your task, carry on your work with greater speed,' the intercom buzzed every now and then with such clipped commanding voices. Somen could now well define the relationship between an employee and the employer. He delved deeper into understanding the role of a probationary executive, his social standing in a corporate set-up.

Files piled up on the table like flying birds sitting in a row on an electric wire. The bearer of the files could do nothing but dump them before Somen and walk away.

'Sir. Namaste... Files.' The watchman too came with a bunch.

'Why all these... damn it,' Somen burst out. The amount of office documents made his head spin.

'Sanctioning a loan from IDC is not in our job description,' commented a colleague.

'But if a person is underworked, the employer can assign any task to him,' replied Somen in a stern way. Although the employee didn't want to listen to such a dialogue, he couldn't raise his voice against company interest. Although discussions floated around everywhere, no one could voice it publicly apprehending reprisal from the management side. Gradually Somen felt lonelier, as unlike him, no one wished to shoulder any burden. No one had the same commitment to work. Was it because everyone lived like a drop of water on the lotus leaf? How did the sense of detachment creep into their minds? What for?

Somen had no mind to dissatisfy either his colleagues or his bosses. But he couldn't keep his foot in both the camps. The dissatisfaction against the authorities couldn't douse his spirit. He stood unruffled. Instead, he took the ruling tide at the flow. This time he was more concerned with the bread and butter and decided not to seek any help from others.

Somen took a copy of the PR to IDC. Prior to that, the MD had already succeeded in convincing the senior officials there to expedite KSF's loan proposal. Through his intervention, the process reached its final stage. Knowing the obstacles, the MD intervened to find a quick solution. 'The matter must be expedited,' he told Somen and other key players of the company with keen interest. He said they must go ahead whatever might be the expenses. 'I am giving you a blank cheque under the "entertainment" head.' Like the centre forward of a soccer team Somen made all efforts to score at the goalpost. He had to seek an appointment with the Chairman-cum-Managing Director, the highest voice of IDC. His private secretary made him wait for about an hour.

'Damn it,' he blurted out. His voice contorted with utter disgust. He repeated his request to the private secretary. But the secretary imperiously asked him to wait a bit.

Somen simmered like a boiling pot of water. However, he couldn't sit there in silence.

'What are the qualifications required for an appointment with the CMD then?'

'Why such a question?' the PS replied repulsively. 'I will send you in when it's time. He is not in his chair now.'

As Somen stood near the entrance, a middle-aged babu came out and slipped into a car. A few men hovered around him. Somen tried to recognize him.

'Is he the CMD?' Somen asked.

'He has just left for the airport to receive one of the VIPs from the centre,' said the private secretary.

'That's great!' Somen replied solicitously. He didn't feel like talking to the PS any further and walked out. He wiped the drops of sweat from his face with his hanky. He was feeling more and more dissatisfied. The atmosphere became nauseating for him. He saw persons coming and leaving at will whispering closely with the PS. Many of them entered the office chamber of the CMD.

'Has the CMD returned from the airport? How come I didn't see him?' Somen was puzzled over the circumstances.

'We can't explain so much to you,' replied the steno attached to the PS.

Both of them had attended frequent telephone calls promptly. Somen could guess their beaming mood during the conversations. He loitered heavily as if with a sense of defeat. Exhausted, he left the place and returned to the factory.

Somen was disappointed. What would he say to the MD? That a man dreaming to conquer the entire surroundings had bowed down before a private secretary?

On hearing of Somen's return, the MD called him to his chamber. 'Hello Somen. What about the progress?' he asked urgently.

Somen didn't open his mouth to say a word. This provoked the boss to wield his sword.

'Hah! Why couldn't you push through the proposal at IDC?'

'There was little that I could do, Sir!' he said apologetically.

'Tell me, what were your basic problems?' MD asked.

Somen went into the details of his encounter with the IDC staff to convince his boss. He told him about the unfriendly reception he had received at the CMD's office. The motive was obvious. Vested interests were so deeply entrenched; it was really difficult to get through them.

That was what the MD had inferred much earlier. No doubt, the efforts of Somen went in vain. He sat there looking exhausted. The MD wanted to cheer him up. He immediately rang up the private secretary of his counterpart in IDC and spoke in a sugary tone.

'Very well, then... Please see that nothing goes wrong this time. Okay... Bye.' The MD put the receiver down in a very optimistic manner. It implied that he was never at a loss in such transactions.

Within no time Somen could rebuild himself. He wanted to have a stronger rapport with the IDC staff this time.

'Good luck... Let success be with you', the MD told his young officer cheerfully.

'Thank you Sir!'

'And take Seshadri, my personal assistant, to coordinate there.' Somen bowed to the command.

The next day at about 10.30 a.m., Somen and Seshadri reached the main office of IDC. Perhaps with a solid aim to feed quality grass to the roguish-eyed human horses, who had earlier stalled the progress of their chariot of success. As such, the profit-seekers wanted this to happen. They were not interested in anything except lining their own pockets. On reaching there, the PS greeted Somen cordially, 'Hello! Please come in... Are you new to KSF?' 'Yes... I am a probationer,' replied Somen shaking hands with him.

'Okay... Very well! May I know a little more about you?'

'I am Somen Roy from Odisha.'

'But your accent sounds Bengali.'

'Although we are originally from West Bengal, my parents have settled down in Odisha.'

'Oh nice, Roy... You can go and meet our CMD. He is there alone in his chamber. Please...'

Somen looked at the chameleon hero of officialdom. How much he had changed within twenty-four hours. Half of the heart so crafty and cunning whereas the other half so welcoming. Somen entered and took a closer look at the chair to convey his regard. 'Namaskar.'

'Please take a seat,' said the CMD.

'Thank you Sir,' replied Somen.

The sweet aroma of the CMD's cologne wafted across the room. Somen didn't like the smell but had to sit quietly. Although middle-aged, the man looked highly stylish. A pair of power glasses rested on his nose. Before Somen could utter anything, the man began to harangue him about how forms were to be filled up, how there should be a neat calculation of the total requirement of capital, the expected quality of turnover after modernization and expansion of KSF, so on and so forth. He didn't wait for Somen to reply, and continued, 'But you must strive hard to ensure your future security. Unless you achieve the best possible standards, your unit will remain imperfect.'

'Sir, all your advice will be followed meticulously,' said Somen.

'Very good. Your MD should know that I am always eager to help your cause. But one thing, your documents, plans must be neat on all fronts. What do you say? Am I not right? How many MDs think like me?'

Somen had to digest each of the utterances. Seeing him responding to his sermons, the CMD went a step further saying, 'Look gentleman! You are young and have a long career ahead of you, but always work hard with sincerity. There has been no substitute for it so far. Only hard labour and nothing else, it is the sole key to success.'

'Hard labour', those two words went like a merry-go-round through his mind. Did he mean that the agricultural workers engaged in the fields for the whole day were not doing hard labour? Could he, then, show them the key to their success in life?

Somen had to carry the weightage of words silently as he preferred not to retaliate to such corporate jargon. But his sixth sense went on defying such maxims.

'All bogus, agents of the ruling class,' Somen shouted to himself. But he maintained an outward calm throughout.

'Where is your PR?' the CMD asked.

'This one ... Sir.'

The CMD leafed through it for a while, but then he became repulsive. 'You should realize that I have granted you maximum time. See I am already preoccupied. Please meet the Chief Finance Manager with this PR. He sits on the top floor. I will tell him right now to talk to you on this.' Saying so, the CMD turned his face downward.

Somen felt his manner to him had been irksome. He was a man to speak and not be spoken to by anyone. He was not happy with the outcome, as he wanted to have the time to convince the CMD of his total devotion to the expansion programme. But the latter had dismissed him. Perhaps he didn't want to hear any kind of success story from such a petty junior officer. He spoke out apathetically, 'All right. I shall talk to your MD on this.'

The whole incident dejected Somen. Was it a fact that the junior could do nothing other than to listen to the blowing of the trumpets of seniors? Was Somen one such sycophant to bow down before the seniors?

An attendant took Somen to the office chamber of the CFM. Seshadri followed both. On seeing him, the CFM's private secretary examined him carefully from head to toe perhaps with a 'give me something smile'. Somen was not acquainted with such facial expressions. The attendant exchanged glances with the assistant. Both acted in an underhand manner purely in the spirit of middlemen. Their attitudes repelled Somen but he had to bear with the same for the fruit. A fat envelope, yes, it had eyes like any sensible living being. It had wings to fly from one pocket to another. In a way, it was the booster to convert the near impossible to possible! The king of happiness to keep everyone hale and hearty!!

The PS made everyone wait. Somen was not even offered a chair to sit on. He saw many persons with grave looks sitting around. Somen got disheartened once again and looked around. A thought took hold of Somen's mind. 'Damn it.' Somen sighed and went up to the PS.

'Murty Babu...'

'Yes... please.'

'I am S Roy, Probationary Executive from KSF,' Somen said, about to hand him his card. But the PS declined to accept it.

'The CMF is busy. Please wait or come back later.'

'What do you say? The CMD told us to meet him straight away.'

'Maybe, but did the CMD tell you to meet the CFM right now? Impossible as he is busy finalizing the annual report of the Board meeting,' the PS replied in a casual manner.

Somen noticed his obstinate mood. 'All right, let me wait here then,' he said.

Somen kept throwing dissatisfied glances all around. Although the whole set-up looked polished and illuminated, the service providers were shrouded in darkness. Famous quotes of several prophets on love and compassion covered the walls, but the reality was the reverse.

As told by someone, Murty had an unemployed son-in-law who was to be employed by KSF. The earlier lip assurance of the MD was to be translated into reality. Murty was now at the vantage point of such a smart bargaining.

'So what was the point of deputing me then?' Somen grumbled. He tried to maintain his cool in a public place, but wordlessly he brooded over devising a new strategy to combat this hopeless situation. KSF should be beyond the pale of an ignominious character like Murty or might be his son-in-law. What a shady fellow who couldn't look beyond personal interests!

'ID, the super benchmark of success!'

Somen looked bitterly at this big hoarding. Such a hoax! He walked across the corridor and cast his pale look on both sides.

The walls were lined up with quotations: 'Honesty is the best policy', 'Service at the doorstep', etc., as if IDC poured down all blessings on its burgeoning customers. 'Bloody shylocks!' Out of bitterness, Somen sat on a chair and gnawed at his fingernails. He met Murty once again. But met with the same response again. He stood like a hapless guy before an individual who wanted to settle personal scores.

Mr Murty was wearing a talisman on a dark thread around his neck. He had applied a small spot of vermilion on his forehead. The right side of his table had some flowers while the left had some *mahaprased*. So it was to be presumed that he was a pious man.

Somen was getting impatient. Murty looked more and more unapproachable. He avoided Somen as if he were an infiltrator. Like an old tout the private secretary wanted to rip him off for his petty gains. How long would Somen go on pestering him against his will? The patience seemed evaporating. Somen wanted to be rude but confined himself within the four walls of gentility.

'Mr Murty, I have been in the line for the last one hour, waiting for my turn—'

The telephone rang suddenly. The PS picked it up. His voice grew excited at once. He said something about a precondition. An abrupt smile flickered on his face. Was it the culmination of a healthy bargain?

'Your DGM, please,' Murty handed the receiver to Somen.

'Yes Sir.'

'Please go ahead. Murty is convinced. I am there to take care of it,' the DGM said.

Somen had to keep mum. He couldn't ascertain if the DGM was aware of the below average capability of Murty's son-in-law. How would he occupy a post in KSF? Merit would become an empty syndrome then. All quality control exercises would have to be thrown to the winds. His idealistic vision of KSF would vanish so quickly, Somen screamed within himself.

Before such a thought haunted him further, Somen discovered a peculiar welcoming sign on the face of Murty. A sudden happiness seized Somen's heart and he began to reciprocate Murty's look. The moment came like a drowning man striving hard to catch a log of wood floating nearby. How come all of a sudden the diabolical face of Murty turned benign? What a transformation within the blink of an eye!

'Please go…finish off your task.'

'Okay. Thank you.'

Somen entered the cabin with a gentle precaution. The tension in him remained.

'Good morning Sir.'

'Yes please,' the CFM asked him to sit down.

'Thank you Sir.'

While handing over the PR for scrutiny, Somen wanted to explain the hard work that was involved. But his mood was roughed up by something other than this. The officer started squeezing him point blank. His superiority was obvious. Somen had a feeling of déjà vu like history repeating itself.

'Where are the tabulations on your market study?'

'This chapter, Sir.'

'Silly! No concrete picture emerges from here.'

Somen somehow smelled the CFM's preconceived notions. Otherwise how could he voice such opinions?

'See. Your report seems too sketchy, lacks a detailed market survey. There should be specific columns for each case study.'

How could Somen speak on all the points bypassing the other professionals who had worked on the report? After all he was not the mastermind. However, he tried his best to convince the CFM but he was not prepared to be convinced at all.

'Where is your techno-economic report?'

Somen wondered what this new objection was. It aroused further anguish in him. What the hell did it mean? 'Sir, I shall communicate all your observations to my bosses,' he said.

The CFM didn't ask any further questions. He noticed Somen's helplessness and changed the style of conversation,

'I think you are a fresher in this job.'

'Yes Sir.'

'Is that why your experienced bosses didn't turn up and sent you instead?'

'I can't say, Sir.'

'Where are you from?'

'Odisha... Sir.'

'Your institution has availed of sufficient equipment finance and term loans but are quite slow in repayment.'

Somen felt himself a victim, both helpless and bonded. Why was he being questioned so much? Had he joined a company whose credibility was at stake? How to get rid of such a hostile atmosphere? It was as if IDC had nothing but objections.

'Go fill in the missing information and come back,' said the CFM to Somen.

Somen returned to his factory and informed the MD about what had happened at the meeting. The MD's chamber turned into a war room as everyone started arguing loudly. They vividly dissected organizational inertia and Somen like a skilled surgeon took the lead.

'What the hell do they mean?' the MD asked the others. He intoned further, 'I shall float equity shares with higher offerings of interest to combat this game plan of IDC. If necessary, I shall seek foreign capital from NRIs.'

However, the DGM and others pointed out Reserve Bank of India restrictions. But the MD continued, 'I shall leave no stone unturned to arrange capital for my factory.' Many senior executives came forward to offer their opinions. They acted like drumsticks playing on the war drum thereby adding vitality to the beleaguered wings of Somen to take his flight to further heights in IDC. Some new pillars sprang up to exert prop support to the relationship between KCF and IDC.

But by now Somen had reached a decision. Embarrassed, he spoke out, 'Sorry Sir, I can't pursue this matter. Please entrust someone else to do it.' On hearing this, the MD became angry. 'What has made you say this?'

Somen struttered, 'I may not be in a position to understand their true minds, Sir.'

'It is a shame that you call yourself an executive and won't take responsibility in this matter. If that be your spirit... better go elsewhere to pursue your career,' the MD snapped with wild anger in his voice.

Somen stood submissively before his boss. The rhyme of bread besieged his ears. His unemployed days flashed through his memory. Nevertheless, he straightened himself saying, 'All right, Sir! If you are not satisfied with my performance, you may relieve me at once.'

His words stunned everyone. What a stubborn mind! So blunt and straightforward!!

'Somen! Be calm. You are ahead of anyone's pursuits. Nobody can question your sincerity. Don't be short-tempered. A corporate job needs patience,' one DGM who was present tried to pacify him.

The MD looked composed. He had already cast aside his furious mood and mellowed down appreciably. And so had Somen. He too had surrendered to the situation. He offered himself wholeheartedly to shoulder all responsibilities and was determined not to bend under any challenging circumstances.

'Sir, I am ready to undertake any responsibility you will assign me,' Somen told the MD.

The MD smiled. Perhaps he wanted this kind of commitment from one of his subordinates.

'Dear Somen! I know your sentiment. It is unfortunate that I spoke to you in that language. I have a distinct hope that you will bring glory to my factory.'

The MD's words filled Somen with happiness. The poisonous brew of hot-tempered dialogues could be contained. The MD and other staff members relaxed and returned to the cause that had been neglected so far. As such, the MD's frowning bore fruit that would win over all hostile situations lying ahead.

KSF's Board of Management met in the mini-conference room. A special group was formed under the chairmanship of the DGM to coordinate all the issues on this. All set to work to galvanize the whole process. Somen became the focal point, the loan emissary to IDC, to expedite the matter. The MD patted him saying, 'Get ready once again. I am there with you. Good luck.'

'May we sit for some more time to finalize things,' Somen asked the DGM.

'Oh! Why not? Let us go to my room then,' he replied.

There, both talked to each other in a free and frank manner. Somen detailed what had happened in IDC on previous occasions. Murty's case of wanting a job for his son-in-law was a priority.

'Be sure to carry the appointment order tomorrow with my signature. I am processing the file right now,' the DGM said emphatically.

'But Sir, between you and me, it should be purely on a temporary and ad hoc basis. Otherwise the employees' union will pounce on us,' said Somen.

'Please don't worry. That is my lookout.'

Somen had no alternative but to carefully adjust to the mighty establishment. He jumped into action with the sole aim that Arati would come one day from Beethalgarh to share his life in Bangalore.

77

SOMEN LIKE A warrior reached the final stage of his battle. His interaction with IDC was eventually successful. The hidden motives of assistants couldn't thwart the whole process of granting a term loan to KSF any more. However, Somen brought the objections he had faced to the attention of the MD, IDC. 'Sir, you speak about the simplification of paperwork, but please see.' The MD went through the objections raised by his own staff and issued a warning, 'If there is such a tendency to halt a process, very few entrepreneurs would come forward to avail of a loan from us.' As a result of this warning, the staff acted more diligently with general clients.

Somen had a major breakthrough. Many employees in the IDC office wanted to consolidate their friendship with him. They were full of praise for the way he handled his task. Somen would rise to become the right arm for both KSF and IDC. He was truly worth his weight in salt. He had toiled hard and now he was reaping the rewards. One day, he accidentally came across a Record Keeper who belonged to Odisha and with whom he could converse easily in his native Odia.

'Can you find an old record for us from your Record Room?'

'Of what kind, Somen Babu?'

'Any covering an earlier sanction of a loan.'

'Oh! Why not,' the Record Keeper replied gently. 'After all you are from my own state. Can't I do this much?'

The Record Keeper even found out compliance of other parties. Like a sharpshooter, Somen piled them up on a separate table and leafed through every detail attentively. From then on, he didn't cling to any particular seat but moved from one place to another, even from one floor to another to expedite sanction of the loan. Dialogues were exchanged strictly on a commercial basis. Emotions were kept hidden so that they could not to be measured through any sensitive barometer. Somen tried to keep up his stand not to be brushed aside by officers holding key positions. He began to act intelligently and made every effort towards a dedicated move. He kept himself prepared for the final assault.

'Listen, here everyone has a motive,' said the Record Keeper. 'If you fall into their trap, then you are gone.'

Somen could feel the veracity of the statement. But he didn't allow his confidence to be dented.

'What do we do then?' asked Somen.

'Nothing but a cocktail party,' replied the Record Keeper. Both of them spent some time gossiping over a cup of coffee. When Somen tried to pay for it, the Record Keeper refused. 'After all, we belong to the same locality. Allow me this courtesy.' Somen noticed that the Record Keeper's shirt collar was frayed and his hawai chappals were worn out. But unlike the others, he had the human touch.

On reaching his office, Somen briefed the MD about his efforts. He was full of praise for the MD, IDC. 'We can certainly bank on him, Sir.'

A smile swept across the MD's face. 'Oh, are you sure of your assessment of human beings! Okay... tell me in detail of your contacts so far.'

'With the majority of the officers, Sir, from the lowest to the highest authority,' Somen replied.

'Now you can know why I smiled.' Saying so, the MD pulled out a sheet of paper from his diary and handed it over to Somen. It was an indent for about thirty silk saris.

Taken aback, Somen raised his face. 'Who ordered you, Sir?'

'It is a guarded secret between us. But as you can imagine this is from the same person whose integrity you rate so high.'

Somen was left to wonder. He was severely shocked by the reality of facts. He became partially wordless as his mind absorbed the truth. Then he said spontaneously, 'Sir, what is the need to worship the bull when Shiva himself is ready for the same? And, Sir, how would this be taken care of?'

'You, who would be more suitable than you?'

'Okay, I am not opposed to the idea. I have absolutely no hesitation in doing this, but let me take one attendant for the purpose.'

'Oh sure,' replied the MD wholeheartedly.

The MD asked one responsible staff member from the Production Department to attend to this. Choosing and packaging the saris were to be taken into account as well as their delivery by the attendant to the residence of MD, IDC. Somen was to supervise the whole exercise. But Somen had a genuine concern about his ability to carry out a task of this kind. He didn't want this improper deal to impact his public life later. He certainly wished that KSF's tent should be fixed firmly but not with the support of a corrupt rope. The MD had understood what was going through in his junior's mind, even though he had agreed to do the same. He didn't exert any further pressure since he too wanted to uphold the untainted pride of his junior.

The MD pondered over whom he could find as a substitute for Somen. But the more he thought the more he realized that to find such a person was an impossible task. He knew that it wasn't easy to find a person whom one could trust. There were people everywhere, but there was no one who had integrity.

When Somen turned to look at his boss, he was surprised to see how helpless he really was. He wanted to say something to console him but it was unbecoming on the part of a subordinate to do so.

Somen had second thoughts, not knowing whether to say yes or no to his new assignment. His conscience began to prick him. He didn't know whether or not he should remain like the serene petals of a lotus sprouting from a slushy pond.

He looked at himself, the contradictions building up in his mind and piercing every thought without allowing them to sail smoothly.

78

INITIALLY, SOMEN FOUND it difficult to comply with the queries raised by IDC. How awful were the points raised one after the other in the objection slips. It was like extracting every bit of his mind to answer every odd query. A group of employees provided timely help to beat such silly paras. 'Where are the old compliance reports of different loanee organizations?' he asked one or two office assistants. Soon, those were piled up on his table. Such documents helped him unravel the process involved. The MD himself waited anxiously to go through the fresh submission. There was little resting time for Somen, his workload and the demands of his bosses kept him fully occupied. In spite of such a heavy load, the sweet memory of Arati couldn't take leave of him. His mobile phone kept ringing, diverting his attention. It was the only medium connecting them. Somen worked non-stop, determined to finish his task. He would quietly puff cigarettes one after the other, dictate notes to his steno or shout out for papers to be brought to him. Often, a burst of laughter could be heard from outside. It came like a speck of light in a zone of darkness. Some were seen congratulating a bearer for bringing hot refreshing food for them. Such generosity was a trick played by the management to stretch out the duration of the work to its maximum.

The computer professionals, typists and others had to satisfy their burning appetites with such fast food. The supply provided genuine entertainment for many. Somen rushed to each one's table to check if they were being served. This pained a few who didn't appreciate the idea of working under the leadership of a petty junior like Somen. At times, they used to throw crude and unsavoury comments at Somen.

'See, why is this chap from Odisha being given such a big responsibility?' one executive whispered to another. Such secretive conversations came to the notice of the MD, but he didn't turn away from his decision.

79

A GROUP OF employees from IDC wanted KSF to host a dinner for them. This annoyed the management. Although the MD felt uncomfortable, he contacted the heads of both the finance and administrative wings of his factory to find a solution. Fearing his excited mood, the heads didn't advance any arguments but authorized the funds to meet such expenses without insisting on the vouchers.

'I am happy you have found a quick solution,' the MD told them both. Once the funding was granted, the MD swaggered around making adequate arrangements for the get-together. 'Listen, my friends. Let us discharge this burden wholeheartedly. *Atithi deva bhaba*. We should rise to the expectations of our guests. We must not appear inadequate in any manner.' With smiles on their faces, the employees went ahead with the preparations to diffuse the tension in the MD's mind.

The opportune moment arrived. The organizers had laid out enough to eat and drink. And as the drinks flowed, satisfaction mounted in everyone's hearts. The dining hall in the guest house took on a festive air as the evening progressed. Bowls of food appeared on the table, their aromas tantalizing each guest. Somen's eyes flitted across the pomp and ceremony of the dinner party but he heartily wished he were elsewhere. The smell of alcohol was revolting to a teetotaller like him. He stood quietly by himself and declined to participate even when his colleagues pleaded with him to do so. Somen was adamant that he did not want to betray his own philosophy of life.

'Are you tired?' Somen heard his MD speaking quietly to him.

'No Sir...not at all.'

'Please come on...join us at least. You are the key man here,' the MD added further.

Somen couldn't refuse a request from his boss. It pulled him into a trap. He walked up slowly to join the team as though it was a torture.

The tables spilled over with dozens of French and Indian wines—red, white and champagne. Plates of cashew nuts and other dry fruits were placed here and there. It was obvious that many of the participants couldn't have dreamt of such varieties or even eaten them in their daily lives, leave alone the perfection of the culinary skills.

When dinner was served the guests were persuaded to drag chairs nearer to their tables while the serving staff went around with the dishes.

Somen sat silently like a mute participant looking calmly at others. The coolness within him became a marked feature.

The drinks were passed around.

'Somen Babu... Have a drop at least,' pleaded someone.

'What! You don't take. Are you sure? Oh please!'

'A very rare night. Come on, please. Cheers.'

'No...no I am all right,' Somen replied with smile. 'It will lead me nowhere,' he said in a voice that reached everyone's ears.

Having no way out, Somen sat through the dinner eating some chapattis, vegetable curry and a glass of milk. Although he was sufficiently alienated, he looked controlled. Like a small fish frantically trying to get out of the beak of a crane, he saw that even his suite was occupied by a horde of invaders. How to get rid of such unwelcome elements? 'Oh, please spare me,' he cried from within. It were as if all roads of exit were sealed for him.

80

THE DINNER PARTY worked wonders and quickened the process of removing the obstacles that stood in the way of sanctioning the capital loan. The erstwhile objection slips were pushed into cold storage. The banquet brought fresh intimacy between the two groups and now all negotiations were carried out in a light-hearted, optimistic manner. There appeared to be a complete reversal of roles. Murty, the cunning master, was seen carrying KSF files earnestly from CFM to MD and again the other way round. How successfully could he feather the nest of his son-in-law there? Somen looked at him dryly without a sign of love on his face. But Murty's interaction with him was something extraordinary.

'Hello...good morning.'

'Morning.'

'What yaar...you were not seen that night. Perhaps brawling in a secret corner.' Somen didn't reply.

'Feel sorry for my behaviour. But, Somenji, what really happened to you?'

'No... nothing like that. Why do you want to know a reason for my behaviour when I myself didn't feel any difference?'

'Was that your normal face, then?'

'Certainly. I am what I am. How can I change the appearance of my face deliberately,' Somen said to Murty smilingly. 'But Murtyji, did you pay attention to our file or leave it as it is?'

Mr Murty stopped for a while to remember but he couldn't recollect where the file was.

'Our file?' Somen repeated.

'Look, I have it. Please wait. I am just coming from the Assistant Finance Manager.'

After some time Murty came out from the chamber of his boss with the same file that appeared to have been lost somewhere. He, however, opened the file and became a little inquisitive.

'Somenji, where are the lowest quoted prices of tools and machines? Your PR has quoted prices that don't match with the quotations submitted by the foreign suppliers. Why is that so?'

'My goodness, is that really so?' Murty's words burst upon Somen like arrows. He quickly glanced through the comparative statement. The defects looked glaring. What could be the reason? A sign of anxiety hit his mind again and again. What led to such wrong documentation? How did it happen? Somen was completely perplexed. The production officer had accompanied him to IDC. He told him straight: 'I am afraid we can't rectify such defects in the PR. The battle of compliance has to be continued till the PR is considered expedient.' He took the matter personally without charging anyone from KCF for such a visible lapse. Was it the company policy to drag him from a remote village only to clean debris out of its path?

The spirit of compliance had to accelerate. The last phase shouldn't crush his ability.

The production officer seized the chance to talk. He uttered quietly: 'This might be the way to evade both customs and excise duties.'

'That's right. What kind of a corporate administration is this?' Somen spoke out in anger. The other officer asked him to be quiet. 'The MD won't take this lightly,' said he. Words like excise evasion, foreign exchange violations dropped into his ears like crackers. 'Dammit,' he exclaimed.

Mr Murty wished to say something to him in private. But Somen took exception to this and said, 'In public service, is their anything secret?'

'Of course,' replied Murty.

Somen asked, 'What are those things, then?'

'Oh! Not so loud, please.'

Somen followed him to a corner.

'If your organization sincerely wants the storm to blow away, you better take back these quotations. Ask your foreign suppliers to inflate the same quoted prices by a minimum of 20 per cent. Also add some unlevied items to avoid tax burden. You may not bring those at the time of actual installation,' Murty said to him quietly.

Such words angered Somen. He lost control of himself. He

wanted no part in such a loan-fixing racket. How is it that Murty felt no qualms about asking for a kickback?

'Ours is only 20 per cent, Somenji.'

'What is that?'

'PC...'

'Meaning what?'

'P...e...r...c...e...n...t...a...g...e!' 'You have to part with a minimum of 20 per cent of the total loan component that would be sanctioned in your favour,' he said.

'Don't you understand my words,' he added further.

'Oh no! My problem is not to understand a business of this kind. But what to do, I have no way out,' said Somen.

'Very good, then, I had no prior idea of you. Nobody told me either. Anyway it is up to you and your company,' said Murty.

'Oh, what a bargain!' Somen said to himself.

81

THE NEXT DAY the sun was shining in the sky like a fluorescent umbrella. KSF was celebrating its anniversary and the administrative building looked festive. The organizers took minute care of food and drinks in order to bring happiness for the employees' families. They were told that the Divisional Railway Manager, Bangalore Division, was to grace the occasion as chief guest. For Somen, this was a great opportunity to pursue the cause of his wife's transfer. Earlier, he had been to the railway zone office and had met some assistants working in the establishment section, but there had been little scope to meet the officer-in-charge of transfer and posting.

'Hey, what do you want?' an attendant called out to Somen in chaste Kannada.

Somen had never expected such intimacy from a stranger. 'Sectional head of the establishment section,' he replied calmly.

'Come this way,' the attendant told Somen.

'But which sectional head: bill, budget, transfer, which one? Tell me exactly the purpose of your visit,' the attendant repeated.

Somen tried to read the body language of his new guide. He looked unpretentious. A kind of raw innocence sparkled on his face. But Somen had no intention of confiding in a stranger, especially someone who didn't have any power. The waiter repeated his question.

'Be frank. Maybe I can help.'

Somen focused a silent look at him. His dejection became more acute.

'Please don't lose hope. Tell me frankly,' the attendant became more and more curious about the exact reason for Somen's visit.

'Just to pursue a transfer case.'

'Oh! Fine. But whose transfer?'

'My wife's.'

'Nice, come this way.' The attendant conducted Somen to the table of an officer. Without a word, he stood looking at the middle-aged man waiting for his welcoming gesture. The man raised his eyes enquiringly.

'You may talk to him there, he is the sectional head,' said the attendant pointing at the officer.

'Okay.'

'Tell me, in which way I can help you?' said the officer.

Without being offered a chair, he had to stand to speak of his wife's cause. Although embarrassed, it didn't worry him to speak out the reason of his visit. 'I just want to know if there can be any zonal transfer.'

'Whose case do you want me to look at?'

'My wife's. She is an assistant in South-Eastern Railway'. Now the officer's attitude changed. Like the ruler of a mini-empire, he started sermonizing:

'See, we have certain policies on transfer. One should at least be in a place for more than a period of three years.'

'My wife Arati fulfils that criterion. She is at Beethalgarh and has already completed three years of stay in a single station. Of course, she is in a clerical job, moreover, in a separate zone of South-

Eastern railway.'

'I think your wife knows it. In a zonal transfer mutual consent is necessary. That means you have to find an assistant here who would be equally desirous to go there.'

'Is there any vacancy here?'

'That I have to check. Of course if there is vacancy things would be easier.'

'Okay, tell me the place of choice.'

'Bangalore cantonment or Jashwantpur. Difficult indeed as so many stations are falling upon these two. You may opt for some comparatively far-off stations.'

Both fell into discussion to find something suitable. The Section Officer seemed warm-hearted. He offered Somen a chair to sit on while they continued their discussion.

'What about yourself?' he asked Somen.

'I am Somen Roy...an executive from KSF. My wife Arati is in Beethalgarh under the Samastipur railway zone,' Somen supplemented.

Two of the juniors made their way to the SO, perhaps to involve themselves in the conversation. Somen glanced at both of them. Their young eyes looked around peevishly. One of them asked:

'What is your wife's name and her present posting?'

'Why do you want to know?'

Such a question appeared distasteful for Somen. He didn't approve of such inquisitiveness from a young recruit, an apparent novice. He wished them to be less talkative but he had no way to snub them. The SO intervened bluntly, 'No need to ask somebody's name. It doesn't serve any purpose now.' Saying so, he looked at Somen mildly.

However, on insistence from the SO, he pulled out a sheet of paper from his pocket and handed it to him. It carried the details of his wife's posting, designation, present address and the place she desired to be posted.

'Oh, good enough but send me the transfer petition too,' said the SO briefly. Somen handed a copy of Arati's representation to him. However, the SO told Somen to get a copy of it endorsed to avoid delay but cautioned that it should be routed through their zonal office. Somen left the office with a request to expedite his wife's representation at the earliest.

As he was getting into the staff car, one of the young employees came rushing up to him. On seeing him, Somen stopped and waited for him under the shade of a tree.

'Hello Sir... good morning.'

'Good morning.'

'Are you Somen Roy?'

'Yes.'

'I am SV Prasad. I serve here as Legal Assistant.' On saying so, he extended his hand to Somen for a warm shake.

'Is there anything you want to say to me?'

'Actually, my wife Sharada is a senior typist in KSF.'

'Oh, I know Sharada. She is a fine worker.'

Instantly, their conversation became more personal.

Prasad took a step further. 'You rarely find anyone honest and sincere here. Almost everyone seeks their vitamin M, meaning money.'

'But that sectional head with sandalwood paste on his forehead appeared so cordial,' Somen added.

'Oh my God! He is a first-rate boozer. The other two also, even home brewing is insufficient for them. Any quantity would do,' said Prasad in a low voice.

Although Somen was interested in what Prasad was saying, he was in a hurry. He looked at his watch and then at Prasad, frantically wishing for his dialogue to end.

'I know you are in a hurry, you came here to pursue the cause of Madam's transfer. I know... Be sure... It will be done,' said Prasad.

Such a promise encouraged Somen.

'But how come you are so optimistic about the transfer? Don't you know it is zonal and has to pass through several departments both here and there?'

'I know everything, but see the Deputy General Manager in

charge of establishment looks after transfer and posting. He is cordial with me. We are both from the same native state, Uttar Pradesh. I can pursue this case with him.'

Somen beamed at him.

Somen promptly handed over a photocopy of Arati's representation to him.

'I keep this with me,' said Prasad. 'Perhaps you should request the DGM to visit your showroom, or better still, present him with a new silk sari for his wife,' he added. Somen listened attentively to Prasad who seemed like a prophet about to crack the heart of an official bastion. While returning, Somen imagined the calm touch of Arati, as if sitting next to him in the car. As a responsible husband what would be a greater duty than to have his near and dear one beside him? He was thinking of their future together in a software city like Bangalore.

82

SITTING IN HIS cabin, Somen tried to remember the faces and names of his colleagues, both young and middle-aged. Each one of them carried a common motto to widen the business entrepreneurship of their company, labouring assiduously for a secure life. The long-term struggle that aimed at adding flesh to the skull of Judabandh was already a forgotten task. Instead, it had now become a long-term plan invoking inspirational strategy for the resurrection of a corporate house.

All of a sudden there had been escalation in the rates of quotations. The MD, KSF, himself headed the new plan. His team of officials was let loose on this exercise. They started keeping track of foreign suppliers and their agents in India. They ramped up their task while Somen and his team were sidelined into a corner. Their laboured documents were pushed into cold storage. Flashes of PC appeared from the MD's closed bastion. As night deepened further, his office began attracting strangers. The MD swirled around acting like detergent to remove all stains so that KSF could shine in apparent whiteness.

No doubt, KSF was preparing for a big jump from a lesser-known past into a greater future. The onlookers all assembled enthusiastically to see the upcoming swing of their unit. Each one looked at the other to exchange thoughts in private. Tongues wagged with talk of secret deals. From drivers to sweepers, from office assistants to field staff, the two hemispheres came together to speak of what was happening. Doubts and suspicion invaded the sphere. Brokers flooded the office. Like a drop of mercury Somen couldn't be dissolved in this exciting flow. The MD's integrity was constantly questioned by the union leaders in their trade union meetings. Like the wind moving branches, money moved everyone. A silent howl engulfed Somen. 'A man is not exactly what he appears to be, so impure and deceitful!' Somen complained to himself. It seemed everyone wore a mask, the mask of PC. However impious within, the outer façade glittered.

Somen heaved a sigh and peered out from the window. 'All idiots. Your glittering dresses, everything, even your charming glances mean nothing. It's only after the pursuit of PC, he growled.

Somen lay on his bed overwrought. He looked up at the revolving fan and tried to find a solution. He had little love for his job and yet now he was being forced to pay a price for it. No matter... As he had seen, the world belonged to making money and money making alone could be called the mother of all professions.

'Why do you rack your nerves for a cause that you have nothing in common with?' Somen heard a voice from within.

Somen went to his bookshelf with a sense of purpose. He picked up the Bible from it and leafed through its pages. His eyes fixed on a line by Timothy. 'The love of money is the root of all evil'. Such words reverberated through his mind.

Just then the MD's private secretary called and asked him to meet the boss at his residence on some urgent matter. The staff car also reached immediately.

He had no option but to go. Obviously his boss didn't care about how late it was. He felt exhausted but sat in the car. On reaching, he saw the MD sitting outside his house looking serious. On seeing Somen, he started: 'Somen...'

'Yes Sir.'

'We have to work hard on the project. You shouldn't go anywhere and restrict yourself to the guest house only.'

Somen was perplexed. How could his boss's mood oscillate like this, ignoring him and then seeking his service? He replied bluntly, 'I am definitely at your command, Sir, but I can't be made responsible for those below me, particularly alerting them beyond office hours.' His words came like arrows, interrupting their conversation.

The MD just smiled. Perhaps he knew that there were many who would pay lip service to please their boss but then not prove their worth in the field.

The MD went inside his house and brought a fresh jacket-bound copy of the PR and said: 'This is the new one... See if there are any anomalies in it. If okay, we can resubmit this one.'

'Sir, right now?' Somen asked cautiously.

'Do not worry, take your time. We will make use of the rapport between KSF and IDC to the maximum. No problem will stand in your way any more.'

'Sir, are you asking me to do the company's work during private hours!' Somen spoke offhandedly. He disliked pressure of this kind. The MD tried to convince him.

'See Somen... I am giving this to you because you have no family. Look at it whenever you have time to spare,' he said emphatically.

'Come on, Somen Babu, have a drink,' a senior officer interrupted with a glass of whisky in his hand.

'No please... thank you,' Somen said and left with the PR after saying goodbye to his bosses.

Somen heartily wished to work in a better environment where he didn't have to be constantly bombarded by the dictates of bosses. He was like a commodity, a product that was being used until it eroded. Did any better set-up await him? Somen sat in the car to return to his guest house feeling utterly exhausted. 'Is this your choicest job, for which your parents tended your body and mind so carefully?'

His conscience put him in the dock again and again.

'Perhaps your wish was something else,' he said to himself.

83

AFTER A FEW days, towards late evening, a special messenger from IDC brought an important letter for the MD. It was the loan sanction order. The employees knew its contents because the letter had been sent earlier through email. The messenger was given a ride in the company car to move here and there with some other letters. As a result, the employees, en masse, rose to their feet in celebration. Even the staff of the production unit of silk yarn wanted to press the red button to stop their spinning wheels but the Chief Production Manager strictly stopped it. Instead, all inspectors and JEs, including machine men, were told to mutually manage their duties, rotating hour-wise. In all the break-rooms, food packets and drinks were supplied in plenty much to the satisfaction of everyone.

Now it was the turn of the organizers. The MD told them emphatically: 'Let us have a banquet in the guest house but strictly for officials from both IDC and KSF.'

'Somen, what has happened? The loan is sanctioned perhaps,' asked one of the colleagues.

'Can you imagine? So much jubilation. What could it be other than this?' Somen remarked to a colleague.

'Bravo!' The latter gestured with his hand. Somen gave a smile. He didn't want to appear proud before his colleagues.

'I have noticed how hard you have worked. In fact labour never goes in vain,' another colleague interjected.

The sanctioning of the loan made everyone in KSF very happy. It seemed like the end of a long road journey. But only Somen leaned back in silence. No enthusiasm...nothing. He left his office for the guest house, entered his room and tiptoed within it. Then he called softly to the waiter for a cup of tea.

He tried his best to make excuses not to join the high tea party because he didn't want people to question his health and mental condition. 'I am okay,' he said with a smile.

'Somenji, you ought to join us. It is your success after all. All of us are honestly acknowledging your months of hard labour,' said a colleague.

Observing the mood of his colleagues, Somen agreed to join the party but said, 'Please allow me some more time to get ready.'

Finding himself alone the thoughts of Arati, his parents and Minati whispered in Somen's ears. Similarly the words of Prasad. They all flashed across his mind simultaneously. The representation of his wife was yet to reach the Zonal Manager. Was he then to bury the fate of his family under the heel of the railway administration? How to overcome the apathy and sluggishness of the railway clerks? Could Prasad, a small-time employee, cope up with the movement of files, avoiding their cunning eyes?

Somen's eyes swam across the framed photo of Arati on the table. He saw his wife's smiling face and suddenly felt as if she was talking to him.

'And, my dear husband! Is this your ultimate strength? Your masculine urge to find a new social order? But are you capable of organizing a transfer?' A voice seemed to be coming out of the sweet beaming photo.

Somen felt a sense of defeat. Without dissolving into his earlier melancholy, he looked at the photo entreatingly. 'Please Arati, allow me some more time, I promise...Arati...I really promise.'

'What promise? Can't you feel the anguish of my bleeding heart? How a married lady is thrown into the corner of a village. Yes, like worn-out garments.'

At once, Somen grabbed hold of the photo and held it close to his chest. 'Arati! Excuse me. Wait a little longer.'

Somen held the photo frame close to his lips and kissed it again and again, as if it was his only companion in this solitary room.

'Why have you come here?' he asked himself. Somen didn't want to interfere with the rights and privileges of any human being nor look at their self-centredness. How had he become so small before these urban dwellers, almost like losing his self-dignity? But Somen didn't allow himself to brood any further. Instead he wanted to be optimistic, to dream and plan his future so that he could leap out of the darkness to arrive at his shining area. He would plan his own dream house in Bangalore city and hire the services of any architect irrespective of his fees. He would choose every boulder or brick, marble or tile for the construction of the house, inviting masons even from his own hometown, if required. With his wife Arati, Baba, Maa and at times, his sister Minati and other such close relatives. Then his life would really become meaningful for him and not this guest house living. In the balcony, the drying Sambalpuri saris of Arati and Maa would give him more comfort than bolts of silk from his own factory. Dreams flashed by one after another like tidal waves occupying his oceanic mind.

But Prasad had not turned up. How long would he nurse the hope of Arati's transfer and wait for the order? His thoughts turned sour again. Would he have to begin the transfer process again? The subject called Arati was an endless story for Somen.

He left his room and found his way across the lawn. Not being sad any more, he sought nourishment from the flowery show on both sides of the lawn. He revisited his thoughts and murmured, 'Everywhere there is the smell of graft, red-tape but certainly not in the rosebuds and their leafy wings.'

Deep in thought, Somen found himself in a distant corner, a little away from the guest house.

He heard a waiter calling him, 'Sir, officers are waiting for you in the hall.'

'Oh sorry, I strolled around and accidentally came this way. Is it late already? Has the MD arrived?'

Somen hurried to the venue escorted by the waiter.

On joining the group, his colleagues congratulated him. Even the MD and other senior officers showered epithets of praise on him.

But again, the voice of his dearest, prompted from within, 'Where is your success unless you show it to me? Don't forget your promise.' Somen moved around, shaking hands with people, but the voice of

Arati didn't run away from his ears.

Suddenly, a bip...bip came from his cellphone. Looking at the screen, he knew that it was a message. It was from Prasad. Somen opened the message box at once to read:

'Arati madam transferred to Bangalore.'

What great news! Somen initially didn't believe his eyes. He went through the message repeatedly. Even though he was at an office gathering, he went to a corner and replied to Prasad: 'Dear Prasad, Thank you so much, Somen', and immediately forwarded the SMS to Arati.

Even though he was at a party, Somen started thinking about packing and shifting his personal effects from Beethalgarh to Bangalore. Time came like a healing factor. The estate section of his company would provide him with new accommodation within the VIP zone of the campus. He could foresee an assured future for both him and Arati in Bangalore. To his good fortune, the same officer was just standing near him. He requested him for an allotment of company quarters in his favour and the estate officer assured him that it would be done at the earliest.

Arati, on the other hand, received the SMS from Somen as the most laudable prize in her life. Soon both Somen and she would be together. Their long-distance relationship would end and they could look forward to the beginning of a new dream, a new future. Perhaps even the arrival of a child and life in a metro instead of a small town.

What a brilliant coincidence that this should happen at a grand party that had confirmed his foothold in the KSF and the city as well! It was as if the darkness of his past had disappeared unable to withstand the light of his coming days.

He came forward joyfully to meet his colleagues, keeping his fingers crossed for a new set-up.